Kidnapped Hearts

by
Morgan Elliot
Erin Wade

Copyright 8/2020
ISBN: 9798669249793

Edited by Dalia Redmond

GW00809073

Kidnapped Hearts

by
Morgan Elliot
Erin Wade
Copyright 8/2020
ISBN: 9798669249793

©7/2020 Morgan Elliot & Erin Wade
www.erinwade.us
www.morganelliot.com

Independently published
By Morgan Elliot & Erin Wade

DEDICATION

To our wives who have tolerated our late-night writers' conferences and endless requests for proofing. They allow us to write our stories and they read them endlessly. We would be nothing without them. They light up our lives.

Morgan & Erin

~~~

ACKNOWLEDGEMENT

A special "Thank You" to our wonderful and witty "Beta Master," **Julie Versoi**. She makes us better storytellers.

~~~

CHAPTER 1—The Pitch

If I could only live at the pitch that is near madness, when everything is as it was in my childhood, violent, vivid, and of infinite possibility!

Richard Ghormsley Eberhart

Tuesday April 7

Sophie tasted the dust before she caught a glimpse of it rising over the oiled dirt road leading up to the house. She knew what was coming, even though her view was obstructed by the large knoll covered with scrub pine. It was unusual to have an unannounced visitor at this time of the year and this evening, she was alone, the sole sentry at White Bark Ranch.

Finally, the vehicle crested over the last rise of the driveway before it flattened out to a circular drive at the foot of the main house. A minute later a large sable colored SUV with tinted windows pulled in front of the house. She did not recognize the vehicle but didn't feel particularly apprehensive; she was annoyed. *Not this again! When in the hell is that asshole going to stop sending me developers that want to turn my ranch into a resort for the rich and irritating? He does this just to piss me off!*

She stepped inside the screen door to grab her shotgun, just in case the unexpected guests were not the friendly type. *Better safe than sorry,* she mused to herself. Sitting in a rocking chair on the porch, her body positioned slightly behind one of the large porch pillars, she waited.

The SUV was smack dab in front of the steps to the huge wrap-around porch, where Sophie had been sitting enjoying a rare warm spring evening. A well-proportioned woman, dressed in a blue pencil skirt, white crisp blouse and a matching jacket, elegantly swung her legs out of the SUV. Her head was down, as if she were watching where her feet were going to land. When she stood, Sophie pegged her at about five feet seven inches tall and wished she could see her face. Before turning toward the steps, the woman bent into the cabin of the SUV and talked to her companion, a hulk of a man from what Sophie could see.

After pulling out a briefcase, she turned toward Sophie. Sophie's eyes widened. The woman was stunning. Her hair was black with mahogany tones and hung straight down to mid-back. It was cut flawlessly. Sophie thought, *the haircut alone tells me she sure isn't from around here!* Sophie had been in Montana for thirty-six years and had yet to find anyone who could cut her hair to her satisfaction; but then nothing rarely was to Sophie's satisfaction, unless she herself choreographed it. Sophie ruefully smiled.

The woman squarely faced Sophie and mistook Sophie's slight smile for friendliness, returning it with her own.

"Hi, I'm Jules Law. Are you Sophie Martini?"

Sophie nodded her head. She couldn't stop staring. Ms. Law's skin was a lovely shade of olive splashed with golden undertones, smooth and without blemishes. Her cheek bones were prominent, but balanced with a gently sloping nose, a warm and inviting mouth, that when she smiled, announced a slight dimple in her chin. She was a woman who appeared to be comfortable, self-possessed, and confident. But it was her eyes that drew Sophie in. They were dark, intelligent, piercing, though not menacing, and they seemed old, as if they had seen a lot, in comparison to the woman's chronological age. Sophie wasn't sure, but from Ms. Law's facial structure, she thought she might be part Middle Eastern.

Finally, Sophie nodded her head, her thin smile disappearing, and said, "I am. Are you lost?"

Jules did not move toward the steps, but answered a polite, "No we're not lost." She recognized what Sophie had in her arms and was pretty sure that the shotgun was not just for show. She made a quarter turn and motioned to her companion in the SUV.

Sophie heard the driver-side door open and shifted her eyes from Jules to a man who stepped out. He was big and well-muscled, maybe six feet six inches tall at two hundred and fifty pounds. Well-groomed with closely cropped hair, he was dressed neatly and professionally.

Definitely not from these parts! The proverbial red flag was waving in Sophie's face. He looked military, police, covert. She wondered if he was carrying a weapon under his well-tailored jacket. She pondered her own paranoia. *You've been watching too many Law and Order reruns and reading too many murder mysteries over the winter.* Sophie refocused and observed him come around the car to stand next to Ms. Law.

He said, "Howdy ma'am. I'm Jake Lawrence. Jules and I drove down from Missoula to see if we could talk to you. May we come up?"

Despite Jake's friendly and homey approach, Sophie's cautiousness did not dissipate. She shifted the shotgun in her arms, ready for action. Before Sophie could answer, Jules quickly said, "We're not here to cause any trouble but would like to discuss a business proposition we think you may find interesting."

Not another real estate developer, Sophie groaned inwardly. In the last year, she had been hounded by developers who wanted to turn her property into a mega resort with multi-million dollar estates. The ranch was over eight hundred acres bordering the Selway/Bitterroot Wilderness Area, the third largest wilderness area in the lower forty-eight. U.S. Forest Service Lands surrounded the ranch on three sides and the ranch's high meadows provided excellent grazing from late spring to early fall. Located about one hundred and twenty five miles southwest of Missoula, the ranch was accessible, yet remote enough for privacy making it a prime target for high-end development. Who wouldn't like to wake up most mornings and from the mesa, where the main buildings were located, look out over the wooded valley surrounded by a halo of snowcapped mountains? On a clear day, Trapper Peak could be seen from the west side of the porch.

Damn Keith Woods and his fascist bank, deliberated Sophie. He could never keep his trap shut about Sophie's financial problems and the very real possibility that she would soon have to sell off the majority of her property to avoid losing the family ranch to the bank. Woods would love that. He was in bed with a local relator and stood to make a sizeable finder's fee if Sophie decided to sell. The property was worth between ten and fifteen million dollars. Sophie loathed Woods. He was the most unethical man she had ever met, so he occupied the position of 'major scum' on Sophie's slime list. If Sophie could find a way to neuter him without going to prison, she'd consider it.

Pack of wolves, she muttered to herself just before addressing Ms. Law. "Look, I don't know where you got your information, but I am not interested in selling the ranch to anyone, so get back into your vehicle and leave!" Thinking about Keith made Sophie angry, but she managed to modulate her voice and not come across as a raving lunatic.

Jake, with an *okay boss, what do we do next look* turned toward Jules, waited for her to take the lead. Jules quickly corrected Sophie's impression.

"Ah, Mrs. Martini, we don't want to buy your property. We're not real estate developers. We're from a security firm out of Los Angeles and need your help. We're prepared to make it worth your while."

Jules waited for her words to sink in. She was hoping that Sophie would be intrigued. When the ranch personnel were vetted, Sophie's profile told them that she was high-spirited, swift to jump on the bandwagon for a worthy cause, principled, hardworking, inquisitive, and the first to help out a friend in need. She also couldn't stand being kept in the dark. Jules was betting on Sophie's curiosity. Remaining quiet, Jules knew that if she spoke first Sophie would probably tell them to get lost again, punctuating her displeasure with a round from her shotgun.

Sophie's eyes were flashing. She was trying to imagine what kind of business proposition these strangers could have for her that didn't involve selling her ranch. She took her time in answering. "Do you have any kind of identification?"

When Jake and Jules made a move for the interior pockets of their jackets, Sophie, said, "Slowly, nice and easy. I don't know what you've got in there besides your IDs. Hold them up in front of you."

Both Jake and Jules gingerly reached into their inside jacket pockets, pulled out their IDs and held them up in front of them at chest level. Sophie couldn't really see them in the fading light from the porch and Jules knew this, so she waited patiently for Sophie to make the next move.

Sophie said, "Ms. Law, walk over to the steps with both your IDs, please."

Jake handed his ID to Jules and holding both in front of her, Jules walked slowly to the steps, never taking her eyes off the shotgun. While she didn't think that Sophie was a real threat, under duress people could panic and do foolish things. Jules had seen this many times when she was in the military. Sophie came out from behind the porch pillar, moving a little closer to the top step and motioned to Jules to come up. She reached out and Jules offered the two IDs, which Sophie promptly took.

The IDs looked legit, but now-a-days you could get anything printed up. In the top of the wallet folder of each ID, there was California PI license. The bottom part of the bifold held an identification card with their respective photos for a company called Intelligent Security Services, with both a Los Angeles and Washington, DC address and phone number. Sophie thought about calling the number, but she knew that any number they gave her could be bounced and answered anywhere in the world. She was going to have to rely on her intuition, which right now was conflicted.

She couldn't quite wrap her head around the vibes she was getting. She was not particularly fearful of Jules and Jake per se, rather she was nervous of what they represented and what might follow. While they were friendly and professional, something seemed to walk in their shadows that gave her a shiver. Sophie shook off the disquieting feeling and turned her attention to Jules who immediately spoke.

"I see you still have some doubts and I probably would too if two strangers just showed up out of the blue way out here. What can we do to convince you that we mean you no harm and all we want to do is talk about a mutually beneficial business deal?" Jules mentally crossed her fingers. Her expertise was in managing operations, not people and she was nervous that she would make a mess of the proposal she had been entrusted to make.

If I were in my right mind, thought Sophie, *I'd tell these strangers to leave and come back tomorrow when Rick and the ranch hands returned. They'd come back if they had legitimate business, right?* But Sophie was not in her right mind. She was very intuitive though sometimes a bit reckless when boredom set in and right now, boredom and curiosity were in the driver's seat. It was dusk and Rick would be back soon, so Sophie felt she had a cushion of safety. She backed up and leaned against the support post to the left of the steps. Looking at them she said, "Both of you, take off your jackets and put them in the car."

Jake and Jules looked at each other and complied without argument.

"Now, leave your firearms in the car and maybe we'll talk," directed Sophie.

Neither Jake nor Jules were surprised that Sophie had guessed they were carrying weapons. It was a logical conclusion. Jake raised his pant leg slightly, carefully unholstered the pistol, opened the car door again, and laid it on the seat.

Sophie was pleased with herself and said rather arrogantly, "Okay, Ms. Law now you, and don't tell me you don't have one."

Jules' mouth turned slightly upwards in a furtive smile. *Sophie may be a back-water rancher,* she thought, *but she's no dummy.* Still mildly amused, she slowly pushed her skirt up her left thigh until the holster was visible and removed a small automatic pistol. If either Rick or Alex had been there, they would have appreciated the unintended seductiveness of Jules' unholstering. Jules walked to the open car door and laid the pistol on the seat, next to Jake's.

Sophie said, "Ms. Law, lock the doors, come up here, and bring the keys with you."

Jake handed Jules the key fob. Jules clicked the lock button, went up to the top step, and held out her left hand with the fob to Sophie, ready with her right if Sophie should get crazy with the shotgun. Sophie, outwardly composed, reached out swiftly taking the key fob and told Jules to sit down in the rocker next to hers. The porch was about fifteen feet deep, so Sophie positioned her rocker where she could keep both Jules and Jake in sight.

Sophie looked Jules over again, appraising her trustworthiness. Jules was not uncomfortable with the penetrating gaze. Men and women ogled her all the time, and in her profession, she was often "sized up" by potential clients and potential enemies. She waited patiently until Sophie said, "Okay, you have ten minutes to get my attention. Start talking."

Jules nodded and began. "Thank you, Mrs. Martini. As I mentioned, I work for a security company based in Los Angeles. Most of our clients are celebrities, high profile businesspeople, insurance companies and government agencies. We provide typical security services, including body-guarding, business security, PI services, intelligence gathering, hostage negotiation and rescue services."

Sophie did not interrupt, so she continued.

"About eight months ago, a woman from Los Angeles was kidnapped and held for ransom. She is the young adult daughter of a very wealthy and successful international businessman who owns multiple munitions factories."

Sophie interrupted. "You said, 'She is the daughter.' I take it she survived the kidnapping."

"Yes, she did," voiced Jules.

Sophie once again interrupted. "Was her father one of your clients?"

"Not prior to the kidnapping. As I was saying, her father, George Bentworth, owns munitions factories in multiple countries. There are always rumors with this kind of business, though nothing illegal has ever been charged. Anyway, Claire, his daughter, disappeared from the dressing room of a department store. She was shopping with her stepmother who had left her to go to another area of the store, returned an hour later and couldn't find Claire.

"Mr. Bentworth was out of his mind. He reported her as missing, but the local police failed to turn up a single clue that pointed to a kidnapping, so they treated it as a voluntary disappearance. Basically, they did nothing. He called the FBI, but they concurred with local authorities that there was nothing to be done until there was solid evidence that it was an abduction.

"Bentworth refused to accept law enforcement's interpretation of the events. Apparently, he had a contact in Washington who knew one of the owners of our company and was referred to us. We stepped in and treated it as an abduction based on Mr. Bentworth's feelings, but knew that if it had been a kidnapping, the chances for a good outcome were slim. Typically, in an abduction, if there is no ransom call within the first twenty four to forty eight hours the chances of an adult victim surviving are small. He hadn't received a ransom call in the four days that she had been missing.

"The afternoon we were hired, a ransom call came in. The demand was for $6 million. Bentworth was able to get the cash right away. He and his family were covered under a kidnap/ransom/extortion insurance policy with Lloyds of London. Lloyds already had an agent on site that was authorized to proffer the money."

Jules paused, waiting for Sophie to catch up, then picked up the story again, sparing no details of the steps they took to rescue the girl.

Sophie asked, "How old was Claire?"

Jules answered, "Twenty-two, but she was very sheltered. Her father is an extremely controlling man with overdeveloped protective tendencies which he seemed to have taken to the extreme after his wife was killed in a car accident over four years ago. He mapped out her every move, even hired bodyguards to follow Claire around her junior year abroad in Italy. I suppose, in all fairness, he was doing what he thought was necessary to protect his only daughter."

Jules paused to assess Sophie's interest.

"Mrs. Martini, the ten minutes you gave me are up. Shall I continue?"

Sophie smiled slightly, knowing that Jules was maneuvering her, but nodded anyway.

"There's a multitude of details that we can give you later if you are interested, however the gist of the rescue efforts entailed dropping the money at sea and picking Claire up at a different location. We had covert teams at the drop and pickup locations, but it proved fruitless. The only conclusion we could draw was that the kidnappers never had any intention of releasing Claire or that something had gone wrong at the holding site. Jake and I were still convinced that the holding site was near the water, even though the rescue or pickup location's coordinates were miles from the ocean."

At hearing Jake's name, Sophie remembered that he was still standing by the car. She turned her attention to him and asked, "Why did you think they had Claire stashed by the water?"

Jake moved to the steps, stopped and answered, "It was a hunch, but at the first light of day, we really got lucky! One of our people who was assigned to monitor the news media, saw that there had been an explosion and fire some hours prior at an abandoned warehouse by the water. Jules and I rushed over. The fire investigator was able to tell us that he believed the explosion was due to a gas line leak. He speculated that the line was purposely disconnected allowing gas to leak into a room on the second floor. He still wasn't sure what sparked the fire and subsequent explosion, but he hypothesized it might have been a candle set on top of a cabinet about five feet higher than the gas leak because there were no traces of an accelerant. Also, there were no signs of human remains. So, we operated on the assumption that if Claire had been there, she must have gotten out or released and refocused our search, ultimately finding her."

No one spoke for a moment, then Sophie with pursed lips said, "I'm glad she is alive and I'm really sorry that this young woman had to go through such a terrible ordeal, but I fail to see how this is has anything to do with me."

Jules took a deep breath and looked at Sophie. Sophie continued to rock back and forth for a few moments, deliberating on whether she wanted to hear more. Finally, she motioned for Jake to join them on the porch. "Sit down," said Sophie laying the shotgun against the wall in the alcove. Sophie asked again, "So what does this story have to do with me, Ms. Law?"

Jules shifted in her seat, pulling her skirt over her thighs. She desperately wanted to come across warmly and with concern. "It's getting late and we have a long drive back to the motel, so I am going to give a synopsis of what happened after Claire was found. We can fill in details tomorrow if you like."

There was no objection from Sophie, so Jules told her that Claire was physically and emotionally injured to the extent that she had to have surgery to repair the injuries to her shoulder and leg. She was also diagnosed with Post Traumatic Stress Disorder. Her concentration was impaired. She became hyper-vigilant, exhibited an exaggerated startle response and demonstrated emotional numbness.

Sophie didn't have a good feeling about what would follow, but she tried to remain relaxed. All she said was, "And?"

Jules put her elbows on chair arm rests, rubbed her temples, then looked up to Sophie and in a matter of fact, straightforward manner said, "We want Claire to continue her recuperation here at your ranch."

Sophie jerked back in her chair. Her mind was spinning, reeling. Anger slowly replaced the blood that had drained from her face, leaving her wan and worn out. She wasn't as introspective as some people, but she knew enough about herself to realize that when her mind was careening out of control, she shouldn't speak until she managed to calm down. Tonight, she was successful in holding her tongue. Jake could feel the tension. It seemed like an eon to Jake before Sophie broke the silence.

"You never found the kidnappers, right? So that means you want to hide her here while you hunt them down."

Jules ignored Sophie's question and answered obliquely. "Her shrink thinks that Claire would benefit from getting out of the surroundings where the trauma took place. We think that this is a perfect place for Claire to continue her recuperation."

"Why here?" asked Sophie, not liking the idea at all, but keeping a rein on her inclination to blurt out *Hell, no!*

Jake chimed in. "Mrs. Martini, we checked out many places against several criteria and your ranch is the best place. There are a lot of tabloids looking for a story, so we want her somewhere that is remote, difficult to reach, and not on the top ten vacation destinations list. It's located smack in the middle of the Bitterroots, one of the roughest mountain areas in the U.S. The way the main buildings are laid out on top of this mesa, backing to the mountains and overlooking the valley, provides a natural sentinel location. Finally, the river is deep and provides somewhat of a natural barrier to casual interlopers, like, uh, reporters."

Jake shot Jules a look that was not missed by Sophie. Jules deftly piggy-backed on Jake's pitch.

"There is another factor, Mrs. Martini, perhaps the most important factor. Everything we have heard about you, tells us that you and your operation might be a good match. We did in-depth research on the top three locations that met all the security and privacy criteria, but your ranch was the only place with a potential environment that we think might be helpful to Claire's emotional state."

Sophie's anger had downgraded to agitation, but it spiked again. "What do you mean you did in-depth research? I don't like the idea of people digging around in my personal business."

Jules' stomach tightened, then lurched, but she remained outwardly unperturbed and explained that she understood Sophie's concern. She clarified that it was necessary for Claire's safety. She reassured Sophie that everything they found was strictly confidential. Looking at Sophie's body language, Jules knew they were in for an eruption that would rival Mt. Vesuvius.

Sophie was fuming and cut Jules off before she could continue. "You are very adept, Ms. Law, at minimizing the fact that you investigated the ranch's personnel and invaded our privacy. Right now, I have half a mind to boot your PI fannies right out of here!"

Jules reached over and put her hand on Sophie's arm. Sophie shrugged her hand off and got up, pacing the long porch. Without warning, she spun around on her heels leveling a venomous look at the two of them. Jake was sure she was going to throw them out. Sophie continued pacing the porch, shaking her head and muttering something in Italian. Jules and Jake barely breathed. Just as quickly as she had gotten up, she stopped pacing, came back, and dropped down into her rocking chair before leaning forward snapping, "You said you had a business proposition. Let's hear it."

Jules and Jake were flabbergasted. They didn't know what to make of Sophie's sudden and unpredictable change in her attitude and demeanor. All Jules could surmise about Sophie's change of heart was that although she was furious about the investigation, she had put two and two together and figured that they knew her financial situation and thus expected a pitch involving money. Either way, Jules was not going to look a gift horse in the mouth.

"It's simple, Mrs. Martini. Claire comes out here for a few months and we make financial arrangements beyond what you would receive from a normal guest stay. We can go over all the details tomorrow."

"Now," hissed Sophie.

"The short of it is, if you decide to let Claire stay here, we are prepared to take care of back mortgage payments, pay the mortgage payments the months she is here and when she leaves, make a lump sum payment equal to the remainder of the mortgage."

Jules thought Sophie might slap her across the face for laying out the deal in such a direct and brutal manner.

Sophie, emotions bouncing between fury and incredulity, spit out, "I'm assuming that you know how much that amounts to, being that you did your investigation!"

Neither Jules nor Jake rose to the blatant bait, which was dripping with sarcasm and hostility.

Sophie continued, "What's the catch? Where's the hidden clause? Where do I find the small print?"

She looked toward the shotgun but didn't reach for it, crossed her arms in front of her chest, and glared at the two of them. She looked like she was careening out of control, but Jules wasn't going to soft peddle the arrangement to Sophie and was fully prepared to detail the conditions and expectations, though she was exhausted. She had often spent days at a time without sleep under enemy gun fire but hadn't experienced this type of emotional weariness for a long time.

Sophie was tough, but if Jules was right, she would be a fierce ally, if they could convince her to take the deal. And that was a big if.

"Sophie, we'd have a contract with everything spelled out, no hidden agendas, no small print. Claire stays here for up to six months. Bentworth provides the financial resources and, of course, we provide the security. We'd have our people on site, perhaps as guests for the summer, and Claire would have a psychologist so that her treatment could continue while she is here."

Jules waited for the barrage of objections she surely thought would follow her summary, but Sophie was oddly quiet, even introspective. She seemed to be studying the pattern of the porch floor.

Jake looked at his watch, then at Jules. He stood up, muttering, "Excuse me, Mrs. Martini," and walked toward the far end of the porch. He thought that maybe Sophie would talk more openly with just Jules there.

Jules finally stood up and awkwardly put her hand on Sophie's shoulder. Sophie looked up startled. Jules looked into her pale green eyes and soothingly said, "We went over a lot tonight. Why don't you think about our offer and tomorrow we can go into more detail on the logistics plus answer any questions you may have."

Sophie made no response at all. Jules, unsettled and with a gnawing sensation of anxiety pervading her body, decided to take the lack of response from Sophie for tonight

"Good night Mrs. Martini. Jake and I will be by tomorrow afternoon. Thank you for your time. We'll leave."

Quite out of character, Jules bent over and gave Sophie a timid side by side hug, taking the keys from Sophie. Sophie continued to sit on the porch, numb from the night's events. She heard the SUV doors close followed by the starting of the engine.

Jules and Jake headed down the road on their two-hour drive back to Missoula. Jake told Jules that he thought things had gone relatively well. Jules nodded but rolled her eyes, a gesture not lost on Jake. They turned off the road from the ranch and headed north on Route 93. Jake had been working with Jules long enough to know that she was preoccupied, and it might not go well if he interrupted her. He decided to do it anyway.

"When are you going to tell Sophie about Alex?" Jules groaned and sunk down in the seat, quiet the rest of the way back to Missoula. Jake knew better than to risk asking again.

The phone rang only two times before it was answered. "Hadn't heard from you in a week or so. I've been waiting for your call. I take it you think it's time to try again."

The voice on the other end of the call answered, "Yes, and I have an idea how to get it done without complications, but we'll have to move soon. Bentworth has those ISS people hanging around at the estate. I found out they are looking for a safe house to stash her."

"When can you get away?"

"Thursday noon, usual place at 1:00 p.m." replied the voice on the phone.

"Fine. I'm running out of cash. Any chance you can advance a few thousand?"

"I'll see what I can do. I'll have to juggle some things. Bye for now."

CHAPTER 2—Phoenix Rising

A mythical bird that never dies, the phoenix flies far ahead to the front, always scanning the landscape and distant space.

Feng Shui Master Lam Kam Chuen

Wednesday April 8

When Sophie was sure that they had left, she grabbed the shotgun, walked into the foyer, and locked the door. She went back to the kitchen table and sat down with her head in her hands, trying to settle her emotions and look at it from all angles. Sophie was a dichotomy: Wild, passionate, short fused, yet intensely logical. She was often in conflict with her own personality and emotions.

She was still brooding when she heard Rick's truck pull up to the back. Looking at the kitchen clock, she realized she had been sitting for over an hour. It was past midnight. She waited for him to walk through the back door into the kitchen. Moments later he dropped his duffle bag in the doorway, said, "Hi," and with one look at Sophie, immediately knew that something was wrong. Sophie looked worried and out of sorts. He strode over with his usual purposeful gait and when he reached her, she stood up throwing her arms around him. Though Sophie was affectionate, this was not usual behavior.

It must be bad, thought Rick. He pulled away gently, holding her upper arms and said, "Are you okay? Is Alex okay?" Sophie nodded "yes" and told Rick to sit down.

He joined her at the table, and she recounted the events of the night. Rick listened intently, seldom interrupting, knowing that Sophie had to get her tale out. When she had finished the story, she realized that Rick had her hands in his and was gently rubbing hers with a soft soothing touch. Without knowing it, Sophie had calmed down and much of the agitation she was feeling had subsided. Rick saw the signs that Sophie was exhausted and hoped that she would agree to go to bed.

"Let me walk you up to your room so you can get some rest. Then I'm going to go down to the office and do some research on this ISS, the kidnapping, and Bentworth. In the morning I'll call a couple of friends I have in D.C., then brief you so we can figure out the next steps, okay?"

Sophie nodded and headed toward the back steps to the family quarters. Rick was glad that Sophie had not given him an argument. She could be headstrong. He followed closely behind and went into Sophie's suite after her. Sophie had a sitting room, which she used mostly for sewing, a bedroom, and a bathroom. They were standing in the sitting room when Rick asked her if she wanted him to sit with her until she fell asleep. Sophie told him she would be okay, so he touched her arm briefly, gave her a peck on the cheek, and left with a "see you in the morning," over his shoulder as he made his way back down the stairs to the office.

The office was located to the right of the main entry, across from the great room, just to the right of a small check-in area with two comfortable leather chairs that faced the registration counter. Next to the office, were Rick's quarters, a small bedroom and bathroom.

Rick's official title was 'Business Manager', however, he wore many hats, including Sophie's closet friend, confidant, and lover. He booted up the office computer and while he was waiting for Windows to come up, he went into the small bathroom and splashed water on his face. Opening a small refrigerator in the office, he pulled out a cola. He would need the caffeine to get through this night. Settling himself in front of the computer, he opened the Internet browser. As soon as Google came up, he typed in Intelligent Security Services. There were over a hundred thousand references to the company. He started reading and after an hour, was convinced that ISS was a legitimate operation.

Beginning a new search, he typed in Jake's name. A few references came up citing Jake's military career as well as his affiliation to ISS. He had served as a Navy Seal for most of his career, receiving various service medals, including the Navy Cross, an award for valor in action against an enemy. He retired with a Commander rank. Rick was also able to find an article from a local newspaper in upstate New York, where Jake grew up. The article detailed Jake's rescue of a young boy from drowning in a semi-frozen pond when he was a senior in high school. Jake had gotten a scholarship to Syracuse University as a starting running back and volunteered his time at the local nursing home. An all-American boy!

Jules was another story. Not much came up on her except for her affiliation with ISS and a few news articles about her involvement with ISS operations, including the Bentworth kidnapping. He found very little on her prior to her association with ISS. Rick thought that the absence of information was just as telling as an abundance of information. He guessed that she might have been with one of the government intelligence or covert organizations. Jules Law might not be her real name.

There was lots of information on the Bentworth kidnapping. He read every article and newspaper report that he could find before his eyes started to swim. Getting up from the computer, he retrieved his address book, which he kept locked, along with his firearms in a built-in wall safe hidden in the closet. Thumbing through the book, he found the two names he wanted. It was now about 3:00 a.m. Montana time, 6:00 a.m. on the east coast. He dialed the first number and waited for an answer. The automated response instructed him to leave a message. He did and about ten minutes later one of his cell phones rang.

"Daniel, how the heck are you? You up all ready?" said Rick jovially

"Rick, you son of a bitch, where the hell are you? You fell off the grid a few years ago and no one has heard from you."

"I'm still out here on the ranch in Montana. Don't miss all the saluting and groveling."

"Isn't it like 3:00 a.m. out there? What in the dickens are you doing up? Even roosters don't get up until the sun comes up! How's your girlfriend? Isn't she from Montana?"

Rick ignored Daniel's question and got right to the point. "Daniel, I need your help."

Daniel heard the seriousness in Rick's voice. He responded, "What do you need buddy? You know I'd do anything for you, as long as it doesn't get my butt in a sling."

Rick briefly outlined what he needed, information on ISS and their relationship to covert agencies. He also asked for financial or contractual data if Daniel could get his hands on it. Daniel listened then asked Rick, "Are you somehow tied into this organization?"

Rick, stretching the truth a little, told Daniel, "They want me to do a job for them."

Rick couldn't see Daniel, but he correctly surmised that Daniel was nodding his head up and down, understanding Rick's caution before accepting a job with any organization that might have covert ties with the CIA or any other government agency.

"How fast do you need this?" asked Daniel.

"Unfortunately, I need information in a few hours."

Daniel hesitated a moment and quipped, "For you, I'll put a rush on it. Don't know how much I'll get, but I'll call you back in a few hours. Let's be careful, just in case."

"Thanks Daniel, I'm on a prepaid cellular. Don't think it can be traced back to me. Did your ANI capture the number?"

"Nope, bye, Rick," and the phone went dead.

Rick did not make the second call yet. He decided to wait to hear from Daniel. Daniel was well connected with the various covert organizations in Washington, but sometimes, they didn't want to share information, so Rick wasn't holding out too much hope. He laid down on the bed, set his wristwatch to go off at 5:45 a.m. and let his mind wander to thoughts of Sophie.

Alex had convinced him to come to Montana the Christmas of 2015. Both were stationed at Camp Dwyer in Afghanistan. He was reluctant to go, not because of the subzero temperatures of Montana winters, rather he got overemotional around the holidays and didn't want to subject anyone to his melancholy. Mary, his wife, died in April of 2013, only a month after he had arrived at his new post as Brigade Commander. It was especially hard for him around Thanksgiving and Christmas. However, Alex kept hounding him and, in the end, made him feel guilty.

He had received orders from the Marine Corps Intelligence Division (MCIA) to send troops to the south of the camp in the Hemland River Valley, a hot spot for Taliban Insurgents, drug, and child trafficking. Air support was also dispatched to support the regimental combat troops to quell the latest uprising.

Rick had sent Alex, who was the camp psychologist, to help out with any children that were recovered as part of the comprehensive mission. While there, Alex got caught in a crossfire during a skirmish and suffered serious injuries. Although Rick knew it wasn't his fault that Alex got hit, he irrationally felt culpable.

So, when Alex told him that his help was needed to make the trip, he couldn't refuse. Both had thirty days of leave, so Rick packed his gear and hitched several military transport rides to the U.S. Naval Hospital in Yokosuka, Japan, where Alex was recuperating after emergency treatment at the 31st Combat Support Hospital adjacent to Camp Dwyer. He expected much worse than what he saw. Alex only had a slight limp. Rick just shook his head and smiled, knowing that he had been conned. He didn't mind.

Newly minted Captain Alex Martini became his friend, his confidante, and his rock during the months after Mary's death. Alex was not invasive, never pushed Rick to talk about his emotions, but somehow had a sense of what Rick needed. Often, he had difficulty sleeping when the emotional pain was too much to bear and prowled the camp during the early morning hours. Alex started appearing at his door, standing there until Rick noticed, then sat down on the bench outside of his quarters. Rick would come out and the two of them would sit there for hours, watching daybreak, sometimes not exchanging a word. He was convinced he owed his sanity to Alex. The least he could do was help on the trip to visit Sophie, Alex's aunt in Montana.

They bussed their way to Tokyo, flew commercial to Seattle, then hopped a flight on Alaskan Air to Missoula, where Dean, Sophie's foreman was waiting for them. Alex was right, the trip was grueling. It had taken them over 24 hours to get to Big Sky Country, which was under a siege of snow, wind, and bitter cold. Rick, who had been raised in Virginia and lived there most of his life, didn't know how the airplane landed on the frozen runway without skidding out of control, let alone how anyone drove on the snow-covered ice.

Rick was exhausted and stiff as he helped Alex into a huge dualie outfitted with chains. He could only imagine how Alex was feeling, but Alex was Alex and you never heard any complaining, no matter how bad it got. Dean had hot coffee in a thermos for them, offered sandwiches Sophie had made, and told them to catch some shut eye if they could, because sure as shooting, Sophie wasn't going to let them go to bed without thoroughly interrogating them.

They finished the sandwiches and coffee and despite the caffeine, promptly fell asleep. Alex was stretched out on the back seat of the quad cab and Rick had reclined his seat, his head almost touching Alex's feet. Dean didn't mind. He'd be better off without any backseat drivers in this storm.

When the truck pulled in front of the house, both Alex and Rick woke up. Rick hadn't shaved in more than 24 hours and his extra-heavy five o'clock shadow had evolved into a scraggy stubble. Great impression he was going to make. He rubbed his hand across his jaw and shrugged his shoulders.

Alex laughed, and said, "It'll be okay. Aunt Sophie knows we've been traveling for more than a day."

Rick quipped back good naturedly, "Oh sure . . .just because you don't have a five o'clock shadow!"

Alex punched his arm and Rick jumped down from the truck to avoid further jabs. He had expected to see Alex's Aunt Sophie in the doorway, but she had not come out.

Damn cold at ten below zero. Can't blame her, he thought as he stiffly walked toward the porch. He stopped in mid step, remembering that Alex might need help getting out of the truck. He went back to offer his arm, hoping that Alex wouldn't act all macho and refuse his assistance.

Dean was long gone, having deposited the bags inside the house and was headed down to the bunk house before Alex and Rick went inside. Alex opened the door, motioned Rick to follow, and both walked into a small foyer with coat hooks on the right side. They shrugged off their coats, put them up on the hooks, took off their fatigue boots, and went through the second door that opened to a huge great room. It smelled wonderful, a cross between evergreens and spices. In the corner stood a fifteen-foot Christmas tree decorated beautifully with a host of lights and ornaments. On the mantel of the oversized fireplace there were boughs of pine and holly.

Then Rick saw a nice-looking woman he guessed to be in her mid-forties, though he would learn later that she was ten years his senior. Her red hair, swept up in a bun of some sort, complimented her green eyes which were framed with arching eyebrows and a few crinkly crows' feet. Her nose was straight and sat squarely in the middle of her rosy cheeks, but oh her mouth. He could barely breathe. Heart shaped, perfectly symmetrical, with plump lips, slightly parted in anticipation, did him in. He was surprised by the unexpected stirrings he felt.

Without a word she took Alex into her arms, holding on tightly, as if she were never going to let go. Alex didn't shrink from the embrace, rather relaxed into it and let Sophie take all the time she wanted. Finally, Sophie kissed Alex on the mouth and both cheeks before letting go. Before Alex could introduce Rick, Sophie turned, and grabbed him in a fierce bear hug, her head against his chest, resting just below his nose. He swooned from the smell of her hair against his nostrils...*sandalwood, musk, and orange*, he thought as he breathed in deeply to enjoy the exotic fragrances. Unconscious of his movements, he lifted his arms to loosely hold her around her back. She held him for several moments, then released him and passionately said, "Thank you for bringing Alex home alive!"

Rick was thunderstruck, confused. Tears were running down his face, and he couldn't seem to move his feet. Head spinning and knees rubbery, he was at a total loss of what had happened, what to do, what to say, and how to handle the tears. Surges of emotion scuttled through his chest. He was no longer thinking; he was just trying to keep breathing.

Sophie looked up at him, quickly took his hand in hers, and led him right past Alex. They walked through the reception area to a little office and into a bedroom. He let her lead him because he didn't know what else to do. She turned to Rick and said, "Dean already brought in your bag.

Why don't you wash up, maybe get a quick shower and shave, then come into the kitchen for a midnight snack? Sometimes the altitude, if you're not used to it, can make you a little dizzy and weak in the knees."

Lying on his bed in the same room right now, he pondered what Alex might have told Sophie before his arrival and thought that someday he'd ask. His visceral reaction to Sophie had left him shaken, feeling embarrassed and relieved at the same time. He also was grateful that Sophie had given him an out and time to compose himself. She may not have known what caused his emotional display, but he was sure she knew it had nothing to do with the altitude. He remembered digging into his duffle bag, finding his shaving kit, and doing just what Sophie had told him to do, shower and shave. After putting on clean clothes, he made his way into the kitchen. Alex was sitting at a table, dressed in a long-sleeved Henley and some sort of pajama bottoms.

"Aw, I thought you might be wearing your Big Dog pajamas!" Alex joked.

Rick blushed, bowled over by Alex's brash teasing in front of Sophie. He didn't want Sophie to get the wrong idea about Alex and him.

Sophie came toward him, put one hand on his shoulder and said "You never mind. Alex is always misbehaving." She handed him a glass of scotch, picked hers up from the table, said, "Cheers," and downed the entire contents in one gulp. He looked at her, she smiled and nodded slightly, and he followed suit. He was appreciative that she had not asked if he was feeling better. She poured another glass for both, sat down at the table next to him and began asking about their trip.

Rick woke groggily to the alarm on his wristwatch. He got up, used the bathroom, and was drying his hands when one of his cell phones rang.

"Rick, I've got your information. Ready to take notes?" Daniel was talking in a low voice, not quite whispering, but low enough that Rick had to strain to hear. Daniel was hurried but organized. After he finished, Rick thanked him and promised to keep in touch. The information Daniel gave him wasn't much more insightful than what he learned from public sources, except for two things; the political connections and Jules Law.

ISS was a well-established business with three owners. Greg Paulson, a retired Navy Admiral, who was the front man. He was very skilled in getting government contracts. The second principle was retired Senator Baluchi. He handled the money, which was a logical extension of his service on the Appropriation Committee in the U.S. Senate. *No conflict of interest, right?* He had put up most of the capital to launch ISS, though Paulson and Law had put in a chunk. Rick was not surprised to learn that Jules Law was also an owner. All three had appeared as owners on ISS's website.

What he didn't know was that she was in charge of Operations and unlike Paulson and Baluchi, who were located in Washington, she was based in Los Angles. His instinct about her background had been right. Her dossier included a stint with Marine Intelligence, special assignment to the National Security Council, and unspecified covert assignments. Her upbringing was also interesting. She was born and raised in Glendale, Maryland, a stone's throw from where Rick grew up. Her mother was Iranian, born in the states, and her father was an Anglo with a well-positioned civil service job with the IRS. Jules was fluent in Farsi, probably learning it from her mother or maternal grandparents. Rick new that Farsi was the most widely spoken Persian language in Iran, Afghanistan, and Tajikistan. She was also fluent in Kurdish, spoken in Turkey, Iraq, Iran, and Syria. No wonder she was valuable in the intelligence community!

Seemed pretty logical that Jake's connection was to Admiral Paulson, both doing stints in the Navy, but he wondered how Jules fit in with the good old boys. Daniel was quick to answer that there were rumors that she and Senator Baluchi had been 'close' friends, all innuendo and nobody particularly cared, because neither of them were married. Daniel also confirmed that the ISS group had ties to the NSA, Army intelligence, and occasionally did intel work for the CIA, known in the intelligence community as 'the Company.' Rick asked him if there was any indication that ISS had been contracted by the CIA to provide cleaning operations. Daniel said there was no indication, however, it could be hidden deeper than he was able to go without arousing suspicion. He doubted that Paulson and Baluchi would play in that sand box, but everyone had their price.

The last piece of information that Daniel provided was about Bentworth. He had a strong relationship with the Senate Armed Services Committee, making sure that they were wined and dined, all within legal parameters. It was possible that Bentworth knew Baluchi, and word on the street was that a current member of the Armed Services Committee referred Bentworth to ISS. Again, nothing that seemed unusual on the surface.

Daniel abruptly said, "Gotta go," and the phone call was disconnected.

Rick was about to make the second call, when his phone rang again. Daniel was back on the line.

"Listen, Rick, sorry about that, but I gotta make this quick. Just got word that Bentworth is tied into more than the Armed Services Committee. He's the CIA's errand boy. That's all I can say right now. I'll get back to you when I can."

He disconnected once again.

Rick understood exactly what Daniel was saying. There were conflicts going on all over the world and while the U.S. picked and chose its public battles, often covert monetary resources were funneled through the Company and more often than not, munitions were supplied to assist in protecting U.S. interests, economic or geographic in conflicted areas. The best-known example of covert operations was what happened in Chile. As a result of the declassification of CIA documents from 1970 – 1976, there was no doubt that the CIA had significant involvement in the military coup of 1973.

U.S. companies were heavily invested in Chilean copper, making it Chile's largest export. By 1930, U.S. investments were staggering. Between 1938 and 1963 there were various political parties in control of the Chilean government, none of them presenting a threat to multinational and U.S. economic interests.

Then in the presidential elections of 1964, there was clear danger to U.S. interests posed by the socialist candidate, who's plan included the nationalization of foreign owned industry. To prevent a victory of the socialist candidate, Salvador Allende, the U.S. poured twenty million dollars through the CIA into the campaign to get Allende's opponent elected in hopes of staving off financial disaster for U.S. companies.

Six years later economic conditions in Chile worsened and the 1970 election for president was a three-way contest. The CIA and interested multinationals put less money into the campaign than they had in 1964 thinking that Allende would lose, and the U.S. interests would be protected. However, Allende won and began the Chilean Path to Socialism, including ending the power and control of multinational corporations and large landowners.

By the end of 1971, one hundred fifty industrial plants were usurped and transitioned to state control and in July of 1971, U.S.-owned Anaconda and Kennecott Copper mines were nationalized. Henry Kissinger, in a now famous, but arrogant quote, fired off the current sentiment of the U.S. government concerning the actions of the Chilean government.

"I don't see why we need to stand by and watch a country go communist due to the irresponsibility of its own people."

A covert plan was put into place to replace the democratically elected Marxist president, Allende, with a military government sympathetic to U.S. interest, solely with the purpose to halt any further expropriation. First, the U.S. cut off all loans and blocked the World Bank and other sources of money to Chile. This economic war failed. Then, the CIA waged covert smear campaigns through conservative newspapers and radios, playing on the fears of communism. This too failed, leaving only one option.

On September 11, 1973, four branches of the Chilean Armed Forces, led by Pinochet, violently overthrew Allende, beginning seventeen years of violent military rule, flagrant civil rights violations, and the "disappearance" of thousands of people. The coup was successful and secured economic stability for U.S. interests.

Rick conjectured that Bentworth might be, at the behest of the CIA, a supplier of munitions to allied factions protecting U.S. interests. This put a whole new spin on the kidnapping!

It was 6:30 a.m. and he heard Sophie in the kitchen. He would wait to make his second call until he talked with her. Rick quickly washed up, pulled on a clean shirt, and headed to the kitchen.

As he came up behind her and put his arms around her, he asked, "Were you able to sleep at all?"

Sophie kept working at the sink while responding, "Surprisingly, I did. What about you?"

"About two hours, while I was waiting for east coast bureaucrats to wake up." He had gotten himself a cup and was pouring coffee.

"Are you ready for a cup yet, Soph?"

"In a minute. Thanks. What do you want for breakfast?"

Rick loved breakfast. He could eat it three times a day, so he didn't pass up Sophie's offer. "You bet I'm ready! How about a couple of eggs over easy, a side of bacon," he said with a straight face, "and whole wheat toast with some of those strawberry preserves you made last summer?"

Sophie turned and faced him with a forced smile. "I'll make the eggs, but you will be lucky to get 4 slices of bacon. You'll have to make the toast and while you're at it, put in a couple of slices for me." Though she had slept, she was still preoccupied.

Rick got up, readied plates, napkins, butter, the preserves and dropped four slices of bread into the toaster. Sophie was already frying the eggs and bacon. Rick sipped his coffee while he waited for the toast, appreciating the fact that Sophie wasn't rushing him to share what he had learned. If Sophie had a fault it was her tendency to be impatient. However in all fairness, occasionally she knew when to hold back, if and only if, it suited her purpose. Once they were both seated at the table with their food, he began telling Sophie what he had learned. He was careful not to identify his source.

"Bentworth's connection to the CIA may put a whole new face on the kidnapping. Here are the options as I see them. One, the kidnapping was random. In other words, some thugs targeted a rich guy. Two, the kidnapping was personal. Someone Bentworth crossed, either personally or in his business dealings, was trying to get back at him. And three, Bentworth ticked off the Company and they intended to teach him a lesson."

Sophie fully knew what The Company meant. She interjected, "Door number three sounds ominous. Do you think that ISS' involvement is part of the subterfuge?"

Sophie never failed to surprise Rick. She had a quick mind and could put things together rapidly to see the big picture.

"Good question. I don't think that ISS is working on behalf of the Company, but either way, if door number three is the right door, keeping the Bentworth woman here would be dangerous and risky to us and our summer guests."

"So, are you saying that we should turn down the proposal?"

Rick scratched his head, rubbed his jaw, and leveled a serious look at Sophie. He was so decisive about most things, that his wavering threw Sophie.

"Sophie, you and I know what the cash infusion could do for the place, but are you willing to take the risk of opening the barn doors and letting all the horses run out to get the cash?"

Sophie appreciated the metaphor, nodding her head in understanding. "Rick, do you think it would hurt to try and call ISS' hand?"

"What did you have in mind, Sophie?"

"Well, Jules and Jake are coming back after lunch. What if we play blackjack, show our hand, let them know what you've found out and force them to show what they know. I would bet that they know more than they told me."

Rick considered this as he got up to pour another cup of coffee for himself and Sophie. "I think that might be a good tactic, but I would like to make one more call to a friend in DC before we decide. I can see the wheels turning, Sophie. What else?"

"What if ISS is on the level and they don't have any involvement with whomever abducted the woman? Even if this is true, do you think that Bentworth is going to shell out the kind of money they're talking about just to stash Claire here for a few months? There's got to be something else."

Score another for Sophie. It was exactly what Rick had been turning over in his head. "Let's say that ISS is on the level and they are not embroiled with the CIA in this situation. Maybe the real mission is not just to provide security services and treatment for Claire. Suppose it is to track down the people who planned and executed the kidnapping and deal with them outside the legal system. Bentworth may be the type of fellow that wants his own brand of justice. It would be easier for ISS to get the job done if Claire were tucked away in a safe location, don't you think?"

Sophie nodded and finished her coffee. When she got up to clear away the breakfast dishes, Rick said, "I think I had better make that call now. Talk to you in a few."

Once Rick was back in the office, he dialed Senator Thane's office. The phone was answered by one of his aides who questioned him on the nature of the call. Rick tried to be polite and sidestep the question, however the aide told him that she would not put the call through without a name and reason for the call. He told her to tell Senator Thane that Colonel Rick Hidalgo was on the line and it was a matter of personal business which he would only discuss with the Senator. His hackles up now, he also told the aide that if Senator Thane found out he had called and he wasn't put through, he was sure that she would be joining the ranks of the unemployed. She asked him to wait a moment. Two minutes later, Senator Thane came on the line.

"My god, the Phoenix rises! Is that really you, Rick?"

"Guilty as charged, Senator. Thanks for talking to me."

"I had no choice. You scared the hell out of my aide! What can I do for you?"

"Senator, you know I wouldn't be calling unless it was important, and I had struck out everywhere else."

"Rick, I owe you a lot for saving my son's ass. Tell me what you need, and I'll see what I can do."

"Senator, you don't owe me anything. Tyler was young and stupid. I just used a little influence to get him straightened out. How is he?"

"Tyler is doing fine. Just about ready to graduate from Wharton Business School and start a job with some wall street investment firm."

"That's great. I'm glad to hear that, Senator. I'm always at your service, anytime."

"I'll be sure to remember that, Rick."

The Senator was subtly reminding Rick, that there would be a price to be paid in the future for his help now. After Rick had pulled Tyler's ass out of the proverbial fire while he was a snot-nosed kid in the Marines, a discrete three months later, Rick got a promotion from Captain to Lt. Colonel. Rick knew how it worked and accepted the quid pro quo.

"Any time, Senator, any time."

"Okay, what do you need?"

"Senator, any reason to have your office phones bugged or recorded by anyone?"

"Naw. Even so, I have them swept regularly. You probably know that I sit on the Homeland Security and Government Affairs Committee now. We're extra vigilant lately."

"Senator, I'm talking about the home team."

"Yeah, I figured. We're okay."

Rick briefly described the situation, the players, and what he already knew. He asked the Senator if he could, without rocking the boat, find out if Baluchi or Paulson were in the CIA's pocket. Senator Thane didn't answer right away. When he did all he said was,

"Wow. You sure are playing in the big pond. Is this a life or death situation for you?"

Rick was honest. "It isn't right now but could be depending on the decisions my family and I have to make."

"All right, Rick, but I'll have to be careful. If they are, I don't want to tip off any of the Company boys, or for that matter, Baluchi and Paulson."

"Thank you, Senator. You have my number and please, don't do anything that will cause you grief."

Returning to the kitchen, Rick reported what he had done. Sophie was not surprised that Rick had friends in high places. He was a man of integrity and very resourceful.

CHAPTER 3 – Into the Fire

Double, double, toil and trouble; fire burning and cauldron bubble.

William Shakespeare

Wednesday April 8 (cont.)

Just as Sophie was laying out soup and sandwiches on the table for lunch, Rick came in and washed up in the kitchen sink instead of using the lavatory sink. She hated that, but it was practically his only vice, so she stopped complaining long ago. They were both tired, Sophie from anxiety and Rick from not sleeping the night before.

"Sophie, you know I love you, don't you?"

"Rick, what brought that on?"

"Oh, I don't know. Guess I'm just in tune with my manly emotions today."

Sophie laughed. "Rick, you're always in touch with your emotions. You just don't express them too often, unless of course we're in—"

Rick cut her off before she could finish her sentence, hoping to keep her from embarrassing him. "All right, all right Sophie. You made your point. No need to get graphic. But you do know that Alex and you are my family and I would do anything for you, right?"

"Of course, dear. Both Alex and I know this."

"Sophie, I think we need to talk to Alex about this whole situation."

"This is why we get along so well, my darling. We're almost always on the same page. I was thinking of calling but didn't want to add any more stress. Remember? Paper signing today. I'm sure that it is going to stir up some unpleasant feelings."

"Right, right," mumbled Rick. How Sophie kept all those details in her head, he could never figure out. He was the one with the almost photographic memory, yet Sophie retained miniscule facts his mind refused to deem worthy of remembrance.

Alex was discharged from the Army in September of 2016 shortly after Rick had retired and moved out to the ranch with Sophie.

Alex started out in the Navy ROTC program while at the University of Montana in Missoula, then delayed entering the Marines for two years in order to get a Ph.D. in Forensic Psychology at the University of Denver. After an honorable discharge, Alex came back to the ranch for a short time, then moved to Seattle to take a job as a forensic psychologist for the court system.

Shortly after moving there, Alex met and fell in love with Reggie, short for Regina, a lawyer with some hot shot firm. They had been together over three years, but the last year of the relationship had been stormy, to say the least. Reggie was increasingly absent and finally told Alex that it was over just before Christmas last year. After several months of negotiation through Alex's attorney, Alex was buying out Reggie's interest in the home they had bought together.

Rick knew that Sophie was secretly hoping that Alex would agree to put the house on the market, split the proceeds with Reggie, and come home. He wondered, *Is today more traumatic for Alex or Sophie?* He had to admit that it probably would be hard for Alex to be in the same room with Reggie, who had moved on and was already involved with someone else. To top it off, Alex would have to empty the legendary piggy bank to buy Reggie out and Rick knew how uncomfortable Alex would be without a nest egg stashed away.

"Earth to Rick, earth to Rick. Where are you?"

"Oh, I was thinking about Alex and that floozy Reggie. I still think we need to call and get some input, even if it's a tough day. Think we could entice Alex to come out here this weekend?"

"Who knows? You know Alex as well as I do. Once Alex goes down one path, it's hard to change course."

"Ah, Sophie, the apple doesn't fall far from the tree."

Sophie swatted him, laughed, and started to clean up the table when Rick's cell phone rang. He answered it while walking out of the room.

"Rick are you by any chance on a secure line?" asked Senator Thane.

"I'm on a burner cell phone."

"Okay I guess it will have to do. We seemed to have stirred up some, ah, discomfort. Don't think you are in danger, though, but why tempt fate? Get rid of the phone and get yourself another one. Turns out your two boys are not in bed with the Company. They regularly turn down certain assignments that don't meet their operational criteria. Some sandboxes are too full of shit. You know what I mean?"

Rick promptly answered, "Yes I do. Was there anything else?"

"Yeah, two more things, one of note, the other just background. Bentworth took over the business from his father, when he became ill about fifteen years ago. His father died shortly after that. There is speculation that the father may have been involved in some covert activities in South America, but I can't get confirmation without ruffling big feathers. I don't think this has anything to do with your current, ah, situation, but I decided to tell you so you'd have an idea on how ingrained Bentworth might be with the Company. The other, well, I'll let you decide. Rumor has it that Bentworth refused to do an errand for the Company, but as it turned out, the Company now seems to be okay with his refusal. The Company's intel was wrong, so when Bentworth refused the job, it probably avoided egg on their face. They should be grateful, though they'll never admit it."

"You sure about that, Senator?"

"Yup. It was easier to ask questions about Bentworth than about your other two boys. Got it on good authority."

"You think they were telling you straight, or just what they thought would be good for business?"

"My take is that I got the skinny, but you've been around long enough to know that even seasoned ducks like myself can fall prey to a duck hunter's call. Catch my drift?"

"Sure do. Better watch my tail feathers."

"Exactly, my friend. Take care and if you are ever in DC, call me for dinner. You're buying."

"You bet."

Rick hung up and walked back into the kitchen to relay Senator Thane's information. At first, she looked at him quizzically, then her brain synapses kicked in and her face lit up with recognition.

"So, the kidnapping was either random or personal, not CIA related?"

He nodded his head in the affirmative. "What time was Alex signing papers?"

Sophie told him it had been scheduled for early this morning.

"Soph, I think we should call now before Jules and Jake show up."

"Okay, you do it. I'll sit with you."

He pulled out a different cell phone from his pocket, found the number in the contacts, dialed, and put it on speaker phone.

"Dr. Alex Martini's office. How may I help you?" answered a perky voice. Rick said, "Would you please tell Dr. Martini that Rick Hidalgo is calling from Montana."

"Rick!! Is that you?" Alex was on the line a moment later.

"Alex how are you, my dear?" chirped Sophie.

"Fine. I just got back to the office. It went better than I had imagined. Aunt Sophie, are you okay? You sound funny."

"Oh yes dear. Just fine. Rick and I are on the speaker phone. Say, we were wondering if you might agree to hop a flight this weekend and come out to the ranch. We have some things we want to talk to you about."

"Really, Aunt Sophie, I'm fine. Stop being a mother hen."

"Alex," piped up Rick, "Your aunt is not being a mother hen. We've got something serious to discuss, and I'm sorry that the timing is so bad."

"You haven't decided to sell, have you Aunt Sophie?" asked a slightly panicked Alex.

"No, no, but we've received an interesting business proposal we'd like you to review."

Both Rick and Sophie knew that Alex wouldn't be satisfied with that explanation. They prepared for Alex's typical relentless pestering.

"What do you mean a business proposal?"

Rick said, "Are you sitting down? It's kind of wild."

"Yeah, I'm sitting, but if you don't tell me what's going on, I'll be pacing."

Rick cut to the chase. "Yesterday, Sophie was asked if she would be interested in having a high-profile guest here for a few months. In exchange, Sophie would receive enough money to pay off all the ranch's debts."

Alex, equally as direct, responded, "Who is this high-profile person?"

"Do you remember reading about the kidnapping of a California woman, Claire Bentworth, several months ago?" asked Rick.

"Vaguely. Why would they want this woman to stay at the ranch? I mean, you know I love the ranch and it is a great vacation place, but why are they willing to settle all the ranch's debts for her to stay there? Do they want you to cancel all the other guests for the summer?"

Typical Alex, three questions in the same breath. Rick tried to slow the interchange down and patiently explained.

"First of all, we don't have to cancel any of the guests who have already booked. Secondly, they like the remoteness of the area, away from photographers and reporters."

Sophie continued, "There are a lot of details that we can't go over right now, that's why we want you to come out and—"

Alex butted in, cutting off Sophie, "I get the sense that you two are not telling me the whole story."

Rick tried, "Alex, the deal essentially comes down to her staying at the ranch, we protect her privacy, and the mortgage is retired."

"Who are the people that made the offer? Relatives?" continued Alex.

"Her father hired a security firm and people from the firm made the offer. I checked them out with my contacts in DC and the firm is legit," explained Rick.

"Now I remember the case. What did they say about her medical condition?" pushed Alex.

"She had to have some surgeries to repair injuries she suffered, but she is well physically," Sophie replied.

"And emotionally? Did they tell you about that?" Alex pressed on.

"Yes. She was diagnosed with PTSD. However, she has had extensive therapy and is doing better. Her psychiatrist thinks a change in environment would hasten her recovery," answered Sophie tolerantly.

"You guys, PTSD can be tricky. I don't think that either of you are equipped to deal with some of the behaviors associated with PTSD." Alex shot back.

"They said she would have a companion with appropriate psychiatric training to handle any complications from the PTSD," responded Sophie.

"Man, I'd really like to be there to talk to these people. I don't want you two getting involved in something that could be disastrous for you, the ranch, or this woman. When do they need an answer?"

Sophie and Rick exchanged looks. Better than what they had hoped. Alex was interested.

"They're coming back today to provide us more detail, but they haven't given us a drop-dead date to make a decision," answered Sophie.

"Can you get them to stick around a few days so I can get there? I might be able to catch a flight out tomorrow or the next evening. Let me call you tonight to let you know if I can rearrange my schedule for Thursday and Friday. If I can't get there, we'll have to set up something over the phone. Promise me you won't accept their proposal until I can talk to these folks and the woman's doctors," said Alex with finality.

Alex's demand was unmistakably framed with concern, but Sophie recognized that Alex was on the hunt, impassioned with a new challenge. Sophie promised that they wouldn't make any decision until all questions were answered. They said goodbye and would wait for the call tonight.

Sophie, mildly amused, looked at Rick. "Well, that was easier than I thought, I mean the part about getting Alex to come out here. At least this will provide a diversion from thinking about Reggie."

"Sophie," Rick started, still trying to decide if he would butt in, "I think Alex hasn't been in love with Reggie for a long time but is still fuming over the infidelities and betrayals. The dream of a happy household evaporated a while ago. Alex has such high standards that it's difficult for people to live up to them and for sure, Reggie just didn't share the same aspirations."

Sophie shook her head. "You talk like this is more than conjecture. How do you know this, Rick?"

"I think sometimes Alex tells me things that because, well, let's just say, some things are easier for Alex to tell me than you."

"That's nonsense. I'm very accepting and tolerant! Reggie was always welcome here. I never passed judgement," replied Sophie with a slight hint of indignation.

Rick had to be careful here, because Sophie wasn't always tolerant, though she liked to think she was. "That's true with most things Sophie, but remember Alex is trying to hold herself up to your and Mario's example. How long were you married to Mario? Did Alex ever see you fighting? To Alex, you had the perfect relationship, even if it wasn't."

"I don't want Alex to use Mario and me as a measuring stick, Rick. Times were different then and there weren't as many choices, and just for the record, no relationship is perfect," responded Sophie, her hackles definitely ruffled.

"I know, I know, Sophie, but you can't change what was imprinted on Alex. After the death of Carlo and Franny, you and Mario became Alex's world. When Mario passed, you became the only connection to everything Alex had known. Alex is trying to invent a world in which to live, but the only model available, is what was learned here."

Sophie sighed heavily, put her arms around Rick and kissed him on the lips. "Sometimes I wonder just who the shrink is in this family!"

God was she lucky that this dear man had walked into her life. She remembered the night they met. Mario had been dead for several years. He had succumbed to lung cancer after eighteen months of aggressive surgical, chemo, and radiation therapies, leaving Sophie and the ranch in dire financial trouble. He died early in Alex's senior year at college and it was always Sophie's contention that Alex delayed military service for another two years, so that Sophie wouldn't be alone. At least at graduate school in Denver, Alex was close enough to get home for long weekends and vacations.

When Sophie gave Alex a welcoming hug the night they arrived years ago, she caught a glimpse of Rick in the corner of her eye. Sophie had good observational powers. In an instant she concluded that he was good looking, about ten years older than Alex, dark hair, closely cropped, strong shoulders tapering to a slim waist, and muscular thighs. His face was a classic roman face, chiseled brow, nose, and chin. His mouth was hard to describe. He kept pursing his lips together, a duck out of water in her house; ruggedly handsome, but terribly uncomfortable, and maybe a bit broody, thought Sophie.

When she hugged him and he fell apart, she was powerfully drawn to him. It was astonishing to her. After Mario died, Sophie had many opportunities to remarry. Droves of local, and some not so local, men were interested in courting her. None made her feel more than amused. But this man, several years her junior, hit a nerve. She remembered thinking, as she left him in the bedroom, *Great, I've been like an old prune for years and now the juices start running again with Alex's boss.* Sophie could be crude in talking to herself, but rarely was this self-deprecating side of her visible to others.

Her attraction to him was a torment the entire time he and Alex were at the ranch. Every time she was close to him, she wanted to touch him. Every time he laughed; her heart flip flopped. She loved interacting with his quick wit and dry sense of humor. By the second week, after she had observed Rick's and Alex's interactions, Sophie decided that Alex and Rick were close and probably shared more than talk about baseball and girls. Finally, one night when Rick had gone down to the barn to help Dean on some winter project, she had time alone with Alex.

"Alex, I just wanted to let you know that I think Rick is a wonderful man. You two seem very close."

Alex had a blank look, not yet connecting the dots. Finally, Alex laughed, "Oh, Aunt Sophie, what do you want to know about him?"

Sophie was almost positive that Alex wanted to say something else but decided not to. Maybe Alex had noticed how Sophie felt around Rick and was hesitant to say anything but as usual, Sophie plowed ahead. "Alex, you don't have to tell me if you don't want to, but is he with anyone?"

Sophie wondered if Alex would be truthful with her.

Alex groaned, fidgeted in the armchair, put the book down on the side table, got up and started pacing. "Oh, my god, Aunt Sophie! You like him!" Sophie's face must have given her away. Alex chortled and said, "Oh my gosh. After all these years, finally there is someone who's gotten you hot and bothered."

Sophie's face burned red. She twisted in embarrassment. Alex kept laughing in disbelief. The mild teasing had made Sophie uncomfortable, so Alex went over to her, sat on the arm of the chair and said, "I'm sorry, Aunt Sophie. I didn't mean to make you uncomfortable, though it is nice to turn the tables now and then. I think this is great! It is wonderful to see that someone can still turn your head. Go for it! I know he likes you too."

Rick had gone outside to wait for their guests. He saw Dean and the boys ride in. Dean would fill him in later and let him know if they had encountered any problems on the drive up to the spring meadows. Getting a herd of cattle from one place to another wasn't the smooth going portrayed on TV. Rowdy and Ruby, the two Red Heelers came running up the road and leapt up the steps into Rick's outstretched arms. Squatting on the porch floor, he rubbed both of their heads, hugging them, talking to them softly.

"Did you have a good trip? Did the cattle behave? Did Jeanne cook you something good for dinner last night? Don't tell Sophie. Are you tired? You had a long walk. Want to take a nap? Maybe Sophie will give you a special treat for all your hard work."

The dogs lapped up the attention and tried to sneak in a few wet kisses before he dismissed them with, "Go see Sophie."

Still full of energy after a four-hour run, they said their goodbyes and raced around the back of the house to see if Sophie was there. No doubt the dogs were thinking that they could bribe Sophie with kisses to get some leftovers.

Rick got up off the step and moved to a rocker on the porch. He saw the dust rising in the distance and waited patiently for the SUV to pull up to the house. Both Jake and Jules got out of the car at the same time.

Jules saw Rick on the porch and said, "Good afternoon, Colonel," not trying to hide that she knew who and what he was. She extended her arm for a handshake and said, "I'm Jules Law." Jake came up behind her, offered his hand with a simple, "Jake Lawrence, here."

Rick accepted both handshakes with a simple, "Rick Hidalgo. Nice to meet you. Let's go inside and talk. Sophie's waiting for us."

All three of them walked into the kitchen. Sophie was already at the table. Looking up, she greeted them, and asked them to sit. She wasn't sure how to proceed, but she needn't have worried. Jules immediately took control.

"Mrs. Martini, have you had a chance to fill Rick in on our proposal?"

"Yes, I have. He's up to speed," answered Sophie succinctly.

"Great. Why don't we spend some time answering any questions you might have and then we can move on to talk about the mechanics of the deal. Will that work?"

Sophie said yes and looked at Rick. Rick felt like he was in a relay race and Sophie was handing him the baton. He didn't want to fumble and drop it.

"Uh, is it okay if I call you Jules and Jake?"

"Certainly. That would be fine," answered Jake good naturedly.

"Okay, well, Sophie and I have been talking about your proposal and of course, we called Alex this morning. I'm assuming you know who Alex is?"

Jules purposefully didn't look at Jake, but knew he was thinking the same thing. Since Rick broke the ice about Alex, they wouldn't have to. She nodded, "Yes, we do."

Rick picked up a slight deviation in Jules' body language and paused to study her. Maybe he was mistaken, so he continued. "We do have some questions for you and hope that you can answer them truthfully." He stopped for a moment to let the word 'truthfully' sink in.

"You see, if we move forward with your proposal, we would want a clause in the contract that gives us the ability to cancel our involvement and still receive compensation, if you don't fully disclose any, shall we say, liabilities or dangerous situations that could arise from the deal."

Sophie glanced at Rick and gave him a silent thumbs up through ESP, or so she thought. Jake looked like he swallowed a snake. Jules remained cool, non-plussed, no emotion crossing her face, and no telling body language changes. Jules smiled inwardly. Rick had done his research. Paulson had advised her to not react if something like this came up, but to take it as a sign that she was dealing with competent people.

She was expecting this Rick thought. *Now she knows that we did our homework and the game is on.*

"We'll answer any questions you have to the best of our ability with the information we have today and if that information should change down the road, we'll disclose it to you. We don't want you entering into an agreement unless you are one hundred percent comfortable and committed."

Back in my court, thought Rick.

"Let's start with what your company is going to do while the Bentworth woman is here. We think this is an awfully expensive venture, just to keep the press and paparazzi away."

"Mr. Bentworth hired us not only to protect his daughter, but also to find the culprits who planned the kidnapping. He has not been satisfied with law enforcement's efforts and wants to see the perpetrators brought to justice. We've gotten some small leads that might pan out, and we are prepared to run with them."

"I see," said Sophie. "So, while Claire is here, you are going to be playing cops and robbers?"

"More like Sherlock and Watson," quipped Jake. This was the first sign that Jake had any sense of humor, corny as it was.

"Why do you need Claire stashed away somewhere, while you play Maggie and Fritz?" asked Rick.

Jules was impressed with Rick's reference to fictional female – male detective characters Maggie McGuane and Fritz Thieringer. She genuinely laughed at his joke. The reference was lost on Jake and Sophie, but perhaps this would serve to launch a bond between Rick and her.

"As we continue to investigate, we might ruffle some feathers. You know about that, don't you, Rick?"

Rick wondered if she knew the specifics of his research the last eighteen hours or if she was just talking in generalities. He'd admit what he had done, in a generic sense, if she asked him, but for now, he simply nodded his head.

Jake picked up the beat. "Truly, we want to see her safely tucked away where the chances of a repeat attempt are unlikely."

Sophie shot out the next question, perhaps a little too aggressively, but no one seemed to notice, except Rick. "We'd be in a lot of danger if whomever was responsible for the kidnapping found out she was here and wanted to grab her again, or worse, kill her. How likely is this?"

"We've given that a lot of thought, Mrs. Martini, and have made every attempt to cover our tracks and not attract attention. The ranch is remote, not a likely place that Claire would go, and we've got a pretty good cover arranged, just in case. Plus, we'll take security measures, including having our people here at all times. If we get Claire up here without anyone noticing, and we think we have it worked out how to do this, there shouldn't be a way for anyone to find out."

"But you cannot guarantee that, right Jules?" asked Sophie.

Jules acknowledged that they couldn't guarantee it, but the likelihood of a repeat attempt at the ranch was very, very small.

Rick chimed in. "I imagine that you have eliminated Company as suspects in the kidnapping?"

This time, Jules' eyes opened wider, but she answered straightforwardly. "We considered that it might be a possibility with Bentworth's, ah, activities and business practices, but were able to rule that out. What we have not been able to rule out is the possibility that it was a business associate of Bentworth. However, the small amount of evidence we have, points to a more personal connection."

Rick said, "Do you think that because the evidence points to a more personal connection, the risk for Claire and the folks here at White Bark Ranch is less?"

"Honestly, yes. I think the threat is minimal in any event, but I'm not going to lie and minimize the possibility of something going wrong."

Score one for Jules. She had told the truth. Rick was beginning to feel a little provisional trust with her. He peeked at Sophie. Her face was placid, and she showed no sign of agitation at this time.

"Jules, Jake, I think we need to get to some of the details now," responded Rick.

Jules dipped her head and Jake took over, spelling out the security provisions they wanted to implement, the cover that had been arranged for Claire, the personnel they would have at the ranch, how they would make sure that the ranch guests were clean, and an extraction plan if something did go wrong. Jake spent the better part of a couple of hours going over details, while Rick listened and occasionally asked questions.

When Rick was satisfied, he came full circle from where he started, telling them that he and Sophie had talked to Alex.

"Folks, Sophie and I have a lot to digest. There is one more request that we have. Alex, who is in Seattle, wants to talk to you, Claire's medical doctors and her psychiatrist before we make a final decision. Alex is concerned that we may not be equipped to handle the emotional or behavioral dangers that Claire might present."

"Is Alex able to get away from work and fly out tomorrow? We can arrange a private flight from Renton Airport, a few miles north of Seattle."

Jules looked at Rick with expectantly raised eyebrows, not at all hiding that they had considered Alex a key player in this and had made tentative arrangements for transport. Rick waited for Sophie to answer.

"We're supposed to get a call tonight."

"Okay. May we stay at the ranch and wait for the call? We'd like to see the facilities you have here if that is possible," Jake requested.

Sophie and Rick simultaneously agreed, though Sophie wondered why they wanted to see the facilities if they had already done an in-depth investigation. Rick knew. They had already done most of it by satellite, and they wanted to put the finishing touches on it by doing an advancement survey, a quasi-military term that means an in-person scouting. Jules asked Sophie if there was somewhere she could catch up on overdue work. Sophie invited the two of them to have dinner with them, then led Jules to the office.

An hour later, Rick and Jake were still out on their sojourn across the main facilities of the ranch they called the "Compound." Sophie went to let Jules know that dinner would be ready in about thirty minutes. Jules looked up from her computer and saw that Sophie had more on her mind than a dinner announcement. She turned toward Sophie and gladly waited.

"Ah, Jules I was wondering if you had a moment? I need to talk to you woman to woman."

It sounded funny, clichéd, and old fashioned, but Jules didn't let on that she was amused.

"Of course, Sophie. Any time. What's on your mind?" Jules motioned her to go on.

"I know you said that the risk for people here at the ranch is minimal. I guess I feel better that you'll have people here as guests or ranch hands, but I can't help thinking that our paying guests could be in mortal danger if something went wrong. What do you people call it—collateral damage?"

"I think the way we can eliminate almost any chance of this happening would be to have Claire stay in the main house, if possible. I really think that if anyone wanted to try something, it would be done under the cover of night. There are just too many people around and experience tells me that if there is another attempt, the kidnappers won't want to draw attention to themselves. Remember that she disappeared from a dressing room and it was an hour before anyone noticed. No witnesses, no collateral damage."

"Jules, I could never forgive myself if anything happened to our guests."

"Nor could I," responded Jules, trying to break out of her operational mode, which often came across as results oriented and cold. Sophie needed comforting and reassurance. "I honestly believe that with the proper planning, we can minimize any danger. I would not have agreed to this, nor would my partners at ISS, if we thought there could be any fall out. Aside from the ethical considerations, it would be bad for business."

With unerring sincerity, Jules continued. "Sophie, we have never lost a client, we've never caused the death of anyone but the bad guys, and we certainly aren't going to endanger our record at White Bark Ranch." Jules attentively looked at Sophie. Sophie held Jules gaze through worried eyes, then pulled herself together, said thank you, and returned to the kitchen.

Dinner was a quiet affair. Everyone appeared to be talked out. Sophie and Jules were clearing the table, Rick was washing dishes, and Jake was drying, when the phone rang. Sophie picked it up.

"White Bark Ranch, how may I help you? Oh, hi, Alex." Sophie listened, with an occasional, "uh huh" punctuating the otherwise silent kitchen. It felt like a long time had passed before Sophie actually spoke in more than one-syllable words.

"Listen, Alex, don't worry about a flight. The people we told you about can arrange a private flight late tomorrow afternoon out of someplace called Renton. Do you know where that is?" Sophie listened, then hesitated a moment, finally saying, "Oh, I see. Let me put Jules on the line with you to work out the details."

Rick heaved a heavy sigh. Alex was coming. Jake went back to drying dishes, and Sophie handed over the phone to Jules. She introduced herself, spent a few moments with the required niceties, then pulled out a piece of paper from her pocket. She read the flight arrangements to Alex and provided her phone number in case there were any problems. She cautioned Alex not to tell anyone about the trip. Then she became silent, listening intently. Sophie, Rick, and Jake had no way of telling what was going on, but it obviously was a one-way monologue. The call concluded with, "I'm looking forward to meeting you and spending some time with you, but you had better take that up with your aunt."

Jules handed the phone back to Sophie, who briefly listened, then said, "I'll discuss it with Rick." She hung up the phone and turned to Rick, "Would you go for a walk with me? There is something Alex wants us to consider. Jake, Jules please excuse us for a while."

Rick dried his hands and headed for the door, trailing Sophie who was already on her way out. They headed toward the pond that was really a natural widening of the river. The tributary ran fast down from the mountains, but it was slower here and perfect for pond-side picnics, swimming, and fishing.

They walked arm in arm on the lighted trail until they were out of hearing distance from the house. When Sophie felt comfortable that no one could overhear them, she told Rick that Alex wanted Jules and Jake to stay at the ranch. Alex had mentioned it on their call earlier today, but for the life of Rick, he couldn't imagine why it was so important to have them stay on the property. Must be some kind of psychological thing. They discussed the pros and cons, and finally decided to go with Alex's instinct.

They lingered by the side of the pond under the cover of the tall White Bark pine, the ranch's name sake. Holding Sophie's hands in his, he teasingly asked Sophie if she was going to invite him to spend the night with her. She could be as flirtatious as he could. "Why, I could use a little bit of comforting with all that has been going on."

He kissed her on the lips, obviously wanting more, but neither of them cared to leave Jules and Jake alone longer than was necessary.

Walking into the kitchen, they saw a sight they found amusing. Rowdy and Ruby were in the kitchen with Jake and Jules. Rowdy was sitting on the floor next to Jake's chair, getting his ears rubbed. Ruby had somehow convinced Jules to sit on the floor so she could lay in her lap and get her belly rubbed. The dogs were used to having strangers around, and they were generally polite, but usually kept their distance, especially with kids. However, tonight, they had settled right in with the two strangers.

"Uh, Sophie, I hope it's okay, I mean about the dogs," muttered Jake, acting like a schoolboy caught doing something naughty.

"It's fine. The dogs are usually well behaved, so we let them come and go through their dog door as they wish," answered Sophie, for the first time feeling more comfortable with the two sleuths. The dogs had proven to be pretty good judges of character.

Jules got up from the floor, much to Ruby's displeasure.

"All the travel arrangements have been confirmed. Jake will pick up Alex in Missoula tomorrow around 7:00 p.m. and drive back here. It's getting late, so we had better shove off, unless you have any more questions."

"Hold on just a minute. I'm not sure why, but Alex wanted us to invite you to stay here at the ranch starting tomorrow. I don't know if you planned to stay past tomorrow or the next day, but Alex was pretty adamant about you being here." Sophie realized that her invitation left much to be desired in the way of politeness, but she had already put her foot in her mouth, so she waited for a response.

Picking up the uncertainty of the invitation and practicing her diplomatic skills, Jules asked Sophie and Rick, "How do you feel about us staying here?"

Rick, trying to recover from Sophie's back handed invitation, attempted graciousness and responded for both himself and Sophie.

"We think it would be just fine, but the cabins aren't open yet, so you'd have to stay in the upstairs guest rooms." He hoped he sounded sincere because Sophie was already looking for a glass of water to wash down her foot.

Jake attempted to ingratiate himself. "That's very nice of you. It would help us if we didn't have to spend four hours a day traveling. One other thing, Rick, I'd like to finish as much of the tour tomorrow around the main compound, then take a ride up into the surrounding land if possible."

"I'm available all-day tomorrow," offered Rick. "Jules are you coming out tomorrow morning too?" He wanted to keep track of the two of them as much as possible.

"I'm going to spend some time in Missoula tomorrow, so I won't be here until later in the afternoon."

"How will you get out here if Jake has the car?"

"Don't worry, Sophie. I'll get arrange a car for tomorrow morning before Jake heads out here. Thank you for dinner. It was delicious. Have a good night."

CHAPTER 4—The Decision

Once you make a decision, the universe conspires to make it happen.

Ralph Waldo Emerson

Thursday April 9

Midnight had come and gone and now daybreak was a breath away. One of Jules' talents, and she had many, was that she could sleep almost anywhere and anytime, but Jules couldn't settle. She wasn't looking forward to telling Sophie the real reason ISS had chosen the ranch. She knew it could torpedo the whole deal.

She swore to herself that this was the last time she would compromise her ethics on this job, no matter what. Looking at the clock on the hotel nightstand, she sighed and decided to administer a little self-therapy in hopes of relaxing and getting a few hours of sleep before she walked into the lion's den.

It was another balmy spring day. As Rick and Sophie were finishing up their pancakes and bacon, they heard Jake's voice. God, he must have gotten up before sunrise to get here at eight in the morning. Sophie called to him and he appeared in the kitchen dressed in jeans and a fancy cowboy shirt. Sophie stifled a laugh and Rick, trying not to chuckle, asked if Jake had eaten, as he poured him a cup of coffee.

Jake laid three large bags of groceries on the table and said he had eaten. Sophie raised her left eyebrow, a tell that trouble was brewing. *Oh, here it comes*, thought Rick and shot Sophie a warning look. Sophie didn't like the smell of charity, unless she was on the giving end. Sophie leveled her gaze at Jake and said, "What's this?"

"Uh, Sophie, you've been so nice and fed us, so I, um, thought I'd bring some groceries by. Hope they're what you like."

"Well, now, Jake, that was very nice of you. I'll put them up while you two boys go to work."

Rick and Jake knew when they were being dismissed and bolted out the back door as quickly as they could. Ruby and Rowdy, loyal to the grocery bags, stayed with Sophie.

Lunch time came and went with neither Rick nor Jake showing up. It wasn't a big deal; she had made an "Everything Soup" to serve with her fresh baked whole grain bread. As a child, Alex had dubbed the soup made with all the leftovers in the refrigerator, "Everything Soup" and the name had stuck.

Sophie called down to the bunk house and Jeanne, the cook for the ranch hands, answered the phone. Sophie asked her how the trip was the day before last and listened to Jeanne's tales of on-the-trail culinary challenges. Jeanne was Dean's wife and oversaw the feeding of the ranch hands and goading them into keeping the bunk house relatively clean.

Sophie bided her time and when Jeanne took a rare breath before chattering on, Sophie cut in. "Jeanne, did you feed Rick and his guest this noon?"

"No. Who is Rick's guest?

Just like Jeanne to be her usual Peaky the Elf, from the Beaky Peaky Tip Top Elf Books, sticking her nose in where it shouldn't be. Sophie said, "Thanks, Jeanne. I must go. I'll try to stop by later."

Sophie had no intention of stopping by to visit with Jeanne. She told her that solely to preempt Jeanne from coming up to the main house. The only reason she put up with her was because she was Dean's wife. Mumbling under her breath to no one in particular, *Lord knows how he puts up with her, but she's part of the package, so I gotta cope.* She started some light cleaning and made up rooms for Alex, Jules, and Jake.

After finishing, Sophie sat down for a mid-afternoon cup of coffee and cookies, thinking about what she was going to prepare for dinner. She, Rick, and most likely Jules would eat around 6:30 p.m., but Jake and Alex wouldn't be in until 9:00 p.m. tonight. No choice but to make a stew that could be reheated. She started getting her ingredients together.

The Learjet25 screamed down the runway at precisely 4:30 p.m. Pacific time, lifting off smoothly. The pilot told Alex that the flying time was approximately an hour. He also told her to sit back and relax, that they anticipated a smooth ride all the way. After takeoff, the co-pilot came out and offered Alex a drink.

"Maybe a nice Merlot," Alex suggested, half joking, thinking that they'd only have those little bottles of liquor served on commercial airlines with usual red or white. The co-pilot nodded, walked back to a tiny galley, and in no time, brought, in a real wine glass, not plastic, presumably a Merlot.

Alex hated flying. As a small tyke, Alex got car sick frequently and never seemed to outgrow the motion sickness that caused her so much anxiety. Wine probably wasn't the best choice for motion sickness, but after asking for it, it would have been embarrassing to tell the co-pilot not to bring it. Trying to relax, Alex leaned into the plushy padded leather seat, thinking that an hour wouldn't be so bad on this little baby.

Reclining, Alex tried to bring some order to the events that had taken place in the last few months. Existence with Reggie had been exciting at first, but those things that had attracted them to each other in the beginning, were the same things that caused the downfall of the relationship. Reggie thrived on excitement and Alex, though sometimes a participant, more often enjoyed the quiet. She was a homebody. Reggie's need for continued and heightened excitement caused a rift between the two of them, presumably leading to Reggie's dalliances. While intellectually Alex understood the situation, raw emotions trumped. They started living strained parallel lives. Reggie put an end to their three-year relationship in December and struck out to find the next unsuspecting victim. *What was I thinking when I fell for Reggie?* While Sophie had shown the utmost courtesy toward Reggie, Alex knew that Sophie didn't like her. Sophie's tolerance for Reggie was based on her love for Alex. Rick wasn't as ingratiating. Though he had remained neutral, not offering an opinion one way or another, his neutrality should have been enough of a tip off to Alex. *Guess Aunt Sophie is right about my pig headiness.*

Sophie and Mario couldn't have kids. Alex never knew if it was Uncle Mario or Aunt Sophie. When Alex's parents were killed in a freak car accident, just shortly after Alex's tenth birthday, Sophie and Mario became legal guardians and treated Alex as their own child. Maybe they overcompensated because of the tragedy, giving Alex a lot of freedom and space to make decisions early on. *That's probably why I became so headstrong,* rationalized Alex.

Thoughts of Reggie pushed their way back into Alex's consciousness. She wasn't operating under any illusions about Reggie but was still nursing wounds from Reggie's cavalier behavior during the last year they had lived together. Not only was Reggie insensitive to Alex's feelings, the one-night stands and affairs were out in the open. Reggie didn't have the decency to try and conceal them. *God,* Alex thought. *I can't believe I came out to Aunt Sophie for Reggie!* Fuming, the anger inundated her conscious mind like a spring torrent that made the river in front of the ranch swell, churn, and spit. Alex, her stomach roiling with a mixture of anger and nostalgia, remembered the day.

She had come back to the ranch from Seattle for Memorial Day weekend, resolute in having the dreaded conversation. Alex was edgy and sick to her stomach. She didn't think that Aunt Sophie would stop loving her, however she was terrified that Sophie would stop respecting her. Late Saturday night, she asked Sophie to take a ride with her in the morning up to one of her favorite spots in the woods, north of the house. They rode for an hour, tended to the horses, and sat down to eat a picnic breakfast by the side of a pool. She knew that Sophie could tell something was brewing, though Sophie didn't inquire.

When Alex was agitated, she tended to pace. After they finished eating, Alex got up from the blanket and started pacing, rubbing her hands in front of her. She dropped to her knees in front of Sophie and said that she had something important to tell her. Sophie reached for her hands, but Alex drew back.

"Aunt Sophie, I've kept something from you for a long time and I no longer can hide it." She got up and paced again.

"What is it, Alex?"

"It's not like I've lied to you or anything, but I feel like I've been deceitful in not telling you. I feel dishonest and cowardly and I can't live like this any longer. I just have to get it off my chest, even though I'm afraid."

Sophie carefully inquired, "Sweetie, is it something that happened in Afghanistan?"

Alex again dropped to her knees in front of Sophie. "No, no, not Afghanistan."

Sophie continued, "Then what? There isn't anything you can't tell me."

Alex, fear seizing her, took a deep breath then said, "I don't know, Aunt Sophie. You're not going to like this. I've met someone that's important to me." Sophie had a confused quizzical look on her face, so Alex blurted it out. "It's a woman. Reggie is her name."

Sophie hadn't expected that at all. Alex had a string of boyfriends in high school and her fair share during her undergraduate years, though she rarely brought any of them around more than once, and now that she thought about it, Alex wasn't particularly affectionate with any of them. She could see that Alex was suffering, waiting for her response.

"Alex, you've caught me off guard. Give me a minute here."

Alex got back up and started pacing again. Sophie took her time to carefully frame her answer. "Alessandra, here's what I think, and wait until I'm finished before you interrupt, okay?"

Alex nodded, afraid of what she was going to hear.

Sophie continued. "To be honest with you, I'm not thrilled with this news, but not for the reasons you might think. I would imagine that you've already experienced the difficulty trying to live this life in a discriminatory climate caused by the narrow mindedness of people. I don't wish this on anyone, least of all you, the person I love the most in the whole wide world. Look how afraid you've been to tell me, someone who accepts you unconditionally."

Alex couldn't stay silent any longer. "You don't understand, Aunt Sophie," but before she could continue, Sophie kindly said, "but I do. I understand this isn't a choice for you, that it is who you are, and that to be happy, you have to act on your feelings. I just can't bear the thought of this hostile world heaping more than your share of pain and suffering on you, but, in the end, love is love and there is so little love in this world that I don't care whom you love, just as long as that person loves you back."

Alex seemed to have been flash-frozen in mid pace. Tears flooded her eyes. Just as Alex dropped to her knees for a third time, Sophie reached for her and pulled her to her breast. Alex rested her head against Sophie while Sophie stroked her hair. Some time passed before she pulled away and simply said, "Thank you, Aunt Sophie. This means the world to me. I've been so ashamed."

Sophie's head was swimming, but she knew she had to maintain her composure for Alex. She thought that for all of

Alex's strength, she was as fragile as she had ever been in her life. "Ashamed of what, sweetie?" Alex, still crying, choked out, "Ashamed that I was such a coward to hide who I am from you."

"I'm the one who should be ashamed for not providing you a safe enough environment to tell me." Sophie's answer was most unexpected and rocketed Alex into uncontrollable sobs.

When Alex's sobs subsided, she told Sophie that she could ask her anything. Sophie, regaining her composure, asked Alex easy, mundane questions. Where did she meet Reggie, what did Reggie do, how long had they been together, would she like to bring Reggie out for the fourth of July, and did Rick know? Alex knew the not so easy inquiries were still to come.

On their ride back to the house, Sophie, breaking the dense silence of the forest, peppered Alex with the questions that had been smoldering in her skull since they sat at the pool. "Alex, um, when did this, uh, change take place? You always had a gaggle of boyfriends following you around?"

"I knew in high school, but I kept dating boys, hoping that one would prove me wrong and make me feel something."

"Have you ever slept with a man?"

Oh Christ, thought Alex. *I'm going to have to deal with the whole sexual side of this now.* She answered Sophie, "I've had a few experiments. I could never seem to find a man that I could bond with emotionally."

"You seemed to have bonded with Rick, though," mused Sophie.

"Yes, but that was different. I just never felt the emotional and sexual connection like you do with him. He was more like a big brother to me," answered Alex.

"Sweetie, I want you to be happy, of course, however, I've got to ask this question. Are you sure?"

"Yes, Aunt Sophie, I'm sure."

"How do you know?" ventured Sophie.

"The same way you're sure that you're heterosexual and like men," answered Alex without sarcasm. Alex was dreading the next question she knew would be coming and Sophie didn't disappoint her.

"Ah, Alex, if you don't mind me asking, what do the two of you do in bed?"

Alex was tempted to say, "Sleep", but she knew that Sophie wouldn't find it funny right now. She also didn't want to be crass. While she guessed that Sophie could be very passionate in bed, she knew that Sophie's public persona was conservative.

"The mechanics aren't much different than being in bed with a man." Fleeting confusion passed over Sophie's face. Alex knew she'd have to be more graphic. "You just substitute fingers for a penis."

"Oh, I see. Right, right," Sophie uttered nervously, the blush spreading from her neck up her face.

Alex giggled. Sophie took off her hat and swatted Alex on the upper arm. They rode side by side for a while until Sophie's brain came up with the next series of questions.

"Alex you said up at the pool, that Rick knew. Did you tell him?" Sophie wasn't asking to make sure that it would be okay to share this with Rick if he didn't know. She wanted to find out if Rick had been guarding the secret from her.

"Not exactly. He caught me sneaking out of a doctor's tent in the early morning hours."

"A woman doctor?" inquired Sophie

"Uh huh," was all that Alex said.

Impatiently, Sophie asked, "Well what happened?"

Alex sighed, then began. "We were in camp, waiting around until the next mission. Rick was prowling around that night because he couldn't sleep. It was so damn hot. As luck had it, he was passing by, just as I was leaving her tent. He was cool, though. I'll never forget what he said."

"Lieutenant, you must be feeling pretty bad to rouse a doctor in the middle of the night."

"He was so proud of himself to have made a play on words."

Intrigued, Sophie asked, "What did you do?"

"I saluted and said, 'Yes sir.'"

"Then what?" Sophie prompted.

"He told me, tongue in cheek, to get back to my quarters and rest so that I would be feeling better for morning report."

"That was the end of it?" inquired Sophie.

"No, not by a long shot. Later in the day, he called me into his office, closed the door, and told me to sit down. I was scared," answered Alex, shrugging off the anxiety laden memory.

"I'll bet," consoled Sophie.

"Then he said, 'Look Alex, I don't agree with all the policies, but there are people who do, and you have a good career ahead of you if you want it. And personally, I don't care with whom you spend your private time, but you had better confine your doctor's appointments to off-post furloughs, if you catch my drift, and then you had better be darn careful.' He went on to reassure me that the conversation ended there unless I did something stupid."

"What did you do?" Sophie was getting irritated. She was having to pull the story out of Alex.

"I told him 'yes, sir', saluted and left as fast as I could."

"Did he ever say anything again?"

"Yes, but not what you are thinking, Aunt Sophie. Three months later, she was killed in a helicopter crash in the Hemland province, near Camp Dwyer where we were stationed. I never did find out what she was doing on that Black Hawk medevac helicopter. She shouldn't have been on it."

Alex didn't have to explain much about Afghanistan to Sophie. Wherever Alex served, Sophie had a map and learned more about the region than most intelligence agencies did. She tracked Alex's moves based on codes they had developed.

"It was a rough time for me. Rick helped me through it, gave me a safe outlet, and made me use my own psychological skills to regain a healthier viewpoint. He got in trouble, though, for spending so much time with a female subordinate, me, after-hours in his quarters. His CO called him in and read him the riot act for conduct unbecoming of an officer, supposedly, improprieties with a subordinate officer. That is one thing about the military I don't miss. Guilty until proven innocent.

"Rick, probably unwisely, took him to task. As Rick tells it, after he explained that he was providing support for a soldier that had lost a comrade in battle and that he was not having any kind of inappropriate relationship, asked the general if the general would be having this conversation with him if I had been a man. I think the conversation with the general probably was part of the impetus for Rick taking retirement when he did."

The co-pilot roused Alex from her thoughts and said to buckle up. They had started their approach to Missoula and would land in about ten minutes. She asked him if there was time for another glass of wine. He returned with a refill and a slip of paper. Surprisingly, it turned out to be a 1996 Ignoble Charmant (Merlot) from a small vineyard in Deming, New Mexico. Alex mused to herself, *I'll just bet there will be many more surprises to come,* as she sipped the wine slowly this time.

The scent of stew permeated the entire house with a delicious tomato and onion bouquet. Sophie heard a car door slam, followed by, "Okay to come in?"

Jules had arrived and was making her way to the kitchen. Jules knew that she'd gain five pounds if she stayed the rest of the week, but oh hell, it was worth it. She loved to eat and appreciated home cooking as much as gourmet fare. When she settled herself in the kitchen, she made idle talk with Sophie until Rick showed up twenty minutes later.

"What time did Jake take off?" Jules inquired.

"Around 4:00 p.m. this afternoon. I'm surprised your paths didn't cross on Route 93," answered Rick as he washed up in the sink.

"Do you two still have more work to finish?" continued Jules.

"Yes, we never made it up to the mountains today. We were thinking of going out tomorrow, camping and coming back Friday afternoon. Want to come?" invited Rick.

Before Jules could answer, Sophie chimed in, "Where did you and Jake eat lunch today?"

"Sorry Sophie, I should have called you. Jake picked up a couple of sandwiches and cookies when he bought the groceries this morning."

"No problem. Just didn't want you boys to go hungry. Would you please set the table and figure out what you all want to drink?"

"Sure thing," answered Rick good naturedly. He had never minded Sophie's manner of asking a question but clearly meaning there was an expectation of compliance.

It was 7:00 p.m. when Jules' phone rang. Looking at the caller ID, she recognized the call coming from Jake.

"You got her? Any problems? What time do you think you'll be here? Sophie has dinner for the two of you, so I hope you didn't ruin your appetite with a McDonald's run. Okay, see you in a few." She turned to Rick and Sophie, "Jake's got her, no problems with the flight. They'll be here soon."

A few minutes after 8:00 p.m., Ruby and Rowdy flew out their dog door long before Rick, Jules, or Sophie heard the SUV. "Must be coming up the drive," muttered Rick, as he got up.

Jules' phone rang and after looking at it, she abruptly got up, excused herself and went into the kitchen. Rick and Sophie went out to wait for Jake and Alex. The dogs were flanking the SUV, trying to herd it, then when it stopped, stood guard at each side. Rowdy greeted Jake with a dusty jump up on his jeans. Alex was smarter and squatted down as soon as she got out of the SUV, so Ruby wouldn't try and jump up for a kiss. Once Rowdy realized that Alex was on the other side of the car, he raced around and bullied his way in front of Ruby. By the time the dogs' excitement was contained, Jake had carried in both his and Alex's bags. Rick showed him the way to his room.

Sophie ran down the steps and hugged Alex. Alex held Sophie at arm's length and inquired how Sophie was doing with all the excitement. Sophie asked Alex if Jake had briefed her at all, though Sophie didn't think even Alex would get much out of Jake.

"Nope, he didn't. Kept saying that he thought it was better to hear everything from Rick and you. I am beginning to wonder what kind of shrink I am if I couldn't get this guy to talk the entire trip."

"Speaking of the trip, did you get air sick?" asked Sophie.

"No, not this time, so I'm ready to eat. That is," Alex said tongue in cheek, "if you have something ready."

With linked arms, and dutiful dogs following, they made their way into the kitchen. Rick came down from settling in Jake and Jules who had made her way upstairs after her call.

"Are the two sleuths coming down?" asked Sophie.

"Jules said they'd join us in about an hour," responded Rick, appreciating their sensitivity in allowing Rick, Sophie, and Alex time alone.

"Alex," started Sophie, "I hope you don't mind, but I put Jake in your room with the private bath and have you and Jules in the rooms with the connecting bath. I didn't think it was proper for Jake and Jules to share a bathroom."

"You and Rick share a bathroom," teased Alex.

Rick groaned and slumped down in his chair, wishing he could hide under the table with the dogs. They had kept their relationship quiet and clandestine for several years, or so they thought. Everyone at the ranch knew but never said anything, respecting their privacy.

Sophie indignantly, and with a bad fake British accent, shot back, "My dear, we may share a bed on occasion, but we never, ever, share a bathroom!"

Rick, laughing, just shook his head, while turning beet red. Alex laughed until she had tears in her eyes.

"All right you two clowns. Enough of this tom foolery. Let's get down to business." Sophie slid a bowl of piping hot stew and two slices of her home baked bread in front of Alex. "Would you like something to drink?"

"Dr. Pepper, please."

While Alex ate, Rick and Sophie laid out details of the proposed arrangement. Alex ate steadily, listening carefully. By the time Rick and Sophie had covered all the bases, Alex was eating a brownie with pecans Sophie had made earlier in the day.

"You're uncharacteristically quiet. No questions?" asked Sophie.

"Oh, yeah, lots, but only one for you two. Right now, without any more information, what are your guts telling you?"

Rick answered first. "I think there is some risk, but minimal." Sophie remained quiet until prompted by Alex.

"Alex, I agree with Rick, but I can't help shake the feeling that it's an opportunity we can't pass up."

"Aunt Sophie, if you don't do this, realistically, what are the chances of keeping the ranch intact?" Alex knew that

Sophie had to mortgage the ranch to pay for her uncle's cancer treatments and with improvements they had made to turn the ranch into a part-time dude ranch, there was a pretty hefty financial obligation. However, she had no idea how serious the situation had become.

"Alex, we're facing having to sell off a good portion of the ranch for development without this deal," Sophie answered straightforwardly, deciding it was not the time to hem and haw.

"Aunt Sophie, why didn't you tell me? I could have given you what I had in savings instead of buying Reggie out. It would have been okay moving to an apartment," groaned Alex.

"No sweetie. You went through enough trauma. You didn't need to be chased out of your house."

Alex dropped her head, shook it left to right, then focused on Rick. "And you, why didn't you clue me in?" she said angrily.

"You know why Alex," Rick answered non-defensively.

Alex continued to shake her head with pursed lips, but this time it was with an up and down motion, signaling Rick that she knew his hands had been tied by Sophie, probably upon pain of not letting him back in her bed again! She let it slide and returned to her next question.

"One more question. Since you called me, I am assuming you two want my input. Is that a fair statement?" she asked. Sophie and Rick were nodding their heads. Alex continued, "Well then, it looks like we have to do some more work to make sure we're all in agreement, one way or the other. I want to meet this Jules, tonight, but not do any heavy talking. I'll take her out on the property tomorrow, sort of get relaxed, you know, and get a sense of her."

Rick was rolling his eyes, anticipating some psychobabble bullshit about how getting to know Jules would give them clues as to her real motives. Alex stared him down.

"Look, you gecko, don't go putting down any of my psychological techniques. They served us well in Afghanistan, so just "f" off!"

Although Alex had said this good naturedly, Sophie turned from the sink and playing indignant, sharply said, "Alex, watch your language."

Alex muttered "I'm sorry Aunt Sophie" and Rick performed a mock salute to Alex, "Aye, aye, General Shrink," and they both laughed.

Ruby and Rowdy got up from under the table. It looked like Alex was finished eating and no more surreptitious scraps would be coming their way. They were headed outside, when they turned and looked up at the back stairs. Alex had her back to the stairs and did not see Jules coming down. Rick only noticed because the dogs were looking. She was very quiet, probably not wanting to intrude, or maybe it was an occupational habit. Rick invited her in. "Jules, come meet Alex."

Jules walked toward the alcove and got to the table as Alex was getting up to turn around. Sophie turned from the sink to observe. One of Alex's skills Rick had profited from while in Afghanistan, was her uncanny ability to size up someone quickly. Ninety percent of the time she was right.

Jules extended a hand, warmly saying, "You must be Alex. I'm glad you came."

Alex took her outstretched hand but didn't speak. She just stood there holding Jules' hand, laser eyes locked on hers. Jules didn't move either, meeting Alex's gaze straight on. Rick and Sophie threw each other a look; they felt a current surging through the air. Something inexplicable seemed to suspend the women in time and space.

Sophie clocked the scene. Jules was dark, slim, athletic, lithe, like a dancer. Alex was the antithesis. She was shorter and had softer curves, the pale creamy skin of northern

Italian descent, collar length blond hair with strawberry and light brown highlights. Her eyes were a gentle hue of sage and moss with specs of cinnamon giving them a soothing look, and her soft cheeks framing a voluptuous mouth, made it appear that she was always about to break into a smile.

Alex was the first to punctuate the reverie with a subdued, "Do I know you from somewhere?"

Jules didn't make a move to disengage from the handshake. "What gave you that impression?"

"Your eyes. There's something familiar about them," said Alex, stumbling over her words a little, feeling oddly embarrassed and at the same time electrified. Her hand was tingling.

Cool and composed, still holding Alex's hand, Jules told her, "Hmm, that's interesting, but I don't believe we've ever been introduced prior to this evening." Jules had chosen her words carefully, avoiding an outright lie.

Alex, reluctant to break the handshake, finally gave up trying to place Jules and shakily pulled out a chair for her. Jules, eager to avoid any more questions from Alex, moved the conversation along as a parent does when trying to get a reluctant toddler to bed.

"Alex, you've had a long trip, and I know that Sophie and Rick filled you in on the basics, so I thought that you and I could spend some time together tomorrow getting your questions answered and contacting Claire's doctors. What do you think?"

"Sounds okay to me." Alex was still distracted and had the strong sense that she knew this woman from somewhere.

Jules continued, "I'd really like to see the trails that are used with the guests. Are you game?"

Rick, no stranger to Alex's 'tells' saw that she was not fully focused on what Jules was saying. He chimed in to give Alex a moment to regroup. "Jake and I will be taking ATVs over a good portion of the property and then camping out, unless you need us for something."

Alex's attention snapped back. "Terrific idea." She'd get to talk to Jules without Sophie and Rick around. "I'll have a couple of horses saddled and ready to go right after breakfast. You do ride, right?"

"Well, I haven't ridden recently, but I'm up for it."

"Is 8:00 a.m. too early for you? I don't know if that gives you enough time for your beauty rest," Alex mildly joked in an attempt to be friendly. "Be sure and bring a jacket. It's still cold in the mornings."

Jules said goodnight and excused herself, going back upstairs. Alex followed on her heels, eager to get to bed. She was tired. Rick and Sophie were left in the kitchen contemplating the whole scene, when Sophie asked, "Rick, did you feel it too? What just happened?"

Rick shaking his head said, "Hell if I know, but something electrifying is brewing."

CHAPTER 5—Flashback

Those with the greatest awareness have the greatest nightmares!
Mahatma Gandhi

Friday April 10

It was 2:00 a.m. At least that's what the clock on the nightstand said. Jules woke up to muffled sounds coming from Alex's room. She had forgotten to close the door to the adjoining bathroom and could hear Alex's vague moaning sounds. Lying there, she listened as the sounds intensified. Getting out of bed, she made her way through the bathroom, and cracked open the door that went into Alex's room. The full moon was waxing, and Alex had not closed the curtains. Moonlight immersed the room and Jules saw that Alex was thrashing in the grasp of a nightmare. She waited a few moments, not wanting to intrude, though Alex's laments were becoming louder and more coherent, as coherent as a nightmare would allow.

"Take cover, get down. God damn it, get your asses down!" She wasn't quite screaming, but her tone was fiercely intense and urgent. She twisted and turned in the bed, throwing herself face down. "I'm hit, I'm hit," she cried out in pain. Flopping again on the bed, she lay on her side, in a semi-fetal position, repeating, "Stay where you are; that's an order!"

Alex was having a flashback. Jules made the decision to wake her, even if she would catch guff later. Sitting on the bed and holding Alex's shoulders, she pulled her up to a sitting position, put one arm around her back, the other on the back of her head, not out of tenderness; she just didn't want Alex to sock her in the face with her flailing arms or hit her head. "Wake up Alex. Wake up. You're having a nightmare. You're safe. Wake up."

Alex stopped struggling and went slack in Jules' arms. She was drenched in sweat, yet still smelled of rose and chamomile. *How can that be?* Laying Alex back down on the bed, Jules, her lips close to Alex's cheek, whispered, "It's okay, you were having a bad nightmare."

Alex was still a bit disoriented. Though Jules had never experienced flashbacks herself, she knew that sometimes people who did were disoriented for a little while after the episode. She waited. In a minute, Alex said, "Was I shouting? How did you hear me?"

"I left the bathroom door open. You were loud enough for me to hear you. I'm sorry if I invaded your privacy, but I recognized the signs of a flashback."

"Thank you. I'll be all right now."

Jules had been dismissed, but she didn't take it personally and asked, "Do you have flashbacks often?"

"No, not since I got out of the Marines. I can't imagine what triggered it."

Jules watched Alex, who seemed to still be groggy. She didn't want Alex to be pulled back into the nightmare, so she got up, went into the bathroom, and wet two washcloths with cold water. Sitting back down on the bed next to Alex, she laid one of the washcloths on Alex's forehead. With the other, she wiped down her cheeks and neck.

"Would you like a drink of water, Alex?"

Alex looked up at her and nodded almost imperceptibly. Jules found a paper cup in the bathroom, filled it with water and returned. She took the washcloth off Alex's forehead, put her left arm under Alex's shoulders, and helped her up far enough that she could drink without spilling it. Taking one more look at Alex, she thought she was okay

"Alex, I'm going to return to my room now, but I'll keep both doors open in case you have another episode."

Alex didn't argue. While Alex didn't know what triggered the flashback, Jules had a good idea. Alex may have recognized her on some subconscious level earlier in the evening, which in turn, had triggered the episode. If this were true, it was only a matter of time before the subconscious perception seeped into her waking consciousness.

The next morning, Rick and Sophie were already down in the kitchen waiting for the others. Rick had been up early and fixed scrambled eggs, biscuits with homemade preserves, and juice. Alex came down first.

"Sweetie, did you have a nightmare last night? I thought I heard something, got up, but then, things were quiet."

"Yeah, Aunt Sophie, I did. Sorry to have awakened you."

"Don't worry about that, I just wanted to make sure you were all right," responded Sophie.

"I'm fine and raring to go. Any word from our two guests?" inquired Alex.

"Not yet. Why don't you sit down and eat, while I pack a lunch for you and Jules? Rick, will lunch, dinner, and breakfast for tomorrow be enough for you and Jake? By the way, how did you introduce Jake to Dean, just so I don't contradict you?"

Rick, proud of himself, puffed up his chest and said, "Told Dean that Jake was doing a survey of the property for an asset re-evaluation. You were thinking of refinancing the mortgage and he'd be around off and on during the summer seeing how the place was run. He didn't ask anything more after that."

"That was pretty creative," said Alex between bites of her strawberry jam laden biscuit.

Rick smiled broadly. "Why thank you. There is an element of truth to it, don't ya think?"

Jake came down first, dressed again in jeans, with a fresh cowboy shirt and brand spanking new cowboy boots.

He was comical, trying hard to fit into the surroundings. Jules followed a few minutes later. She had on curve-hugging blue jeans, a nicely tailored button-down blue oxford and paddock boots; a sure sign that she had been around horses more than a little.

After eating, they all picked up their plates, carried them to the sink and headed to the barn. On their way up to the mountains, they would stop by the house and pick up the provisions. Jake and Rick went to the equipment shed, an adjunct to the barn. Alex and Jules heard the roar of the ATV engines, followed by zooming up the road toward the house.

"Dean, can we get Jules outfitted with a horse? We're going to be riding most of the day."

"Howdy ma'am. You a friend of Alex's?"

After a quick look at Alex, Jules answered Dean, "Why yes, yes I am. How are you this morning?"

"Where'd you meet Alex?" queried Dean, ignoring Jules' polite inquiry as to his wellbeing.

Alex jumped in, "We're Marine buddies, both served in Afghanistan." Jules' eyes widened; a movement not lost on Alex. Jules thought that Alex might have remembered and was waiting for the shoe to drop.

Dean seemed satisfied and got back to business. "You know how to ride?"

"It's been a while, but I rode hunter jumper in college," answered Jules.

"Is that like steeple chase, with those skimpy little saddles?" asked Dean.

"Yes, and those skimpy little saddles are much easier on the horse than the twenty-pound Western saddles," challenged Jules.

"You've been out of touch, girlie. We only use neoprene saddles here. Light as a feather." Dean smiled with superiority. Jules, sufficiently rebuked, shrugged her shoulders and caught a quick glimpse of Alex. She was stifling a grin.

Dean picked out a seven-year-old mare that had good manners but still had a little spunk. "This here is Goldie. You'll like her. Real steady but can get down and go with the best of them. Wanna start brushing her while I get Alex's mount? Alex, you want to ride Tommy boy?"

"Sure, Dean. Is he as naughty as ever?"

"For everyone but you, Alex."

Soon the women were saddled up and heading the quarter mile back to the house to pick up the lunch that Sophie packed. Alex watched Jules. She had quiet hands and used her legs to direct the horse, as opposed to yanking on the reins, as most novices do. Goldie, the mare she was riding, seemed to appreciate Jules' gentle hands. They went around to the back of the house and Sophie came out with a saddlebag. In one side she had packed sandwiches, fruit, and cookies, and in the other, bottled water. Alex jumped off Tommy Boy, throwing the reins to Jules. She tied down the saddlebag, hugged and kissed Sophie, remounted, and headed east, down to the river.

Alex and Sophie's affection toward each other left Jules a little sad and wanting. Her childhood, by all accounts, was perfect, except that her parents were cold and doled out affection as a reward, not like Sophie who dispensed warmth and fondness with Alex like an artesian spring, always flowing, never freezing over. She had to admit that she was envious.

The path was still wide enough for the two women to ride side by side. Alex picked up a trot with Jules following suit. Jules rode very relaxed and moved with the horse, sitting deep in the saddle to minimize the jarring of the trot. Alex turned to Jules and asked if she was up for a canter. Before she could answer, Alex cued Tommy Boy. Looking back over her left shoulder, Alex could see that Jules eased Goldie into a slow and rhythmic canter without any problem.

They rode north along the river for fifteen minutes, before the river veered east. The relatively flat trail began to climb and narrow. Alex took the lead, slowing Tommy Boy to a walk. They continued to climb for another fifteen minutes, winding through a mixed conifer and deciduous forest. Jules was glad that she had brought a jacket. It was much cooler in the woods than it was riding along the river. Neither woman spoke. Alex loved riding in the woods. She knew it like the back of her hand from canvassing the property as a child. She had always taken solace in the deep green silence. Jules was quiet for another reason. She was intelligence gathering. When they came to a small clearing, the path leveled out and widened again. Jules rode up next to Alex.

"Alex, are there a series of trails that crisscross each other in this general area?"

"Yes, but they all end up at the same place."

There were two trails that exited the clearing, not including the one that they rode in on. Alex chose the path to the extreme right. The trail steepened almost immediately. Both riders leaned forward in the saddle to help the horses negotiate the uphill climb. They climbed steadily for another ten or fifteen minutes, then the trail cut due east, traversing the hill.

Jules asked if the trails had been cut to challenge both the horses and riders and if the section they were on now, had been designed to give the horse a rest. Alex was mildly impressed with Jules' perception but wasn't willing to give the farm away just yet. Another fifteen minutes passed, and the trail abruptly turned north again. They climbed steadily for another ten minutes, then they broke into another clearing. This one was level; larger than the small clearing they went through forty-five minutes ago. Soft greenish yellow grass was beginning to sprout after a winter nap.

Alex hopped off Tommy Boy, tied the reins to a tree branch and announced, "Let's let the horses rest for a while."

Jules dismounted Goldie, tying her a couple of trees away from Tommy Boy. She joined Alex, who had perched on a fallen tree log and was deep breathing. She loved the musty scent of the forest.

"Alex, I made arrangements for you to talk to Claire's psychiatrist, Dr. Metuchi, this afternoon about four o'clock and then with Dr. Metuchi and Claire together tomorrow."

"Good. Thank you." Alex turned to look at Jules. *She is so beautiful but seems to be unaware of how striking she really is. I wonder if...* Alex filed away her thought as Jules spoke.

"Is there any background information you want from me before talking to Dr. Metuchi?"

"If you're willing. Aunt Sophie and Rick told me what you had shared with them, but I have a feeling that they got the sanitized version."

"They got the whole picture on how she is now, but I had my reasons for leaving out the specifics of her injuries, both physical and mental. There was no need to burden your Aunt with explicit details. I didn't want to paint such a sad picture of Claire as a victim that your Aunt Sophie would have agreed to the deal solely from feeling sorry. In addition, I figured that you and I would have a conversation."

Alex believed that Jules was sincere but decided to challenge her. "Why does it matter if Aunt Sophie agrees to your proposal from feeling sorry about Claire, or for some other reason?"

Lightly touching Alex on her forearm, Jules responded, "That might lead to 'buyer's remorse' down the road if things get rough. I'd much rather give a realistic preview. That way everyone knows what they are getting into."

Thinking that Jules' reason made sense, Alex asked, "Okay, did you sanitize any part of the story?"

Jules easily responded, "No. I told her as much as we know right now."

"I'm sorry if I doubted you, but I have to have all the facts in order to advise my aunt properly."

Jules did not flinch. "I completely understand. Things are a little topsy-turvy right now. This is personal for you. The welfare of the people you love is at stake."

Alex was quiet, recognizing Jules' graceful concession. *This woman is classy, and oh so hot.* "You're right. I'm short-sighted when it comes to Aunt Sophie's wellbeing. Let me see if I can remember what we were talking about. Oh yeah, why do you think the kidnapping was personal?"

"It's just a hunch. I can't speak to the reasons. You're the forensic psychologist, maybe you can provide some insight." Jules' comment was not meant to be condescending or sarcastic, though she feared that Alex would jump to that conclusion.

Thinking for a moment, Alex continued. "Was she raped? God, how I hate that term."

Jules shrugged her shoulders as she said, "She says she was not raped, but then she didn't remember how she got the other injuries."

"Classic repression?" asked Alex.

"Maybe, but I'm not convinced," answered Jules. "She doesn't remember much."

"What did the physical examination show?" Alex was busy formulating a theory and needed additional data.

"It supported her story, that she wasn't raped. There was no semen, no vaginal tearing, no pubic hairs, and no bruising."

Alex was deep in thought. Jules waited patiently.

"Jules, what if the kidnapper used a condom? Would that change the thought that there wasn't a rape? I wonder why she can't remember. Hmm. What if she was in a state of conscious sedation?"

"What does that mean?"

Alex explained. "It's when a pharmaceutical is administered to allow the patient to respond to commands and maintain their breathing without assistance but, probably won't remember anything afterwards. Amnesia is common. That could explain why she insists she wasn't raped. She doesn't remember. There are three primary ways that sedation can be administered. First, by IV, which produces a profound amnesia. Any indication of needle marks, particularly IVs?"

"I don't know that they looked."

"It could have been overlooked," Alex continued. We also have to look at the possibility of External Conscious Sedation, induced by an orally administered drug. Typically, the patient relaxes and falls asleep. It's hard to predict the level of amnesia that can occur, because each person responds differently, but with the right combination, the amnesia can also be profound. I'd rule out the third method, which is Inhalation, used in dentistry offices for years. You know, Nitrous Oxide, or 'laughing gas'. This would have been too cumbersome. One other thing, if the physicians weren't specifically looking for sedation pharmaceuticals, they wouldn't have shown up on a typical tox screen."

Jules didn't respond right away. She was wondering if Alex would come to the same conclusion that a consulting forensic psychologist did. Alex got up and paced, obviously talking to herself. "Jules, I'm sure you have had the best people look at this, right? Besides Metuchi, you probably called in a forensic expert?"

"Yes. We consulted with a retired FBI profiler and forensic psychologist. Do you know Ansel Fahad?"

"I've never met him but know of his work. He's solid. What did he say?"

"I'd be more interested in your thoughts before I tell you what conclusions he drew." Jules wasn't giving anything up at this point.

"Nothing like performance pressure," groaned Alex.

Half amused, Jules' lips curled, as Alex continued. "Without talking to Claire, it's really difficult to speculate. You can't hold me to this."

"Fair enough" uttered Jules.

"Well, then, I'd speculate that one of two things could have taken place. First, the person or persons who were responsible for the kidnapping gave specific instructions to their cohorts who held Claire not to sexually abuse her, maybe under the threat of not getting paid. If this were the case, chances are that the mastermind was a woman. The second possibility is that the mastermind was a man, but the person holding her was a woman. Both scenarios would explain the lack of sexual abuse. I'd bet money that we are dealing with a male-female team."

Jules was impressed. Alex seemed to have a gift. Even hearing information second and third hand, without the benefit of any of the written reports and medical records, or talking to Claire, in fifteen minutes, she came to the same conclusion as the FBI guy did after two weeks of investigation and deliberation.

"I have a few more questions, Jules. Did Claire remember if her captor was male or female or did she have an impression if her captor was male or female?"

"No. The only thing she remembered is that the person was taller than she and always wore gloves. Claire said the hood she was forced to wear prevented her from seeing anything, plus the person never spoke to her. She didn't remember any particular scent, except diesel."

"Then the person holding her could be either male or female," answered Alex. "Do we know if Claire is rebellious? Would she have tried to fight the kidnappers?"

Jules told Alex that Claire was restrained on a bed and allowed to use the bathroom at regular intervals. The tox screen showed low levels of valium, so she probably was mildly sedated to make her easier to control. Then she added,

"Claire was described by both her father and stepmother as passive and non-aggressive. It seems out of character for Claire to resist, unless she got the sense that she was expendable."

Alex thought a moment, trying to pull something from her memory. "That makes sense. Valium combined with Midazolam can induce conscious sedation and Midazolam wouldn't show up on a routine tox screen. The Midazolam has a rapid onset and it doesn't last very long. The presence of valium, which lasts longer, as much as forty-eight hours, could indicate that Midazolam was added to induce the sedation. With that combination, there would likely be no recollection, and meanwhile, the Valium would have kept her mildly sedated to reduce any combativeness. Then something changes, and she senses she is expendable, somehow she rallies and escapes.

"I think this tends to point to a very personal kidnapping, possibly with people that Claire might recognize."

Jules was pensive. Alex waited patiently for a minute or two, then asked, "Shall I go on?"

Jules nodded, interested in Alex's impressions.

"I'm sure your guy at the FBI also considered that Claire might be involved as a perpetrator."

"Yes, but only for a minute," answered Jules.

"What did he conclude?"

"There wasn't a scrap of evidence of Claire's complicity and it also didn't make sense from the ransom perspective. Claire has much more than the six million dollars in her trust fund."

"Hmm, Fahad probably is right, though perhaps the kidnapping wasn't about the money. It wouldn't be too big a leap to theorize that Claire was sick and tired of her father's control and set out to teach him a lesson. This might satisfy a pathological need," offered Alex.

Agitated, Jules jumped all over Alex. "Are you saying that there is a possibility that Claire is mentally disturbed and did this to herself? There's not a lick of evidence that would lead anyone to that conclusion."

Afraid to go down a slippery slope, Alex decided to dole out what she was considering in small measures. "Possibly. Many times, individuals can lead a pretty normal life and still harbor psychosis, that with the right stimulus, can take over."

"Go on," ordered Jules.

"Well, it is possible that she suffers from Munchausen Syndrome and something pushed her over the edge." Alex wondered if Jules even knew what Munchausen's was. Most people had misconceptions about the mental disease.

Surprised and incredulous, Jules, asked, "What? Doesn't Munchausen's usually refer to a parent inflicting injury on a child to get attention?"

"Give the girl an A+," sang out Alex. "Technically, you're right. Munchausen's is typically associated with a pattern of harm and the cases best known, in which an adult inflicts harm on a child, are called Munchausen's by Proxy.

"I think that there could be a possibility of a single-incident Munchausen with Claire as her own perpetrator. I've done enough work to know that it is possible."

Jules caught on right away. Alex appreciated not having to explain in lay terms. "So, what you are saying is that Claire could be both the perpetrator and victim of self-induced Munchausen's."

"Yes, exactly."

"Even if Claire didn't manifest any personality disorders pre-kidnapping, she may still have suffered a Munchausen's episode. Did Fahad even consider this possibility?"

"No, he didn't. You're the only one who has proposed this as a working theory."

"Whoa, hold on Jules. I said nothing about a working theory. I'm just trying to cover all possibilities, even though remote. I wouldn't want to put a line in the sand and stake my professional reputation on this. I haven't even seen the girl."

"Understood, Alex. We'll keep this to ourselves for now, all right?"

"Yes, but as farfetched as this may seem, if there is even a remote chance, and I mean, one chance in a million that Claire is her own perpetrator, then there is no way that I would want her here. Her presence would present a patent danger to everyone around." Alex knew what this meant for Jules. She looked dejected knowing that this was going to be a deal breaker.

Jules, trying to hide her disappointment, reached out and lightly touched Alex's hand. "Of course, I certainly understand, but you yourself said it was a long shot."

Alex could see that this was a huge setback for Jules. She turned her hand over and interlaced her fingers with Jules', "I'm sorry to rock the boat. I know this puts a wrench in your plans. However, just as you pointed out earlier, my first duty is to Aunt Sophie."

"I'd probably have the same concerns if I were in your shoes," offered Jules, trying to be gracious and understanding.

Alex non-verbally acknowledged Jules' sensitivity by squeezing her hand and then asked. "Who diagnosed the Post Traumatic Stress Disorder?"

"She saw three psychiatrists and they all agreed. Metuchi, the one she sees now, is an expert in PTSD." Jules was amazed at how fast Alex switched from a virtual dismissal of the proposal to hunt down additional information.

"Is she on medication in addition to therapy?"

"Yes, she's been on Propranolol, I think that's what it's called, for the depression and Zyprexa."

"Zyprexa is an antipsychotic," interjected Alex, wondering if her theory wasn't as farfetched as she originally thought. "Does she exhibit signs of agitation and hyper vigilance? Sometimes Zyprexa helps, sometimes not."

"That would be a discussion for this afternoon with Dr. Metuchi," responded Jules.

"Is there anything that feels 'off' to you about the kidnapping and her recovery? Try and forget what I said about Munchausen's for now." Alex's mind was grinding.

Jules thought for a moment, then said, "Funny you should ask. There has been something nagging in the back of my head, but I can't put my finger on it. We've been through the particulars of the entire ordeal numerous times and nothing jumps out at me. Maybe I'm just naturally suspicious."

"Ah, yes, Rational Paranoia," joked Alex zinging Jules again. "Speaking of something in the back of the mind, I still can't shake the feeling that you and I have met before. Were you in Afghanistan a few years ago?

"Yes. I was with the MCIA. The intel side of things."

"Were you ever in the Hemland Province? Perhaps Camp Dwyer?"

"I may have passed through the Province, but I was never at Camp Dwyer." Jules hurriedly changed the subject. "What other questions about Claire do you have?"

"You've been around Claire post-abduction. Do you really think this is the right thing for her? I mean, wouldn't she be better off in a private institution? We certainly know she would if she were suffering from Munchausen's."

"Personally, I didn't think she'd be better off in an institution, before talking to you. She's starting to cope with her symptoms and sees the need to reconnect with the world. I'd probably defer to Dr. Metuchi."

"Did Claire choose Metuchi?"

"I don't think so. Why?"

"Jules, it's important to know who chose Metuchi. Can you get that information?"

"Yes of course."

Alex bobbed her head, thinking. Jules saw where Alex was going with this. Butterflies were fluttering up a storm in Jules' stomach.

"Do you know if they have been seen together outside of a professional context before or after treatment began?" inquired Alex.

"Alex, I'm not liking this at all. We vetted Metuchi in the first go around. What have you picked up?"

"Nothing yet, but I want to know with what I'm dealing."

"All right, I don't know, but I'll get someone on it right now. Is there a cellular signal up here?" Jules pulled out her cellphone, ready to dial.

"Coverage is spotty at best. You can make calls on the mesa, where the house is, and to the east. There's no signal to the west, north and south. You might try though, we're high enough."

Jules saw that the signal was weak, dialed anyway, and got through. She asked for Mickey. Apparently, Mickey answered because Jules was outlining what she wanted done ASAP. She ended the call with, "Mickey, don't let Metuchi, Claire or the Bentworths catch you and call me at once, either way." Jules returned the phone to its leather case and turned to Alex. "We set up an appointment for you to talk with Metuchi this afternoon. Do you think it's wise to bring up the idea of Munchausen's?"

Alex shook her head several times, then spoke. "I don't think we should share any of our theories with her right now."

"My thoughts too," answered Jules.

###

Alex held Goldie while Jules slipped her left leg into the stirrup and threw her right leg over the back of the horse. She took the reins from Alex and waited for Alex to mount and lead the way. They continued alternating traversing then climbing the hill for another hour until they could go no further. The hill backed up to a tall craggy peak that stood like a sentry over another sculpted clearing. There was a corral, a good-sized lean-to, and an outhouse. They unbridled the horses so they could munch on hay Alex took out from under a tarp in the lean-to. There was a water trough in the corral. Water flowed in from a diverted creek, then out again, back to the stream, assuring the horses a fresh supply of water.

Jules was walking stiffly, but not complaining. It was only eleven o'clock, but both of them were hungry. Alex dusted off a bench under the lean-to and moved it up against the hay, so they'd have something to lean against. She unpacked the sandwiches, fruit, cookies and water and set them on the bench between herself and Jules. When they finished, Alex asked, "How are you feeling? The air up here is thinner, and some folks get dizzy, or get a headache."

"I feel fine, though my legs are a little stiff."

Alex, grinning, taunted Jules. "Probably from hanging on to Goldie for dear life, when we made the last climb."

Equally as good natured, Jules retorted, "And I've got the ride down ahead of us. I look forward to more clinging."

Alex laughed then got up and from a set of lockers, pulled out a blanket. "Want to sit in the sun? I think it's cold here."

In a flash, Jules was up from the bench. "Here, let me help you."

They chose a spot in full sunlight, spread the blanket, and sat down. Before long, Alex laid back on the blanket. Relaxing in the sun, she dozed off. She was dreaming about her aunt and uncle taking her to the state fair for the first time. She had begged them to let her ride the Ferris wheel, even though she was very susceptible to motion sickness. They finally gave in, but Alex turned green and her aunt had to ask the attendant to stop the Ferris wheel after the very first rotation to let her off before she upchucked her cotton candy. How mortified she was!

Alex awoke to a wispy touch on her face and realized that Jules was on her side, propped up on her elbow, stroking her cheek. "Wake up, Alex. Alex wake up. We need to start back."

Alex just about jumped out of her skin, quickly sitting up. She hurriedly got off the blanket and started folding it as soon as Jules got up.

What is she so tense about? thought Jules. *Would she have preferred that I shake her awake?* None the less, Jules tried to ease Alex's apparent embarrassment. "Deja vu, huh?"

Alex attempted a smile, but failed, thinking, *why am I so nervous around this woman?* Back on the trail again, Alex regained her composure and joked with Jules about her 'wake up' calls. Not stopping at the small clearing halfway down the hill, an hour and forty minutes later, they arrived in front of the barn and led the horses in. "Damn," muttered Alex. "There's no one here to take the horses. Looks like we'll have to unsaddle them and rub them down ourselves." She took a quick look at her watch and groaned just as she heard Jules say,

"Hi, do you work here?"

A ranch hand had come into the barn and said, "Yes. I'm Matt, who are you?"

Alex butted in. "I'm Sophie's niece and this is my friend Jules. You must be new."

"Yeah, I started work here about two months ago."

"Matt, we're in a real hurry to make a four o'clock appointment, so could you unsaddle the horses and rub them down? We'd appreciate it."

"Anything for the boss' niece." Taking the reins from Alex and Jules, Matt led the horses to their stalls.

"Thanks, Matt. We'll put in a good word for you," shouted Alex over her shoulder, as she and Jules raced to the house. They got to the house at 3:35 p.m. and didn't stop to see where Sophie was. Racing through the great room, thundering up the front stairs and bursting through the doors of their respective rooms, they hustled to get cleaned up. Alex was scrambling for her tape recorder when Sophie stuck her head in and asked if everything was okay. Still needing to wash up, Alex told Sophie that everything was fine. Sophie saw that Alex was harried and told her that she'd see her at dinner.

Once Alex found the tape recorder, she knocked on the bathroom door and getting no answer, went in to wash her hands and face. By the time she got downstairs, it was five minutes to four. Jules was already in the office, still in her jeans and boots, but she had changed her oxford to a clean polo shirt. She looked up at Alex. "Do you want me here while you're talking to Dr. Metuchi?"

Thinking about it for a minute, Alex told her yes, then asked if she wanted Metuchi to know she was in the room. Jules bounced the question back to Alex.

"Sure, why not? I think her guard would be down, since she knows you," replied Alex.

"Okay, let's go for it," taking out a phone card and dialing, she waited for Metuchi to answer. Alex spent an hour asking Metuchi questions. She finished the call with the sense that Metuchi was a competent, though conventional psychiatrist. She had taken a very conservative approach with Claire's therapy and on the face of it, there had been progress. Alex and Jules debriefed each other and shared impressions agreeing to listen to the tape again later in the evening.

Both wandered into the kitchen where they found Sophie rubbing three rib eye steaks with olive oil, garlic powder, salt and pepper. She set them aside to warm up to room temperature. Sophie was of the opinion that a cold steak never liked a hot grill.

"Hi, you two. Just us girls for dinner tonight. Thought I'd grill us some steaks and Alex, if you want, I can make the salad you like with grilled potatoes, goat cheese and fennel."

"Yum, want me to slice the potatoes?" offered Alex.

"Do you remember how to season them?" quizzed Sophie.

"Olive oil, rosemary, salt, pepper, and balsamic vinegar."

"Jules, how do you like your steak?"

"Medium rare, please". She asked if she could do anything and when both Sophie and Alex said no, she excused herself and headed back to the office, over her shoulder winking at Alex.

"We'll call you when dinner is ready," Sophie called out.

"Thanks. Looking forward to it," answered Jules from the Great Room.

Sophie and Alex continued to work in silence until Sophie couldn't contain herself any longer. "You like her, don't you?"

"I think so, Aunt Sophie, but I get a little nervous around her."

"You do? Do you know why?"

Role reversal, thought Alex, *Sophie's playing shrink again.* When Alex didn't answer, Sophie plunged on. "Honey, are you attracted to her?"

"Oh, for gosh sakes, Aunt Sophie, just because I'm gay doesn't mean I'm attracted to every beautiful woman I meet!"

"So, you think she's beautiful?" asked Sophie enjoying making Alex squirm a little.

"That's not what I meant, Aunt Sophie. She is beautiful. Actually, she's stunning, but that isn't what attracts me."

"Then you are attracted to her?"

"Aunt Sophie, enough! I'm not attracted to her." *Liar.* "She just makes me nervous, okay?" Alex was frustrated with Sophie and wasn't taking the teasing in stride. Maybe she was attracted to Jules, but there was something else and it was something she couldn't verbalize.

"Does it have to do with you thinking you've met her before?" Sophie added, trying to diffuse Alex's frustration.

"Maybe. I just can't verbalize it yet, Aunt Sophie. Can we talk about something else?"

"Sure. Why don't you sit down and have some coffee with me?" said Sophie, conceding that the teasing was over. They continued to chat about the condition of the trails, the lean-to needing repairing and the new guy, Matt, while they both savored their coffee.

Dinner was terrific, the steaks perfect, the grilled potatoes, goat cheese, fennel and spring mix of greens was as gourmet as one would find in any fine restaurant. They sipped coffee on the porch and watched the sun give up its last hold on the western sky, its apricot hue fading gracefully until it settled below the mountains for forty winks. With the disappearance of the sun, the temperature quickly slipped into the forties. Ruby and Rowdy lay at Alex's feet, sleeping with one eye open, just looking for an excuse to be unruly. Sophie offered to get blankets for the three of them, but Alex and Jules declined, saying they had more work to do.

"All right you two. Go do your work. So much for showing gratitude to an old woman for such a fine meal. At least you washed and dried the dishes. Come on babies, let's go inside. My bones are getting too old to sit out here in this cold." Responding to "Come on babies", the two dogs followed Sophie in, haughtily looking at Alex, then giving in, planting kisses on her dangling hand.

On the way upstairs, Alex told Jules that she was going to get a shower first. About forty-five minutes later, Jules knocked on Alex's bedroom door.

"Come in."

Alex was seated on the bed, wearing a 'Go Marines' T-shirt and boxers. *Cute*, thought Jules. *Very cute.*

Looking up from a yellow pad, Alex saw that Jules had gotten dressed in sweatpants and a T-shirt. Her hair was still damp. "Are you ready?"

"Whenever you are, doctor," quipped Jules.

"Okay, here is what I thought we would do. We are going to listen to the tape again and write down anything that seems to be inconsistent, anything that might lend itself to one of our theories, or something that just strikes us oddly. Handing Jules a pad and pen she turned on the tape recorder.

They listened twice and nothing jumped out to either of them.

"Alex, are her opinions and conclusions about Claire sound?"

"They seem to be, unless we consider the possibility of Munchhausen. She'd be way off base then."

"So, in your mind, did she pass the muster?" Jules watched as Alex pulled up a blanket to cover her bare legs.

"Nice and neatly, but I'd still like to know what your operatives dig up concerning out of office contact." Jules nodded her head in agreement.

Alex leaned over to stow her pad and tape recorder in the nightstand drawer when she asked Jules, "So what is on the agenda for tomorrow?"

"Do you still want to talk to the medical doctors about Claire's injuries?"

"No, I think your analysis is sufficient."

"Why thank you, Dr. Martini," teased Jules.

"I didn't mean it like that," answered Alex, slightly annoyed.

"I know. I just couldn't help teasing you."

"Great," said Alex, her insides twisting.

"Alex, tell me something. Do I make you nervous?"

Terrific, thought Alex. *First Aunt Sophie, now her.* She fidgeted, trying hard not to leap from the bed and start pacing. "Yes. Yes, you do."

"Why is that?" questioned Jules.

God, if this is a bad dream, let me wake up, implored Alex. But god wasn't listening.

Jules asked again. "Why, Alex?"

"Jules, I'm tired. Do we have to do this now?"

"Classic avoidance, huh, Alex?"

"Everyone wants to be a shrink," jabbed Alex. "I can see you're not going to leave me alone until I answer."

"Correct, so you might as well get it over," smiled Jules.

"Gee, thanks. Let me ask you a question first."

"Shoot," said Jules succinctly.

"I assume that if you did a background check on everyone here, I was probably included. Am I right?"

"Yes, you're right," answered Jules evenly.

"Then you know about me," responded Alex.

"I know lots about you Alex," mildly taunted Jules. "To what are you referring specifically?"

"Oh, let's cut the dance short," said Alex with great annoyance.

"If you mean the part about being a lesbian, it doesn't concern me in the least," said Jules.

"Well it might, if I told you what my Aunt Sophie thinks about my nervousness with you." Once it was out of her mouth, Alex couldn't believe what she had just said out loud. *I just left a blatant invitation for her to ask me what Sophie thought! Self-sabotage at its best!*

"Do you want to tell me, or should I guess?" said Jules without emotion.

"Christ, you are a pain," shot back Alex.

"So, I'm told. What does your Sophie think?"

Swallowing hard, Alex blurted it out. "She thinks I'm attracted to you." Alex purposefully held Jules' eyes, though it took a great effort.

Jules, cool and deliberate, without a trace of sarcasm or apprehension retorted, "Well, we now know what your Aunt Sophie thinks; what do you think?"

Alex thought Jules' answer was masterfully clever, so clever her stomach lurched. "I think it has to do with this gnawing sense that I know you or maybe because you saw me when I was vulnerable from the nightmare."

"Why would either of those make you nervous?"

"Oh, come on, Jules. I know you've only spent a few hours with me, but a smart woman like yourself certainly has an idea who I am. For better or worse, I like to be in control."

"That's evident, but it's not a sin. Being in control is fine, but surely as a psychologist you must realize that being vulnerable isn't a sin either."

"Yeah, of course, I know that. It's just not comfortable for me," retorted Alex.

"So, you were embarrassed about your flashback?" Jules tried to steer away from Alex's sense that she knew her.

"Not about the flashback, about you seeing me like that," moaned Alex.

"Like what, Alex?"

"Vulnerable, unable to help myself."

"And, when I woke you up on the mountain today, why were you so jumpy and embarrassed?" Jules had already connected what happened this afternoon with the flashback.

"Well, that's more complicated," groaned Alex

"Is it?" Jules patiently said.

"Fine. I was worried about you watching me sleep."

"I *was* watching you sleep. I noticed by your eye movements that you might be dreaming and wondered if you might have had another flashback," Jules offered.

Alex was trying to get her head around this woman's direct, penetrating, matter of fact style. It didn't dawn on her that she used this very style when talking to patients or suspects. She was just too agitated right now.

"We don't have to talk about this anymore Alex. It's just that I wish I didn't make you nervous, that you could relax around me. We're going to spend a lot of time together and I want you to be comfortable."

The 'we're going to spend a lot of time together' wasn't missed by Alex. She was on the brink of self-confession and was teetering. She jumped. "Jules, up there on the mountain, it was intimate, the way you touched me, it was intimate."

"That's what made you embarrassed; that I woke you up by stroking your cheek?" questioned Jules, truly surprised.

Alex jumped in. "I didn't mean that it was, ah, sexually intimate. I just meant it felt, I don't know, like an intimate connection I don't understand."

"It wasn't meant to be sexual. I wanted to make sure that I awoke you gently and not send you into a flashback by startling you."

Jules signed heavily to which Alex responded, "No, no. I didn't feel it in a sexual way. Don't you see? I could go out and screw someone and not feel a moment of intimacy, but you are virtually a stranger and your concern was very intimate. I don't understand why it spooks me so."

Jules wanted to tell her, to ease her emotional distress, but held back. In Alex's current state, she would jump to conclusions. That already happened once or twice today. She sighed deeply, and Alex took it as a sign of Jules' frustration with her.

Trying to get back into her professional comfort zone, Alex addressed Jules. "Let's call it quits for tonight, sleep on what we heard on the tape and revisit it tomorrow."

Jules got up off the bed and started to leave, but before she reached the door, turned, and went back to the side of the bed. "Listen, Alex. I'm not going to change how I interact with you, so you had better get comfortable with me." She took Alex's head in her hands and planted a chaste kiss on her cheek. "Sleep on that!" She strode through the adjoining bathroom door and closed it softly.

Sophie knocked on Alex's door and heard a cranky, "Now what do you want?"

Sophie opened the door and saw Alex in a heap on her bed.

"Oh, Aunt Sophie, I didn't know it was you. Sorry."

"Jules getting to you?"

"I don't want to talk about it right now. We just finished listening to an hour-long tape twice and I'm really, really tired."

Sophie walked to the bed, gave her niece a light hug and said, "If you need me, I'll be up for a while."

Alex thanked her aunt, said good night, climbed into bed, and vowed not to think about the case until the morning. She was successful. She didn't think about the case once. She spent the night thinking about Jules.

CHAPTER 6 – Sight Without Eyes

There is magic in that little world, home; it is a mystic circle that surrounds comforts and virtues never know beyond its hallowed limits.

Robert Southey

Saturday April 11

When Alex looked at the clock on the nightstand, she catapulted out of bed. It was nine o'clock. She washed up quickly, threw on a pair of blue jeans and light blue T-shirt, grabbing a soft denim shirt from the closet to top it off, as she hustled downstairs. Turning the corner, she encountered a well-rested Jules chatting with Sophie about some papers that were spread out on the kitchen table.

"Morning, Alex. Get some coffee and come join us. There's something I want to show you."

Sighing, Alex poured coffee, offered Sophie and Jules a refill, and skulked into a chair next to Sophie, asking, "What are you two doing?"

"We're reviewing the list of guests for the summer," said Sophie.

"I get it. Jules, in looking at the guest lists, do you see anything that jumps out at you?

"No. Reviewing the list was probably unnecessary, since most of the guests made their reservations more than two months ago, but I like to try and cover all bases "There's no such thing as foolproof."

Alex and Jules knew what each other was thinking. If the kidnapping was orchestrated by Claire or someone manipulating her, then it was possible that she might have somehow found out about the ranch, but Jules preempted Alex's concerns saying, "Most likely, the kidnappers would have to be psychic to know that we were contemplating approaching you. However, if you accept our proposal, then we'd want names of people who call in for a booking or anyone on the waiting list you call back to fill a cancellation." Jules thought for a moment, then continued. "One more thing; when we did our preliminary review of the ranch that boy down at the barn who helped us yesterday wasn't included."

"You mean Matt?" uttered Alex.

"Yes. Matt wasn't here. What do you know about him, Sophie?"

A gloomy cloud flitted over Sophie's face. "He's from Stevensville, a small town off of Route 93 on the way to Missoula." With a tinge of anger, she remembered the day he came wandering on to the ranch looking for work. "Rick was working in the office and answered the door. It was February, still very cold. The boy's boots and jeans were wet, his ears and face ruddy from the cold and he looked tired. He got right to the point and told Rick that he was looking for a job.

"Rick invited him in and learned that the boy had hitched from Stevensville to the ranch's road, then hiked in three miles to the house. For some reason, Rick liked the boy. He had experience working neighboring ranches in the summer, so Rick decided to make a call to a rancher down in Idaho, who Matt used as a reference. Rick told Matt to go into the kitchen and tell me that he had sent him in to get warm.

"I heard a knock on the door frame and saw this sandy-haired gangly kid, with hat in hand, standing in the doorway. He was a little backwoodsman in how he talked, but very polite and respectful. I told him to sit down, gave him a cup of coffee and asked him when he had eaten last. He was shy, but I managed to get out of him that he hadn't eaten since the day before. I asked him why and he told me that his dad had kicked him out for being gay.

"He insisted that he was okay and not to go to any trouble. I made him a couple of grilled cheese sandwiches and heated some soup left over from lunch. While he was eating, I noticed that his socks were soaked. I told him to take them off and I'd throw them into the dryer. He wouldn't let me do that and said that if I'd point him to the dryer, he'd take care of it.

"Matt and I were chatting when Rick came in with a big smile across his face. He told Matt that he'd take him on for two weeks and see how it went. There was such a relief across that boy's face, I thought he was going to collapse in a heap on the floor. Rick asked me if I could take the boy back to Stevensville to pick up his gear, because he wanted to start him tomorrow. I had to pick up a few supplies, so we hopped into the truck and took off. Unfortunately, we had a run in with his drunken father but when I branded the shotgun, he backed off and let the boy get his belongings. Turns out he is a hard worker and has some cooking skills, which always comes in handy during our guest season."

Jules sat there pensively, not sharing her thoughts with Sophie or Alex. Finally, Sophie stepped in and asked if either of them wanted breakfast. Alex said she didn't feel like a big breakfast and was going to have another cup of coffee with toast. Jules also declined breakfast and said she'd have what Alex was having. With that, Sophie excused herself, told the women she was going into town for supplies and that they were on their own for lunch, maybe dinner.

Coffee and toast in front of the two of them, Jules broke the ice. "I'm sorry for last night. I shouldn't have pushed you."

Alex was not going to admit that Jules had gotten under her skin. She could get piqued when her private emotional space was invaded and when she got indignant, she often fantasized about revenge. Of course, she'd never act on it; playing it out in her mind was enough. She ignored Jules' apology and announced, "We need to go out again today. I want to show you something else."

"Horseback again?" asked Jules, inwardly groaning.

"Yup. We'll leave as soon as we're finished here."

Washing the breakfast dishes, Alex asked Jules, "What time is the appointment with Claire?"

"Four o'clock, just like yesterday."

Scrubbing the last butter knife, Alex disappointedly said, "I really wish I could talk to Claire alone and face to face, but I guess this is the best we can do for now. If there is some connection between her and Metuchi, I wouldn't be surprised if Metuchi coaches her during the call. However, if we change plans now, either of the two might get suspicious."

Jules folded the dish cloth and hung it over the dish drainer. "Let's see how it goes, then if you think that there is a hint of suspicion, we'll figure out something else."

"I'll pack some sandwiches for the trip. Tuna okay?" Brownies with pecans?" asked Alex.

"I love tuna. See you in a few minutes, I need to get my boots and grab a jacket." With that, Jules disappeared up the back stairs before Alex realized she had left the room.

Leaving the barn on horseback, Jules asked Alex where they were going. Alex was being furtive, and it was obvious that she wasn't going to tell Jules anything more than that they were going to a spot known only by the people at the ranch. Jules resigned herself to enjoying the ride and memorizing the trail, but there wasn't a trail as she quickly found out. They rode back towards the house then through a few of the cabins located at the north of the house and came to the edge of a thick copse of trees that stood sentry to a thicker, darker forest running along the edge of the sheer mountain walls.

Alex jumped off her horse and motioned to Jules to do the same. "From the ground what you see is the steep wall of the mountain going straight down and ending perpendicular with the mesa here, disappearing into the trees. Right?"

Jules shook her head, 'yes'.

"The forest backs up to the wall of the mountain and runs north and south along the entire façade," Alex explained.

"Yes, that's what I thought when we were approaching," replied Jules.

"Okay. Follow me. We keep all the trails we use for the guests and the cattle groomed and wide enough to be recognized as trails. The trail we're going to follow now is not groomed. That means, we'll be picking our way through the trees, and probably getting swatted in the face with sapling branches."

"Why don't you groom this trail?" inquired Jules.

"Because it's private and we don't want to encourage guests to explore on their own. We'll walk the horses a bit because these two haven't been up here in a while. Alex picked an entry spot between two large trees. The woods were thick, dark and everything looked similar, so Jules kept close behind Alex's mount. They walked picking their way through trees and shrubs for ten minutes or so before Alex said it was okay to mount back up. "We're moving parallel to the mountain wall. The belt of trees we're moving through is about a quarter mile wide at this point and we're climbing slightly."

The horses didn't seem bothered by the lack of a trail and handled the occasional squirrel, bird and untamed branch in stride. Alex and Jules were as silent as the woods and had been, each mulling over her own thoughts. After about twenty minutes, Alex spoke again. "Now we're at the place where the forest belt widens to about three quarters of a mile. It's pretty easy to get lost in here at night unless you grew up here or have a compass."

"And what's the significance of the tree belt widening?" Jules asked curiously.

"You'll see soon enough."

Jules thought that Alex's terseness might be her way of punishing Jules for her actions last night. Keeping tight control of herself was where Alex was most comfortable. Jules understood this and didn't see it as a liability. On the contrary, she saw it as a real benefit in the weeks to come.

About ten minutes passed and Alex turned around in her saddle to ask, "Jules, now pay attention here. Do you hear water?"

Jules listened for a moment, then answered, "Yes, but it's far off."

"Right. Just to the north of us there is a waterfall tumbling from the sheer face of the mountain forming a good-sized pool, then running down through a subterranean chasm which empties into the river at the base of the mesa. We'll be there in about fifteen minutes. I wanted to warn you, because the horses might get jumpy. It gets pretty loud."

They rode in silence until the rumbling of the plunging water was unmistakable. Jules glimpsed dapples of sunlight through the trees and thought they might be coming to a clearing, but she wasn't prepared for what she saw. It took her breath away. The forest gave way to a pool thirty or so feet in diameter, ringed with moss and fallen rocks. Alex moved her horse aside so that Jules could move up next to her even though they'd be crowded. Both women got off the horses, now shoulder to shoulder and soothed the horses who were a little nervous on the spongy ground cover. They quieted quickly with Alex and Jules' gentle urging.

Jules looked up at the plunging water dropping effortlessly into the pool. The pool seemed to beckon the water with outstretched arms of shadows and phantom shapes driven up by the swirling mist. Hardly any direct sunlight made its way in; just yellow dapples here and there. Jules looked up. The trees that encircled the pool had grown tall and thick enough to form a virtual privacy canopy over the pool. The air was laden with moisture that seemed to hover like a bee in a field of English lavender. She felt lightheaded.

Alex led both horses to the pool to drink while Jules, whose feet were riveted to the moss, soaked in the beauty. She wasn't sure what had come over her, but she felt euphoric.

Returning with the horses, Alex caught the look on Jules face and instantly knew what was happening. She took Jules' hand and squeezed gently. "We'd better go now. Here, take your horse. There's something more I want to show you. You're going to get a little wet and the horses could get nervous."

Alex took the lead, walking along the pool's edge toward the falls. She disappeared and so did the horse. Jules heard, "Come on. Careful, it's slippery." Jules followed Alex's path and found herself behind the falls on a ledge about four or five feet wide, just enough for her and the horse. Her horse balked, startled by the spitting water and noise, but Jules gently coaxed him across the thirty-foot length of the ledge.

She thought there might be a cave, but the wall was solid. Looking up in the dim light she could see that the wall had been carved out. It was like a huge 'nicho', a word used in the Southwest to describe a recess in a wall where religious statues or other artwork could be displayed. She saw Alex's horse leave the ledge and go through the trees at the northeast side of the falls. About twenty-five yards back into the forest, Alex was tying up her horse next to a tree-shrouded, three-sided lean-to. Jules tied her horse up, plopped down on the blanket Alex had spread out in the lean-to and tried not to feel so awkward.

Suddenly, overcome with uncharacteristic emotion, tears streaked down Jules' cheeks. She could not comprehend what was happening to her. Alex, who recognized a moment of vulnerability, reached out and took her hand. Jules was learning that Alex could change from one emotional state to another like a multitude of fireflies flashing off and on in the darkest of nights. She had been short with her up until now.

She felt a breath of wind moving ghostly through the trees, whispering its presence with a subtle ruffle of her loose hair. Did she imagine it? Was she now imagining the touch of a hand on her shoulder? She turned to see Alex, her arm around her shoulders, waiting for her. But waiting for her to do what? Alex's eyes, taking on the color of the emerald moss beneath them, looked at her with gentleness.

"Jules, why did you kiss me on the cheek last night?"

Jules moved closer to Alex; their eyes locked. When she was inches away from Alex's face she sighed, then hoarsely tried to speak. They were now so close that Alex could see the flecks of gold and burning fires in Jules' eyes. Alex didn't dare move. Jules, still holding Alex's gaze, reading her for a sign to back off, slowly brought her hands up and placed them on Alex's cheeks and nervously breathed out the words, "Because I couldn't."

Not at all expecting Jules' answer, Alex's breath caught, "Couldn't what?"

"Kiss you like this." Jules touched her lips to Alex's, tenderly, shyly, almost chastely. Sensing no resistance from Alex, she tilted her chin and kissed her top lip, bottom lip, then both. She put her arms around Alex and pulled her closer until their breasts were pressed against each. She traced Alex's jawbone with her lips and the tip of her tongue. Alex tilted her head back, offering her neck to Jules. She was not disappointed. Jules ran the tip of her tongue from Alex's collar bone, along her neck ending at her lips. When Jules stopped kissing her, she brushed her cheek against Alex's making a fluttering motion of her eyelashes.

Breathing heavily, Alex halfheartedly managed to say, "Jules, we have to stop," but Alex didn't pull away. She wanted to lie on the carpet of moss, stare at the top of the trees and watch the night tiptoe in swathed in the arms of this woman.

Jules ignored her, running her fingers across Alex's lips, luring Alex to kiss her again. Just before Jules' lips met Alex's once more, she pulled her head away, pausing for a moment before she passionately covered Alex's mouth with hers as they both fell out of breath to the ground.

Alex still in control of some of her rational faculties, leaned back from Jules and groaned, "Oh my gosh. What have we done?"

"Kissed each other," murmured Jules as she began to continue her loving exploration.

"Jules don't be droll," pleaded Alex. "This complicates things so much. How did we let this happen?"

"I don't know, but I couldn't help kissing you. I was feeling so overcome and you were so beautiful. Your green eyes were overflowing with, well I don't know what, maybe understanding in the moment. I just wanted to share the moment with you."

Alex looked at Jules quietly and said, "No, it's not corny and it's not lame. It's what happens when, for a moment, all things superfluous fall away. Scientists say that the feeling of being refreshed and/or euphoric is from the negative ions that are produced as the water falls down a precipice. These little ions, which are extra electrons, dance around in the spray and mist. This produces feelings of well-being because the oxygen atoms in the air have picked up an extra electron. It is the plethora of these negative oxygen ions that can recharge your physical state or more likely, affect your emotional state."

Jules looked at Alex with a mixture of surprise and relief.

Alex continued. "Science may give us the why, but it cannot begin to explain each individual reaction. You had no idea *you* could feel as open as you did until a few moments ago." Calculating whether she should continue, she took Jules' hand and offered her further insight.

"From the little time I've spent with you, I've observed that you're very pragmatic. Don't get me wrong. I'm not saying it's a fault or a short-coming. It's just one of your personality traits. We all grow up with certain attitudes that are created through our imagination or situational upbringing. Whether these attitudes are good or bad makes little difference because they just are."

Jules, asked her, "How do you know this?"

Alex, tongue in cheek, jokingly said, "Well, first of all, I am a shrink. Second my dad brought me up here when I was eight, about two years before he died. I remember how I felt when I saw this place. Even as a child, I was awestruck. I could feel that there was more here than just the physical beauty. I remember that I felt absorbed, surrounded by something I couldn't describe."

"How could you know that as a child?" said Jules incredulously.

"I don't know. Maybe I'm an 'old soul', but each time I came here I felt the same thing; happy, centered, free. When I came back from Afghanistan, I spent a part of almost every day here before I left for Seattle. I knew then that it was the ions that affected me.

"It became clearer and clearer to me that what I felt here was a mysterious tranquility which jettisoned me beyond my mental confusion and doubt. I don't know if there is some sort of energy vortex or, if like my great, great grandfather thought, this place has some mystical qualities, but the roar of the falls quieted my mind long enough to touch some inner place that had remained hidden in the din of everyday life. It's a paradox to me that the thundering water creates such a stillness allowing us for the time we're here, to brush up against our own soul."

Jules nodded as if she were considering what Alex said. Alex saw a grin spreading across Jules' face. She quietly waited for Jules to speak.

"If you're talking Shirley MacLaine stuff, I don't buy any of it."

"Well, Shirley is entitled to her opinions," said Alex evenly, trying not to giggle, "but that's not even close to what I'm talking about. I'm talking about allowing yourself to feel open enough to examine ingrained attitudes that may be holding you back, not some form of astral projection or other metaphysical practice which takes you outside the body."

"So, what exactly happened to me?"

"I can't say what the experience was for you, Jules. I can only share how I would interpret it based on my own experiences, so it may not be valid. Sit with this for a while. Try not to use your mind to synthesize or rationalize your experience. Just let it sit and percolate. You'll get a flash, maybe today, perhaps tomorrow or next year. I can't predict how this will serve you, but I can promise you it will."

Resolutely, Jules looked at Alex with doubtful eyes. "That's a tall promise."

"You will find that I always keep my promises."

Eating their lunch, Jules inquired, "Alex, how did your family find this place?"

"Well, the story goes something like this. Back in the 1880s when my ancestors came out here and staked their claim on the land, there was a lot of copper, gold, and silver mining, mostly around Helena about eighty miles east of Missoula and a town called Phillipsburg, seventy five miles due northeast of us. My great, great grandfather, Marcello, got it in his head that his property was sitting on a vein of gold after he had an experience up here. Remember seeing the White Bark Pine on the way down to the river yesterday?

White Bark Pines are rarely seen at this altitude. It's a tree that characteristically grows at the tree line, much higher up the mountain, but for some reason, that particular pine tree decided to grow where it did, and Marcello took it as a sign. I'm not sure what kind of sign, but I guess people were more superstitious then. Anyway, he was susceptible to signs.

"Marcello stumbled on the Falls when he was exploring his property. He described his experience here as a 'mystical' experience, but not for the same reason you or I might. It's true he was overcome with its beauty, so he sat down on the moss looking at the falls. While daydreaming or maybe sleeping, he had a vision in the shadows behind the sheet of water. It was a woman dressed in a long golden gown standing there beckoning to him. My dad, Carlo, told me that Marcello almost drowned trying to get to the wall behind the falls to see what the woman wanted. He was haunted by the apparition and over the next few days convinced himself that the lady in gold was telling him that there was a vein of gold ore behind the waterfall.

"He brought his only son with him, my grandfather Aldo, who was in his teens at the time, and the two of them set explosives attempting to tunnel into the face of the mountain behind the falls. The rock proved to be more resistant than they expected. Rock in this area of the Bitterroots is very uniform in composition and texture consisting of mica and other types of granular minerals. However, this mountain face is solid granite. After days of trying to get more than five feet in, they gave up and Marcello tried to save face by saying that perhaps he had misinterpreted the vision. Aldo and Marcello's wife chalked up his 'mystical experience' to a nip too many. Apparently, Marcello liked his 'vino', a lot."

"How come they blasted the entire width of the falls?" Jules shifted position and looked at Alex, hooked on the family- created folklore.

Alex answered, "To see if there might be a weak spot in the rock façade. They weren't explosive experts, but the idea of finding a weaker spot was logical. Only there wasn't a weaker spot. After that, they went back to cattle ranching, but the falls continued to hold some mystical value for Marcello and the location was kept secret, passed down only to family members."

"You spent a lot of time up here as a kid?"

"Yes, it was better than a tree house. No one has ever seen any rattlers around, and bears are rare in this area. In fact, the lean-to we are sitting in, my Dad and I built it when I was nine. We'd camp out up here and he'd tell me the story of Marcello over and over. When my parents died, after the funeral, I stayed up here for three days. Uncle Mario camped out nearby to watch over me and Aunt Sophie brought up food for me and grain for the horses twice a day. Neither of them tried to convince me to come back down. Aunt Sophie would sit a while, ask if I was okay, tell me to try and eat something to keep up my strength. I think that being up here helped me reconcile my parents' death and internalize that I had to accept it and go on."

"You were about ten? Quite a feat for someone so young."

"I suppose one could say that, but I was quite logical and rational as a youngster and had tight control of my emotions, not like in the last two days when they seem to ooze out at the least opportune time. Aunt Sophie told me it drove my mother and father nuts to have such a logical and rational kid."

"You and Sophie are so fortunate to have the kind of relationship you do. I envy the affection and love you have for each other."

"I know I fuss at her sometimes and Lord knows she fusses at me, but I can't imagine my life without her."

"I can see that. Alex, you said that the family had guarded this location since the late 1880s. May I ask why you brought me up here?"

"I don't really know Jules. It was just a feeling I had."

"Would you tell me about your feelings towards advising your Aunt Sophie to let Claire stay here?"

"Jules, you know what happened by the pool a little while ago makes the decision even harder for me. I can't deny that I am drawn to you. Something changed for me and I am still trying to get a handle on it. Let's try and put it behind us for now."

"I don't know that I can, Alex. Can you really put it behind you and go on as if it didn't happen?"

"Unfair question," replied Alex, knowing Jules wouldn't let her get away with it.

"No, it's not. Answer me, Alex."

"Truthfully, I don't know. My whole experience with you had been so unexpectedly intense."

Jules thought, *she doesn't know the half of it. Wait until I ask her to treat Claire professionally.*

Alex looked at her with curiosity but decided not to pursue the delicate line of conversation any longer. She conceded, "Okay, I won't be oblique. My advice will really depend on what I get this afternoon from the call, speaking of which, we should start back down."

They got back in plenty of time to wash up and get ready for the call. It was uneventful; Claire answering questions straightforwardly and Dr. Metuchi offering input only when asked, begging off because of a head cold that she had had for a couple of days. When they had finished, Jules asked, "What do you think?"

"Everything seems to line up. Nothing really deviated from what I expected."

"You don't sound convinced."

"Maybe everything was a little too precise, a little too neat, but I tend to be suspicious. It's probably why I chose forensics. I have to think about this, Jules. I'll let you know tomorrow."

###

Alex spent half the night weighing everything again and again, concluding that even though Jules had minimized the danger, any danger to Sophie was unacceptable. In the morning she would share her thoughts with Sophie and Rick and urge them to turn down the offer.

Jules tossed and turned, wondering if kissing Alex had put the project in jeopardy. *What had gotten into her?* She never, ever crossed professional boundaries and certainly not with a potential colleague or client. And now, she had blown everything to smithereens. Her stomach was twisting, and she kept hoping for morning to come soon.

CHAPTER 7 – Revelation

Cease trying to work out everything with your minds. Live by intuition and inspiration and let your whole life be a Revelation.

Eileen Caddy

Sunday April 12

Alex was up early knocking on Sophie's door. No answer, so she went downstairs to find Sophie and Rick in the kitchen. She asked if they could go into the office where they wouldn't be overheard. When everyone was comfortable, she announced that she had some reservations about having Claire at the ranch. She outlined her reasons, including the possibility that Claire was involved in her own kidnapping either consciously or as a result of a mental illness.

Rick was obviously disappointed. To him this was a way to get the ranch back on its feet and into the black. Sophie was crestfallen too. She had come to like Jules and Jake and even trusted them a little. She was doubly surprised because she had taken Alex's positive interactions with Jules as a sign she was leaning towards agreeing with the proposal. Sophie thought about ignoring Alex's recommendation, but both she and Rick knew that Alex normally had good instincts.

Sophie sat quietly for a minute with her hands in her lap and finally said, "Okay, sweetie, we'll go with your gut and tell them we're turning down the proposal at breakfast."

An hour later Jules and Jake came down with their suitcases packed, prepared for the worst it seemed. Sophie invited them to have breakfast which both refused. She sat down at the table while Rick and Alex lounged against the sink.

"Jake, Jules," began Sophie, "uh, Rick, Alex and I were

up early this morning talking about your proposal. Alex feels that if there is a chance Claire herself may be involved, the risk for us and our guests is not acceptable. So, regretfully we're going to have to turn you down. It really has been wonderful getting to know you and we hope you find another safe location for the girl."

Neither Jake nor Jules tried to talk Sophie out of her decision. Professionally, they were prepared for any eventuality and graciously took their leave as soon as politely possible. Jake put their bags into the SUV and was waiting behind the wheel. Rick, Alex, and Sophie were on the porch saying goodbye to Jules. Rick shook her hand firmly and said, "Colonel, nice meeting you."

Sophie gave Jules a little hug and Alex stood in front of her staring into her eyes, still trying to place her. Alex apologized saying, "I'm sorry, Jules. I hope you understand." Jules nodded and walked down two of the steps when she heard a shriek from Alex, "Wait, wait, Jules!"

Jules turned her upper body to see Alex stumbling down the steps toward her. She kept Alex from falling as Alex sank to the stairs in an emotional daze. Sophie and Rick moved to the edge of the porch, but Jules held up her hand to stop them.

"What is it Alex?"

"I know. I know who you are!" Alex managed to barely choke out.

Jules, sitting on the stairs with one arm around Alex, looked down in dismay. Sophie and Rick looked at each other in shock. Jake got out of the car and stood near the hood, waiting to see if there was something he should do.

"You saved my life," cried Alex.

Jules glanced at the others before answering Alex with a whispered, "Yes." Biting her lip and looking lost, she didn't know what more to say or do.

Alex continued weeping uncontrollably. Jules, a little embarrassed that Alex had chosen this very public moment to remember their encounter, tried to get her to stand up and go inside, but Alex fainted. Rick scooped her up and took her inside where he laid her on the couch.

Sophie followed behind and knelt next to Alex. Jules sat on the couch and placed Alex's head on her lap. Jake, who had opened the door for everyone, went inside to join Rick who hovered nearby.

Alex came to after a few moments. "Why didn't you tell me, Jules?" Alex complained, "I tried to find you. Rick used his influence to try to find you, but we came up empty." Alex was overcome by another wave of sobs, but she managed to choke out a word at a time, "The medics who attended me said that a soldier had pulled me out of a deadly crossfire, patched me up, waited for them, then disappeared. They told Rick that whoever it was knew what they were doing and had saved my life."

"I wanted to tell you, but I couldn't. If you'll let me explain, you'll understand. Can you do that?" implored Jules. She helped Alex sit up by propping pillows behind her. She sat next to Alex, turning her body to face her. "Let me tell you what happened and why I had to disappear." Alex sniffled and took the Kleenex that Sophie offered her. "I was with the MCIA and was out on a recon mission with my troops. We were gathering information from distant relatives of the most wanted Taliban Insurgents, most of them living in the Hemland area."

"We had gotten intel that a skirmish was going on near our intended route, so we changed direction. The intel passed to us was bad. We thought we were heading around your skirmish but found ourselves in the middle. You and your people were pinned down and caught in a crossfire between two Insurgent groups. There was nowhere for you to go. Our mission that day was to talk to detainees, not to engage with the enemy. I disobeyed our orders and directed my team to take out the Insurgent platoon on the east. Then I saw you go down and heard you scream above the gunfire. You kept telling your people to stay down. You must have known they'd be fish in a barrel with the crossfire if they went in to get you.

"Once my team neutralized the Insurgents closest to your position, your people had a fighting chance against the others. I crawled down to the gully under fire cover from my team, dragged you back up a hill and pulled you behind some boulders while I radioed for a medic.

"You were hurt badly, going in and out of consciousness. There was blood on your shirt, so I cut off the sleeve and saw that a bullet had gone clear through your left bicep. I looked into your eyes and told you that you would be okay. You nodded your understanding and I cut away your fatigues at the blood-soaked area on your right thigh. I couldn't find an exit wound. The bullet was still in you. Your fatigues were also blood soaked across your lower abdomen and I couldn't find where it was coming from, so I looked at your body armor thinking it might have been pierced. You were lucky. The Interceptor armor withstood the AK-47 bullets and fragments from a nearby IED.

"I opened the outer and inner vest anyway and saw that the blood was coming from your left side of your groin. I did not see the entry point in your fatigues because you were soaked in blood. I cut open your fatigues with my knife to get a look. You had a metal fragment lodged in your groin. I prayed that it hadn't hit your femoral artery.

"I put pressure on your groin to stop the bleeding and I knew the pain would be excruciating, so I administered an ampule of morphine and in a minute or two you were out of it. I left the metal in your groin, covered it with a heavy surgical pad then put two rocks on each side of the metal shard to apply pressure. I finished bandaging your other wounds and was about to close up your body armor when I saw medics coming up from behind us. I left you in their hands and got the hell out of there before anyone reported that we had engaged in combat without getting permission."

Jules waited for it to sink in. Alex had stopped crying and had all but shredded the Kleenex in her hand. She put a hand over her forehead and eyes, rubbing with slow rhythmic movements. Still not looking at Jules, she conceded, "I understand what happened, but why didn't you tell me this when I first got here?"

Jules gathered herself, looked up to the heavens in silent prayer, and hoped that the truth would be enough. "I didn't want you and your family to make a decision on our proposal based on some misplaced sense of gratitude."

"So, you knew who I was?" There was a warning tone in Alex's voice.

"Sort of. When I opened your body armor, I saw your name on your fatigues. Later that day, I put in a call to your unit, but you had already been airlifted to Japan after emergency surgery. By the time I got through to them the next day, you had been stabilized but still unconscious. It wasn't until we started doing the background checks on White Bark Ranch that I realized you were Sophie's niece. Then it was too late."

"You were counting on me not remembering?"

"Yes, for the reasons I already explained."

Alex had regained control and was mortified that she had allowed her emotions to get away from her. She started to get up forcing Jules to move. "I seem to be very tired. Can you please just let me go up to my room and rest?"

Sophie accompanied Alex and a short while later returned to the great room. Jules thought that Alex might be upset but Sophie thought that what Jules had done was noble. Sophie walked over to Jules and gave her a hug. "This changes everything, Rick. Alex owes her life to this woman and yet she purposely didn't tell Alex in order not to influence her. I'd say that's a very trustworthy person."

"Sophie, you know that I was leaning in favor of taking on Bentworth's daughter, but I respected Alex's opinion. If you think that we can trust Jules and Jake to keep us safe and sound, then I'm with you. You know, though, Alex isn't going to like this."

"I hate to pull rank here, but I am the principal owner of this ranch and have the final word."

"Hey, I've always been okay with that, Sophie. You have a good business head and the perks are great!" Rick was infused with a renewed sense of anticipation.

Disregarding Rick's less then subtle allusion to their relationship, Sophie asked, "Do you think I should go tell Alex?"

"If I were in your shoes," said Rick, "I'd let her rest for a while."

"Okay. Do you want to see if Jake and Jules want something to eat? They passed on breakfast."

"Sure."

Sophie went upstairs and didn't bother knocking on Alex's door. She walked in to find Alex lying on the bed with a blanket over her legs. It reminded her of the night Alex's parents were killed and she had to tell Alex. She shuddered. "Alex, how are you doing? I know this was a tremendous shock for you."

"I'm regrouping, trying to think clearly."

"Honey, sometimes thinking is overrated. Just go with your intuition. I think what Jules did shows her integrity."

"Aunt Sophie, will you do me a favor?"

"Of course, anything," Sophie told her.

"Go back downstairs and send Jules up here. I want to talk to her alone. Thank you."

Dismissed without fanfare, Sophie went back downstairs and conveyed Alex's request to Jules. Jules didn't look too thrilled and was steeling herself for a tirade now that Alex's initial shock had worn off. She knocked and went in before Alex answered. The blinds were drawn, but the darkened room didn't hide the tension. "You wanted to see me, Alex?"

"Yes." Alex wearily asked her to come over to the bed.

Gingerly, Jules sat on the edge of the bed, waiting for the rebuke.

"Not knowing who saved my life left a big hole in me. I struggled with why I was chosen to be saved as opposed to one of my men who also was shot down. I tried to make sense of it in a spiritual way. You know, karma and all, but it's nagged me and, in a small way, made me feel unworthy for all these years. I've always tried to pay back the universe with acts of kindness in hopes that the void would go away someday. But it didn't. Jules, why did you pull me out and not Rob who had been hit near me?"

"I don't know what to tell you. I don't know what will help you?"

"Tell me the truth."

"I saw you both go down. With the route I took into the gully, I got to you first. When I finished patching you up, I went over to him before I backtracked to my unit. Once I saw how he was hit, I knew there was nothing anyone could do for him. He was already dead. Even if I had gotten to him first, there's no doubt in my mind that he wouldn't have survived. Alex, there's no secret meaning here. You survived because of your geographical position."

"You didn't have to choose?"

"No, you were first on the path in."

Tears of release ran down Alex's face. Jules leaned over to brush them away. She felt Alex's warm breath whispering, "Stay with me for a while."

An hour later, Sophie's curiosity got the better of her. While Rick and Jake were talking, she snuck upstairs and carefully turned the knob on Alex's door. Peeking around the door, she saw the two of them. Sleeping. Jules had her chest against Alex's back with both arms around her. Spooning was Alex's favorite position as a child. It seemed like Alex had made her peace with Jules, at least for now. Sophie went back downstairs to join the boys.

"Sophie, everything all right up there? They've been talking for a long time."

"They're not talking, Rick. They're sleeping."

Rick and Jake looked stupefied. Neither said a word.

At noon Jules woke up and stayed quiet, hoping that Alex would wake soon. Her right arm was numb. Alex had been sleeping on it for two hours. A few minutes later, Alex woke up and turned slightly to her left, still against Jules. "What time is it?"

Looking at her watch, Jules told Alex that is was a little after noon. Breathing in the scent of Alex's hair, Jules asked her how she was.

"As well as can be expected, when after almost eight years, you find out that the woman you kissed at your secret place turns out to be the woman who saved your life. Maybe Grandpa Marcello was right, I mean about the place being mystic."

"Alex, what can I do to help you reconcile all of this?"

"Nothing. It will just take time. We probably should get up. I'll bet they're wondering what the heck we've been doing up here."

Sophie had Jake setting the table for lunch. Rick walked in with a plate of hamburgers just off the grill. "Ah, ladies, just in time for lunch. Sit down, sit down, Jake will set a place for you. Did you get everything settled, Rick asked with a raised eyebrow?"

"We're working on it," answered Alex flatly.

Halfway through lunch, Sophie put down her partially eaten burger and addressed everyone at the table. "I've reconsidered Jules' and Jake's proposal and decided to go forward with it. Rick agrees, and I hope Alex will too."

Everyone around the table looked at Alex. With concession in her voice, she told Sophie that she would support whatever she wanted to do. *Not an enthusiastic endorsement,* thought Jake and Jules, *but they'd take it.*

Alex leveled her gaze at Jules and Jake, her voice dripping with steel, and took them to task. "You had damn well better make sure that nothing happens to Aunt Sophie and Rick, or anyone else here for that matter." She didn't have to say the "or else" part. It was implied and understood. Alex didn't expect an answer and neither Jake nor Jules offered one. They simply nodded their heads solemnly.

The five of them spent the rest of the day and into the early evening hours going over plans, talking about alternatives for a communication system that would work across the ranch, the installation of a security system in the main house where they decided to house Claire, who from ISS would be undercover at the ranch as a guest, ideas about an extraction plan and their insertion plan. They agreed that they had to get Claire to the ranch before the regular guest season started. Both Jules and Jake knew there was only one other issue to be resolved before they headed out to put the operation into motion.

###

It had been an intense day, but Sophie was keyed up. She silently checked on Alex, who was already sleeping. *Good, she needs the rest,* Sophie thought as she made her way back down the stairs, across the dining and great room through the office to Rick's room. She knocked quietly and found herself being pulled into the room, smothered by Rick's passionate kisses. With one arm pinning Sophie to his bare chest and the other locking the door, he wasted no time in moving her to the turned-down bed. Usually Rick had a slow hand when making love to Sophie. Tonight, he was in a hurry, unbuttoning her shirt and unhooking her bra to expose her breasts. She didn't try to slow him down and moaned with pleasure when his mouth covered first one nipple then the other. She ran her hands along his bare back and hair, still wet from a shower. Rick alternated kissing her face, lips and nipples, until he couldn't stand it any longer and reached to undo her belt and jeans. He worked his way down her belly with his mouth while she helped him shed her jeans and underwear.

Hardly able to contain himself, he was afraid that if they had intercourse right now, he'd finish before she did. Spreading her legs, he lowered his head. His tongue made her gasp. She loved this. After she had climaxed, she told him to sit up. Wasting no time, she straddled him. He groaned and began thrusting as he kissed her lips, neck and breasts. Sophie reached down and began touching herself as he continued to move, his pace quickening. God, he loved to watch her do that. It almost pushed him over the edge, but he held on until she came a second time. Lying next to each other, they talked for a few minutes until sleep claimed them.

Monday April 13

Alex woke up around one in the morning and couldn't go back to sleep. She got up to get a glass of water from the bathroom and noticed that Jules hadn't closed the door to her side of the bathroom. Quietly, she opened the door wider. Jules had fallen asleep with the bed-side light still on, reading glasses on the nightstand and a manuscript of some sort strewn on the floor next to the bed.

She was on her stomach in a modified frog position with the sheet and blanket covering her from her hips to mid-thigh. Alex thought she detected a scar on her exposed back right along the spinal column. Without thinking it through, Alex walked into the room to have a closer look. She got as far as the side of the bed when Jules grabbed her with her left arm and wrestled her to the bed, ending up on top of Alex. "Jules, it's me." *God, what reflexes this woman has, even asleep, they kick in,* thought Alex.

Jules got off Alex, falling on her back, reaching for the sheet to cover herself. She mumbled she was sorry and that old habits die hard. Alex didn't get up as Jules had expected. She stayed put and turned on her side to look at Jules. Jules wasn't having any luck with untangling the sheet from the brief struggle. Embarrassed, she flipped over on her stomach to hide her exposed breasts from Alex. Alex wouldn't have guessed that Jules was so shy. *Maybe clothes are her armor, like being in control is mine*, thought Alex as she briefly lifted her body to free the sheet. With her body safely covered, Jules turned towards Alex, clutching the sheet to her chest. "What are you doing here?"

"That's a fine welcome," teased Alex. "I thought you'd be glad to see me, considering the way you kissed me this afternoon."

Jules hid her head in the pillow, then poked it out, just enough for Alex to see her face. "Alex, we've only known each other for two days. If I'm wrong, forgive me, but this is a little too soon for me."

"Jules, if you collapse time and space, then the two days are irrelevant." Alex didn't know why, but she was enjoying making Jules squirm.

"I want to, but I can't, and neither can you," said Jules resolutely.

"What do you mean?" countered Alex, forcing Jules to spell it out

Jules sat up, still clutching the sheet around her. She was worn out. Dealing with Alex's emotional swings, her own raw emotions and this whole damn project, had left her more war battered than Afghanistan and Iraq. She summoned the energy to explain it to Alex, fully expecting another one of Alex's outbursts. "I want you to come back to the ranch to continue Claire's treatment."

"What? Are you joking?" exploded Alex. She thought Jules was going to explain why they shouldn't have sex. She never expected this.

"No. I'm dead serious. You know the place; you know how to take care of yourself; and you have a brilliant mind that is tapped into a theory we can't afford to dismiss."

"Jules, you are out of your mind! Even if I wanted to, I can't just leave my job in Seattle."

"Yes, you can."

"No, I can't. I have commitments and besides, they'll never give me a leave for three or four months. There is such a need that they'd fill my position before I could blink."

Jules turned the tables. "Would you be willing to do it if they committed in writing to holding your job open for up to six months?"

Alarms went off in Alex's head. She could feel her skin crawling. *Had this been a masterfully manipulated set up? Had Jules gone behind her back and talked to her employer already?* An eruption bigger than the last one at Mt. St. Helens in the 1980s was about to materialize. One moment Alex wanted to kiss her, the next have sex with her and now, do her great bodily harm! No wonder she felt like a yoyo!

Alex got up and paced, calling upon the last shred of control she could unearth. Threatening, she spat out, "Jules, and you had better come clean with me, have you gone behind my back and already talked to my employers?" Alex took Jules' silence as guilt. She had been duped. Yelling something about betrayal and 'unmitigated gall', she felt Jules' arms come around her from the back. She whirled to confront Jules, inches from her face. "I, I should punch you in the nose," she stuttered.

Jules stifled a chuckle. It was comical that the only thing Alex could come up with was a punch in the nose, but she successfully got out, "Look, you hot head, calm down. You're going to feel stupid having to apologize to me. I did not talk to your employers."

Jules still held her as she struggled to break free, but when Alex realized that Jules was much stronger than she was as well as half naked, she stopped struggling and retorted, "Fine, did someone in your company talk to my employers?"

"No. Let's sit on the bed and I'll share with you why I think it's possible." Jules released her and headed for the bed.

Like a chastised child, Alex sheepishly went back to the edge of the bed to hear Jules out. "Do you really think I'm a hot head?"

"Alex, can we please get on with this? It's almost two in the morning," replied Jules as she reached for her T-shirt. "I'm surprised we didn't wake Jake." Shrugging on her T-shirt, she explained, "I think that your employer would allow you a six month leave under two conditions. One, we have a temporary replacement for you, and two, the request comes from someone high up in the government. You'd be surprised what happens when the Attorney General of the United States picks up the phone and asks for a favor."

"And you can do this, I mean get someone like that to call?"

"I can't, but we know someone who can."

"What about someone to pick up my cases and take on new ones in my absence?" offered Alex.

Good, thought Jules. *She's acting like she's at least considering this.* "Remember when I asked you if you knew Fahad?" Alex said a dubious "yes" and Jules continued. "He's done work for ISS off and on since he retired and while he's not as creative as you are, he is solid and has a good reputation. We approached him about a month ago asking if he would be interested in working with us on a full-time gig. This was the backup plan if you said no."

Pensive, Alex said, "So you already had considered asking me."

"Yes."

"What did he say?"

"He's bored, wished he hadn't retired, and would be interested if the price were right." Jules was facing Alex and could see that she had withdrawn. "What's bothering you, Alex?" Getting no answer, Jules took a stab in the dark and casually said, "Are you afraid that your employer will like Fahad better and retain him instead of bringing you back after the leave?"

Alex's head snapped around. "Do you think I'm that insecure, Jules?"

"No, not at all, but I think it's a valid concern, especially when playing in a good old boy's backyard."

"Well, now that we're on the topic, what's to prevent that from happening?"

"Written agreement, also known as a contract," Jules said without a tinge of sarcasm.

"You aren't that naïve. All contracts can be broken. It's just a matter of how much it will cost," shot back Alex.

Frustrated, Jules reached for a way to sway Alex.

"Then ISS will hire you if you don't get your job back. Okay? I'll put it in writing with a quarter million guarantee. Does that make you feel more secure?"

Alex was incensed. She was determined not to let Jules see the volatility of her anger. In a quietly modulated voice, she called Jules' bluff. "Have your attorneys start drawing up a contract," and with that, she got up from the bed and walked to the door. Just before she left the room, she turned and spat out, "Now I understand why we can't be involved. I just wish you had told me this before you went and kissed me." With that she walked out and closed the door firmly.

Everyone had their own agenda Monday morning. Jake and Jules had to get back to Los Angeles. Alex was scheduled to fly out first thing to Seattle and Rick and Sophie had to start preparing for the summer guests. Jules asked if she could use the office for a while. Rick told her to make herself at home. She called ISS' in-house attorney and left a detailed message with instructions on where to email the contract by close of business today. She'd catch hell from Paulson and Baluchi, if they heard what she had done from the attorney, so in a butt-covering move, she called each of their office numbers and left identical messages. When she was finished, she went to collect Jake from the kitchen. Alex was there too, ready to catch a ride with Jake and Jules to the airport.

Sophie noticed the tension between the two of them. She wasn't going to pry. She had recognized the signs, especially after seeing the two of them sleeping together yesterday morning. There was something between them, but they were so pig-headed, they were doing their best to drive a wedge between themselves so they wouldn't have to deal with their feelings. *They have a long ride back to Missoula, so let the two of them work it out on their own,* thought Sophie as she kissed Alex and flew out the back door on some urgent business to hide the tears in her eyes.

CHAPTER 8 – The Call

You must know that in any moment a decision you make can change the course of your life forever the very next phone call you make could be the one single thing that causes the floodgate to open, and all the things that you've been waiting for to fall into place.

Anthony Robbins

Monday April 13

Alex got into her office around 10:00 a.m. She was backed up with clients and court appearances, so she didn't even get to her email until she got home around 8:30 p.m. She saw an email from law@intelligentsecuritysrv.com with a title line 'Agreement'. The message was short, succinct and impersonal: 'Please review contract as we discussed. Sign and FedEx to the address below.' Opening the contract, Alex was surprised to see it was in plain English and only two pages long. The contract was between her and ISS. It stipulated that beginning on a mutually agreeable date, Alex was to become an 'on-loan' contract employee of ISS for up to six months with salary and benefits at her current rate and, if after six months, her current position was no longer available, ISS would offer her a permanent position, working as a consulting forensic psychologist or a sum of a quarter of a million dollars, her choice. Jules hadn't been bluffing.

She looked at the return address and saw it was in DC. Alex's stomach was queasy. What was she going to do? She had called Jules' bluff, now Jules was calling hers. She thought about talking to Aunt Sophie, but then dismissed the idea. Sophie would love to have her at the ranch. Next on her list was Rick. She dismissed that too. Alex had put him in the middle more than once and was not going to do it this time, plus she didn't think he'd promise to keep this to himself.

Picking up the phone, she dialed and waited for an answer.

"Danny, I hope I'm not disturbing you. It's Alex."

"Alex, no, it's okay. What's going on? Problems with Reggie?"

Daniel Feinstein was the attorney Alex had used when negotiating a settlement with Reggie over the house and common property. She met him at a party and the two of them hit it off.

"No, not at all. Look Danny, how are you with contracts?"

"What kind of a contract?"

"I guess you would call it an employment contract," offered Alex.

"Not my specialty, but I can refer you to someone."

"It's two pages long, and in plain English. It's from a company that's offering me a six-month research job, if I can get a sabbatical from the courts."

"Wow. I didn't know you were considering something like that."

"It came up out of the blue. They approached me."

"Okay, that shouldn't be any trouble at all. You still have my email? Send it over."

"Yes, and uh, Danny, could you look at it tonight?"

"That hot to trot, huh? What's the matter, the city's not big enough for both you and Reggie?" he joked.

"Funny boy. Call me back and Danny, please keep this to yourself."

"Don't worry Alex, you still have me on retainer.

"Thanks".

An hour later the phone rang. "Alex, got a minute?"

"Yes, yes, of course. What do you think?"

"I don't see too many contracts written without the usual lawyerly language. Must be a new trend. Pretty soon, if this catches on, no one will need attorneys," he chuckled then continued. "It's very straightforward, no ambiguity, and as close to ironclad as possible. Whoever this ISS is, they must want you badly. A word of advice, though. Make sure you get your sabbatical in writing before you sign this and before you sign off on the sabbatical, run that agreement by me. Okay?"

"Absolutely. Thank you, Danny. Let's try to get together some night this week for a drink."

"Sure. How does Wednesday around 7:00 p.m. sound?"

"Good. Meet you at Coldwater Bar and Grill, on Fifth Avenue, or would you prefer somewhere else?"

"That's great, Alex. See you there."

Alex had just hung up the phone when it rang again. No caller ID. Probably some telemarketer. She let it go to voice mail. A minute later, the phone advised her she had voice mail. A telemarketer wouldn't leave a message. The message was curt.

"Did you get the contract? Call me. You have my number."

Alex purposely waited another thirty minutes before she called back.

Jules answered on the second ring. "Thanks for calling back. Have you had time to look over the contract?"

"Yes. I've even discussed it with my attorney."

Silence on the other end. "Alex, we wrote it in plain English so you wouldn't have to go to an attorney. Can you trust this person?"

"I don't have any reason not to trust him, but if you want to vet him out," she said with mild sarcasm, "his name is Daniel Feinstein. He handled my property settlement. Danny says it looks good but told me not to sign it until I get an offer of sabbatical in writing. How do you propose I do that?"

"Alex, if you're willing to take this assignment, the U.S. Attorney General's office will make a request to have you loaned to them for a special project. Your boss will get a call tomorrow and, of course, agree to loan you out because he'll have no choice. He will also agree to the terms which include a written promise to hold your job open and maintain your tenure and years of service. You won't have to do anything except say yes to your boss. From this point on we need to be careful. What time are you leaving your house tomorrow morning?"

"7:30 a.m., why?"

"Tomorrow morning at 7:00 a.m. a courier will come to your home with a package. Put it in a safe place and when you get home at night open it and call me immediately. You'll understand."

"Okay, I got it. Open package and call you."

"Good. Also, don't tell Sophie or Rick about this, ah, development and, if you can, try and play hard to get with your boss. Don't make a commitment right away. We want him to be able to report that you weren't too keen, but that he was able to convince you to do your patriotic duty. That shouldn't be too hard for you, should it?"

Was that a dig, or was it simply an innocent rhetorical question? Alex stopped herself before she got annoyed.

"I'll talk to you tomorrow night to get your answer," and Jules was gone.

Tuesday April 14

Just as Jules had told her, a bicycle courier was on her doorstep at seven the next morning. She thought it was odd that he didn't ask her for a signature but sloughed it off and put the package in a locked file cabinet before leaving for work. The day went by quickly with interviews, reports to write and a court appearance. When she got back to her office there was a message waiting for her to go upstairs and see her boss.

Randy's door was slightly ajar, so she stuck her head in and said, "Knock, knock." Randy, her boss of four years, waved her in and quickly dispensed with whomever was on the phone with him. "Alex, would you please close the door? Something has come up and I need to talk to you in private."

"What is it Randy? Is it serious?"

"Just about as serious as it gets." Randy, full of himself, outlined almost word for word what Jules had told her last night. When he finished, she hemmed and hawed, telling Randy that she didn't think she wanted to get involved with the government, but told him that he had made a very convincing argument and would give him an answer tomorrow.

He handed over a letter of agreement, stipulating that she would be granted up to six months of a sabbatical and that her job and tenure would be protected for the six months. He also pointed out that she would be receiving a call from the project's liaison later today to brief her in case she had additional questions. Alex thanked him for the opportunity, said she wanted her attorney to look over the letter of agreement before she signed it and left.

Alex went back to her office and made a list of things she had to do to get ready to hand over her current cases to Fahad. She wasn't sure when she made up her mind to accept the job, but she had, for better or worse. She wasn't afraid of commitment, only all the rubbish that came with it.

By the time she got home, it was after 7:00 p.m. She wasn't hungry, so she retrieved the package, unwrapped it, and looked inside. There was a prepaid cellular phone, presumably to use when calling Jules, a conceal carry pistol with an adjustable leg holster, a Glock nine-millimeter automatic with a clip-on holster, a special NSA carry permit for both and several rounds of ammunition for both firearms. She picked up the phone and called Jules who answered right away.

"I take it you opened the package."

"Yeah, I know how to follow orders."

Jules ignored Alex's snarkiness. "That special carry permit allows you to board aircraft with firearms and skirt security in local, state and federal buildings. Please start carrying one of the firearms tomorrow. Do you know what to do to get past security?"

"I would guess that I pull out the carry permit, flash it and go around the metal detector."

"Exactly. Do you know what to do if anyone challenges you?

"Be an asshole?"

Jules rolled her eyes. "That too, although I was thinking along the lines of asking for a supervisor and making him or her call the NSA number on your carry permit. They'll apologize to you profusely."

"You are one tough lady, Jules. You love it don't you?"

"Not really. It's just a quid pro quo game. I worked at the NSA, so I got to know some folks. Now make sure you use the prepaid phone when you call me or the ranch. The numbers are programmed into the phone's contact list. Rick got a similar package today and was briefed by Jake. Did you notice that there is a box within a box? Pull out the top box, the one the guns were in."

Alex's eyes got wider as she sifted through the contents. There was a Canadian passport that confirmed her entry to the U.S. yesterday from Aden, Alberta through Whitefish, Montana. Her address was a Calgary address. There was also a Canadian passport for Claire with the similar information. In addition, there was an Italian passport for Claire, with the name Clara Rivetti, showing she entered the U.S. through Chicago two weeks from now. Finally, there was a stack of cash and several prepaid credit cards with varying denominations.

Jules had been waiting patiently for a minute or two, listened to the rustling and finally heard Alex say "shit".

"So, you've gone through everything?"

"Yes. Claire's and my alter egos," she tried to joke. The

seriousness of the situation had begun to sink in.

As if Jules had read her mind, she said, "Don't worry Alex. This is just precautionary. Not much of a chance you'll have to use the other identities or even pistols. Remember, though, we want to cover every conceivable possibility. You okay?"

"I will be," replied Alex, not sure if she would be any time soon.

"Lock that stuff somewhere until we're ready to get you to the ranch and when you do travel, have it on your body. With your carry permit, you won't get searched."

"Jules, I got my approval for sabbatical this afternoon and am taking it over to Danny to review. I'll be sending off the ISS agreement as soon as Danny approves the sabbatical letter."

"You made up your mind?" Jules tried to disguise the excitement in her voice."

"Yes, but I have to have your word, Jules, that if any time I want to back out and return to Seattle, I can do it with no penalty."

"I only ask that you discuss it with me before you make that kind of decision."

"Do I have your word, Jules?"

"Yes, and I always keep my promises," Jules laughed, slightly mocking Alex's words the day at the pool.

Alex ignored her and asked, "Have you checked out Danny yet?"

"Clean as a whistle. He squeaks when he walks and he's cute too. None the less it would be prudent to keep up your guard. If he asks why ISS wants to hire you, tell the truth. ISS needs a forensic psychologist to work on a research project for one of their contracts. This is exactly what the Attorney General's office told your boss and local DOJ."

"Oh, one more thing, my boss told me that someone from the Attorney General's office would be contacting me for instructions."

"That would be me. Consider yourself contacted."

"Gee thanks. I had a sneaky suspicion it might be you."

"You've got a lot to think about, Alex, and a lot to do at work to get ready to leave. We'll fly you out of Renton again the Saturday after next. When we get closer, I'll brief you. That's all for now. You can call me at any time for anything. I'll be in touch. Sleep well." She was gone just like that again! Talk about pragmatism.

Alex picked up the cell phone and hit redial. "Miss me?"

"Actually yes, but probably not why you think."

"And what do I think?

Jules couldn't resist, "That I miss you because of your winning personality."

Laughing at Jules' clearly snide remark, Alex retorted, "That's exactly what I thought! Jules, I don't think we thought out how to explain that I'm back at the ranch. I'm supposed to be on this research project. What if someone reports back to my boss or friends in Seattle?"

"We've got you covered. The ranch fits in with your cover. First of all, you can hide behind not divulging the nature of the research you're doing. Second, Montana is a hot bed of potential projects of interest to the DOJ. Did you know that there are over eight hundred prison camps in the States, all fully operational and ready to receive black ops prisoners? They're staffed with full time personnel and operated by FEMA, the Federal Emergency Management Agency. All it would take to activate them is the Attorney General's signature on a proclamation and warrant. It's called the Rex 84 program and there are dozens of Executive Orders to justify the existence of these camps. It's rumored that some of these camps are operational, others are sites for black ops and some standing ready at a moment's notice for a host of other reasons. There's speculation that one exists at Malmstrom AFB in Montana, outside of Great Falls. So, you could be working on this type of project. In addition, Montana and Idaho are hot beds for Patriots or the Militia.

You probably know a lot more about the history of their existence than I do."

"I doubt that, Jules. You are incredibly prepared. I don't remember the chronology well but do know that the Montana Militia evolved from an earlier organization in Idaho after a government siege at Ruby Ridge. The wife and son of a white supremacist living at the compound were killed in the standoff. With the awareness brought to the area by the press coverage, they tried to portray themselves as a human rights group, but nearly all leaders and supporters were white supremacists. The Montana chapter is located at a site up in Noxon, about twenty miles from the Idaho border. It's a couple hundred miles from the ranch."

"Okay, then. If you were forced to talk about your research, you could allude to either or both, but keep it generic. Feel better?"

"Sure, I do," taunted Alex sarcastically. She thought Jules' 'feel better' question was patronizing.

Jules heard the edge to Alex's voice and dismissed the taunting as a defensive mechanism, hiding discomfort and fear. "Alex, this cloak and dagger thing can be unsettling at first, until one learns it's like any other job. I remember how it was for me on my first field intel gathering mission. I was going along as a translator. Our CO briefed us, two others and me, the night before we were to be dropped into Afghanistan. Even though I knew I'd be in the company of two of the best operatives I felt scared and alone, as if a lifeline had been cut, and I was adrift. I didn't dare tell my companions how I was feeling and certainly not my CO. That would have been the end of the career I wanted. So, and not to be patronizing, I would totally understand if this is how you feel. That's why I told you that you could call me anytime, about anything, even if it isn't related to our current activities."

Jules came across sincerely. Alex felt contrite, considering Jules' admission. Alex knew she was going to have to toughen up. "Thank you, Jules. I mean it. I wish you were here." This time Alex hung up first.

Wednesday April 15 through Friday April 17

The rest of the week went without a hitch. Alex met Danny on Wednesday night for a drink, which stretched into dinner. He gave her the thumbs up on the sabbatical document. On Thursday, Randy met with Alex to discuss who would tell Alex's co-workers about her special assignment. Randy thought he should handle it and Alex knew just how he would spin it to make himself look like a hero.

By Friday Alex had all her cases organized and was ready to meet with Fahad on Monday afternoon. They would spend Monday and Tuesday reviewing cases and meeting people in Randy's group. Wednesday and Thursday, Fahad would shadow Alex to get the lay of the land and, on Friday they'd tie up loose ends.

Saturday April 18

Early Saturday morning Alex was feeling antsy and went out for a light jog. She hadn't had any exercise all week. It was one of the rare spring days in Seattle when there was no moisture weighing heavily in the air. Alex's house was in the Columbia City area, located west of Seward Park and southeast of Beacon Hill. The people who lived there took pride in the neighborhood. Because of the shops, restaurants and many community activities like the Farmers Market, the Columbia City Theatre and Beat Walk with live music from May through December, the streets were always full of friendly people. The geographic location couldn't be better. She was minutes away from major highways.

Running her usual loop, she got home in about 30 minutes, lifted weights for a while to keep her upper body toned, then showered and got dressed in casual clothes. She had arranged to meet a group of her friends for an early lunch to say goodbye. She discussed this with Jules and they both agreed that she should act as she normally would. Picking up and leaving without saying farewell to your friends, would raise more suspicion than meeting them for a quick goodbye.

Jules had asked her to start carrying one of the firearms, but she hadn't. Last night Jules explained that she wanted her to get used to the feel of carrying a weapon again and to please follow her instructions. Alex did not carry one on her run. There just wasn't any place to hide it. However, she was now wearing a jacket and didn't have any reason not to honor Jules' request. She chose the Glock nine-millimeter with the belt clip holster. The cut of her jacket didn't allow for a gun at her waist. It bulged and pulled. Quickly she chose another jacket with a more generous cut through the chest and waist. Looking at herself in the mirror, she was satisfied that no one would guess she was carrying. Slipping the carry permit into her breast pocket, she took off for Belltown.

Twenty minutes later she arrived at the Dalhia Lounge, parked, and went into join her friends and co-workers.

Lunch was superb and her friends were genuinely sorry to see her go, yet supportive of her new adventure.

It was close to 3:00 p.m. in the afternoon when she got home. She shucked off her jacket, removed and locked up the gun. Not bothering to change, she plopped down on the couch with a book just before the prepaid cell rang.

"How'd it go with your friends?"

"Fine. They wanted to know more details, but I deflected." Alex wondered if she should talk to Jules about her reaction to carrying a weapon and after a short pause, she asked Jules if she could ask her a question.

"Sure. Go ahead."

"I got the oddest feeling today when I put on the Glock. I can't put my finger on it, but it was surprising to me since I regularly carried a handgun and sometimes an M16 in Afghanistan."

"Hmm, odd, like how?"

"Hard to describe. Off-balance, out of whack, something like that."

Jules was quiet for a moment. Alex thought she could hear street sounds in the background. "Alex, I think it's different when one carries a weapon during war time. It boils down to kill or be killed. I'm guessing that you only used your weapons defensively. In other words, if someone shot at you, you shot back, but you didn't initiate, right? More-over, our government sanctioned your use of the firearms. The Marines told you, so to speak, that the use of the weapons was okay. Would you agree so far?"

"Yes," agreed Alex.

"Now, however, no official government organization is sanctioning the use of your weapon. Consider that you may be feeling an entirely new level of power that can easily, because of your previous training, be wielded whenever *you* choose. The realization that one truly has the choice of acting ethically or not is entirely different than the war-time experience."

"Interesting insight. Does the feeling pass?"

"I can only speak from my own experience. No, it never has passed. In some ways it is liberating to feel protected from the threat of violence, but I constantly find myself assessing my surroundings with a heightened awareness because I know I might have to make a split-second decision on whether or not to use the weapon. This is a heavy ethical responsibility for me."

There was silence on Alex's end. Jules knew Alex was internalizing the information and paused before she went on.

"Alex, are you with me? There has been a slight change in plans."

"Uh, oh. Trouble?"

"No. Just a rethink of strategy. After some discussions with my people, we've decided that I should see you in Seattle and let people see me with you."

"What? You think that is a good idea?"

"I do. We now think that I should be your contact, come to Seattle and brief you. That way, just as you brought up, if anyone sees us together it won't be a big deal."

"But what about the kidnappers?"

"If they know anything about ISS, they'll know that we have lots of contracts. It would be a big leap to tie you to the Bentworth situation, especially with the cover we've established."

"Okay, you're the boss. When are you coming?"

"In about one minute."

"What?" said Alex confused. "Did you say you were leaving in a minute?"

"No. I said I'd be there in a minute. Do you have room in your garage for another car? If you do, open it now please."

Alex raced to the kitchen door that went out to the garage and pushed the button to open the overhead door, turning into the driveway was a late model ubiquitous white sedan, rental no doubt, with Jules behind the wheel still holding her phone to her ear. Alex was about ready to charge down the steps into the garage when she checked herself.

"Alex, Alex," she heard through the phone still in her hand, "You can hang up now," chuckled Jules.

A moment later, Jules got out of the car and went up the stairs into the house. Alex gave her a light hug, closing and locking the door carefully. They stood in the kitchen looking at each other for a long moment.

Too stunned to talk, Alex stared at Jules who looked very sexy in an expensive Prada dove-gray pant suit

3

perfectly set off with a Ralph Lauren pale pink women's tailored shirt. She had gold and diamond earrings with a matching necklace. Jules stared back at Alex's outfit; light-weight wool navy slacks, a powder blue V-neck cashmere sweater that showed off her well-endowed breasts and a string of pearls with matching earnings.

Finally, Alex took one of Jules' hands and lead her into the living room. It was mid-day and the curtains were open. She closed them while Jules looked on, still in a semi-stupor, quite unusual for her. As soon as the drapes were closed, Jules took off her jacket, folded it carefully and set it on the back of a chair that matched the sofa. She removed her clip-on holster and gun.

Alex raised her arms and Jules slowly walked into them, reaching her own around Alex's back. She rested her head on Alex's shoulder and breathed in a light and fresh subtle perfume, murmuring, "Umm." Alex could feel Jules' breasts pressing against her own, making her want more than a friendly hello hug.

"Dolce & Gabbana Light Blue," she told Alex, trying to curb her body's responses.

"What?" said Alex distractedly.

"The perfume you are wearing. Ah, it's nice," whispered Jules, as she turned her head and found Alex's lips.

Pressing their bodies together, their tender, tentative kisses, gave way to more passionate kisses, neither of them able to get enough of each other. They were headed down a slippery slope with no brakes in sight. They both knew it but didn't have the power or desire to stop. Jules backed Alex up to the edge of the couch and leaned over, forcing Alex to sit down as she strained to keep contact with Jules' mouth. Pulling back for a moment, Jules knelt in front of Alex and looked up at her.

"You know this isn't a good idea," said Jules as she brushed a lock of Alex's hair from her face.

Alex's answer was to wrap her legs and arms around Jules, leaning forward to kiss her, right after she said, "I know but my emotions are not always subject to reason."

Jules got up from her knees, sat on the couch and continued kissing Alex until she craved more contact than just Alex's lips. She gently pushed Alex down, picked up Alex's legs and swung them up, then draped half her body over Alex's. Jules, deepening her kisses, threw one leg over Alex's legs and pressed her upper body against Alex, supporting herself with her free arm. She stroked Alex's hair, face and neck with her free hand.

Jules was nervous. She wished this wasn't her first time with a woman. It had been easier to be celibate then to deal with her attraction towards women, come out to her parents, who were very judgmental or jeopardize her career. She now wondered if repressing her longings and desires to protect herself, both professionally and emotionally had been the wisest choice to make. For the first time in her carefully orchestrated life, she allowed longing and wanting to be loved possess her, aching for Alex's touch.

She was drowning in the expectation of how Alex's kisses would feel on the rest of her body. Alex was using both her hands to touch Jules' hair, her face, her lips. She ran her hands down Jules' back, her buttocks and the back of her thighs. Alex used her index finger to gently trace Jules' lips, then slipped her finger into the corner of Jules' mouth, lighting a fire in both of them. Each time Alex did this, Jules captured her finger with her lips, closing them around Alex's finger and sucking gently and moving her mouth up and down the length of the finger.

Lost in the thrill of Alex's tongue sliding across her lips, Jules felt Alex's hands pulling her shirt from her pants. The waist band on her pants was loose so it came out easily. Alex's hands were on her back under her blouse, feather light, skating across her muscles, only stopping to pop open the closure on Jules' bra. Her excitement mounted when

Alex moved her hands along the length of her back, dragging her thumbs the length of her ribs, just skirting contact with her breasts. It seemed to have started a war between butterflies in her stomach and the increasing need at her core.

Jules sat up and reached for the hem of Alex's sweater, lifting it to expose Alex's mid-section. Alex arched her back, then leaned forward to help Jules pull it off entirely. Jules looked down at Alex, with desire and want. She tenderly touched Alex's face, traced Alex's lips with her fingers, then gently fluttered her fingers over Alex's neck, ending on Alex's chest, following the line where lace met skin. Alex heaved in ecstasy, pushing her chest upwards towards Jules.

The realization that she was breaking every professional boundary clamped hard against Jules' chest, but she was already lost in a warm haze of need. She bent her head and traced Alex's stomach with her tongue, moving upward until Alex grabbed her face in both hands and devoured Jules' mouth. Alex looked at Jules with wanton eyes. "Take it off. Take it off."

Jules didn't know what she meant. *What did she mean? My shirt, her bra? Stop thinking and just do it.* She reached around Alex's back, lifted her from the couch and undid the bra, slipping the straps down Alex's arms and throwing it to the floor. Alex laid back down and pulled Jules to her, but Jules resisted. She desired everything, but right now she simply wanted to adore this beautiful creature below her. Alex's golden hair was splayed across a deep maroon throw pillow. The contrast was striking in the low light of the afternoon. Her breasts were the color of heavy cream, buttery and soft. Her face was flushed, her cheeks crimson and lips had taken on a vermillion hue.

She ran her hands down from Alex's bare shoulders, across the upper part of Alex's chest, not yet touching her breasts, then down along her sides, stopping at the waist band of her slacks. Looking at Alex, asking permission silently, she straddled her at thigh level and slowly, purposefully, teasingly, unbuckled Alex's belt, unbuttoned her slacks and lowered the zipper painfully slowly. Alex sat up and pushed Jules' shirt off her shoulders, removed her bra and remembering Jules' shyness, encircled her with her arms so that their breasts were pressed together, hoping that Jules would not back off in shyness.

"I want to touch you, kiss you," breathed Jules, "but—"

Alex cut her off before she could continue. "I want you too, please." Alex covered Jules' mouth with hers as Jules tentatively touched Alex's left breast with the tips of her fingers. She circled her nipple with one finger, bent her head to close her mouth over the other nipple. She flicked the nipple with her tongue causing Alex to arch her back and push her breast further against Jules' lips, moaning her delight. Jules was more excited than she had ever been in her life.

Sitting up again, Alex caught Jules' face in her hands and said, "my turn." She wasted no time with subtlety, bending her head to take Jules' right breast in her mouth and stimulate the left nipple with her fingers. Throwing her head back, Jules shuddered and entangled her fingers in Alex's thick hair, pulling her closer. Alex stopped touching Jules' breasts with her hands and reached down to frantically undo the belt on Jules' pants. Unbuttoning and unzipping the pants, she reached inside and stroked Jules' belly. Jules was writhing, still straddling Alex's legs.

The remaining clothes kept them from feeling what each desired. Jumping off Alex, Jules quickly discarded her slacks and knelt back down next to the couch. In one downward movement, she stripped off Alex's pants. Jules climbed back on top of Alex. Both were lying on the couch, clad only in panties, heaving against each other with unrestrained lust.

"Jules, come with me."

Jules was momentarily confused. *Was Alex ready to orgasm now? Oh my god, what do I do now? I haven't even touched her,* fretted Jules to herself. Alex didn't notice Jules' confusion when she pushed Jules off her and swung her legs off the couch. She took Jules' hand, leading her to her bedroom. Throwing back the comforter and top sheet, Alex beckoned to Jules, who didn't need any encouragement. They lay facing each other, touching, running their hands all over each other's body, kissing with tenderness and abandon. Alex's body was fevered with her desire for Jules. Alex was no stranger to being with women, but she had never been so desperate for someone to touch her. All she could think about was Jules. She wanted Jules to take her.

She turned her back to Jules and pressed herself into Jules' abdomen. Jules, who understood what Alex wanted, slipped her left arm under Alex's neck to caress her breast and ran her right-hand down Alex's arm, side and hip, moving slowly across her belly. Jules nibbled Alex's neck and leaned over to capture Alex's lips. Alex reflectively pushed her buttocks into Jules' groin and bent her right leg up, swinging it up over Jules.

Suddenly Jules stopped and whispered to Alex, "I'm not sure what to do."

Alex realized right away what Jules was saying. *She hasn't done this before.* She turned to her and tenderly asked, "It seems like you know how to kiss, right?" Jules nodded her head. "And do you like how this feels?" Alex took Jules' hand and covered her own breast with it. Jules whispered "yes."

"And you know how to follow instructions, right?" Alex asked. Again, Jules nodded her head. Alex looked deeply into her eyes and said, "Then you know what to do. Kiss me."

Jules did not tarry. She continued kissing Alex as she slipped her hand under the fabric of the panties. She moved her fingers, stroking, skimming over the scar where Alex's leg met her abdomen. As Alex moved against Jules' body, Jules began to feel more apprehension. In Jules' limited experience, which turned out to be only with one man in college, the times with him weren't always so good. But then, she had never been with anyone like Alex.

"Baby, please let me know what you want. Tell me what you want," uttered Jules in short gasps.

Alex, barely coherent, begged, "Touch me Jules, touch me. I'll tell you."

With Jules' free hand and direction from Alex, her panties were history. Kissing her neck and fondling her nipple, she kept moving her hand lower and lower, teasing, building Alex's excitement, until she could wait no longer. She parted Alex's lips and stroked her, feeling Alex's warm wetness. She heard Alex moan from her touch, then Alex hoarsely whispered, "Let me touch you too, Jules."

Jules, afraid that she wouldn't be able to concentrate, gently removed Alex's hand bringing it up to her lips to kiss it, saying, "This is about you right now. Please, I just want to make you happy."

Jules listened to Alex's body, her reactions and moans told her where to touch her in the way that brought Alex the most pleasure. When she thought Alex might be close to finishing, she heard Alex beg, "I need you inside me."

Jules entered her gently and with just a few thrusts, Alex came hard, crying out, heaving and trying to find Jules' mouth. When her climax subsided, Alex tried to move away but Jules held her tightly and began again. Alex stiffened her legs and came sharply a second time, then a third. She was totally spent, barely able to move but Jules didn't mind. She could wait. It was enough right now to cradle Alex in her arms.

A few minutes later without warning, Alex turned Jules on her back and straddled her, bending over so that her breasts were positioned a few inches from Jules' mouth. Jules slowly pulled her down, taking one breast, then the other. Alex was supporting herself with her arms, but managed to position one knee between Jules' legs, pushing up against the soaked crotch of Jules' panties. She pulled away from Jules' warm mouth and started kissing Jules' breasts. She had seen them before but seeing and touching were two different things. They weren't as large as hers but fit in her hand perfectly. She flicked her tongue over Jules' nipples, which instantaneously pebbled and hardened in her mouth.

Jules was moving against Alex's thigh and had become more insistent. Keeping her hands on Jules' breasts, Alex began to move down Jules' body kissing her until she reached the waist band of Jules' panties. She hooked her fingers in the waist band and swiftly tugged them off, returning to kiss Jules' belly and lower. Jules wasn't sure when Alex knelt between her legs and lowered her head. She captured Alex's head in her hands and looked at her with timid eyes.

Alex said, "It's all right, darling. I really want to do this. Don't be shy. Please let me."

Jules let go of Alex's head and surrendered herself before she changed her mind. Alex began exploring with her tongue. Jules gasped and thrust her hips upwards, as Alex flicked her tongue back and forth across Jules' sensitive spot. Alex reached around Jules' buttocks and lifted her, squeezing. With Jules' buttocks in Alex's hands, Jules began to follow the rhythm Alex had set and was soon lost in the building sensation that crept through her lower belly.

Alex felt Jules' rhythm change. She continued to stroke Jules' sensitive spot with her tongue and entered her with two fingers, moving slowly at first then more forcefully, bringing her to a more powerful orgasm that she had ever experienced. Alex kept contact with Jules as she spasmed, over and over, easing her through her climax.

Alex grabbed the edge of the sheet and wiped her mouth before hovering over Jules' flushed body suffused with the sheen of love making. Jules opened her eyes and said, "It's never been like that for me before."

Alex, smiled, kissed her lightly on the lips and replied, "It's all in your head, baby" before she pulled up the sheet and cuddled next to Jules.

Jules chuckled *that's what they must mean when they say that sex is heady,* just before she drifted off.

When Jules awoke, she could hear a shower running. Alex was already up. She languished in bed for a few moments, then saw a neatly folded terry cloth robe on the side of the bed where Alex had been sleeping. There was a note tucked into the collar. "If you were hoping for a rose, then you'll have to wait until next time. I'm hungry, let's eat."

Shaking her head with amusement and remembering how quickly Alex could jump from one state of mind to another, she got out of bed and slipped into the robe, belting it on the way into the bathroom. Alex had left a towel, wash cloth and a little basket of various soaps, shampoos, conditioners and lotion on the vanity. On top of the towel there was a travel size tube of tooth paste and a new toothbrush. *Hmmm, she thinks of everything,* mulled Jules. Standing in front of the vanity, she could see that Alex was still in the shower, rinsing herself.

Alex was finishing up when she turned and saw Jules. "I'll leave the water running. I'm just about ready to get out." She didn't seem to be at all uncomfortable with her nudity. Jules wished she could be so comfortable.

As Alex grabbed a towel from a hook outside the shower and wrapped it around herself, Jules took off her robe and got into the shower, positioning herself with her back to Alex. She was soaping up when she felt a hand snake down her back. Alex was leaning into the shower, asking if she wanted her back scrubbed. Jules must have nodded because Alex stepped back in and began soaping up her back.

Casually, Alex told her that they would probably have to wait at any restaurant in the area, being Saturday night.

Jules said over her shoulder, "We have reservations at 7:30 p.m. at La Medusa, just down the road from you. I thought we could walk."

"You were pretty sure of yourself, weren't you?" teased Alex.

"Anything but. However, your aunt was sure of you," said Jules as she tried to escape Alex's arms around her.

"Not so fast," said Alex with amusement as she held Jules tighter. "What do you mean that my Aunt Sophie was sure of me? My god, did you tell her about us?"

"Heavens no!" Jules said with feigned horror. "It's not enough that I just slept with a colleague who's working on a case with me, which by the way, if my partners found out, would land me in major hot water! Do you think I'd add to that what Sophie might do to me?"

Alex had to smile. "Well then, explain yourself," she said with mock command as she nuzzled Jules' neck.

"I talked to Sophie yesterday. You know, hand holding, but she was fine. She asked if I had spoken to you and I said I had, and you seemed to be okay. Then out of the blue she said to me, 'You know, Jules, Alex is very headstrong, pig-headed. I think that when her parents died, even though she had Mario and me, she made a vow not to rely on anyone again. Sometimes you just have to ignore all the superfluous stuff and just take her, if you understand my meaning.'"

Letting go of Jules and turning her in her arms, Alex laughingly asked, "Oh my god, Jules. What did you do?"

"Nothing. I was afraid to ask her to explain, so while I was sitting in the car outside in your driveway, I made up my own interpretation."

"Yes, yes you did," said Alex as she kissed Jules, "and it was a splendid interpretation."

"Don't make fun of me, Alex."

Teasingly, between nibbles on Jules' shoulder, Alex replied, "Oh, I'm not making fun of you Jules, but I sure did have *fun* with you earlier." They kissed again and almost didn't make it to the restaurant, but in the end Alex's stomach prevailed.

Seated in a corner which afforded a modicum of privacy, they ordered roasted cauliflower gratin with pine nuts and raisins to share as an appetizer, pan roasted organic chicken, grilled fruit and summer greens for Jules and rigatoni, Marsala braised beef ragu for Alex, plus a bottle of 2006 Pinot Nero before settling in to enjoy a relaxing evening.

After some light chatting about Seattle, Alex wanted to get to know Jules. She felt that Jules had the advantage because of the background check. "Jules, I get the sense from some of your comments, that you haven't been with many women." Alex knew full well she probably had not been with any.

Jules groaned, "Was I that bad?"

Alex laughed, "Oh no darling, you were spectacular, more spectacular than I could have imagined. I was just wondering about your past relationships, that's all. Really, Jules, I can honestly say that you have nothing to worry about in the bedroom department."

"So, it was good for you?" inquired Jules with a hint of apprehensiveness in her voice.

Still feeling insecure, thought Alex, so she told her, "No one has ever made me climax so many times. You were better than good." She hoped it would alleviate any self-doubt about Jules' love-making repertoire. Jules blushed and bashfully lowered her eyes. Alex went on with her original train of thought. "It's just that you know so much about me, yet I really don't know a lot about you. It feels a little unbalanced."

Jules talked about her upbringing, her relationship with her parents and a brief relationship she had with a man in college. She told Alex that she had spent a long time lying to herself by choosing not to deal with her attraction to women. Admitting her cowardliness seemed like a great dichotomy to Alex. Jules was a courageous and daring individual in everything she did but couldn't bring herself to accept who she was. Alex wasn't judging by any means. It had taken her years to divulge her identity to Sophie. She just thought that Jules was fearless and wouldn't have been so reluctant to accept and deal with her sexual orientation.

"Do you ever plan on telling your parents?"

"I suppose I would if I wanted to settle down with someone."

"It's not easy, Jules, but I guarantee that you'll feel a whole lot better when you've told them, even if they don't react very positively. Keeping that part of yourself hidden from those you love wears on you, whether you know it or not. I wish I had told Sophie long before I did."

Jules sighed deeply, taking a sip of the wine thinking, *I'd take that risk to be with you.* Instead she said, "You can say that in retrospect and of course your story had a happy ending, but my parents are not at all like Sophie. I wouldn't put it past them to call up my partners and out me, with the intention of embarrassing me to go straight." *What is this with me? I've never felt this kind of connection before.*

Alex was chagrined. "You're right, of course. That was very short-sighted of me, and I'm sorry."

"No worries, Alex. Right now, I'm having to cope with what has happened between the two of us and don't want to pile any more on top. You do understand, don't you?"

Alex nodded her head and she felt a cloud of worry pass behind her eyes. *What if the intensity of the experiences we had together at the ranch and here, are too much for Jules? In Alex's professional opinion, Jules hadn't even come out to herself. Would she abandon the deep palpable connection between them to avoid possible exposure of buried emotions and feelings?*

Jules saw the look on Alex's face and became concerned. "What's wrong Alex? Did I say something to upset you?"

In a split second, Alex decided to try and keep things light. "No, no of course not. I was just thinking that you know a lot about my ex-girlfriends, with your investigation and all, so I'm turning the tables and want to know about your relationships."

Jules ignored the good-natured dig about the background investigation and humbly said, "I'm afraid that you're going to be disappointed. There aren't any juicy details. I had a boyfriend for about a semester in college and I met a woman in the service once but was too afraid of the consequences to make a move. I pretty much spent my entire career celibate."

"You're telling me that you haven't slept with anyone for ten years?" said Alex not quite believing what she had heard.

"Yes, that's what I'm telling you."

"My god, Jules, that's incredible. How did you do that? I mean, even from the perspective of just the physical release, not even talking about the emotional needs, how did you deal with the need to be touched, to be loved?"

"Remember, Alex, I grew up in a non-demonstrative household. There wasn't a lot of touching, so for me, it really wasn't something I expected, but I understand how you, because of your upbringing, might wonder. If I felt needy, I ran until I had exhausted myself."

Without losing a beat and in a completely non-invasive manner, Alex asked, "And after you got out and started the business?"

Okay, safer subject, thought Jules. "Not until I moved out to LA. I felt safer, away from DC and my parents, but I travel so much that it makes it hard. Plus, there's never been anyone that's held my attention past two or three minutes. Maybe I wasn't looking in all the right places, but it seems that I attract one of three kinds of women, present company excluded, of course."

"Of course," smiled Alex, "and what are those?"

"Well, there are women with egos the size of Alaska. You know, full of themselves and their success, but underneath, I think their egos are pretty insecure, because they needed constant stroking. It is exhausting."

Alex was thoughtful. She replied, "Arrogant individuals who appear to have huge egos generally spend a good amount of time inflating their egos to feel better about themselves. Mostly, we really don't like ourselves, so we try to bolster even the smallest accomplishment or pleasure to make us feel better. What's the next category?"

"The black hole. These women don't disguise their insecurity. They come at you straight on and siphon off all your energy. They can't seem to muster up enough ego on their own, so they constantly need someone else to do it for them."

"That's interesting," mused Alex. "Over inflated ego vs. not enough ego. It all comes down to ego, doesn't it? Either too much or too little. That's a pretty good insight, Jules. And the third?"

"Hmm, the plain old garden variety whacko," Jules said, cracking a smile.

"So, you met your share of sociopaths?" quipped Alex, meaning it to be a joke.

"One or two. The worst was a stalker."

"Oh my," responded Alex, realizing that when Jules said whacko, she really meant 'intensely disturbed.' "How did you handle it?"

Jules recounted the story in its entirety for Alex, including how the stalker lay in wait and stabbed her. Jules had warned the intruder twice, then pulled the trigger of her pistol when the woman came at her a third time. Jules hung her head for a moment then looked at Alex with sadness and remorse. "I killed her."

"How horrible for you!" Alex grabbed Jules' hands from across the table. "I can't imagine what you went through!" gasped Alex again. "Oh my god! You're fortunate to be alive! The scar on your back, right?"

"It was awful. I called the police, told them that I had shot an armed intruder because I had feared for my life and that I was injured. Then I called Jake who didn't live too far away. He got there just after the patrol cars did and started barking orders to the two young cops, telling one to get outside and seal off the crime scene and the other to call and find out where the heck the ambulance was.

Once it arrived, Jake stayed behind to deal with the detectives while I was on the way to the hospital. At some time during the ordeal, he must have called Mickey, another person from our office, who met me at the hospital just before I went in for surgery. It took a while to get things worked out, but no charges were filed against me. After that experience, I've not had much desire to get back into the dating scene."

"Jules, I'm sure you considered every other avenue before having to resort to shooting her," consoled Alex.

"The part that really threw me was my not seeing it coming." Jules was shaking her head, blaming herself for the incident. "I missed how really crazy she was and never expected an attempted murder attack."

"If this helps at all, try and remember that it is difficult even for a trained professional to determine if and when a stalker's behavior decompensates. Her break with reality might have been in the works for a long time and something small and inconsequential to you or me, might have pushed her over the edge."

"Thank you, Alex. So now you know why I don't have much of a social life."

The conversation had turned out to be much heavier than either of the two of them could have imagined and they didn't know where to go after Jules' stalker story, so they just sat sipping wine, lost in their own thoughts. The server appeared with their entrees just as the silence became strained. After a few bites and telling each other how good their choices had been, Alex tried to broach the discomfort.

"Jules, the more I get to know you, the more I realize what an incredible person you are. You already know how grateful I am to you for keeping me alive, but I want you to know that I admire you. The things you have gone through would paralyze another person and yet, here you are a fully functional and caring person. I know from experience, that when one talks about traumatic experiences or deeply buried feelings and emotions, it can have a cathartic effect, but afterwards it can cause a person to withdraw even further to counteract the vulnerability they feel."

"Please Jules, trust me. Don't feel like you have to hide." With a final impassioned plea, Alex added, taking a deep breath, "I don't know what I'd do if you did." Alex didn't know how Jules was going to react. It was fifty-fifty; withdraw or stay in the present. It was obvious observing Jules' face that she had called on her reserves of courage to remain engaged.

"Alex, a little while ago I was worried that you would psychoanalyze me. It made me nervous. Now I'm pretty sure that's what you must be doing. I'm on the edge of my seat, ready to head for the hills," confessed Jules with a burst of discomfort.

What would work now for Jules? Would humor help? Would this be the right time for physical contact? Could sharing an experience from her past make Jules feel more comfortable? What do I do now? Alex's mind spat out these questions in rapid succession while Jules nervously waited. Alex went on instinct and prayed it would be the right reaction.

Reaching across the table, past their plates, Alex held Jules' hands. She leaned over the table, making the contact intimate. "Jules, the thought never crossed my mind to psychoanalyze you, but I am very glad that you asked. Lots of people have the impression that psychologists have the answer for everything or that they practice their skills to manipulate people in their personal lives. That's not true for the vast majority of us. Perhaps we can even have some idea on how to communicate better than the average Joe, but I assure you we experience enough trouble and unhappiness on our own without inviting more by analyzing people in our personal lives.

"I've been interacting with you, one on one, person to person, not psychologist to patient. Understand? My personal relationships are just that, personal. You should know that I respect you, have a great deal of affection for you, and that I would never use my skills to invade your psyche. It goes against everything I believe. So, please don't head for the hills. I'd just have to follow you and bring you back. I'm a very good roper, you know," finished Alex hoping that ending on a note of humor would work.

Jules pursed her lips, sat back in the chair a little and nodded her head. Without feeling a need to explain or protect, she told herself that she could trust this woman, whose life she had wrestled from the hands of the grim reaper. Running her hands through her hair from temples to the back, Jules re-engaged with Alex's eyes and announced, "we're having dessert."

Returning home, Alex asked Jules if she had a suitcase. Jules told her it was in the trunk of the car. Alex teased her and goaded her into saying that she didn't want to take it out earlier because she didn't want to be perceived as presumptuous. "But you were, standing there looking all awkward and nervous," countered Alex with a slight smirk.

Jules suppressed a smile and with a straight face, retorted, "Ah, but you are the one who opened your arms to me, and your reaction could hardly be categorized as just a friendly hello hug."

Alex went into the kitchen and took out a bottle of brandy. "Want a night cap?"

Jules followed her into the kitchen saying "Yes, please" to the night cap. "And just so we get the record straight, you're the one who kissed me first."

Alex chuckled warmly and handed Jules a snifter on their way back into the living room. "This isn't going to put you to sleep, is it?

Jules coyly asked Alex what she would do if it did. Alex took her time, looking Jules up and down. *God this woman is breathtaking. She makes my blood boil.* "Well, if it did put you to sleep, I suppose I'd have to take extreme measures with you."

"Like what?" invited Jules.

"Come here, I'll show you."

CHAPTER 9 – The Day After

We are like butterflies who flutter for a day and think its forever.
Dr. Carl Sagan

Sunday April 19

They had made desperate, passionate love most of the night and were still sleeping close to noon when Alex's new cell phone rang. She untangled herself from Jules' arms and legs, answering sleepily. "Hello."

"Alex, I woke you, didn't I?" sang Sophie. "Everything all right?"

As Morpheus lost his hold on Alex, her brain cleared and realized that Jules was lying naked in her bed while her Aunt Sophie was on the line wanting to exchange pleasantries.

"Yes, Aunt Sophie, ah everything is, uh, just fine. I'm still a little groggy. Sorry."

Jules rolled over to face Alex and stifled a laugh knowing that Alex was nervous as a worm being dropped into a recently stocked lake.

"How come you're sleeping so late? You've always been a morning person, even on the weekend," interrogated Sophie.

"Ah, well, I was out late with a friend last night and didn't get to sleep until the wee hours."

"You weren't out with that no-good Reggie, were you? Are you out of your mind? Is she with you right now? You aren't thinking of getting back with her, are you?"

"Whoa there, Aunt Sophie. Don't get all riled up and by the way, I appreciate your loyalty, but I haven't seen Reggie for six months. She didn't even show up at the closing. She sent her henchman instead. For the record, Aunt Sophie, there is no way in hell that I would ever, ever consider getting back with Reggie. She was good for only one thing and that was to clarify for me what I never, ever want in a person!"

"Are you alone?"

"What is this, the Inquisition?"

"No, no, of course not, sweetie. It's just my plain old nosiness. Must have caught a bug from Peaky the Elf! I just called to see how you were doing and to tell you I miss you. I wish I could see you more often. I know Rick feels the same."

"Me too, Aunt Sophie. Actually, you may very well get your wish, seeing me more, I mean. Jules and I were going to call you today—"

Sophie interrupted cutting off Alex before she could explain. "Jules is there with you? Are you in bed with her?" gasped Sophie.

Evenly Alex continued, "Listen Aunt Sophie, we were going to call you via a conference call today to tell you that I've decided to come back to the ranch while Claire is there and continue her treatment myself." Alex didn't hear a sound on the other end and thought the call might have been dropped. "Aunt Sophie, are you there? Are you all right?"

Sophie was too stunned to answer at first. Finally, she spoke. "When did you make that decision, Alex?"

Alex explained that she and Jules had talked about it the last evening they were at the ranch. She admitted that she thought Jules was out of her mind when she proposed it, but the more she thought about it, the more it made sense.

Sophie asked her if she was qualified to treat a PTSD kidnapping victim. Alex didn't get her hackles up because she knew what Sophie meant. Sophie understood that Alex's job revolved around going to court after making a psychological examination and she thought that Alex hadn't really treated or counseled people. Alex assured her that she was qualified and that she was up for the challenge.

Jules had gotten up from bed and gone into the bathroom, coming back in a robe. She wrote on a pad next to the bed and held it up to Alex. "Coffee?" Alex nodded and continued listening to Sophie go on about her reservations of Alex giving up her job. Jules left the bedroom and was clanging around in the kitchen, presumably looking for the coffee pods.

Sophie must have sensed Alex's distraction. "Alex, tell me the truth. Is there someone with you in your bedroom?"

Without hesitating, Alex told her the truth. "Aunt Sophie, there is no one in the bedroom but my sleepy old self." She went on to explain to Sophie what had been arranged by Jules.

When Alex finished, Sophie, whistled appreciatively, "Wow that Jules is something!"

Alex knew that Sophie was baiting her, waiting for a reaction, but what the heck, she'd make her aunt happy. "Yes, she is. You'll get no argument from me."

She was saying goodbye, when Jules walked in with two cups of coffee. Alex sighed heavily and gratefully accepted the cup offered to her. Jules must have been paying attention at the ranch. She had put the right amount of milk in it. "Wow," said Alex after a sip of coffee. "That was interesting. We don't have to worry about telling her now. Aunt Sophie showed the appropriate amount of concern, but I think she is secretly gleeful. However, I don't think she bought it when I side-stepped her question about you being here."

"Are you suggesting we tell her?"

"Which part? The part about you being here or the part where we hardly got any sleep last night? That'd go over well, don't you think?"

Sitting on the side of the bed, Jules ran her hand down Alex's back. "I think you underestimate your Aunt Sophie sometimes."

"Maybe so, but let's just leave our, ah, friendship, or whatever this is for another time. Okay? It's almost noon. What would you say to brunch and a walk? I know a place close by. After that if you like, I could take you sightseeing."

"Sounds fine, as long as we can get in some time to review how we're going to handle my visit to your office tomorrow morning and a few other loose ends."

"You're leaving after that?"

"Afraid so. Wish I didn't have to, but I have other ongoing cases and I need to visit Bentworth and Claire to let them know that the plans are in motion."

They were seated as soon as they got to a small neighborhood restaurant Alex and Reggie had frequented on the weekends. The server who came to their table knew Alex and raised his eyebrow quizzically at Alex after taking a look at Jules from top to bottom.

"Hi Robbie, how are you? What's extra good this morning?"

Flirtatiously Robbie answered, "Nothing as yummy as this gorgeous woman sitting next to you."

"Funny, Robbie. I can always count on you to say the most awkward thing at the most inappropriate time. Bring us coffee with cream and promise to be a good boy when you come back."

"Gee Alex, you're grumpy this morning," he said with a dramatic turn of the heel and a swish to the service bar.

Both Alex and Jules giggled. "At first I thought he was coming on to me," said Jules, "but now I realize he was needling you. You're right about this neighborhood. Seems like people know you quite well." She smiled and moved her eyebrows up and down for effect.

"Speaking of predilections, wise guy, are you okay with what has happened between us?"

Jules was placid. "I'm okay. I didn't think I would be after what I told you and I wasn't sure that we could ever have a normal conversation again, but it looks like I'm not gonna melt away. Alex, this is really all new to me, the emotions, the feelings. I've never experienced the achy feeling in my chest I get with you. It does scare me, and I have to be honest about it with you. I am still struggling with the ethics of it all."

Robbie came back with their coffee and two menus. After he had put the coffee and menus on the table, he put one hand on his hip and the other on Alex's shoulder, and said, "Girl, are you going out of town soon? I'm down to my last ounce of patience with my parents."

"Maybe, Robbie. You want to house sit again?"

"As soon as possible! I'll be back in five to get your orders."

Alex explained that Robbie often house sat when she and Reggie were gone more than a few days. He was neat and clean, didn't throw parties and, in spite of how he comes across, was very reliable. She asked Jules what she thought about having Robbie stay at her house while she was at the ranch. Jules thought about it and said she didn't see any problem with it, but they wanted to vet him out first.

They chatted easily, though Alex got the sense that Jules had a lot on her mind and was slightly detached. It might have been too much for her to tell Alex all that she did. Her body language had changed, and she wasn't making as much eye contact. Alex decided not to press, knowing that if Jules felt pressure, it would drive her away, maybe permanently.

Once they got back to the house, Jules told Alex that she was tired and wanted to pass on the sightseeing. Alex inquired if she wanted to take a nap. Jules answered she just wanted to lie down for a while. Two minutes later, she was out cold on the living room couch. Alex covered her with a blanket and started making a list of things she would have to do before she left for the ranch.

Jules awoke around 5:00 p.m. to an inviting smell wafting from the kitchen. Soft music was playing, classical piano, Chopin for sure, but she didn't remember the name of the piece. After folding the blanket and making a run to the bathroom, she went to find Alex. Alex was dumping what looked like chopped up fennel into a pot already boiling on the stove. She tipped-toed up behind Alex and leaned over Alex's shoulder to smell the soup. In hushed tones, she whispered, "Did I startle you?"

"No, I heard you coming but didn't want to spoil your fun," murmured Alex. Turning, Alex put her arms around Jules' neck and kissed her gently on the lips. Jules didn't resist, but she didn't take advantage of Alex's warm willing mouth. Alex noticed and tried to remain calm and neutral. Before letting her go, she told her that supper would be ready in an hour.

Jules was ready to talk about the case. First, she told Alex what Mickey had found out about Dr. Metuchi and Claire's relationship. Elena, Claire's stepmother, and Dr. Metuchi belonged to the same club, knew each other by name, but didn't hang in the same circles. It was Elena that suggested to Bentworth that Metuchi see Claire. No one at the club remembered seeing Claire with Metuchi prior to the doctor/patient relationship, but it didn't mean that they weren't together at some time. Alex didn't comment on the findings but filed it away. She thought she'd ask Claire directly.

"What's Metuchi's background?" asked Alex.

"She's originally from south of the border. Her mother remarried after her father, a retired military general, was killed in Buenos Aires in the early seventies. Her new family emigrated to New Jersey when her stepfather was awarded a fellowship at Princeton. Following in her stepfather's footsteps, she went on to medical school at Princeton and did her psychiatric residency at Stanford University. She stayed in California and set up a practice with her now deceased husband."

"Siblings?" prompted Alex.

"Yes, a half-brother from her mother's second marriage," responded Jules. "Her brother was in and out of trouble, including a stint in a private psychiatric hospital in Maryland when he was seventeen."

"Hmm, Jules, do you know where he is now?"

"He's out on the East coast and owns a successful business. By trade he is an electrician and his business supplies electricians for commercial renovations," replied Jules.

"Any idea why he was confined in the hospital?"

"He currently has a diagnosis of bipolar disorder. He was interned after a brush with the law and the records are sealed, so we really can't tell. Could bipolar disorder land him in a hospital?" queried Jules.

"It's possible. Years ago, it was a very misunderstood disease. Late teens and early twenties are typically when an individual shows signs of the disorder."

Jules had an agenda and didn't stop when Alex got up to stir the soup. After outlining what she wanted to accomplish at Alex's office in the morning, she briefed Alex on the installation progress of a security system at the ranch, including an 850MHz private channel radio system on towers located in strategic areas of the ranch. The plan was to install small solar and wind power to keep them operational. There was no commercial power on the ranch except at the main compound. The total estimated price tag was half a million.

Alex, whistled. "Geez, Jules, Bentworth must really be pissed off to spend this kind of money to hunt the kidnappers down."

"You have no idea. The guy is worth billions and is sparing no expense. A million here and there is like pin money to him. Frankly, I'm concerned that he might shoot them before we can get them into police custody."

"You mean you are going to tell him first when you find and capture them?"

"Afraid so. He's footing the bill. It'll be more than what they asked for in ransom."

"Don't think I'd want to be on his bad side."

"Wise woman. I don't intend to tell him or Claire where she is going. I want no leaks."

"Understood. Anything else, or are we ready to eat?"

Jules was already in bed, lying on her side, when Alex slipped off her robe and joined her. Jules was facing away from Alex and did not turn around. Alex slid closer to her and propped herself up on her left elbow, tracing her fingers along the length of Jules' back.

"You like this, don't you?" said Alex.

"I love it when you're the one doing it," Jules said into the pillow she had bunched up under her head.

Alex kept stroking Jules' back with feather-like fingers. "Jules, may I ask you something?"

"Uh, not again," replied Jules, slightly wary of what would come next.

"Is that a yes?" persisted Alex.

"Sure, why not, although I can't imagine what more you want to know after this weekend," Jules said sardonically.

"Jules, were you ever really in love?" Alex had been replaying in her mind the conversations she and Jules had had over the last twenty-four plus hours. She had a little red flag lurking somewhere in her consciousness and wanted to flush it out. She was concerned that she might be Jules' first, both in terms of sexual experiences and the first with whom Jules had fallen in love. Maybe she was assuming too much, but all the signs where there, unless Alex was totally deluded.

Jules sighed and rolled over to face Alex. With her face inches away from Alex, she looked for some sign from Alex as to what this was about. *Was Alex going to tell her she had fallen in love with her? Was this the lead into it?* Jules knew how she felt, but she wasn't ready to put any kind of label on it. "That's really a hard question for me to answer. I don't know, Alex. I don't think so. I've been attracted to women, but never got close enough to experience anything deeper."

Alex disengaged her hand from Jules' and laid it on Jules' cheek, kissing her gently. Jules willingly accepted the kisses. When Alex stopped, Jules asked her if it was okay not to make love tonight. Alex was disappointed, not because she had been planning on sex, though she had, but because she somehow thought she had wounded Jules.

"Darling, have I hurt your feelings in any way?"

"No, no, Alex. It's just that I've been thinking that to get through the next few months, we are going to have to compartmentalize this aspect of our relationship, at least for the duration, and for me, I need to start now. I hope you understand, don't you?"

Alex did understand but wasn't happy about it. Jules' emotions were powerful right now and very much tied to making love. She needed time to collect herself to be able to resume her professional perspective early Monday morning. "Jules, I understand that you need some time to take a step back and get prepared for the weeks to come. I just don't know how successful I'm going to be hiding my feelings towards you."

They talked some more, never mentioning the word "love", treading softly, and stepping around it like a woman wearing new Manolo Blahnik's steps around a rain puddle to avoid ruining her shoes.

CHAPTER 10 – Back at the Ranch

Doubters may bet a week's salary against us, but I wouldn't bet the ranch.

John Connors

Monday April 20

The smell of coffee woke Alex before the alarm went off. It was five forty-five. She knew Jules must be up, but lazily reached behind her to confirm her groggy conclusions. Using the remote to partially open the duettes in the bedroom, she dragged herself up to a semi-seated position against the headboard. Jules walked in carrying two cups. *God, she is striking; I can't seem to get enough of her. All I want to do is drag her back to bed and never let her go,* thought Alex.

Jules was dressed in a fawn colored light-weight wool pencil skirt with a matching wide leather belt and shoes. The skirt was hemmed to fall above her knees with just enough leg showing to leave the onlooker wishing for more. The ripe peach houndstooth blouse with French cuffs and pinpoint collar was slightly tailored, drawing attention to her narrow waist and flattering the bust line.

Alex questioned whether she had ever lusted after Reggie as she did with this gorgeous creature. The answer was easy. *Not ever, not like this.* Jules saw that Alex was up. She said good morning, handed one of the cups to Alex, kissed her on the corner of her mouth and sat on the side of the bed with her upper body facing Alex.

Alex replied, "Mmmm, I could get used to this."

Jules thought she meant the coffee and answered halfheartedly, "Well, unless you're expecting Sophie to do this for you back at the Ranch, I'm afraid you're going to have to wait a while for me to bring you coffee again."

Alex picked up Jules' mood and tried to brighten it up. "What? You're not going to do this at the ranch? There's no way that Aunt Sophie would do this unless I'm sick." Alex saw the melancholy spread over Jules' face like soft cream cheese over toast. She wondered what was coming.

"Oh, Alex," Jules shook her head slightly, looking down at the coffee in her hands, "I don't know what expectations you had but, if all goes well, I won't be at the ranch very often."

"I didn't have any expectations, Jules. I was just hoping."

"You don't understand, Alex. I never should have started this whole thing between the two of us. It's all my fault, but I just couldn't help it and now I'm trying to make this as painless as possible."

"Oh, I understand, Jules," responded Alex with an edge to her voice. "I understood last night what was going on, but I thought it would be temporary not forever. You're talking like you're stepping back permanently!" She put her half-finished coffee down on the nightstand and stared at Jules.

Jules saw the flicker go out of Alex's eyes. "No, you don't understand, at least not fully. Leaving you, this, us, is not easy for me either. I swear to you I've never felt the kind of attraction, pain and conflict I am experiencing now. Never have I been faced with choosing between my personal life and the job. Alex, I need you to understand that I'm in uncharted waters here. I know that I have an obligation to the job, but I *feel* I have a connection to you, and it's cutting me in ways I can't even explain."

Jules expected Alex to blow a gasket, get angry and end it by metaphorically stomping off. In some ways she even wished Alex would come unhinged. It would be easier. The room was quiet for a moment, then Alex reached for Jules' coffee cup, put it on the nightstand with hers, lifted Jules' head with a soft touch to her chin, and spoke.

"Darling, I can't pretend to know exactly what you are experiencing, but I know whatever it is, it is difficult for you. I also know that your backing off is your way, the only way right now that you can think of to protect me, you, and the investigation. It's not hard to comprehend that you think our feelings for each other could, if things got rough, compromise decisions and end up jeopardizing the investigation. I'm a pretty smart person, Jules, and you don't have to carry this burden by yourself. I wished that you had talked to me about your concerns before you made this unilateral decision but, even so, I care enough for you to support any decision you make."

Damn, thought Jules. *Not what I was expecting.* Alex did not take the ball and slam dunk it to end the game. Instead, with surgical precision, she lobbed it back into the court of Jules heart cutting deeply. *Now what? Do I just get up and walk away?*

Alex saw the sadness in Jules' eyes replaced by uncertainty. She knew that Jules had expected her to get angry and end it, but she didn't want to end it. Choosing to suppress her innate passion and quick temper, Alex had single handedly without a weapon, rendered Jules utterly defenseless. Benevolently, she wiped Jules' tears from her face, put her arms around her, and softly told her that she wasn't going to make it easy for Jules to walk away. Jules pulled back, looking at Alex with questioning eyes and thought, *was I that transparent?*

Alex went on compassionately. "There's more, isn't there? Even though you say that the risk of danger to my family and me is minute, you're afraid that you might have to choose between Claire and me, and you know that you'd have to choose Claire, because she is your client." With the precision of a seasoned litigator, Alex added, "Isn't it also true that if it came to that and something happened to me, you don't know how you could live with yourself?"

Barely breathing, Jules answered, "Yes," and turned away.

Alex let the sheet fall and bare breasted she wrestled Jules back into her arms. Jules resisted with a hopeless, desperate sob, but Alex was not going to be deterred. When she finally was able to turn Jules around and hold her as she might comfort a child, she spoke. "Jules, what I feel for you is way beyond special. There has to be another way. I don't know how yet or what that way might be but promise me you won't make any hard and fast decisions until we've both given this some thought and come to a joint decision. Promise me."

With her heart feeling like it had been through a meat grinder, Jules sighed, "All right, Alex. I promise you, but we are going to have to deal with this next week. I intend to deliver Claire to the ranch Monday or Tuesday."

Monday April 20 (cont.) – Friday 24

Everything went without a hitch at Alex's office, but Alex was distracted and spent the week brooding about Jules. She was resolute in not calling her, giving her time to sort through her raw emotions. She kept busy getting arrangements with Robbie settled, checking in with neighbors, letting the local precinct know she'd be gone and that there would be a house sitter, pre-paying utility bills and getting her car serviced. She also made an appointment with Daniel to update her will.

By Friday, Fahad was in the thick of it and doing quite well based on feedback from court clerks and the department's secretary, Mary. Mary was one of those people who gave you the unmitigated truth, whether or not you asked for it. Around two, Alex went up to say her goodbyes to Randy.

"Randy, I just stopped by to let you know I'd be leaving soon, and that Dr. Fahad has done remarkably well in the short time he's been here. I think that we're pretty lucky to have gotten a person of his caliber and experience."

"Alex, do you have time to sit down for a moment," asked Randy.

"Sure."

Randy seemed to be searching for the words, so Alex waited until he worked out whatever was troubling him. "Alex, I just wanted to say that I, for one, will sorely miss you. Don't get me wrong, I think this opportunity is fantastic for you and for our department, but I worry that you may not want to come back to such a mundane job after all the excitement with your new assignment."

Wow! Thought Alex. *That's the first time I've seen Randy remotely in touch with what I have contributed to this department.* She carefully responded, "Randy, thank you for sharing your feelings with me. I am honored that you felt you could be so honest. Now I have to be honest with you. I don't know what can happen in six months for either of us, but I want you to know that my taking this temporary assignment which, by the way you convinced me to take, is just that, temporary. I have a house here and a life and I wouldn't look forward to starting over anywhere else." That was as close to a guarantee she could give him now. Ironic, she thought. She had been worried about being replaced and Randy was worried about having to replace her. She said her final goodbye and headed to the grocery store to stock the refrigerator for Robbie.

Saturday April 25

Standing in her foyer, looking at her watch, Alex mumbled to herself, "Where the hell is Robbie?" Jules had arranged a car for her, and it was due on her doorstep in fifteen minutes, but Robbie was nowhere in sight. She tried his cell phone again, but it went directly to voice mail. She was trying to think through what she would do if he didn't show up before the car, when the back-door buzzer sounded. She rushed through the kitchen, opened the door and found Robbie standing there with bicycle in hand.

"What happened to you? Where's your car?"

"Sorry Alex. It wouldn't start this morning and Mom and Dad had left the house already, so I had to pedal over here."

"Why didn't you answer your cell phone?"

Robbie patted himself, searching his pockets. "I must have left it in the car. I'm really sorry, Alex."

"Okay, Robbie. Water under the bridge. Let me give you a quick rundown before my car gets here."

Alex ran Robbie through the paces and was handing over the keys, when she heard a honk in her driveway. She made Robbie promise to set the alarm every time he left the house and even when he was in the house. She hoped that he'd make good on his promise. He helped her carry out her bags and waved goodbye as the car pulled out of the driveway.

The flight was uneventful arriving on time at the Missoula airport. She was feeling refreshed after a short nap on the Learjet 35 and eager to get to the ranch. As she was getting off the plane, the co-pilot handed her a manila envelope. She looked at him questioningly and he just shrugged his shoulders. He told her to open it when she got into the private terminal.

While Alex waited for her luggage, she sat in the quiet terminal and opened the envelope. There were two pieces of cardboard taped together with a slight bulge. She pulled them apart and saw a key fob taped to the cardboard along with a note. She recognized Jules' writing.

"Thought you should have your own wheels while here. Dark blue Jeep Grand Cherokee 4 x 4 outside to the left." No signature. Alex wheeled her bags outside and walked to the left, pressing the unlock button on the remote until she saw taillights blinking. Understanding now why Sophie and Rick had not met her, she shelved her mild disappointment, loaded the SUV and headed to the ranch.

The two-hour trip seemed like an eternity to Alex. She wished she could go faster but stayed within a few miles of the speed limit so she wouldn't chance an encounter with the state police or, worse, the local yokels from the small towns she was passing through. At 1:30 p.m. she turned onto the road that led up to the ranch and soon was in Sophie's embrace.

Sophie got her settled in her old room then fed her lunch. Rick came up from the horse barn and told Alex he wanted to walk her through the security and communications systems that had been completed yesterday. They were testing them today and he thought it would be a good way to get her up to speed. She told him that she'd be available as soon as she unpacked.

They spent the rest of the day reviewing the systems and getting educated on the solar and wind structures providing the power for the ranch radio system as well as backup power for the rest of the ranch in case of a commercial power failure. By nightfall Alex was tired and excused herself to go up to her room. Sophie had explained earlier that Claire and Mickey would be in the rooms with the adjoining bath. Alex had asked who Mickey was, then remembered that Jules had called him when they were out riding a couple of weeks ago. Alex, trying not to feel hurt about being in the dark on some of the plans, brooded until she fell asleep.

Jules returned to LA on Monday and met with the field team that she had put into place to provide security for Claire at the ranch. Mickey, a lawyer turned martial arts expert, had been tapped as Claire's bodyguard. Mickey was drop-dead gorgeous, and no one would guess that he was getting close to forty. He was in incredible shape. They had all discussed the best cover for the operation, settling on Mickey playing Mickey. Jake thought that it was entirely possible for Claire's fictitiously created family, who were rich textile barons from Turin, Italy, to hire a bodyguard for their daughter.

In researching Claire's cover, Mickey had learned that the Turin economy was driven by four industrial sections, including the motor car industry lead by Fiat, the coffee industry, the sparkling wine industry, and the hundred year old textile industry, which employed over six thousand people in Turin and produced over fifteen million garments a year. The textile industry would provide the tie to Sophie. She had worked in the industry before immigrating into the States.

The only problem with this approach was that Mickey could be traced back to ISS. Too many coincidences for Jules' taste. Mickey who liked the idea of not having to hide who he was, cautiously suggested, "We leak that I had some sort of disagreement, I quit and went freelance. What do you think?"

Jules nodded her head and Jake said, "I'll get going on it immediately and make sure all finances are in place. Let's go over Bill and Marcy's cover and make sure it's going to work."

Bill Trehorn and Marcy Contrares were playing the role of a couple on their honeymoon at the dude ranch. The other guests would understand if they didn't want to take part in group activities. Bill had been with ISS for six years and was one of the best undercover operatives they had. Before coming to ISS, he had been a CHIP officer, experienced with motorcycles and ATVs. He was still quite attractive with his ever-present tan and graying temples. Marcy was from the

DC office and didn't have much field experience but was a crackerjack computer expert. She was a natural blond, buxom, half Bill's age, so with the current trend of older men searching for half-their-age second wives, they made a plausible couple.

When they finished, Jake took over and showed aerials of the ranch, schematics and actual photos of the security and communication systems, extraction plans, and other information that Jake thought necessary to fully brief them. They broke for lunch then returned to wrap things up.

Jules powered on the computer and started showing them pictures of the Bentworths and key ranch personnel. When she got to Alex's picture she quickly looked away from the screen. Jake noticed that she stumbled a little when talking about Alex's role. He shot her a look and she nodded almost imperceptibly that she was okay. When they finished, Marcy and Bill picked up their new identities and background material and made plans to rehearse before they went up to the ranch mid-week.

Jules was stowing the laptop in her bag when Jake asked her if she was ready to go out to the Bentworth's estate. In the car he asked if she was having reservations about Alex. *What an understatement*, she thought, *but not for the same reasons Jake might have.* She told Jake that the time she had spent with Alex in Seattle had heightened her level of comfort with Alex's ability to do the job. Jake chewed on that for a while, not at all convinced that everything was ok back at the ranch, so to speak.

###

Bentworth was expecting them. One of the household staff showed them to Bentworth's office which had just been swept for bugs that morning by ISS personnel. Bentworth was very anxious. Jules had called him on Tuesday to let him know that they were ready to execute the plan to move Claire to a safe house, but she failed to give him any details and set up this meeting instead.

"Jake, Jules, come in, please. Have a seat," said Bentworth, motioning to a couch and chair grouping around a table in the corner of his home office. Once Jake and Jules were settled, he sat in one of the chairs. Bentworth was a man used to being in charge. He got right to the heart of the topic. "So, where are we?"

Jules took the lead. "Mr. Bentworth, we're ready to move Claire within the next few days. First of all, allow me to apologize for keeping you in the dark these last couple of weeks. We felt, and still feel, that the least number of people knowing where Claire is going makes it safer. I'm sure that no one here would purposely tell anyone where Claire is, but they might inadvertently slip and provide a clue. We're pretty sure, Mr. Bentworth, that the kidnapping was personal so any potential for a leak must be addressed." She let that sink in for a moment then asked if he had any questions about the way they wanted to operate. Bentworth, though visibly unhappy, said he understood.

"Good, then." Jules went about explaining the precautions at the ranch and a little about Alex, to Mr. Bentworth. There were no questions; Mr. Bentworth, was chewing his lip nervously.

"There is one other thing before we talk about how we want to get Claire out of here. Mr. Bentworth, as part of our plan we need to make sure that Claire isn't in communication with anyone during the time she is in the safe house, unless we arrange it in advance. I know this is going to be a hardship for both Claire and you, but it is essential. If anyone even has an inkling where to find her and I remind you that there are sophisticated listening devices that can pick up a whisper a mile away, it could compromise the entire operation. Finally, we've installed a secure server at the safe house location, but even email is risky. We need to have your one hundred percent compliance with this. Will you guarantee this?" Jules thought, *I'll put money on Bentworth blowing up right now!*

Bentworth was red in the face but remembering the small stroke he had in the past, restrained himself. He was being asked by these people to cut off all contact with his daughter. "Would someone from your office be calling to update me on a regular basis?"

"Yes," answered Jake. "Either Jules or I will touch base with you two or three times a week to give you an update on her wellbeing. Mr. Bentworth, I hope I'm not out of line here, so I'm going to take a chance and hope you'll forgive me if I crossed some boundary. I've been to the safe house. In fact, I supervised the installation of the property-wide radio system and security system and feel very confident that your daughter will be safe. In addition, I spent time with the two principal owners of the property, and I can tell you without reservation, that they'd sooner sell their souls to the devil before they'd put your daughter in harm's way.

"One of them is an ex-military man with combat experience. He's smart and knows how to handle himself in a crisis. I know it's difficult putting your faith and trust in the hands of strangers but Mr. Bentworth, if you want us to catch those bastards who took your daughter, then you've got no choice. We either do it Jules' way, or we don't do it!"

Man to man talk, thought Jules as she surreptitiously rolled her eyes. Bentworth got up and walked around the office, pouring himself an amber liquid from a sideboard full of crystal bottles. He was looking out the window across the ocean for a moment then turned, downed the rest of his drink, and went back to the conference area where he sat down and addressed both Jake and Jules.

"All right. We'll play it your way, but you had better catch those bastards so I can—" He trailed off, afraid to share what his plans were once the kidnappers were apprehended.

"Good man," said Jake sincerely. "We can talk to Claire and Elena now, if you're ready," said Jules.

Bentworth picked up the phone on his desk, dialed a three-digit number and said, "Would you please get Claire and join Ms. Law and Mr. Lawrence in my study? Thank you, honey. Yes, yes, I'm really fine."

Bentworth paced while Jules and Jake waited patiently for Elena and Claire. Three or four minutes later, time enough for Bentworth to down another drink, Elena rapped quietly and came in with Claire trailing behind her. Jules hadn't seen Claire in a few weeks and got up to give her a brief hug. Claire said hi to Jake and sat down between Jake and Jules, facing her father and stepmother. "What's going on?" Claire said.

"Honey," began Bentworth, "Jules and Jake are here to go over plans to move you to a safe house while they finish the investigation into your kidnapping. They told me they found a great place and that it is very safe."

"Where is it, Daddy?" asked Claire with mild curiosity.

"Jules and Jake feel it's better that none of us knows the location for now, but if you don't like it when you get there, we can see about doing something else, okay?"

Jules and Jake shuddered in their shoes. *What kind of a stunt is this?* They both thought simultaneously. Jules butted in. "Claire, we've gone to a lot of trouble to find this place for you. Both Jake and I spent several days there, and I know you are going to like it. I think you should go in with the expectation and commitment that you are going to give it a real shot for at least four weeks. If after that you don't feel the same way Jake and I do, we can have a pow wow with your father and Elena to figure out alternatives. How do you feel about this?"

"I think it's fair. I can go with that," answered Claire a little cavalierly.

God, a potential disaster averted, thought Jake. *Thank heavens that Jules is quick on her feet.* Before Bentworth could do more damage, Jake took control of the conversation.

"Okay, Claire, here's the plan. First of all, you should pack today and have your bags ready to leave at a moment's notice. We plan to move you out on Monday or Tuesday. Your father will get a call from us when we're in route here to pick you up.

Jake and Jules tag teamed the explanation of the extraction for the better part of an hour. When the logistics were out of the way, Claire piped up. "So, what do I pack?"

Jules pulled a printed list out of her lap-top bag, which Claire skimmed quickly. "That's all? Jeans, shirts, underwear, tennis shoes, sweaters, jacket, toiletries, and medications?"

"That's right. You really won't need anything more and if you do, we can get it for you. If you want to add a pair of riding boots and gloves and take your iPod, you could throw those in, too."

"Where are you sending me, to wilderness camp?" asked Claire.

"Hardly," answered Jules. "Just trust me on this. Just make sure you have your stuff packed by tomorrow at noon in case there is a change of plans. Anything else folks? Claire?"

No one spoke up, but it was apparent that they all had one big question; *Where were they taking Claire, and would she be all right?*

Bidding them good day, Jules and Jake made their way into the hall when they encountered the Bentworth's housekeeper, Rosa. Jake and Jules left without further ceremony and held their thoughts until they got on the highway back to the office.

"Gosh Jules, do you think the housekeeper overheard anything?"

"Jake, I sure hope not. We have no idea the length of time she might have been standing there. We had better rethink our plans here."

"Maybe you're right. Even if the destination is confidential, and if she is in league with the kidnappers, they'll know about the extraction plans. Can you get the flight moved up on such short notice?"

"I don't know Jake, but I'm going to try right now. Can you please call Mickey? I don't think we need to move up the departure time for Bill and Marcy. They made their calls without worrying about anyone overhearing them. All ISS vehicles were equipped with a 'Briefcase Bug Detection System' and nothing but their cell phones were recognized and allowed. Anything else that tried to breech, was locked out.

Jules got home around ten and called Alex. She hadn't talked to her since she left Seattle on Monday morning. *Oh, shit, maybe it's too late. It's eleven in Montana,* thought Jules, but Alex answered.

"Hi! Thought you had written me off."

"Not yet," answered Jules, taking Alex's barb seriously. "I take it you found the SUV?"

"Yes, thanks. It's nice not to have to beg to borrow my aunt's truck if I want to go somewhere."

"Well, that was partially the reason we sprung for the car."

"So, it's really a get-a-way car should we need it," joked Alex.

"Precisely," answered Jules gravely. "Under the front mat on the driver side, there is a compartment with cash and a Glock with clips. You need a five-digit code to open it — without a crowbar, that is. Ready to memorize?"

"Yes. Go ahead."

"Four, one, one, two, zero," read Jules.

"Any significance to that number?"

"Think about it. If you guess, you win a prize," snickered Jules.

Alex ignored Jules' supposedly cute riddle and asked, "What's up?"

"I called for two reasons. First to tell you that I need you to be at the Camas airport in Missoula at 10:30 p.m. tomorrow night. Bring Rick and no one else. We've had to change plans and get her out tomorrow."

"Something's gone wrong, hasn't it?" Alex couldn't hide the concern in her voice.

"Not really. We're just taking precautions. Wear your handgun and make sure Rick is armed. You can tell Rick and Sophie what I've told you tomorrow late afternoon, but no sooner. Okay?" Jules didn't wait for an answer. "Now listen Alex. Just before we're ready to come out of the terminal, I'll call you. Drive the SUV past the terminal entrance, turn around and head the opposite direction, stopping a little to the right of the door. Unlock the doors and pop the hatch. Claire and I will get into the back seat while Mickey loads the luggage. As soon as Mickey jumps in, drive off normally unless I tell you otherwise. We'll need Rick to keep a vigilant eye while Mickey loads."

"Okay. I got it. Are you sure you're not worried?"

"No, not at all," Jules fibbed. "What's the saying? A good defense is a good offense."

"Something like that. What's the other thing you called about?" asked an inquisitive Alex.

Jules glossed over Alex's question. "Do you want to go over the plan again just to make sure?

"No Jules, I got it. What else is going on? I feel like you are avoiding something."

With a sigh, Jules said, "How are you?"

"I'm okay Jules. I miss you, though." Alex wasn't going to tip toe around the whole situation.

"And are you doing okay with your Aunt?"

"Yes, she's as spectacular as ever, though she has done some mild prying as to whether you and I are getting along okay. Remember? We left for the airport in quite a huff."

"Mm-hmm. I remember. Alex, I'm beat and almost falling asleep on my feet. Tomorrow is going to be a very long day for both of us, so I'm saying goodnight. I'll see you tomorrow and we'll talk, okay? Don't forget the code."

"I won't. Four, one, one, two zero. Right?"

"Yes. Sleep well, angel."

Alex remembered what her mother used to say to her every night as she tucked her into bed and kissed her good night. "Dormire con gli angeli." Loosely translated it means sweet dreams, but literally it's "Sleep with the angels." Alex drifted off with warm thoughts hoping she hadn't deluded herself.

"I just got a call. They plan to move her in the next couple of days. No, I can't talk any louder. Pay attention. The plan is to move her either Monday or Tuesday. I'm betting they'll use the cover of night. We need to be ready to intercept them. Yes, I'm sure. Fine. Let's meet tomorrow. 4:00 p.m. at the usual place? Yes, tomorrow, Sunday. Listen, no screw-ups this time."

CHAPTER 11– The Extraction

Surely you do not disbelieve the prophecies, because you had a hand in bringing them about yourself. You don't really suppose, do you, that all your adventures and escapes were managed by mere luck, just for your sole benefit?

J.R.R. Tolkien

Sunday April 26

With less than two weeks before the first round of paying guests were scheduled to arrive, and more importantly, just a couple of days before the Bentworth entourage was due to arrive at the ranch, Sophie and Rick were working at a feverish pitch. There were cabins to deep clean and get ready.

Sophie totaled up the guests who would be with them during the first and second week of the season with the intent of ordering sufficient supplies. She put her menu together, based on a survey they did last year. A short time later, the computer spit out a list of supplies and provisions needed. The software program was pretty slick. It even emailed the supply list to various suppliers she regularly used.

Her summer help was due to arrive Wednesday, May sixth for a few days of orientation before the guests arrived on Sunday, May tenth. They were college kids who lived in nearby towns and counted on the summer job to earn their tuition and living money for the fall semester. Jeanne would take care of feeding them and if they wanted to stay at the ranch, there were extra bunks available.

Sophie was coming out of the office when Alex came down. "Morning sweetie. How did you sleep?"

"Like an angel," replied Alex with a genuine smile.

"Were you thinking about Franny?"

"Mm-hmm. Last night I remembered what she always said to me before I went to sleep. Remember?"

"Dormire con gli angeli," said Sophie. She felt a moment of melancholy followed by an ache in her chest. Franny, short for Francesca, had married Mario's brother Carlo six years before Sophie threw caution to the wind and moved to Montana to marry Mario, whom she had known only for a short while he was in Italy on an extended visit to relatives.

Franny was born in upstate New York, had gone to college and had an education degree. She was teaching in the elementary school in Missoula when she met Carlo. He fell hard. He was smitten with Franny and spent as much time with her as he could for weeks. A year later they were married. Alex was born eighteen months later and was already quite the hellion when Sophie arrived at the ranch to marry Mario.

Franny could have been resentful when Sophie arrived. Two couples living under the same roof could have been a recipe for a catastrophe, but Franny made it easy for Sophie. Franny spoke Italian and helped Sophie learn English which she spoke now with hardly any accent at all.

Franny was never jealous, never resentful of Sophie's occasional moods, taught her the business end of the ranch and allowed her to take an active part in Alex's upbringing. The two of them became very close. Sophie loved Franny more than she did her own sisters. When Franny and Carlo were killed, Sophie wanted to die and would have given anything to exchange her own life for Franny's, but knew she had to pull herself together for Alex. Franny would have expected nothing less.

Sophie tried to be a substitute mother and when she put Alex to bed, she'd say, "Dormire con gli angeli," until two weeks after Franny and Carlo died, Alex asked her to stop, explaining in a manner, way beyond her years, that it wasn't the same and it made her sad.

"Aunt Sophie, Aunt Sophie, where did you go?"

"Just thinking about your mother. God, what an extraordinary person she was, just like you!"

Slipping her arm around Sophie's waist, noting the tears in Sophie's eyes, Alex walked her towards the kitchen, trying to focus on the mundane. "Have you had breakfast yet?"

"Nope, I was waiting for you. Let's go see what we can scrounge up." Sophie, slowly recovering from her poignant memories, asked Alex if she would give her a hand in cleaning up a couple of the cabins.

"Sure. I think we ought to do the same in the two extra rooms upstairs. I'm expecting Claire and Mickey in any day now," offered Alex, hoping not to pique Sophie's curiosity too much.

"Okay, let's start in the house after breakfast. Do you think they'll be here tomorrow or Tuesday?"

"Hard to tell Aunt Sophie. Where's your better half this morning?"

"Rick? Don't let him know you think he's my better half. His head is big enough as is," teased Sophie. "He's down at the barn going through whatever it is he does opening season." Sophie knew exactly what he was doing, as she had her finger on every pulse of the ranch, just like Franny had taught her. "He'll be back up for lunch around one. Did you need to talk to him?"

"Nope. Nothing in particular," Alex fibbed.

Sophie made oatmeal and toast. They ate then went upstairs to get the two adjoining guest rooms ship-shape. Working together, they got both rooms ready in under an hour. When they finished, they grabbed a cart from the laundry and service area and headed for the first cabin south of the house.

The cabin hadn't been used since last fall. It was dusty and needed deeper cleaning. Sophie and Alex worked well together and in two hours, they were heading back to the house to start lunch.

Rick came up shortly before 1:00 p.m. He washed up and asked if there was anything he could do to help with lunch. Sophie waved him to the table and Alex served the sandwiches and fruit. Rick and Sophie drank iced tea and she had her favorite, Dr. Pepper, and not the diet stuff.

After a few bites of her sandwich, Alex cleared her throat and said, "I need to tell you some things. Let me start with the fact that this is confidential, to be kept between the three of us right now. Jules called late last night to tell me that they are bringing in Claire tonight. She wants Rick and me at the Camas airport at 10:30 p.m. to pick them up."

"I thought you said it would be Monday or Tuesday," Sophie mildly complained.

"The plan got changed. I'm not sure why, but I'm sure Jules will explain when we get back tonight."

Sophie asked who was coming in besides Claire, Mickey and Jules.

"I think that's it right now, Aunt Sophie."

"Okay, then. We'd better get to those other cabins and have them ready, just in case."

With that, they all scattered to attend to their duties. Sophie and Alex finished all the guest accommodations and came back to the house to make dinner. Rick joined them about six o'clock. He told Alex that they'd better leave around eight, to plan for contingencies like a flat tire or accident on the road. Alex excused herself to take a shower and said she'd be ready shortly. Rick and Sophie lingered over coffee and small talk.

"Is this change in plans something we should be worried about, Rick?" Sophie was wary.

"I don't think so, Sophie. I think Jules wouldn't be moving Claire at all if there were any danger. I'd guess that the real plan all along was to move her today and the Monday/Tuesday thing was a red herring."

"I hadn't thought of that," said Sophie. "Makes sense." She relaxed until Rick said,

"But just to be sure, when Alex and I leave, I want you to go down to the bunk house and hang out there until we get back."

"And what's my reason for going down on a Sunday night? Don't think so, Ricky-boy! I'm coming with the two of you." Rick didn't see any reason why she shouldn't come along, so he didn't argue, but didn't exactly say yes.

"Mr. Bentworth, this is Jules. Don't ask any questions, just listen and do exactly what I say. Are you alone? Okay. Do you have a radio or TV you can turn up?"

Bentworth answered, "Yes, I'm watching basketball."

"Turn up the TV. Loud. Good. There's been a change of plans. In about five minutes a catering van is going to pull up to the gate. Instruct your people to let it in. When it gets to the front door, go outside and talk to the two people in the van. Point towards the garage and give them instructions to back in. Are you with me so far?"

"Yes, but what's going on."

"Just listen," snapped Jules. "After you've talked to them, go back inside the house and open the garage door of an empty bay. Wait for the van in the garage and when they start backing up, make like you're directing them. Once the van stops, go back inside and put Claire's bags by the door. Then wait. Got that?"

"Yes. I understand."

"We are moving Claire right now." Jules succinctly explained the remainder of the plans and hung up.

Three minutes later, Alfie's Catering van pulled up to the gate. One of Bentworth's employees at the guard shack asked the nature of their business and called up to the house. Mickey was driving, Marcy was riding shot gun, and Jake was ready to grab Claire. Bentworth must have given the order to let them in because in a minute the gate opened, and they were on their way up to the house without a search.

Bentworth was wound tightly, but gave a credible performance had someone been scanning with a laser long-distance listening device or watching with a high-powered scope. Ten minutes later the van was on its way out of the Bentworth estate.

Claire was obviously confused, but a reassuring nod from Jake settled her down in the van. Getting out of the estate wasn't a problem but getting out unnoticed might be another thing entirely. Marcy and Mickey were super vigilant, watching for anything that could signal an attempt at hijacking the van or their cargo. They drove until they picked up the Pacific Coast Highway, heading west towards Oxnard until they reached their turn off. They turned north and headed for Camarillo Airport, where a private jet was waiting for them. A few minutes later, they were on Aviation Drive, pulling up to a double gate near the terminal. Mickey showed the guard identification and the gates opened. Everyone was on high alert. A sniper shot was not out of the question. Mickey maneuvered the van with its rear facing the steps of a Learjet 45.

Jules ordered a Learjet 45 because of its extended range. It could go twenty-one hundred miles without refueling if necessary. Missoula was about fourteen hundred miles from Malibu. That left them a cushion of seven hundred miles should they have to head to an alternative location. Jules fervently hoped they wouldn't need it.

Earlier this morning the usual charter service filed a flight plan to Dallas according to Jules' orders. With new software, it would be a matter of minutes to revise the flight plan once on board and get clearance to head to Montana.

Mickey and Marcy got out of the van and opened the back doors forming a screen between the van and the bottom of the jet's stairs. Mickey got out first, sandwiched Claire between Jake and himself, and hurriedly marched her up the stairs to the comparative safety of the cabin. Jules was already on board. Jake and the co-pilot loaded the suitcases in to the baggage area, then Jake got back inside the van.

Jules was leaning into the cockpit, giving the pilot instructions to change the destination from Dallas to Missoula, when the co-pilot got on-board, invited Jules into the cockpit, and closed the door. Neither the pilot nor co-pilot was fazed by the last-minute change request. They had flown extensively for ISS and knew that everything was subject to change at the last minute.

Mickey sat in the aisle seat next to Claire, who still looked dazed. When the pilot gave the thumbs up to Jules, she left the cockpit and returned to the cabin, taking a seat facing Claire. The engines started and the plane began to move. Looking out the window Jules saw that the van had pulled away but was waiting by the gate until the jet headed towards the runway.

The co-pilot came out and asked them to fasten their seat belts for takeoff. She had been on the crew of many of Jules' flights and had a crush on her. Before she returned to the cockpit, she laid her hand on Jules' shoulder and let it linger while she told them she'd let them know when it was okay to unbuckle the seat belts.

Mickey made gaga eyes at Jules, who rolled hers. Five minutes later the jet lifted off and Mickey exchanged a relieved look with Jules.

Claire asked, not addressing anyone in particular, "May I talk now?"

Mickey told her she could chatter up a storm if she wanted. Someone else might have taken Mickey's comment as patronizing, but Claire didn't seem to be bothered. "Can either of you tell me why plans changed? I was expecting to leave tomorrow or Tuesday."

"Claire," began Mickey, "just a simple precaution in the event that somehow our plan had been discovered."

"So, nothing to worry about?" Claire said halfheartedly.

"Absolutely not," answered Mickey in his best convincing voice. "Why don't we all relax for a while, get something to eat and drink, then we'll go over your cover story. I think you're going to like it! Okay?"

"Okay, is Mickey your real name?"

"Yes, it is."

"Will you be using your real name wherever we are going?"

"Yes, and I'll be using my real profession, bodyguard extraordinaire," he said with an infectious laugh.

With that Claire smiled then turned towards the window to watch the lights of the greater Los Angeles area disappear as the plane rose sharply and banked to the right. The co-pilot came out, informed them that the flying time was just short of three hours and then took their drink orders.

She returned and brought Claire a soda, a Johnny Walker Black for Mickey and a Glenlivet for Jules. It was a rule of ISS not to drink while on duty, but it appeared that Jules, as an owner, had given a special dispensation when she asked for "Glenlivet." Mickey had never known Jules to get rattled, let alone drink anything but wine. *Maybe there was more at stake than appeared.* He'd have to keep his eyes open.

Color was coming back into Claire's cheeks and she seemed to be relaxing. However, both Mickey and Jules knew that with PTSD a flashback episode could strike at any time. They needed to keep her focused on some sort of task but didn't want to go over her cover story too far in advance and create more anxiety

The co-pilot came out again and asked them if they would like anything to eat. *Terrific, thought Mickey. This might divert her attention for a few more minutes.* The choice wasn't great, but it gave them something to joke about. Jules asked for the chicken salad sandwich with carrot sticks, Mickey chose the oversized roast beef with kettle chips, and Claire wanted the club with pretzels.

When they finished, Jules excused herself and tapped on the door to the cockpit. The co-pilot slid it open. Mickey and Claire couldn't hear what she was saying, but she seemed relaxed when she came back, the love-sick co-pilot on her heels. She removed the remnants from their dinner and asked if they wanted their drinks refilled. They all declined.

Jules got up and retrieved a briefcase from the seat behind her. "Okay, Claire, ready to learn your new identity?"

"Sure," she said nervously. "Who am I?"

"You are Clara Rivetti, a distant cousin of Sophie Martini who owns a cattle and dude ranch. You have come from Italy to spend the summer with her family." Jules painstakingly went over the details several times until she was confident that Claire would be able to live the legend.

"Tonight, Sophie's niece, Dr. Martini and Sophie's partner Rick will be picking us up at the airport, then we have a two-hour drive to the ranch." Jules heart ached when she said Alex's name.

"Dr. Martini, the one I talked to over the phone?"

"Yes. She agreed to leave her practice and treat you at the ranch. She was brought up there and knows every inch of the property. You won't be stuck in a room out there."

Claire, suddenly animated, asked, "So, this Sophie speaks Italian?"

"Yup, she's the real thing. She came over to the states when she was twenty to marry a fellow named Mario."

"Where is Sophie from?"

"Turin," answered Jules. It looked like Claire was getting into the cover, so she let her lead the conversation.

"Torino, huh? What did she do before she came to the states?"

"She was a seamstress, working in one of the better-known design houses there."

"And she gave all that up to marry this dude Mario and move to Montana sight unseen?"

Without the slightest bit of sarcasm in her voice, Jules said, "I guess love renders the head useless."

Mickey and Claire laughed. They had no way of knowing that Jules was referencing her own situation.

Claire, showing off, asked her next question in Italian. "Potro avere a parlare Italiano?" *Will I be able to speak Italian?*

Jules, surprising both Claire and Mickey quipped back, "Solo se si desidera." *Only if you wish.*

With astonishment, Claire exclaimed, "Jules, I didn't know you spoke Italian!"

"I picked up a little when I was stationed there years ago."

Changing the subject, Claire stated, "I can't believe my father agreed to all of this. Who convinced him?"

"Your father wants to try and help you begin to put the kidnapping behind you and have a chance at some normalcy. It was Dr. Metuchi, who convinced him," answered Jules truthfully.

Claire wrung her hands in her lap and didn't say anything for a while. Remembering Alex's thoughts about Claire's potential involvement, Jules scanned Claire's face for any signs that could tip them off to Claire's reaction. Her face didn't change, though she appeared to be pensive. She sat quietly for a minute or two, then resumed the briefing.

Once again, Claire asked multiple questions until the co-pilot announced that they would be landing in twenty minutes. Upon touching down, Jules asked Claire how she was doing. Claire said that she felt pretty good. Jules hoped that she was telling the truth.

At 8:00 p.m., Alex came downstairs. She had changed into snug black jeans and a pinpoint light blue shirt that showed off her curves. Playing the red neck cowboy, Rick whistled, "Who you getting all gussied up for, me?"

Alex ignored his teasing and said, "Let's roll."

Sophie came out from the kitchen and grabbed a jacket from the hooks in the foyer. It dawned on Alex that Sophie thought she was going along. *Oh great!* she reflected to herself. She reviewed Jules' instructions. *You and Rick come alone.* Alex groaned inwardly, *how am I going to handle this?*

"Aunt Sophie, uh, Jules told me that just Rick and I should go to the airport. There won't be room with three of them coming. The SUV only has room for five."

Rick responded, "Alex, I don't want Sophie here alone. Jules can go pound salt. Sophie is coming with us, even if she has to sit on my lap!"

Christ reflected Alex. *This is going to be one long summer.* She replied to Rick, "Rick, may I see you for a moment?" He begrudgingly nodded and followed her into the office, leaving Sophie in the great room with her mouth hanging open.

"I understand your concern about leaving Sophie here alone, but Rick, I think she really would be safer here than with us. I'd bet dollars to donuts that Jules is worried about how Sophie might react in a difficult situation. You and I, well, we've been faced with life and death decisions and know how to handle ourselves. I don't think we want to take any chance with putting Sophie in a, ah, stressful situation, if you catch my drift. Let's get Matt, she seems to like him, to come up and sit with her."

Rick thought about it and finally, not liking it a bit, acknowledged that Alex had a valid point. "Maybe you're right. Let's go break the news."

It wasn't pretty, but Sophie relented, and Rick called down for Matt. Rick turned to Sophie and said, "Just tell him that you have some work for him to do. Make him do inventory or something but keep him here until we call you. Promise?"

Sophie resentfully promised and gave Rick and Alex stingy kisses. Her goodbye was chilly.

The trip was uneventful, and they arrived just before 10:00 p.m. with thirty minutes to kill. "Want some coffee?" asked Rick. Alex agreed and input information into the navigation system, hoping for a coffee shop close to the airport.

Mickey left the aircraft first, followed by Claire, then Jules in rapid succession. They went directly into the terminal, Mickey's hand on his gun concealed under his sports coat, the entire time. Mickey waited for their luggage, while Jules and Claire went into the rest room. When they returned, the luggage had arrived. He took a quick trip to the men's room, while Jules acted as sentry.

Jules dialed Alex who picked up on the first ring.

"Ready Jules?"

"Yes, come and get us."

Jules saw the SUV pass by the doors, turn around and then stop exactly where she wanted. She pushed open the terminal doors, looked to her left and right and took Claire's arm, almost dragging her to the SUV. Rick was already out of the SUV and stood with his back to it, keeping an eye out for potential trouble. Mickey got the last bag loaded, scurried around to the other side of the car and jumped in at the same time Rick backed his butt into the front seat.

Alex didn't waste a second. She took off smoothly and expertly maneuvered the back roads to State Route 200, heading west to pick up Interstate 90, then State Route 93 South. Landing at Camas added another half hour to the trip but traffic in and out was a lot less than at Missoula County Airport, making it easier to observe and identify potential problems.

Jules made the introductions, shook hands with Rick and squeezed Alex's shoulder. No one relaxed, except for Claire, who quickly fell asleep with her head on Jules' shoulder. Jules and Mickey recounted the details of the extraction from Malibu and before they knew it, Alex was turning south off of Interstate 90 on to Route 93. If anyone were going to attempt to hijack the car, it would have been on the back roads from the airport to Route 200 or now, anywhere along Route 93.

"Alex are you doing okay? Driving under this kind of strain is tiring," said Jules with genuine concern.

"I'm good so far, Jules," said Alex, suppressing her desire to abandon the wheel and jump in the back seat and ravish Jules. *Tsk, tsk,* she admonished herself. *How immature can I get?*

They almost made the drive to the ranch without any incidents. About five miles from the ranch turnoff, they blew a tire. The pop startled them all. Alex skillfully handled the Jeep while Jules pushed Claire to the floor. Alex calmly pulled the SUV over to the shoulder and both Mickey and Rick warily jumped out, guns in hand.

Alex's peripheral vision detected a movement in the back seat and swung her body and arms to the right until she was facing toward the back. Claire had a gun and was pointing it toward Jules. Alex hadn't expected that at all. A moment later, regaining her composure, she ordered Claire to give her the gun.

"Give me the gun, Claire. Claire, hand me the gun right now, honey. Everything is okay. Rick and Mickey have things under control. Claire, do you hear me? Hand me the gun. You're okay, now."

Claire was non-responsive, frozen in a shooting position with the gun trained at Jules' head. Alex kept talking to Claire. "Claire, it's me, Dr. Martini. I'm going to reach for your gun, and you are going to lower it. Okay? Nice and slowly." Alex extended her right hand and reached for the barrel of the gun. "I'm just going to lower the gun, Claire. I won't take it from you."

Alex slowly pushed the barrel of the gun down towards the floor, talking quietly to Claire. Jules sprang and in an instant grabbed the gun from Claire's hand without resistance. Once Jules had wrested the gun from Claire's hand, Alex tried to assess what happened. *Did Claire mean to do Jules harm as part of her possible participation in the kidnapping scheme, or was she having a PTSD melt down and gotten confused as to who the good guys were.*

After the tire was changed, Rick took over the driving and Mickey rode in the front passenger seat. Alex and Jules had just gotten settled in the back seat with Claire who was still in a semi-catatonic state, between them.

As soon as they got back on the road, Jules asked Mickey if he had been able to tell what caused the blow out.

"No, ma'am, but it was on the sidewall. We'd better take a look at it tomorrow, when its light. Could be just a defective tire with a sidewall separation. If not, something hit us, maybe on purpose."

"Claire, how're you doing? Looks like we had a false alarm," said Jules, hoping indeed that it was a sidewall separation. Claire managed an "okay", but it was clear that she was still in shock.

Monday April 27

Thirty minutes more and they pulled into the ranch road. Rick called Sophie to let her know that she could send Matt back down to the bunk house in five minutes. He checked to see if anyone was hungry and he told Sophie that no one wanted anything to eat. They were all tired and ready for bed. Adrenaline waning, they pulled up in front of the house shortly before 1:30 a.m. Rick helped Mickey with the bags while Alex and Jules helped Claire into the house.

Sophie was waiting for them and knew right off that something was off kilter by the way Jules and Alex were flanking Claire. She gave Alex and Jules a hug and gently introduced herself to Claire, who looked unmistakably fatigued and barely able to stand on her own. Alex offered to take her up to her room.

Alex led Claire into the room that was connected by the Jack and Jill bathroom with the other bedroom where Mickey would be staying. "Claire, I know you don't know me yet, so maybe it will be hard for you to follow my instructions, but I'm asking you to give me the benefit of the doubt. It's been a very stressful day for you, and I want to make sure you take all of your medication. Is it someplace handy?"

"In my carry-on," mouthed Claire.

Alex brought the bag to her and she pulled out three prescription bottles. Alex went into the bathroom and returned with water. Claire took the water and dutifully downed the pills. Alex sat on the edge of the bed next to her. "If you still can't sleep even with the sleeping pill, wake up Mickey and he'll get me. We can try some relaxation techniques."

"Okay, Dr. Martini," said Claire numbly.

Alex put one arm around her shoulder and told her to try and relax, that the ranch was very safe and not to worry about what happened tonight. Everything was okay and they'd talk about it tomorrow.

Tears were streaming down Claire's cheeks. "But Dr. Martini I could have killed Jules!" she wailed.

"Claire, I understand what happened. Please don't let it worry you now. We'll dissect it tomorrow. You have got to get some rest."

"You're not angry with me?" cried Claire.

"No, Claire. I'm not angry with you."

Claire turned to Alex, and through her tears and whimpering said, "I'm so very sorry. I don't know what came over me."

"It's all right. You acted out of self-defense and what you did was perfectly reasonable for a person who has suffered what you have. Now I need you to let go of this right now," Alex said more sternly.

Wiping her tears and sniffling, Claire said that she would try. Alex offered to help her get ready for bed, but she said she was okay now. Hearing Mickey in the next room, Alex felt it was safe to leave her. She left the bedroom and locked the door from the hallway with the newly installed lock, so that Claire would have to pass through the bathroom and Mickey's room to leave.

When Alex got back to the great room, Sophie was deep in conversation with Jules. Jules looked at Alex, then back at Sophie. "I was briefly telling your Aunt about our encounter with the tire blow out and how it upset Claire." Alex got Jules' non-verbal message and knew she hadn't told Sophie about the gun incident.

Sophie said, "Poor girl," then changed the subject. "You two look beat. Jules, we've got a cabin all cleaned up a short walk from the house. I'll take you so you can settle in."

"Sophie, Claire doesn't really know Mickey yet and with the upset this evening, I'd rather stay in the house if I could, but I don't want to inconvenience anyone. The couch down here is just fine."

Alex tried to sound casual. "Jules, if you don't mind, you could bunk in with me. The room is big enough, so we won't be cramped. That way, we'll both be close if we need to tend to Claire. I will warn you, however, that I snore sometimes." Alex tried to end on a light note hoping to throw Sophie's finely tuned radar off the trail.

"Alex, that would be great, if you don't mind. That way, people can come down here and not have to tip toe around me. Good night Sophie, see you in the morning."

Jules started up the stairs without a backward glance at Alex. Alex told Sophie that she was going to turn in too and hugged her goodnight. Sophie didn't let Alex escape from the hug until she spoke softly in her ear. "I see you two girls are getting along pretty well now."

"Why yes, Aunt Sophie, we are. Seems this 'spook stuff' serves to bond even the most ardent rivals," she said with just a little bit of cheekiness. She dragged herself up the stairs and said good night to Rick as he was coming down from depositing the luggage in the rooms.

"Sophie I'm really tired, but I want to tell you what happened tonight," Rick said.

"Jules already did."

"She did? What did she tell you?" Sophie briefly recounted the sanitized version that Jules offered. He wondered if it was wise to tell her that Jules was held at gunpoint by Alex's patient. He decided against it for now. "It really was a good idea that you didn't come. Before I try and find my bed, I want you to know that you raised a magnificent young woman. She handled the Jeep and the girl like a professional."

Sophie looked at him with arched brow, but he was already leaning down with a kiss to her cheek. Sophie lingered a moment longer and decided to follow him.

Alex tapped on the door to her own childhood bedroom across from the rooms Mickey and Claire were occupying, and went in. Jules was sitting on the edge of the bed talking on the phone. "Yes, Mr. Bentworth. We arrived safely. She's fine, sleeping now. No, Mr. Bentworth, there weren't any problems. Yes, I remember what I promised. I'll arrange a call later this week. Certainly. If anything changes I'll let you know. Thank you, Mr. Bentworth. Good night."

By the time Jules was finished with the call, Alex was in the shower. She made it quick, toweled off and came out in a woven cotton, waffle patterned bathrobe. Jules had laid her suitcase on top of Alex's desk and was rummaging around for something. "You can hang your things in the closet if you like and I'll make room in the dresser too." Jules smiled and thanked her as she walked into the bathroom and closed the door.

Alex moved T-shirts out of the bottom drawer of her dresser, then pulled down the comforter and sheet. Lying in bed, she tried to read print outs from the web on new experimental treatments for PTSD, but who was she kidding? She couldn't concentrate. All she could think about was the distance that Jules had created between the two of them. Tonight's events probably would serve to widen the gulf more. She knew that when there is emotional closeness, the physical distance between two people shrinks, but Jules was using the physical distance between the two of them to blunt the emotional connection.

Alex shook her head in frustration then, without knowing why, remembered the tag line from the movie, 'The Painted Veil'. "Sometimes the greatest journey is the distance between two people." It seemed that Jules was not ready to take that journey with Alex.

Jules came out in an oversized T-shirt that reached mid-thigh. Alex caught a whiff of her bath gel, transporting her back a week ago when they were entwined in each other's arms. An ache passed through her chest as if she had lost something that she could never get back.

"It's a Ruger LC 380 semiautomatic. It wasn't racked." Jules said. "She probably got it from her Dad, or if she is complicit with the kidnapping, from one of her partners. That leaves me a little cold. She must have traveled with it in her carryon and put it in her coat pocket when we went to the restroom. This is one contingency I didn't plan for," said Jules.

Alex could tell that Jules was deeply disturbed. "Did you tell Bentworth?"

"No. I'll have Jake go over tomorrow and talk to him. I don't want him yanking her out."

Alex didn't know what more to say, so she asked, "Will you be okay Jules?" she said moving closer to her. "I know you're conflicted, and the incident tonight probably hasn't helped."

Jules covered her eyes with both hands and groaned, "Alex, I can't do this. Not now. You know I'm agonizing, and I've got to keep my distance until everything is resolved. Tonight, just proves that I'm right. What if she had pointed that gun at you?"

Alex, taking a hand in hers, said, "Jules, I think tonight proves that even though we have feelings for each other, we can still be logical, professional, and work together."

"God, Alex, you have no idea how I felt when you reached to lower the gun!"

"How did you feel?"

"Like if anything happened to you, how could I live with myself, dragging you into this." She took her hand back from Alex and bent over covering her head and eyes again.

"What else, Jules? What else did you feel?"

In an agonizing voice barely above a whisper, Jules hoarsely said, "Like I just found you and you might be gone in an instant."

Alex was surprised. Jules, by her own admission, always had a tight lid on anything that remotely resembled an emotion, but now her emotions were on the loose, running around a corral like a horse trying to evade a bridle. She gently took Jules' right hand away from her eyes and made Jules look at her. "But honey, did you feel like you had to make a choice between Claire, yourself or me? Remember, last Sunday in Seattle, you told me that is what you feared, and this is why you couldn't be involved?"

Barely moving her lips, Jules said, "I remember. No, I didn't feel like that."

"Darling, you can't let feelings of future guilt stop you from caring about a person. Even if we had met under different circumstances, without all this intrigue, in a nano second, either of the two of us could be taken from each other." Alex let that sink in before she continued. "In situations like tonight, I'm always going to defer to you. You're the expert and I trust you. I also know that you'll defer to me when it comes to Claire's mental state because I am the expert and you trust me."

Jules was unable to combat Alex's logic. She just sat there immobile.

Do you want me to set up the roll away cot or do you want to sleep in the bed with me?" asked Alex again.

"You know what I want Alex, but I can't—"

Alex stopped Jules from finishing her sentence by putting two fingers across her mouth. Jules looked at Alex with longing. Still wrestling with her emotions, she flung herself into Alex's arms. Their mouths met in a hungry kiss and their bodies melted against each other. Alex reached for the hem of Jules' T-shirt and pulled it off her. Laying her down on the bed, she continued kissing her, while Jules reached up and untied the belt on Alex's robe.

Running her hands over Alex's smooth shoulders and breasts underneath the robe set Jules on fire. Alex couldn't wait any longer to feel her skin against Jules' skin. She shrugged off the robe and fell upon Jules, who was only too happy to feel Alex's body pressed against her own. They heaved with passion, hands and mouths exploring each other's fevered bodies. Jules rolled Alex off of her and sat up pulling Alex onto her lap. Alex wrapped her legs around Jules and laid her head on Jules' shoulder, nibbling gently.

Jules ran her hand through Alex's silky hair while she bent her head to kiss the crook of Alex's neck. She alternated between kissing and dragging her tongue from Alex's neck to her collar bone. Moments later Alex felt Jules' hands on her breasts caressing her nipples until they were so hard it seemed that they would burst from the pleasure. Reaching forward and sliding her hand between Jules and herself, she began touching Jules, eliciting a fevered moan. Jules responded by sensuously moving one hand down across Alex's stomach, lingering for a moment, before dipping between her slightly parted legs. Alex was more than ready.

They were covered with a sheen of sweat and their bodies were surging against each other. Jules thrust her fingers into Alex, sending her into spasms. Losing track of time, Jules sped up, following Alex's rhythm, while Alex continued to touch Jules with insistent fingers. They were in tune with each other's body, each of them wanting to give pleasure to the other, not concerned with their own gratification. Without words they rode each other's waves of passion until they both cried out together.

Lying in bed, facing each other still flooded with sexual and emotional release, Jules stretched to turn off the light. When she burrowed back into Alex's arms, she said, "We have to talk about this tomorrow or at least one of these days."

Alex smiled, kissed her tenderly and joked, "talk is cheap."

With resignation Jules said, "But this," referring to their emotional involvement, "could get expensive down the road." Alex understood. Jules was talking about the toll it would take on their emotional state.

###

"George, was that the people from ISS?"

"Yes Elena. Everything is fine. Jules said that Claire was at the safe house and sleeping."

"George, I wish that I had known that they were taking her today instead of Monday or Tuesday like they told us. I didn't even get a chance to say goodbye."

George knew that Elena was in a snit and that she probably didn't believe him when he explained earlier that he didn't know they were coming. He knew it wouldn't be worth reviewing the facts again. Once Elena was in this kind of mood only time helped. "Elena, I'll try to arrange a call between you and Claire so that you can talk to her. All right? Can we go to sleep now?"

"Thank you darling," Elena responded, kissing Bentworth on his lips and snuggling into him.

CHAPTER 12 –Cat and Mouse

A mouse does not run into the mouth of a sleeping cat.

Estonian proverb, translated by Ilse Lehiste

Monday April 27 (cont.)

Mickey went to bed around 2:00 a.m. and set his watch alarm to go off at two different times. He got up twice to check on Claire. Each time she was sleeping soundly. Even though he had less than five hours of sleep he got up, showered and shaved. He remembered what sharing a bathroom was like. No telling how long he'd be waiting with a full bladder if Claire had gotten up first. After getting dressed in jeans, flannel shirt and tennis shoes, he plugged in his laptop to review the ranch layout. He opened up an email with the security system pdf attachments he had sent himself before they left. He was hungry and could use a cup of coffee, but he didn't intend to leave Claire. There was a faint tap on his door. He opened it and found Rick with a steaming cup of coffee. "How'd you know?"

"Your room is right over mine. I heard footsteps, then the shower going, so I thought I'd see if you needed a cup of coffee as badly as I did."

"Bless you my child," said Mickey. "Want to come in?"

"No thanks Mickey. Sophie will be up soon, and I want to help her get breakfast for everyone. She planned on a buffet around 8:30 a.m. or so. Truthfully I don't remember if she told everyone that last night."

"She did. Thanks, and I mean thanks for last night too. You and Alex are real pros. See you downstairs later."

Rick was filling the large coffee urn with water when Sophie came in. "Hi my love," she cooed. He stopped what he was doing and held his arms open for her. She snuggled against him. He nibbled her neck and murmured, "Darling, I'm your sous chef all week. I'll check on ranch happenings between chopping and slicing! Besides, it will give me a reason to stick close to the house."

"Well, then, let's get cracking. Matt and I made a breakfast casserole, biscuits and banana bread last night. The kid's a pretty good cook. Want to finish with the coffee and then give me a hand with the plates and silverware?"

Rick said with a suggestive smile and a bit of a leer, "The answer, for you, Sophie, is always yes." He laughed lightly at Sophie's blush, turned and lugged the coffee urn into the dining room. Next he went to the pantry and got napkins, swatting Sophie's rump as she was bending to put the casserole in the oven to heat. When he finished, he returned to the kitchen, where Sophie had little containers of jam, honey and butter ready for the table. He juggled them expertly on a tray and tossed out over his shoulder, "Sous chef, ha! More like a mule!" Sophie laughed and swatted him back with a dish towel.

After getting everything else into the dining room, they sat together at the kitchen table to enjoy what probably would be their last quiet cup of coffee until fall. Rick groaned in delight after his first sip. "Where did you get the Segafredo?"

"Online of course. It's not like they carry it at the corner grocery store. We're lucky to get Starbucks in Missoula."

"Sophie, I knew a long time ago that I was deeply and irrefutably in love with you. Must have been because you are Italian, like the coffee."

###

Mickey could hear Claire. He discreetly called out and asked if she needed anything, to which she replied that she was fine. Twenty minutes later she knocked on the bathroom door that lead into his room. Claire was dressed, also in blue jeans and a pastel plaid shirt. She had on some sort of boots. They exchanged small talk and headed downstairs for breakfast. Sophie and Rick joined them at the buffet table, not waiting for Alex or Jules.

Alex woke up around 7:30 a.m. She intended to get up to help Sophie with breakfast, but she heard Rick and Mickey talking so she knew Rick was helping. She lay quietly in bed, her legs entwined with Jules' relishing the closeness. She did not want to disturb Jules, who was sleeping soundly.

Alex kept reviewing the incident in the car trying to memorize the sequence of events and Claire's reactions. Part of her job was to diagnose if Claire was acting or if she'd had a bona fide PTSD episode. She didn't know what Jules had planned today but she wanted to spend several hours with Claire reviewing the treatment notes that Dr. Metuchi had forwarded and getting a feel for Claire. Alex knew she was good at her job, but nevertheless was having serious doubts on her ability to handle Claire if it turned out she was truly pathological. She soothed herself, *Just pre-therapy jitters. I can do this.*

Jules woke up just after 8:00 a.m. She stretched quietly and untangled her legs gently, then rolled over to see if Alex was awake. "Morning. Have you been awake long?"

"About half an hour. I've been going over the gun incident with Claire. If it fits with what you have planned for today, I want to spend several hours with her."

"Sounds like that would be a good idea. Alex, do you think the episode in the car was related to her PTSD or did she mean to shoot me?"

"I don't know Jules. She sure exhibited all the signs of a PTSD episode but maybe she's just a good actress. Give me some time with her and I'll have a better idea."

"Fair enough," replied Jules, as she grabbed her T-shirt slipped it over her head and arms and headed for the bathroom.

Bentworth was coming down the main stairs with a suitcase in hand. "Good morning Rosa. How are you today?"

"Just fine Mr. Bentworth. Are you going on a trip?"

"Yes, afraid so."

"Where to this time?" chatted Rosa amiably.

"Just up to San Francisco for a couple of days, Rosa."

"You want some breakfast before you go, Mr. Bentworth?"

"No thanks, Rosa. I'll have something on the plane. Would you please tell Mrs. Bentworth that I expect to be home around 8:00 p.m. tomorrow night?"

"Of course, Mr. Bentworth. Will you want dinner when you get home?"

"Yes. How about asking Serena to make that old fashion pot roast I like?"

"Okay. I'll tell her. One more thing, Mr. Bentworth."

"Yes Rosa, what is it?"

"I noticed that Miss Claire is not here. Is everything all right?"

"Yes, Rosa. She left yesterday to enter an intense treatment program. She's just fine. I got a call last night."

"Is it nearby? Will we be able to visit her?"

"I'm afraid not, Rosa. I know how much you and Claire like each other, but it's a total immersion therapy. No visitors for three months."

"I hope it works. Miss Claire just hasn't been herself."

"Thank you for your concern and all your help these last months, Rosa. It would have been much harder without you."

"Thank you, Mr. B. Try and have a good trip."

As soon as Mr. Bentworth closed the front door, Rosa dashed back to the kitchen to give the cook Mr. Bentworth's dinner request. She told Serena that she had a little errand to run and she'd be back in an hour in case Mrs. Bentworth asked for her.

###

Everyone was still at the breakfast table when Jules and Alex came downstairs. "Good afternoon," teased Rick.

"Morning," Alex and Jules said in unison.

Sophie told them to help themselves and join the rest of the group. Alex filled her plate. She was not a shy eater. She purposefully sat where she could observe Claire. While she and Jules ate, the rest of them continued to chat about ranching. Alex was surprised to hear Claire ask a question about methane production. Few people knew that cattle are huge methane producers, contributing significantly to the greenhouse effect. Sophie explained that the ranch had reduced the number of cattle and was in its fifth year of making the transition from a cattle ranch to a full-time dude resort but, because of the short summer, financially, it was difficult to do overnight.

The rest of the morning Rick reviewed the communication and alarm system with everyone and passed out walkie talkie-like instruments as well as a pocket size panic alarms. He explained that the system was intelligent enough to determine who had pushed the panic button, the approximate location of the person who pushed it and that each of them would receive a voice alarm on their walkie talkies. He made them raise their right hand and swear that each of them would have both their walkie talkies and panic button device on their person at all times. It was a little over-the-top, but they got the seriousness of it all.

Rick switched from communications guru to ranch manager. He told Claire that she'd have part-time responsibilities helping with the grooming and exercising of the horses two to four hours a day, and once the guests arrived, assisting them tack up their horses. Rick called Dean who showed up ten minutes later to give her a tour. Sophie introduced Claire as a distant cousin from Italy who would be spending the summer with them. Mickey was introduced as her companion. Dean shot a look at Rick, as if to say, *you are going to owe me big for this.*

During the hour Claire and Mickey were gone, Jules and Alex talked to Sophie and Rick about what was off limits for conversations with Claire. Not knowing if Claire was involved with the kidnapping, they chose to keep extraction plans and Bill and Marcy's stay at the ranch among themselves.

"Hello. What's up?"

"Plans have changed. They moved Claire yesterday."

"I thought you said Monday or Tuesday?"

"Isn't it obvious that their plans changed?"

"I guess so. Any idea where?"

"I've got a sense she is in one of two places."

"How do you know?"

"I'll explain later."

"What now?"

"You can stop watching the estate."

"What about some cash?"

"Like we planned. I have to go now. Bye."

Claire was sitting on one of the chairs in the office, Alex in the other. Claire looked nervous.

"Claire, how was your tour of the barn?"

"Good. Dean is kind of a grumpy guy, but I think I can get along with him."

"Don't take anything he says or does personally. He's the same with everyone, except maybe Sophie," Alex smiled. "How are you feeling?"

"A little shaky right now," responded Claire.

"From the tour of the horse barn?"

"Ah, no. Umm, from being in here with you."

"Do you know why Claire?"

"I guess it's because I don't know you and ah, you're so different from Dr. Metuchi. I guess I just feel out of sorts."

"That's understandable. I feel a little nervous too," offered Alex in hopes of inducing a sense of confidence in Claire especially if she were complicit in the kidnapping.

"Really? How come?" asked Claire in disbelief.

"It's always a little nerve wracking for me to meet new patients. I want us to get off on the right foot because if we don't, well then there isn't much chance for the therapy to work."

Claire visibly relaxed with the response. "So, you are nervous because you want me to like you?" Claire's response was a huge tip off to Alex. First, she misinterpreted what Alex actually had said, twisting it slightly to create a level emotional playing field with Alex, her therapist. Second, it clearly showed her need to have her opinion validated and finally, she craved attention. Not good signs.

"Claire, let me clarify. We all want people to like us, but what I was talking about was being able to establish a trusting doctor/patient relationship so that we can make progress towards meeting your treatment goals." Alex watched Claire's facial features and eye movements. Sometimes neurolinguistic programming and eye movements gave insight into how a patient thinks, although its efficacy had been controversial since the 1990's.

"Alex, I'm sorry I misunderstood," said Claire with apparent sincerity.

"No worries," answered Alex warmly. "Now, let's cover a few things up front. I'm afraid that you're going to have to put up with a one-way monologue for a few minutes. Okay?" Claire nodded and Alex continued. "First thing on my list is that I'd like you to sign a release so that I can inform Dr. Metuchi of your treatment progress. How do you feel about that?"

"That's fine," answered Claire rather blandly.

"By the way," continued Alex, "did you know Dr. Metuchi from the club before you started seeing her?" Watching Claire's face and body language, Alex picked up a little 'squirminess'.

Claire answered, "Not really. I knew she was a member because I had seen her name on tennis and golf tournament rosters and even bumped into her once or twice, but we never spoke beyond polite greetings. Why?"

"Seems you didn't make much progress with the two doctors before she took over your treatment. I thought that if you knew her, that might be the reason you got better so fast," punted Alex still wondering about the 'squirminess'. "Okay, would you also be willing to sign a release to have me discuss with Jules anything I feel would be helpful in assisting her to locate your kidnappers?"

"I guess so," replied Claire, much more tentatively.

"You're not so sure about that?"

"Umm, like what kind of things?" said Claire.

"I'm talking about something you might remember in the course of therapy that might help with the investigation. For example, maybe you'll remember if your captor was male or female." Alex watched keenly. There was no apparent reaction from Claire.

She held Alex's eyes, then said, "I guess that's okay too."

Alex thanked her then asked if she wanted her father to be kept informed. Claire reeled at this suggestion. "No way! I don't want him knowing any specifics. All you can tell him is that I'm okay. Dr. Martini, do I have your word on that?"

"Of course, Claire. You're in the driver's seat when it comes to what information is released. You know that the only time I can divulge any thing about your treatment to others without your written consent is if you were going to harm yourself or someone else." Alex purposefully baited Claire. It was clear that she had some animosity towards her father.

"Dr. Martini, sorry about that, it's just that my dad thinks by controlling my every move he can keep me safe. What he doesn't understand is that by managing everything, including the therapeutic environment, he is suffocating me and contributing to my neurosis."

"Is that what Dr. Metuchi told you?"

She looked down momentarily. "It's just what I feel."

Alex didn't believe her. She noted Claire's articulate description of environmental control and wondered if she had read it somewhere or if it was Dr. Metuchi's analysis. However, she didn't convey any misgiving to Claire. "Is that one of the reasons you decided to agree to leaving California?"

"Yes and, of course, there were just too many bad memories there."

"Okay. I get what you're saying," replied Alex. Normally Alex would have taken advantage of her patient's discomfort or anger to probe, but she decided not to do that now because she didn't want to risk an adversarial relationship right off the bat.

Alex wanted transference to occur as rapidly as possible. In this case, what she was shooting for was the transference of Claire's past feelings, conflicts, and attitudes into the present doctor-patient relationship. This way unresolved or unsatisfactory experiences in relationships with her parents or other principal figures, could be resolved by the therapist acting as a new principal figure, supplanting old behavior and attitudes. Some called it re-parenting.

"Claire, the next area I want to cover is treatment goals. I'd like to hear what your goals are for the next three or four months."

Clearly, Claire was in a quandary. She didn't seem to know how to answer the question. Finally, she said, "I don't know what you mean."

"What do you want to accomplish as a result of you continuing treatment out here?"

"Get better, of course," Claire impatiently responded.

"What does 'getting better' look like to you?" countered Alex.

"I get it. Okay. Uh, I want to stop being afraid. I want to stop being startled. I want this constant anxiety to go away, I want the flashbacks to stop and I want to understand why I seem to have lost interest in things that I liked prior to the kidnapping. Is that what you mean?"

"It's a good start," encouraged Alex. "What I want you to do tonight before you go to bed is write down those goals across the top of a sheet of paper." Alex demonstrated on a pad that was on the desk. "Then I want you to list a few things that you think you can do to accomplish the goals under each one of the headings. Questions?"

"Yeah, Dr. Martini. How am I supposed to know what to do to stop these things from happening? You're the doctor. Isn't that your job?" she challenged.

Hmm, a little hostility, observed Alex, *but nothing I wouldn't have expected from the assignment.* "Claire, those are *your* goals! I am confident that you have some ideas on how to go about accomplishing them."

"Well I don't," answered Claire, crossing her arms across her chest, like a petulant child.

"How about if we start off with one right now so that you can get an idea of what the exercise is all about?"

"Fine," Claire answered, clearly still resistant.

"Which one do you want to pick?"

"Getting rid of this anxiety," answered Claire sullenly.

"Okay. That's a good one. First of all, can you identify the anxiety? Is it all the time, is it free floating, does it happen in response to certain stimuli?"

"It's all those, but I'm talking about getting rid of the anxiety that is always there, just below the surface."

"Great, Claire. Now think about what you just said. What is a possible way to combat this 'under-the-surface' anxiety?"

"You mean like the relaxation techniques I learned?"

"That could be one of your answers, what about another?" prompted Alex.

"How about keeping a diary of when the anxiety seems to be at its worst and when it seems to be minimal?"

"That's a tremendous idea!" encouraged Alex. "You'll want to make sure you capture your thoughts, feelings and any behaviors that go along with either the low anxiety or the high anxiety times."

"More homework, huh?" Claire complained.

"Yes, Claire. More homework. I think the goals that you set out are achievable, but not without your total commitment to hard work."

"I guess that's why I'm here. I can't stand living like this any longer," Claire said with an edge of desperation replacing the sullenness in her voice.

"Don't lose hope, Claire," said Alex acknowledging Claire's emotional state. "I have every confidence in you. The final thing on my agenda is to talk to you about the incident in the car last night with the gun. Are you feeling up to it?"

"I don't know. Let's give it a shot." Claire realized the pun she had unintentionally made and quickly apologized to Alex. "Oh my god, I didn't mean it like that. I'm so sorry. That was insensitive of me."

"Claire, it's a common saying. Don't worry about it. Okay? If you can't forgive yourself, then use my permission to forgive yourself". Claire was bouncing all over, moving rapidly from being nervous to seeking attention, from being hostile to challenging, resistant to apologetic. Alex made a note then continued. "Now, first of all, where did you get the gun?"

"My father gave both Elena and me one after the kidnapping."

Geez, thought Alex. *Bentworth must be nuts giving an emotionally disturbed victim of a violent crime a gun. What the hell was he thinking? Jules will go ballistic! Ah Jules...I wonder where she is? When she touches me like—focus Alex.*

"Claire, did it make you feel safe?" resumed Alex.

"Sort of, but I worried that if I pulled it out, someone might take it away from me and use it on me."

"That's a very valid concern, Claire. Did you have that feeling in the car, that Jules or someone else would take it from you and use it on you?"

"I don't know."

"That's okay. Don't worry. Tell me why you decided to pull out the gun?"

"When Jules pushed me to the floor after the loud bang, I got scared. I couldn't breathe and couldn't move. I tried to think how I could get up again and I remembered the gun."

"You said you couldn't breathe and move. Were you afraid when the tire blew out or was it the act of Jules pushing you to the floor that frightened you?" asked Alex.

"I think the loud bang was what first scared me and, then when Jules pushed me down, I couldn't breathe, and I remember not being able to breath when I was taken. I could only think about getting away." Claire was breathing with quick shallow breaths. Alex told her to sit back in her chair and take some deep breaths. After a dozen or so deep breaths, she stopped hyperventilating and Alex continued, remembering the hood that Jules had alluded to a couple of week ago and that Claire had remembered something about her abduction. "Then what?"

"When she got off of me, I reached into my coat and pulled out the gun. I don't remember what was going through my head."

"What happened next?"

"I don't know. I remember you talking to me about dropping the gun, I remember Jules taking it from me, but I honestly don't remember why I pointed it at her."

Alex tried a shot in the dark. "Did you confuse her with one of your assailants?"

Claire hesitated and thought for a moment. "I don't know. Maybe."

"All right, Claire. You've done very well this afternoon. The incident in the car could be related to suppressed memories of your kidnapping. You might experience increased anxiety and possibly a flashback. This wouldn't be all bad because it could give us an insight into aspects of the kidnapping you don't remember."

Alex continued. "Now, I can give you an additional drug to prevent or reduce the severity of a flashback or you can knuckle down and see what happens. Your choice." Many clinicians would not have agreed with Alex's approach of letting the patient decide, but Claire had been so adamant about her father controlling her environment that Alex, weighing all the factors, decided that allowing Claire to make a key decision would be therapeutic. It really didn't matter which choice she made.

"Umm, Dr. Martini, I think I want to see what happens, get this thing that's crippling me out. Will there be someone nearby if something happens?"

"Yes, Mickey is there, and Jules and I are just across the hall. Now don't go setting yourself up for anything to happen. Professionally, I think the chance is very small. I just wanted you to be prepared."

Claire nodded her head in understanding, though Alex could see she was still troubled. "All right, I've had enough indoors for now. Would you like to go for a walk? Maybe we can swap stories about our mothers."

"Is your mother still living?" inquired Claire.

"No, she and my father were killed in a car accident when I was a child. I was raised by my Aunt Sophie and Uncle Mario."

"I see," said Claire with a hint of empathy in her voice. "My mother died too."

They walked down to the pond, followed by Mickey who had finished with Rick and Jules. Alex did not get any more useful information from Claire, other than she learned that Claire had loved her mother deeply, and was now very attached to Elena.

Late afternoon, Alex was changing into running clothes when a tap on the door was followed by Jules coming in. "Going for a run?"

"Yes. I want to clear my head and sort through the session I had with Claire. Want to come along? I don't know that I'll be able to keep up with you though. Your legs are longer than mine and you look like you're in better shape than I am."

"Don't worry about that. A nice slow run would be good." She winked at Alex.

"I'm not that decrepit!" Alex stretched while she waited for Jules to change into sweats. Jules put her carry pistol in a fanny pack, along with the walkie talkie and panic button device. "Lord, if I have any more to carry, I'll have to switch to a backpack. How far are we going?"

"Jules, do I have to take my gun and walkie talkie too?"

Jules shrugged her shoulders and said, "I don't think both of us have to lug them around. So how far are we going?"

Alex responded, "I follow a trail down to the river, then west, then we'll loop around coming back up past the barns. It's about thirty to forty minutes."

"Let's do it," Jules said as she charged out the door leaving Alex in her wake.

They headed south towards the river following the path down by the White Bark name sake pine tree. It was downhill, so neither exerted too much energy. At the pond, they veered right, running west following a path cut out by the side of the river. Dodging piles of road apples left by the horses as their offering to nature, they fell into a rhythm comfortable for Alex and easy for Jules. Neither spoke, enjoying the silence punctuated only by spring birds and the churning river water.

To the west the mountains formed a snow-covered backdrop, contrasting with the trees that were greening with spring leaves. Jules picked up the speed just a little and soon Alex was trailing her, lost in her own thoughts. Jules ran hard for another ten minutes, then doubled back to pick up Alex and continued side by side past the horse pastures, hay fields and, finally, looping around to the north, heading back to the bunkhouse. Just before the trail delivered them to the compound, they slowed to a jog.

"I'd like to talk to you in private," said Jules.

"Me too," countered Alex. "We can go up to my room after dinner. It's too hard for me to talk and run at the same time."

They jogged east up the hill past the cattle barn, horse barn, cabins and got to the house with plenty of time to clean up before dinner. Claire and Mickey were sitting on the front porch playing chess. They greeted Alex and Jules, then returned to their competition, taking endless delight in taunting each other.

Dinner was at 7:00 p.m. and they were finished by 8:00 p.m. Alex and Jules excused themselves, Jules going upstairs and Alex following Sophie into the kitchen.

"Aunt Sophie, Jules and I need some privacy this evening for me to brief her on information I discovered in Claire's therapy session."

Sophie said it was fine and humorously told her not to roll around on the bed. Alex frowned at Sophie, shook her head and equally as cheeky said, "Don't worry, you know how motion-sick I get!"

Sophie laughed at Alex's retort and said she'd save a piece of pie for them if they wanted it later.

###

Alex opened the door to her bedroom, where Jules was waiting. "What did you want to talk about?"

"I wanted to fill you in on Claire's sessions today. She's signed releases for me to share information with Dr. Metuchi and you."

"Did you come to any conclusions?" asked Jules, curled up with her legs under her.

"Oh yes. First of all, she's smart and extremely well read. I suppose you'd expect that from an individual that had all the privileges money could buy. Secondly, she's needy and manipulative."

"How did you come to that conclusion?" Jules inquired.

"I experienced her attempts."

"I see. How does this help us with the investigation?"

"It doesn't right now, except that she could be much more skilled and potentially dangerous than we thought."

Jules nodded her head and Alex continued. "It's also very clear that she harbors resentment towards her father. She refused to give me permission to share her treatment progress with him."

"Enough resentment for her to participate in her own kidnapping?" interrupted Jules.

"Not enough information yet, but you are going to find what I tell you next, very interesting. First promise you won't blow a gasket."

Jules looked warily at Alex and reluctantly promised she'd try not to blow a fuse.

"Ready for this? Bentworth gave her and Elena guns after the kidnapping." Alex dropped the bomb and waited for Jules to renege on her promise.

"Son of a bitch!" yelped Jules. "Of all the stupid things to do! I ought to ring his neck! Damn!"

"Well, at least you didn't rupture a blood vessel," Alex mildly teased.

"It's like giving crack cocaine to someone who just got out of rehab. How could he have been so stupid? Obviously, he didn't discuss it with her doctor." By now, Jules was up vigorously pacing in front of the bed. "I guess there's nothing we can do about it now, except make sure she doesn't get her hands on another weapon."

"Amen to that," said Alex. Also, I thought you'd find it useful to the investigation to know that she has more suppressed memories of the kidnapping than we thought."

"Really? In one session you discovered that?" replied Jules incredulously.

"Well, in all fairness to the other doctors who worked with her, I think it was the gun incident in the car that opened a portal. She said she felt unable to breathe when you pushed her down and could only think about getting away. That sparked her to pull out the gun. The sensation of not being able to breathe might have been from the hood or something they used to subdue her; maybe a hit of chloroform. The effects of chloroform dissipate after one or two days, so it wouldn't show up in a tox screen."

"Interesting. Did she say why she pointed the gun at me?" Jules was intrigued.

"Not exactly. She said she didn't remember. Then she remembered me asking her to put the gun down and you taking it away from her."

"This doesn't seem to point to anything specific, though." Jules was disappointed.

"Jules, she confused the danger of the moment with the kidnapping event. She pointed the gun at a woman, you, instead of the guys right outside the car doors! Buried somewhere in her subconscious, I think she knows that one of the kidnappers is a woman."

"Hmm." Jules was not as elated with Alex's unearthing of Claire's repressed memory as Alex thought she would be. However, before Alex could mull over Jules' reactions, Jules asked, "Alex, are you in the mood for doing some 'what ifs?'"

"Sure. What did you have in mind?"

"How did the kidnappers get Claire out of the store totally undetected?"

"Funny you should ask, because I was thinking about this when I was running this afternoon. Would it have been possible for a woman to impersonate a store employee?"

Jules answered, "Yes, sure."

"What if a woman, disguised as a store employee approached Claire and told her that there had been some sort of, uh, accident or medical emergency with Elena? Claire, though smart and worldly in some ways, may not have a lot of street smarts. The woman could have lured her down a freight elevator telling her that Elena was in an ambulance and didn't want to go to the hospital alone.

"Maybe this is farfetched, Jules, but it's the only thing I can think of as a reasonable explanation of how the kidnappers got her out without anyone noticing, unless, of course, she walked out on her own because she was part of the scam."

"Okay, Alex, then once she gets to the door with the mystery woman and sees that there is no ambulance, what happens?"

"Mystery woman tells her that the ambulance couldn't wait any longer and left, but she would be glad to drive her to the hospital."

"Alex, you've forgotten that Claire had a driver. She most likely would have declined the offer."

"So, out comes a whiff of chloroform, the mystery woman pushes her into the car or van with her accomplice waiting. The accomplice puts a hood over Claire's head and before she shakes off the effects of the chloroform, administers a shot of valium. Mystery woman jumps in the driver's seat and drives off."

"You have quite the imagination, don't you?" said Jules clearly amused.

"Jules, are you making fun of me?"

"Not really. Your theory is plausible. So, let's see what we've got. First, at least one of the kidnappers is a woman. Two, Claire was either lured out of the store or she walked out on her own. Three, we know she was drugged, and we also believe that the kidnapper administered additional conscious sedation drugs during her captivity. Four, one of the kidnappers would have to have medical knowledge to administer the conscious sedation drugs. Five, in Claire's physical condition, she couldn't have walked as far as she did without help. Six, Claire is hostile towards her father. Seven, you think Claire has more memories floating around in her subconscious. Did I get them all?"

Alex didn't want to let this go. "Now, how do we go about finding the mystery woman?"

"Alex, in any case like this we have to look at family members. That means we looked at Elena, the household staff, especially those close to Claire like Rosa, Claire's regular tennis partner and a few other people with whom she socialized. We couldn't find anything tying them to the event. There was nothing that even remotely suggested they were participants in the kidnapping."

"But Jules, maybe these people, on purpose or unwittingly, provided information to the kidnappers. Because we've theorized that there was a woman participant, it doesn't mean that the mystery woman knew Claire prior to the abduction. In other words, if the principal kidnapper is a man, he could have enlisted, say, his girlfriend, as his cohort."

"You're right. We did the same kind of vetting with the male members of the household, Bentworth's Country Club and the guys she dated up to a year prior to the kidnapping. Zilch."

"I'm sorry, Jules, but something is missing. Something. I just feel it."

Jules' back was up because her team was noted for their thoroughness. Miffed, she said, "Alex, we didn't miss anything with the information we had at the time. I'm hoping that you will be able to unearth additional information, like you did today, then we can narrow the scope of the investigation."

"Come on Jules, I didn't mean to impugn your team's ability. Poor choice of words, okay?" soothed Alex.

"Okay, okay. Guess I am overly sensitive about this investigation because we keep hitting the same walls and get nowhere. I've got to be honest. I don't have much patience when I'm stuck in a maze without a way out."

"Ah, that's the pragmatic streak in you, Jules."

Though Alex had only known her about a month, she read Jules' looks and moods fairly accurately. "Jules, I have an idea. Want to hear it?"

"Ah, what did you say?" answered Jules coming out of her thoughts.

"I have an idea, maybe not worth much, but do you want to hear it?"

"Certainly," placated Jules.

"What if we were to pick the likeliest mystery woman and work backward? Retro-reconstruction."

"Backwards deduction?" countered Jules. "So, you're suggesting that we pick a likely suspect, design the plot around that person and see if we can make it fit? Could be dangerous. Lazy cops do it all the time."

"Yes, Jules, you're right, but the difference here is that we're open to being wrong. The danger is minimal if we consider this a methodology rather than a means to an end. What do you think?"

"I suppose it has possibilities," conceded Jules, "but do we really have a good mystery woman at this time?"

"I think we do. I'd stake my reputation that if Claire was involved, she couldn't have organized the whole thing by herself. At best she would have been a supernumerary."

"How so?" asked Jules.

"If she were a participant, then she was a pawn for someone more powerful."

"Powerful?"

"Personal power. Someone like you. When you walk into a room, everyone listens to you. True?" Without waiting for an answer, Alex went on. "I also don't think any of the house staff can be the mastermind and if they did participate, they too were pawns."

"Well, that leaves Elena, Metuchi or some other mystery woman and I'm telling you, there doesn't seem to be a motive."

"Not that we know of. It doesn't mean there isn't one. What would it hurt to look again?"

"Nothing, I guess. I just don't see it, but I don't want to discount your idea of retro-reconstruction, so we will look again."

Alex could see that Jules only agreed to take another look at Elena and Dr. Metuchi to placate her, but she didn't care as long as it got done. "Jules, what else did you want to talk to me about?"

Jules said, "Huh?" Her mind was already working on something else. "Oh, uh, I just wanted to talk about your session with Claire."

"Really, that's all?"

"Yeah, for now."

Tilting her head with mild disbelief, Alex chided Jules. "I don't think you're being totally truthful, but I'm sure you have your reasons for changing your mind. In your time, then."

Jules got up from the edge of the bed and came up behind Alex's chair, putting her arms around Alex's shoulders. "Do you think we could find time tomorrow to ride up to the Falls?"

"Of course, but why?" Before Alex could ask any more questions, Jules lifted her from her chair and carried her to the bed. Talking wasn't on her mind.

CHAPTER 13 – Mist of the Falls

To stand at the edge of the sea, to sense the ebb and flow of the tides, to feel the breath of a mist moving over a great salt marsh, to watch the flight of shore birds that have swept up and down the surf lines of the continents for untold thousands of years, to see the running of the old eels and the young shad to the sea, is to have knowledge of things that are as nearly eternal as any earthly life can be.

Rachel Carson

Tuesday April 28

Jules was watching Alex sleep. Last night's lovemaking was slow and tender, yet full of heightened yearning and arousal. Alex woke a little later with Jules cupping her breast, soft fingers stroking her nipple. She pulled Jules closer and murmured, "I thought I was imagining this."

"No, it's real. I'm sorry, I didn't mean to wake you."

"Then what did you mean?" Alex whispered, already turned on.

"I can't keep my hands from you. I don't want to stop touching you."

Alex found Jules' mouth with her own kissing her deeply. Their mutual desire and passion washed over them and merged with the dappled sunlight streaking through the window.

Sophie, Rick and Alex laid out the Tuesday morning buffet; French toast, scrambled eggs, cut up fruit and ham. Claire was due down at the barn around 10:00 a.m., so Alex would only be able to get in an hour with her.

"Claire let's meet right after breakfast, so you can get down to the barn by 10:00 a.m.. Then we'll get together again around 4:00 p.m. this afternoon. Will that work for you?" Alex asked.

"Yup, that would be great," responded Claire. "By the way, no flashbacks or nightmares last night."

"Glad to hear that. I think just the fact that you were willing to suffer an episode signals great progress."

Rick had already eaten, excused himself and gotten halfway through the kitchen, when persistent knocking on the door got everyone's attention. Sophie went to see who it was. As soon as Rick heard Sophie raise her voice, he turned and flew through the dining room and great room to encounter Sophie and Keith Woods engaged in heated conversation. "It's none of your god damn business, you, you misogynist! Now get the hell off of my property," Sophie yelled, still in control of herself, but on the brink of a total melt down.

"It is my business, you hardheaded—"

He stopped whatever he was going to say when he saw Rick come through the door.

"What's going on? We have guests inside, Woods." Rick attempted to be the voice of reason, though he hated Woods as much as Sophie.

"Look here, Rick. I stopped by as part of my fiduciary responsibility to the bank to see how things were going. It seems that you've been able to clear all of the back payments and I wanted to know if this trend could be expected to continue," said Woods heatedly.

Sophie, daggers flying from her eyes, took a step closer to Woods, her face only a foot from his. "Look, you no good vermin, I told you it's none of your business. You have no reason to be here, so get out before I call the Sheriff and report you for trespassing!"

The confrontation had gotten louder and hearing it, Mickey stopped heaping seconds on to his plate and motioned to Claire to follow him. He took Claire upstairs, locked the doors and monitored the situation through the window of his room, which faced the driveway. He cracked it slightly so that he could hear.

Alex recognized Woods' voice and hurried out to the porch. She had her pistol clipped to the back of her jeans and hoped that Sophie wouldn't see it and try to use it!

Woods saw her and immediately changed his demeanor. "Why Alex, I heard you were back. It's nice to see you again. Will you be staying the whole summer?"

Within the realm of strained politeness, Alex answered, "I haven't decided yet, Mr. Woods."

Woods, besides being a true asshole, was also a big gossip and often used his position at the bank inappropriately. Today was no different. "Well, I'm sure your aunt just loves having you here and, of course, loves it that you're helping out financially, too!"

Surprised and thrown off guard, Alex stammered, "Why what do you mean, Mr. Woods, even though it shouldn't concern you how your bank gets its money?"

Woods, smug and confident replied, "Well, girlie, it is my concern when all of a sudden, months of back payments are made, and money is coming from a bank in Seattle." He was fully aware that the 'girlie' epithet would unhinge Alex. He loved the prospect of insulting her. Heaping on more insult, he continued. "You know, we have to make sure we're not dealing with drug or mob money!"

Pointedly, he looked at Sophie when he made the reference to 'mob money'. Although there were scores of Italian cattlemen and women in Montana, Woods carried his white supremist prejudices right out in the open for all to see. Rick caught Sophie's arm, which was cocked and ready to knock more than the chip off of Woods' shoulder. He stepped between Sophie and Woods, finding himself inches from Woods' face.

Woods didn't back away from Rick, even when Rick snarled at him, jabbing his finger into Woods' chest for emphasis.

"You are a disgrace to the human race, you parasite. I can guarantee you that First Territorial will continue to receive regular mortgage payments from legitimate funds, but the next time you question Sophie's, Alex's, or my integrity, I'll bring you up on charges with the Federal Reserve Board as well as file a civil suit for slander. There's plenty of evidence. Don't think for a moment I'm bluffing, you son of a bitch." Rick's chest was heaving.

The blood drained from Woods' face. He was pale and began sweating. Rick was significantly taller than Woods' five-foot seven stature and it appeared that Woods wasn't going to chance a boxing match. Rick, reeking from the smell of sweaty, testosterone-fueled anger, had averted an assault on Woods from Sophie. Alex saw that it was only a matter of time before Rick clocked him.

She took Woods' arm, turned him around and walked him down the steps, delivering him to the driver's door of his Escalade. "Mr. Woods, I think you should leave now. Be a shame to have to explain to your bosses in Chicago why we filed complaints against you."

Woods loathed these people but knew when to retreat and regroup. He got into his car and peeled out, stirring up an immense cloud of dust. Sophie, still shaking with rage, thought, *that puff of dust doesn't taste half as bad as the taste he left in my mouth.*

Mickey, Claire and Jules came down the stairs shortly after Woods was forced off of the ranch. Jules said good morning to no one in particular, filled her plate and, when seated, said, "I heard there was a bit of excitement this morning while I was on the phone. Mickey filled me in."

Sophie was still quivering with resentment and the vein in Rick's temple was throbbing, so Alex answered. "There's a banker, Keith Woods from First Territorial who has had it in for Aunt Sophie for many years. It started when Uncle Mario got sick then died. We had to mortgage the ranch and Woods was a loan officer at the time. After Uncle Mario died, he tried to court Aunt Sophie several times." Smirking, she continued, "I guess Aunt Sophie turned him down one time too many for his ego to handle. Short-man syndrome, I guess!" finished Alex.

Sophie turned her head to hide her reaction. No one saw that there was another emotion lurking under her resentment of the man. Rick excused himself and headed down to the barn with Mickey and Claire, skipping her morning session with Alex. Alex reminded Claire that she wanted to see her in the afternoon. Jules wolfed down her breakfast and asked Alex if they were still going riding this morning.

"Where are you headed?" inquired Sophie.

"Out on the trails. We had some ideas last night on an alternative approach to the investigation and want to talk about it. Okay if I pack a lunch for us?"

"Sure. I can do it for you if you like," answered Sophie, calming down from the run-in with the odious Woods.

Jules thanked Sophie for breakfast, told Alex she'd be back in ten minutes, carried her dishes into the kitchen and took off up the stairs. Sophie and Alex were left alone.

"Aunt Sophie are you okay now? I know what an asshole Woods can be," commented Alex.

"You have no idea, sweetie. He's not only a jerk, but also very dangerous. I'm fine now that he's gone. I can't tell you how much I loved seeing him intimidated!"

Alex knew about the bad blood between the two of them but couldn't help wondering if Woods had done more than try to financially ruin Sophie, as if that in and of itself were not enough. "Aunt Sophie, that's not like you, or at least I don't remember you being so vengeful."

"Some day when you're old enough, I'll tell you why it would give me the utmost pleasure to see that man rot in hell." In an effort of self-preservation, Sophie quickly turned the tables. "What's happening between you and Jules? One moment you treat each other like friends and the next, the two of you are as cold as frozen turkeys."

"I wish I knew how to explain it, Aunt Sophie," answered Alex.

Sophie had just enough residual anger from the encounter with Woods that she unwittingly channeled it towards Alex. "Well, sweetheart, you are the psychologist. I'm sure you've thought about it." Sophie wouldn't relent.

"It's complicated," answered Alex trying to deflect Sophie's meddling.

"Are you going to try and talk about it on your ride?"

Alex sighed deeply. "Maybe. If she's open to it."

"Alex, I know you think I'm prying and that it's none of my business. I just think you two need to get to a place where you can work with each other without all the melodrama! It's really beginning to get on my nerves!"

Alex was surprised with the tone in Sophie's voice. She was as aggressive as a Cottonmouth during mating season, as Alex had discovered when one struck her boot, while she was stationed for a short time in South Carolina. "Geez, Aunt Sophie. You said it. I'm the psychologist. Let me handle it. All right?" snapped back Alex.

Sophie, partially chagrined, hugged Alex, said she was sorry and kissed her on the lips. When Alex turned to leave, she saw Jules standing in the kitchen doorway. Alex waited until they were out of Sophie's hearing range. "You saw that didn't you?"

Jules flatly said, "You mean the kiss? If she only knew where your mouth had been!"

Alex groaned. "How much of the conversation did you hear?"

"I heard you say, 'If she's open to it.'" Jules thought that Alex looked like a kid with her hand in the cookie jar but didn't comment.

"Jules, Sophie is very observant. She asked me what was going on between the two of us. She said that one moment we were treating each other like friends and the next, we were as cold as frozen turkeys. She wished we could figure out a way to work with each other without the melodrama."

Jules burst out laughing. "Cold as a frozen turkey? That's rich. What did you say?"

"I told her it was complicated. That's when she asked me if we were going to talk about it." Alex kept walking, her sighs punctuated by the chatter of the blue jays swooping from tree to tree as she and Jules made their way to the barn.

"Jules do you want to hang out here or go over to the camp site?" asked Alex before she dismounted.

"Here, please."

Alex tied up the horses and tossed Jules the saddle bags that contained their lunch and a blanket. They settled on the east side of the pool, quietly absorbing the essence that swirled around them.

After a while, Jules broke the silence. "Anything useful from your session this morning?"

"Nope. We didn't have a session because of the interruption with Sophie's favorite banker, but I've got a game plan for this afternoon". Alex rolled over to face Jules. "Jules quit stalling. What is it you want to talk about?"

"Um, I don't really know how to start off. See, I don't want you to think I'm taking advantage of your professional skills, but I have some things I'm trying to work through and need some advice."

"You want a therapy session?" asked Alex, flabbergasted, yet intrigued with Jules' request.

"Not exactly," said Jules with heated embarrassment. "It's just that I need your insight in a couple of areas and was hoping that you might help me out. Could you, ah, remain neutral?"

"Alex's curiosity was piqued. "I'm all ears."

"Okay. I hope I'm not making a big mistake."

"Jules both of us feel like yoyos. If this is going to help resolve this teeter totter act between us, then I'm all for it. Go on."

"I wish I had deliberated more, but I haven't been able to sort out my own thoughts. I'm afraid they are all jumbled up."

"That's okay. We'll sort them out."

"Okay, here goes. First, you know that crossing of professional boundaries makes me feel like I've compromised my ethics. Second, you know that how I feel about you is a heavy burden for me, thinking I might have to choose between the job and you."

"Yes, I know, Jules. You've got to be emotionally honest with yourself," said Alex. "You are quaking with a sense of loss of control over your neatly arranged life. Only you can make the choice of living in utter emotional desolation or embracing this other side of you that is overflowing with promise."

"I know I keep myself tightly locked up and it has served me for many years, but you, you have turned my world upside down."

Jules was agitated. She rushed to stand up and began pacing in her bare feet across the moss. In a burst of energy, she ripped off her T-shirt and shucked her jeans before she dove into the pool. The pool was deep, so it wasn't likely that she would hurt herself but, none the less, Alex rushed to the side, waiting for her to surface. A full minute later, Jules hadn't come up. Alex stripped off her jeans and T-shirt and was poised to dive into the pool, when she caught a movement through the mist followed by a primordial sob.

Jules had swum under the water and climbed up the ledge behind the falls. After putting her jeans and T-shirt back on, Alex picked up the blanket and walked towards the falls. When she reached the ledge, she saw Jules sitting head on her knees, gripping her legs with her arms. She didn't look up but caught hold of the blanket as Alex laid it across her back.

"Come on, honey. It's damp back here". Alex helped her up and adjusted the blanket around her, leading her back to the edge of the pool where they had been sitting.

"Alex, I don't know what happened. I just couldn't sit there; I had to move. It's like my body just took over."

"I know, I know. All your emotions and mental tendencies were in turmoil and that's how your physical body coped. It's okay. With her arm around Jules' blanketed shoulder, she just sat quietly and held her.

Jules hadn't spoken for a few minutes, but finally said, "Alex, I feel so tired. Do you mind if I lie down and rest for a while?"

"Of course not. We can wrap you in the blanket."

Jules laid down while Alex checked on the horses. They had munched on all available leaves within their reach, so Alex moved them to a new spot teeming with fresh buds then returned to the Jules' side. An hour later Jules woke up with a start. She shook herself awake as if trying to dispel a chill that had engulfed her.

"What is it, Jules?" asked Alex, alarmed by Jules' quick movement.

"Nothing. Nothing is wrong. I'm just chilled."

Alex didn't press. She knew it might take a plethora of emotional experiences for Jules to integrate the conflicting emotions, but she wasn't about to burst the balloon right now. She reached for her hand, hoping that at some level the physical contact would serve as a bridge from whatever was happening in Jules' subconscious while sleeping to her conscious mind.

Alex's session with Claire that afternoon was frustrating. Claire was resistant, though not overtly. She refused to talk about anything other than her post trauma state of being. Alex couldn't decide if this was Claire's attempt to stay with topics she knew, if she didn't see the value in discussing pre-kidnapping behaviors, or something else. It nagged at Alex

Alex wanted to speed things up and was considering using hypnotism. There were no indications in Claire's records that either Dr. Metuchi or the other two who had treated Claire had used or considered this a viable treatment option. She left a message with Dr. Metuchi's answering service to call her tonight or tomorrow.

"Jules, Bentworth's wife is driving him crazy," complained Jake. "She wants to talk to Claire. Says she didn't get a chance to say goodbye. I can't see the harm in it, if we set some ground rules."

"If you think you can control Elena on that end, I'll deal with Claire here. Go ahead and set it up for tomorrow." Jules changed topics. "Jake, I'm leaving here on Thursday, heading back to LA. On Sunday, I'll chase down some things Alex feels we should look at so I'm flying out to South America for a few days, then to Afghanistan for another few days. Do you think you can meet me Friday at the office to go over some ideas on focusing the investigation in a different direction? Also, I want to brief you on Afghanistan. Got a call from Paulson a little while ago. I'm bringing in a high value Taliban Insurgent who wants to defect."

"Why you and not some Company or military guy?"

"Paulson said the Afghani government asked for me by name. He got a call from the Company."

"Sounds dangerous, maybe even a set up. You going alone?"

"Yeah. Condition of surrender and defection."

"Geez. No offense Jules, but doesn't it seem strange that they'd ask for a woman? These folks aren't exactly a pro-feminist group."

"True, but I'm supposed to get briefed when I get to Pakistan. I'll let you know more then."

"So, I'll see you Friday morning here in the office?" asked Jake.

"Yes. Talk to you again tomorrow morning before the call with Claire and Elena," concluded Jules.

Claire, Sophie, Rick, and Mickey were playing Trivial Pursuit. Girls against the boys. It was a pretty even match-up, but what made the game fun was each side's constant taunting of the other. Jules observed for a while, noting that Claire seemed relaxed, unguarded, and actually having fun. *Hmm*, she thought to herself on the way upstairs. *Maybe this was a good idea after all.*

Alex looked up from the desk when Jules walked in. "Hi, finished your call?"

"Mm-hmm," responded Jules.

"Got a moment? I have a question for you. Do you know if anyone considered hypnosis with Claire?"

"No, sorry. Do you think it can help?"

"I'm leaning heavily. It might shave off weeks of therapy sessions. Hypnosis is a recognized treatment option for PTSD, especially to treat war-related post-traumatic conditions. More recently, it's been successful in cases of sexual assault and car accidents. I'm really surprised that Dr. Metuchi didn't consider it."

"Are you qualified to do it?" asked Jules.

"Yes, I'm licensed in Washington. Licensure is mandatory there. When I moved to Washington, I maintained by licensure in Montana. However, before I take this step, I want to talk to Dr. Metuchi."

"Umm, okay. I can arrange a call. Let me know when."

Alex looked at Jules. She could see that Jules was bothered, distracted. "Jules are you still warring with yourself?"

Jules angrily said, "Yes, and there is nothing you can do to change that."

Alex went for the jugular. "You know what I think, Jules? I think you are clinging to some self-imposed code of conduct that tells you it is wrong to sleep with a colleague. You're not in the military anymore, so forget the non-fraternization code of conduct, and I'll bet there is nothing in your corporate code of conduct that spells out it is wrong to have a relationship with a colleague. It would be different if I were a client, but I'm not. So it boils down to you either thinking that sleeping with a colleague could compromise an operation, or you use it as an excuse. Yes, that's right, an excuse not to have to deal with your own desperate desire to keep your feelings locked away where they can't be hurt!"

Alex took a breath before passionately continuing, "So if you really think sleeping with me is going to compromise this operation, then fine, I will accept that, but don't you dare use it as an excuse to protect your fragile feelings!"

Alex knew she had taken a huge gamble. She watched Jules with a practiced eye, but she couldn't tell which way it might go. Would Jules begin to resolve her internal conflict, or would Alex's approach launch Jules into another confrontation, which could be even more destructive?

Jules didn't look at Alex. She got up and walked to the door, turning only when she grabbed the doorknob. "You think that helped? Well it didn't. No one is going to force me to do something I don't want to do!" Jules stalked out, leaving Alex to believe she had pushed Jules too far.

It was colder tonight than it had been most of the week. Jules could see her breath as she briskly walked down the lighted path towards the pond. With each angry step, she told herself that she was the master of her own fate and no one was going to tell her how to think. By the time she reached the edge of the pond, she felt an inner pressure to reestablish her control and self-determination. *Let's just cut through this crap,* she told herself. *It's wrong to sleep with a colleague. This whole thing is over. It ends here and now. How could she possibly think I'm using this as an excuse? It's ludicrous. God, I hate shrinks! It doesn't matter how I feel, it's not something I'm going to let continue.* She marched back to the house with a renewed sense of bravado fully anticipating putting an end to the agony. Without knocking on the door, she swung it open to find Alex sitting on the bed reading. Alex looked over her reading glasses at Jules, scrutinizing Jules' face and her body language. Jules was coiled and ready to strike.

"Alex," Jules started, waiting for some reaction from Alex. There was none, so she plunged ahead. "I've decided that I can't continue a relationship with you. It's causing me too much distress and it's not fair to you to have me ping ponging back and forth." Now that the words were out, Jules was sure that she would feel relief. Instead she was unexpectedly drowning in feelings of panic. She was experiencing an emotional pileup.

While Jules was gone, Alex had more than a premonition of what was going to happen. She had already decided not to try and talk Jules out of her inevitable decision. She was sure she loved Jules and that Jules had deep feelings for her but, there was no use trying to talk Jules out of a decision that she felt compelled to make. Alex understood that Jules didn't know any other way except to insulate herself. Sadly, she replied, "If you feel this is best for you, Jules, then I don't have any choice but to accept it, do I?"

Jules hadn't expected Alex to give up so easily but was relieved that it wouldn't go on all night. Before Jules could respond, Alex got up and as she walked past Jules, she placed her hand on Jules' shoulder and started to say something, then thought better of it and just left. Jules was forlorn, lost. As the saying goes, she felt as if she had won the battle but lost the war and had absolutely no idea how or why.

Alex knocked on Sophie's door and waited for Sophie to invite her in. "Aunt Sophie, would it be okay for me to stay with you tonight?" Uncharacteristically, Sophie asked no questions as she pulled back the comforter for Alex.

CHAPTER 14 - Farewell

That Farwell kiss which resembles a greeting, that last glance of love which becomes the sharpest pang of sorrow.

George Eliot

Wednesday April 29

The next morning Jules called Jake to finalize arrangements for the phone call between Claire and Elena. She also filled him in on Alex's thoughts about redirecting the investigation around Elena. Jake, like Jules, was hesitant but agreed because the trail had run cold. They discussed whether or not they would need Marcy and Bill at the ranch. Jules thought that between Mickey, Rick, and Alex, no further security measures were necessary, but before making that decision, she wanted Jake to get Bentworth's input.

Before ending the call, Jake asked if she had heard any more from Paulson about the Afghanistan mission. Jules could tell he was worried, and rightfully so. Even with the best of conditions, it would be perilous. Last night, unable to sleep, she had racked her brain trying to find a connection that would tell her why she had been requested.

"Jake don't worry. If I feel something strange is going on, I'll bail."

Though Jules couldn't see, Jake was shaking his head. "Sure, you will. Ha! That's a good one. When have you ever bailed on anything?"

Jules felt her stomach drop to her feet. *If he only knew!*

###

Alex had just hung up the phone with Dr. Metuchi when Jules knocked and came into the room. They barely looked at each other over breakfast, Alex because she thought she was going to well up with tears and Jules because she didn't want to suffer what she felt when she looked at Alex. Jules looked out the window when she asked Alex, "Did you get hold of Metuchi?"

"I just hung up. Seems her summer cold just won't quit. She blew her nose throughout the conversation." Alex was listless. Her voice was flat. "Dr. Metuchi said she often uses hypnosis to enhance the potency of psychotherapeutic methods, but in this case, Claire was adamantly opposed. I asked her if she knew why Claire rejected it. She said it boiled down to control issues."

"Claire thought she would lose control under hypnosis?" asked Jules, still staring out the window.

"Something like that. Even when Dr. Metuchi emphasized the permissive nature of the trance state and that she would never make Claire do things she didn't want to do, Claire refused."

"Has this changed your mind on trying it with Claire?" inquired Jules.

Alex thought for a moment and said, "No. I'm even more convinced that it's the right course."

Jules turned around and walked over to the desk, looking down at Alex. "Alex, I don't want to leave feeling bad. Is there anything I can do for us to gain some closure?"

Alex looked up at Jules and felt a ripple of wretchedness pass through her chest. "Not unless you've changed your mind."

Jules turned back to the window. As if she were speaking to the glass, she said, "I have to follow up on some of the things you thought we should look at and I'm going to South America for a few days before leaving for the Middle East," Jules said dejectedly. "I'm leaving this afternoon instead of tomorrow."

It didn't surprise Alex to hear that Jules had moved her "escape" date up. "How long will you be gone?" inquired Alex, wondering if she would ever see Jules again. Jules had not left the impression that calling an end to their relationship was temporary.

"Two weeks, Alex. I'm afraid I won't be able to call or email once I leave for the Middle East.

"Am I driving you to the airport?" hopefully asked Alex.

"I think it would be better if you stayed here. I ordered a car this morning."

Keeping a tight rein on her emotions, Alex asked, "Do you still want me to email you with updates on Claire's progress?" Alex knew she was grasping at straws, trying anything to keep a door open.

Curtly, Jules said, "You can, but I won't be checking email once I leave for the Middle East. Better you email Jake and he will let me know if there is something important." She motioned for the pen that Alex was holding and wrote Jake's email address on Alex's pad.

The tension in the room was more than either of them could bear. It seemed all-encompassing, laden with hopelessness, leaving room only for one course of action. Jules excused herself with the bogus excuse of having to work with Mickey until she left that evening. Alex, equally as lame, said she wanted to get in several therapy hours with Claire and she'd see Jules before she left.

###

At 11:00 a.m., with Claire in the office, Jules dialed Jake's phone and waited for him to pick up. He was waiting with Elena and Bentworth for her call. "Hi Jules. We're all here."

"Okay. Let's get started. There are some ground rules we need to follow." Before putting the phone on speaker, Jules gave a rundown of the conditions for the call. "First of all, no one asks Claire where she is and Claire, you are not to tell your father or Elena where you are. Second, and this is for Claire, no description of where you are." She looked at Claire who nodded her head in agreement. Is everyone in agreement?" She heard the Bentworth's say yes, followed by Claire. "Okay, it's all yours."

"Sweetheart," broke in Bentworth, "how are you feeling?"

"Pretty good, Dad. I'm sleeping better and working with the horses keeps me busy."

"Claire, I miss you and I'm so sorry that I wasn't there to say goodbye to you," interjected Elena. "I feel pretty miserable about them moving you when I wasn't home."
"Oh, Elena, I don't want you to feel bad. It was hard enough leaving Dad and if you had been there, it would have been doubly hard leaving." Claire's response was heartfelt.

"I'm really fine here and think this was a good move for me. Before you know it, I'll be back and ready to whip your butt at tennis!" She tried to end on a positive note. It appeared her affection towards Elena was genuine.

"We'll see about that!" said Elena, picking up on Claire's bright mood. "Claire, I hate being a stepmother hen, but are you taking your medication?"

"Every day, but I do miss not being able to have an occasional drink. Elena, you know how I love the Club's Pomegranate Martini's!" Jules' ears pricked up with the reference to the Martini's. Was it some code that Claire and Elena had worked out or was it innocent girl talk?

"Claire," interrupted Bentworth, "you said you were working with the horses. What exactly are you doing?"

"Dad don't worry. It's nothing dangerous," countered an impatient Claire. "In the morning, I help with the feeding, then start grooming, you know, brushing them, checking their hoofs. Then in the afternoon, I exercise them. Sometimes I ride them, but most often, I use a lunge line. You remember what that is Dad?" said Claire, with an obvious challenge in her voice.

"Are you suggesting I could ever forget all those trips to your riding lessons? Let's see now. Even a feeble old man couldn't forget an eight-year-old out there in the ring with a huge horse on a long line running circles around you while you gave it commands!"

"Wow! I never knew you were paying attention. You always had a phone glued to your ear!" exclaimed Claire.

Elena mentioned that she had seen Dr. Metuchi at the Club the other day and she asked her if Claire liked her new therapist and was she adjusting to her surroundings.

"She's nice, but a task master, and she's really different from Dr. Metuchi."

Bentworth didn't like the sound of this. He jumped in, "What do you mean? Aren't you getting along? Don't you think she's competent?"

Working hard at not overreacting, Jules waited for Claire to answer.

"Oh, we're getting along fine and I think she knows what she's doing. It's just that this is the first time someone has forced me to write out treatment goals. That's the difference."

Bentworth seemed mollified. "I see, her style is different."

"Yeah, Dad, that's all I meant."

Jules jumped in and asked them to take a few minutes to wrap up. They said their goodbyes and Elena asked if they could do this again next week, to which Jules gave a vague answer knowing she would be out of the country.

"I think she sounded good, don't you Elena?" said Bentworth once they had hung up from the call.

"Yes George. I think she sounded good, excited for a change. However, I don't have the trust that you do with the ISS people. I really think we need to know her location, just in case there is a problem. I can't sleep nights not knowing where she is. Will you please make a phone call tomorrow and see if we can have that information?"

Bentworth, the father and husband, agreed with Elena. He'd been feeling disconnected not knowing where Claire was, but Bentworth, the munitions mogul, knew it was better that neither he nor Elena knew. Even so, he agreed to see what he could find out.

"King County Superior Court. How may I direct your call?" answered an obsequious receptionist.

"Would you please connect me to the office of Dr. Alex Martini?"

"Certainly, it'll be just a moment. Okay, I'm transferring you now, Sir," replied the receptionist before she was on to the next call in the queue.

"Court Services. This is Mary."

"Dr. Martini, please."

"Ah, sorry Sir. Dr. Martini is on a leave for a special assignment. May I put you through to Dr. Fahad?" The phone went dead before Mary got an answer. *People are so rude now days. Not even a 'thank you'. Oh well, I'm not going to let that prick ruin my day.*

Closing the office door behind them, Alex asked Claire how the grooming and exercising was going. Claire said she liked it a lot, Dean pretty much let her do her thing, and it was fun having Mickey as her gofer. They were getting along well.

"How's the anxiety?" asked Alex, formally kicking off the session.

As Claire pulled something out of her back pocket she said, "I started keeping a diary. I know it's only been a couple of days, so maybe the information isn't too useful yet."

"Do *you* think it's useful?" countered Alex.

"It does help me focus," replied Claire.

"How?" Alex wondered if Claire was talking about what happens when a person is concentrating intently on a project and as a result the hyper focusing shuts out noises and other distractions.

"Sometimes I notice that there is no external stimulus for the anxiety," offered Claire.

"Do you mean that there is no apparent reason for feeling the anxiety?"

"Other than what happened to me no, there is no other reason." Claire liked how Dr. Martini tried to understand her.

"Does the thought of being kidnapped again cause you any anxiety?"

"No. I feel safe here," replied Claire.

If this is what Claire feels, thought Alex, *then why did Dr. Metuchi's notes contain several references to hyper-vigilance and an exaggerated startle response? Very curious.* Alex didn't think that after a few days at the ranch those symptoms would spontaneously evaporate and, once again, Claire was directing the conversation back to the kidnapping. It was clear that she didn't want to discuss pre-kidnapping. *What's going on here?* Alex decided it was time to confront her impressions.

"Claire, I get the distinct impression that you don't want to talk about yourself and how you were prior to the kidnapping. Why is that?"

"I just don't think it's relevant," replied Claire guardedly.

"You may not think it is germane, Claire, however it might be very useful in helping us find a way to relieve the anxiety about the kidnapping." Claire did not respond. Alex didn't talk either. She was thinking and not liking the conclusions that were quickly surfacing.

Finally, Claire spoke. "Dr. Martini, I'm not trying to purposely derail your plans. It's very hard for me to remember what I was like pre-kidnapping. The experience seems to have taken me over."

Alex nodded her head up and down for a few moments, made a split-second decision, and spoke to Claire. "So, it seems you're saying that you're stuck emotionally."

"Something like that," agreed Claire. She couldn't have hoped for a better opening. "I've been giving a lot of thought to a technique that might help get you unstuck, help you reconnect with the past and move you forward into the future. It will only work if you are sure you want to let go of the experience. Are you interested?" Alex waited for Claire's response. *Would it be consistent with Dr. Metuchi's feedback?*

"I don't know. What is it?"

"Hypnotherapy," replied Alex.

"Could you explain how it works?" asked Claire.

Alex couldn't assess whether or not Claire's mild interest was lip service. "Let's start with what hypnosis isn't. It's not putting a subject to sleep. It's assisting a patient to attain an intense focused concentration that is so absorbing it excludes peripheral phenomenon. When you mentioned that keeping a diary had helped you focus, I thought doing this on a deeper level could help."

"Would I lose control?" queried Claire, giving surface credence to Dr. Metuchi's conclusions.

"No, not at all. Hypnotherapy is not like entertainment hypnosis. That kind of hypnosis is hardly ever done with consideration to the subject's needs or vulnerabilities. Hypnotherapy is different. It could help you think clearly, because the kidnapping incident will be virtually excluded from your consciousness while in a trance state."

"Whoa, what are you talking about, a trance?" Claire was agitated. Again, consistent with Dr. Metuchi's assessment.

"People experience a trance state in different ways. It's just a term to describe the time the individual is under hypnosis. Some people experience a state of relaxation that can run the gamut from a mild relaxed feeling to ultra-relaxation or even floating. Others just experience a sense of security or feeling safe. We could focus on those specific issues that might be causing the anxiety to linger and, what I think is so exciting about this approach, is that the patient can often learn to use it him or herself.

"The relaxation techniques that Dr. Metuchi taught you could be described as a mild trance. If you allow us to explore a deeper trance and you learn how to use self-hypnosis, you could gain more control over your anxiety." If control were the real issue for Claire, learning that she could gain more control, might provide a motivation for her to agree.

"I have to think about this, Dr. Martini."

"Claire, what are you afraid of?"

"I'm not certain. Maybe it's because I'll find out something I don't want to know."

Alex pounced on the direction that Claire had unwittingly established. "What kinds of things wouldn't you want to know, Claire?"

Claire looked down and shook her head from side to side. "I don't know. Maybe who the kidnappers were, maybe why they kidnapped me, or if they planned to kill me. You know, that sort of things."

Excitement rolled through Alex. She had been right about Claire harboring more repressed memories than anyone thought. "Claire, with hypnosis we could create a 'selective' memory for you, excluding areas of discomfort until you were ready to remember."

"You mean you could do something so I wouldn't remember when I came out of the trance?" inquired Claire.

"Precisely! What do you say, are you up for it?" Alex crossed her fingers.

"Okay, but can we start next week? I finished my homework and want to take a couple of days to go over it with you."

Claire tried to conceal her reluctance, but Alex knew she needed time to let the whole idea settle in, so she didn't push for an earlier start. "Okay, then we have a deal. We'll start Saturday. Why don't we meet this evening after dinner for an hour and you can show me your chart? Now, off you go!"

Lunch had been a maudlin affair for Alex and Jules. With the table cleared and Claire and Mickey gone, Jules with resignation said, "Alex, Rick and Sophie, I'm going to have to leave this afternoon. A project I'm working on got moved up. However, before I go, I'd like to hear your thoughts on how things are going with Claire here."

"From my perspective," offered Rick, "things are going well. She seems to have settled into a routine, actually enjoys working down at the barn and, it appears, she is getting along with Mickey. I don't see any problems."

"Sophie?" prompted Jules.

"Same here. I haven't observed anything that would cause me concern." She turned to Alex and asked, "What about you? What do you think?"

Taking a deep breath Alex responded, "Nothing overt, but I can't shake the feeling that there is something just under the surface."

"Like what?" asked Sophie.

Alex's eyes were trained on Sophie and Rick as she said, "I have no doubt that she has repressed memories that have not yet come to the surface and, when they do, there could be behavioral issues. Right now, she is on a 'honeymoon' but if she remembers, things could change drastically."

Rick, fully aware that guests were due to arrive in a week, asked, "What kinds of behavior?"

"She could experience flashbacks, withdraw, become combative, go into a depression…stuff like that."

"Alex, could she be a danger to herself or others?" Sophie liked the girl but didn't ask the question out of concern for Claire. She was worried about the guests and the ranch personnel. An adverse incident could destroy their business.

"Not likely towards other people. Any change would likely be self-destructive," answered Alex with a great effort.

Sophie picked up on Alex's dejection. "Is there something you're not telling us? You seem awful worried."

Wishing she had taken an acting class, Alex summoned up a reassuring tone. "I've given you a fair picture on Claire. I don't think there is anything we can't handle. The best news is that she likes and respects Mickey and, we're making progress in her treatment."

"You can tell there's progress in a few days?" asked Sophie.

"What kind of progress?" interrupted Jules.

"She's agreed to an alternative treatment that I think will help her put the incident behind her." Alex was purposely vague, trying to maintain the doctor-patient confidentiality in front of Rick and Sophie.

"Good," replied Jules and after thanking them for their hospitality, excused herself to get her suitcase.

###

Sophie and Alex heard a horn honking, correctly assuming it was Jules' ride to the airport. Rick was already outside talking quietly to the driver when Jules came outside followed by Sophie and Alex. While the driver stowed Jules' bag in the trunk, Rick extended a hand to Jules which she took and shook warmly. Jules then turned to Sophie and hugged her, reassuring her and thanking her for everything.

Alex didn't know what to expect but had told herself she was not going to cry. Jules turned to Alex and, with a pained expression on her face, glanced into Alex's eyes as if she were looking for them to reflect what she should say. Tentatively, Jules encircled Alex with her arms, resting her chin on Alex's shoulder. She felt Alex's arms coming up her sides, grazing her jacket at hip level and ending up around her back. Alex held her tightly and whispered to her as tears streamed down her face, "I love you. Come back to me."

Jules kissed her cheek and let her go. She rushed down the stairs and dove into the back seat of the Town Car. Alex excused herself and hid out in her room for the greater part of the afternoon until Sophie called her for kitchen duty. It was the last thing that Alex needed right now but, nevertheless, she dutifully dragged herself down to the kitchen dreading what she knew was coming.

Sophie was in rare form. She didn't waste any time. "Sit down, Alex. I want to talk to you." Without protest, Alex sat down and waited for the onslaught. Slipping a cup of coffee in front of Alex, Sophie settled herself at the table. Sophie had her 'Mother Superior' look and wasted no time launching into a stern diatribe.

"Alex, I know you're not telling me everything. I've kept quiet for the last couple of days in hopes that whatever it is, you'd work it out or tell me. Now I want the truth. What's going on? What are you holding back? We're not leaving the kitchen until you tell me."

Alex looked at her watch. She had a therapy session with Claire at 4:00 p.m. and tried to come up with a plausible way to make her encounter with Sophie as brief as possible. She recognized her own struggle with anguish since Jules had uttered the words which delivered the greatest adult sorrow she had ever felt. Telling herself that she had better become engaged pretty damn quickly if she had any hope of staving off Sophie's demands for the truth, she began.

"Aunt Sophie, I have told you the truth concerning what I think about Claire. The aspect that continues to distress me is not knowing if she was involved with the kidnapping. This is weighing on me heavily."

Sophie sat back in the chair, the 'Mother Superior" look fading. Nope, it was back, but this time disguised as concern. *Damn,* thought Alex, *here it comes!* Sophie took a deep breath, looked at Alex then took a sip of her coffee before she said,

"You know I'm not talking about Claire. Nice try."

"You're talking about Jules and me."

"Yes. Now spit it out and don't give me any bullshit!" commanded Sophie.

Alex thought for a moment. *It would probably feel good to unburden myself to Sophie. However, I can't do it now, so I had better punt*

"Aunt Sophie, I don't know if Jules told you where she was going, but I have the impression that it's someplace dangerous. I'm feeling very concerned and afraid for her." Alex rationalized that what she said was true. Jules was going to the Middle East. It was dangerous and she was concerned. *Right keep telling yourself that and you might even begin to believe it.*

"Okay, sweetie, if that's really it but I want you to know that you can feel safe talking to me. You don't have to walk on eggshells or choose your words." She got up, leaned over and put her arms around Alex. "Baby, I love you so much. It hurts me to see you suffering."

Alex was stupefied. Just when she thought she had Sophie figured out, Sophie threw in a monkey wrench. *Go figure.*

"First Territorial, how may I direct your call?" answered the Bank's receptionist.

"I'd like to speak to the President or Branch Manager, if that's the appropriate term for the person in charge?"

"Certainly, let me transfer you to Mr. Woods' assistant. Thank you for calling First Territorial," replied the receptionist moments before transferring the call.

"Good afternoon, Mr. Woods' office. This is Esmeralda speaking. How may I help you?" answered Keith Woods' assistant.

"Good afternoon," spoke the voice over the phone. "I'd like to speak with Mr. Woods, please."

Esmeralda was the gatekeeper, polite, and efficient, screening all of Keith's calls. "May I tell him what the call is about?"

The voice on the phone answered evenly. "Tell him it's about a lot of money. Millions, in fact."

Esmeralda said that she would check to see if Mr. Woods was available. The person on the phone waited, then heard a slightly nasal voice say, "This is Keith Woods. How may I help you?"

Brother, they must have some sort of 'how may I help you?' campaign going on at the bank, thought the caller. "Mr. Woods, this is George Bentworth. Do you know who I am?" asked the caller with arrogance.

"I'm afraid that I don't Mr. Bentworth. Why don't you tell me?" said Keith with a sing song solicitous voice. Woods hurriedly Googled Bentworth while he listened to Bentworth describe himself as a successful entrepreneur with a net worth of somewhere around nineteen billion dollars. "Ah, yes, Mr. Bentworth. I see that you are a very successful entrepreneur with many global holdings," fawned Woods, hardly able to control his excitement. "How can I be of service to a man of your stature?" asked Woods, not at all trying to hide his deliberate sucking up.

"Look, Woods," continued the man on the phone, "I've checked around and you seem to be the man in the know around the Missoula area. Is that right?"

"Yes, yes. Of course, that's the case. Being here at the bank gives me access to much of the financial activities in the area and, of course, since we describe ourselves as a community bank, I'm a member of many local organizations. I'm sure you'd find my connections helpful." Woods gloated over his self-stroked sense of esteem.

"That's exactly what I'm hoping," registered the voice on the phone. "What do you know about a Dr. Alex Martini? I understand that she's from your neck of the woods."

"That's right, Mr. Bentworth. Her aunt has a ranch, ah, called White Bark Ranch, south of here." *Here is my chance to stick it to Sophie,* a thought he relished as if he had dripping fangs. "She grew up at the ranch, went off to college, then went into the service. I understand that she was dishonorably discharged," he lied.

"I see," continued the man on the phone. "What else?"

Lying again Woods picked up another nail and hammered it into the coffin. He said, "Heard that she had some problems here when she returned from the military. Rumors were that she had to move out of state and surrender her license to avoid some sort of malpractice suit and sanction from the State Board. Are those the types of things you want to know, Mr. Bentworth?"

"Yes, exactly. That's helpful. She's currently treating my daughter and I was thinking that maybe I had better get some local information about her. The people who arranged for her to treat Claire only presented her credentials from the state of Washington. Although they were good, I had a gut feeling something was wrong."

"Mr. Bentworth," dripped Woods, "I hope I'm not out of line, but I was just down at the ranch this morning. I'm assuming your daughter is there, since I had a conversation on another matter with Alex. I didn't see anyone else but ranch personnel, although they said they had guests. Would you like me to keep an eye out for her?"

"Ignoring Woods's offer, the voice on the phone continued, "What can you tell me about the ranch? I want to know if it's a nice place for my daughter. Of course, she says she likes it, but I want to know for myself."

Woods not certain where Bentworth was going with his question, decided to be straight with him. "It's very nice. Best property around and the family has done a lot of upgrades to the facility. While it's not a luxury resort, it is quite comfortable. However, they have been struggling financially."

"You know, my wife and I would like to come up to visit Claire and also look around. I'm trying to diversify my holdings, maybe go into real estate development. Would it be too great a favor to ask you to get us connected to the right people?"

This is better than sex, thought Woods. "Mr. Bentworth, if you don't mind, I'd suggest that you stay away from any realtors right now. They'll beleaguer you with follow up calls and a man of your importance doesn't have time for that. I know most of them and can line up a tour which I'd be glad to conduct myself!" Power surged through Woods' veins as he waited for Bentworth's gratitude.

"That's very accommodating, Mr. Woods. However, I haven't gotten this far in business without knowing that nothing is without strings. What's in it for you?"

Obviously Bentworth was nobody's fool. Woods answered proudly. "I really am the best person to take you around. I know what ranches are experiencing financial troubles, which means you might get a great deal. I also am familiar with all sorts of things that aren't a problem in typical urban development but can be out here. I'm talking about things like mineral, water, and grazing rights. What's in it for me? Well, Mr. Bentworth, to be brutally honest, I'm hoping that you will want to do business with the bank."

"That's all?"

"I also get a huge bonus if I can sell foreclosed property at no less than 85% market value." Woods hoped that his frank ambition would be attractive to Bentworth.

"All right, Woods. Give me your fax number and I'll have my assistant fax you my requirements. Of course, if you think I've missed something, you'll let me know, right?"

Woods bade Bentworth goodbye and with a hard-on as he had never experienced before, started plotting how to sell

Sophie's property out from under her. That would show her, and her dyke bitch niece who was boss!

Jules was aimlessly dragging a washcloth across Alex's shoulders and breasts, as Alex leaned against her in the tub. She wrapped her legs around Alex's waist, drawing her closer, as she kissed her shoulders and softly said, "What are we to each other?"

Alex lazily answered, "What do *you* think we are?"

Jules stopped kissing and with an impatient shake of her head, replied, "That's a typical shrink response. Can't you just answer the question?"

"Turning her head so she could see Jules' face," Alex, a little breathless, answered, "I think we are two people who are falling deeply in love with each other."

Jules didn't respond, but they held each other floating on their love, until the water got cold and chased them into the warmth of Alex's bed.

Then Alex woke up reaching for Jules, tears streaming down her cheeks. Jules was gone and so was her dream.

CHAPTER 15 - The One

The strongest principle of growth lies in human choice.

George Elliot

Thursday April 30

The ranch was awash with activity. Alex was thankful for the constant parade of food and supply delivery trucks that kept Sophie busy most of the day. Earlier Alex and Claire had met for an hour after which she and Mickey joined Rick at the barn where the Ferrier was already engrossed in a three-day task to change out each horse's steel horseshoes with a non-skid version. While the expense for the non-skid shoes was three times that of the steel shoes, the safety factor justified the expenditure during the guest season.

Tomorrow the Veterinarian was due on site to examine the horses and certify them for a summer of hard work. During Rick's first summer at White Bark Ranch, he negotiated a multiyear incremental flat-rate contract with both the Ferrier and the Vet, which he then took to the liability insurance carrier in hopes of negotiating a multiyear declining rate premium for a clean safety record. This year the savings from the premium would cover the increased cost of non-skid horseshoes and the vetting out of the entire horse herd.

After dinner Mickey, Claire, and Rick decided on a movie. Unfortunately for Claire it wasn't a chick flick, or even a family movie. The men had opted for a Spaghetti Western, "A Fistful of Dollars" starring Clint Eastwood. Rick explained to Claire that Spaghetti Westerns were a sub-genre of Western films that emerged in the 1960s, most of them produced by Italian studios and shot primarily in the Andalusian region of Spain because it resembled the American Southwest. Claire said she adored Clint Eastwood. Mickey and Rick rolled their eyes, but as soon as the theme song started, they turned their attention to the TV screen. *How appropriate*, thought Alex as she listened to the theme song, *'Requiem for a Dream'* before she started up the stairs hoping to avoid any alone time with Sophie.

Hidden in her room, Alex attempted to gather the cascade of clashing feelings that had whirled around her all day. She was tired of dancing with heartbreak. It wasn't difficult to articulate her disillusionment with love and all its promises. As long as she could remember love had been a constant train wreck in her life. Some people couldn't love or didn't love enough. Alex was convinced her fault was loving too much. She never guarded her heart and so, when the disillusionment of love came roaring in, she not only grieved for the lost love, but also for the losses of the past leaving her stressed, sad and small.

She knew that in the long run attempting to suppress feelings with the hope that they would fade away on their own doesn't work too well and only serves to block the natural progression of the grieving process. *I wouldn't doubt that Jules is continuing to block her emotions,* thought Alex.

In one last ditch effort to regain some semblance of normalcy, Alex willed herself to review the therapy notes she made from the last week. When her phone rang, she answered and was surprised to hear from Robbie.

"Hi Alex. I just wanted to call and let you know that everything is fine here, except for something weird that happened yesterday."

"What was it Robbie?" Alex asked with mild concern.

"Your phone rang while I was here, so I picked it up and it was this guy, kind of rude, who asked for you. Said he was from your bank and needed to talk to you about some account."

Alex's antenna went up. "Did he say what he wanted?"

Robbie told her that the dude wanted to know when she would be available. Alex barely let him finish when she pounced, "What did you tell him, Robbie?"

"Chill, Alex. I didn't tell him squat except to say I was just the house sitter and didn't know anything."

"What did he say?"

"Well, he left a number for you to call."

Alex was concerned, but not yet alarmed. *Probably just some over aggressive telemarketer.* "How did you respond to that?"

"Well, duh, I took down the number, but I gotta tell you, this guy sounded weird, like he was ready to snap, you know, come unglued." Robbie was not in the least bit troubled, so Alex tried not to over react.

"What's the number, Robbie?" Robbie read her the number which she copied down with the intent to call immediately. "Robbie, one more question. What time did the call come in?"

"About seven o'clock. Tonight."

Alex didn't want to startle Robbie but thought it best to be prudent. "Robbie, if you feel like you are being watched or followed or you get any more calls like this, I want you to leave the house and go home."

"What kind of assignment are you on? You working for the spooks?" said Robbie laughing.

"Let's put it this way. I'm on special assignment to the U.S. Attorney General and although I'm not handling anything that would cause any particular group or person to target me, one just never knows. Okay? So, let's play it safe. If you sense anything weird or hinky again, go home. Promise?"

"Okay, okay, Doc. I promise, but I don't like it."

"You don't have to Robbie. You just have to do it."

"God, Doc, you sound just like my mother," whined Robbie.

"Robbie, while you are a royal pain in the ass, I still like you. So, if you want me to keep liking you, you'll do what I'm asking. Got it?"

"All right Doc. Best friends forever?"

Alex smiled and responded, "Yup. BFFs, Robbie."

She dialed the eight hundred number, which was answered by an automated response, "Thank you for calling National Bank Services. If you know your party's extension, you may dial it now or stay on the line for an operator. Alex hung up before she dialed the extension. She opened her browser and typed in 'National Bank Services'. Clicking on the first reference returned by the search engine, she was directed to their web site. After quickly scanning the site, she learned that National Bank Services was an Internet virtual bank offering much the same services as a brick and mortar bank does, with the convenience of lower fees.

She redialed the number and this time entered the extension number when prompted, getting a voice mail response. "Hi, this is Thomas. Please leave a message and I will call you back as soon as I can." She breathed a sigh of relief. *Just as I thought… some over-zealous telemarketer. Maybe.*

She picked up her phone again and called Jake, relating the story to him. He told her not to worry that he'd check it out and get back to her one way or the other but meanwhile, she was to tell Rick and Mickey to be on the alert. She liked Jake. He didn't take chances, nor did he brush off her feelings of concern.

Well, I'm at the computer so I might as well try to organize my therapy notes, thought Alex. She had to admit that the conversation with Robbie, and subsequently with Jake, had taken her attention off her wounded heart.

"Sorry to disturb you but I just had a call from Alex. I don't think it's anything to worry about but thought you should know." Jake recounted the incident to Jules who listened dispassionately.

"I'm with you but no harm in checking it out. Was Alex worried?"

"She didn't sound alarmed. More like she was trying to cover all bases," answered Jake. "I wasn't sure if you made it back last night. What were you up to today?"

"I had some personal things to catch up on. Seems I've barely been home in the last month. I'll be in tomorrow for a while as we planned." Jules said goodnight to Jake then stared at her phone, until she reached for it and dialed. "Hi, Mom. I'm sorry it's so late, but I wanted to let you know that I'm leaving the country and will be gone for a couple of weeks. I didn't want you to worry if I didn't return your or Dad's calls."

Jules was both relieved and disappointed that her parent's answering machine picked up her call. She was not in an emotional state to withstand their typical cross examination, pontification, or complaints that they never saw her. Feeling guilty she vowed to herself that she'd swing by and see them when she returned from Afghanistan.

She decided that she had better pack for South America and Afghanistan. When she finished, she carried a pile of clothes into her living room, where they would spend the night until she took them to the dry cleaners tomorrow. Before leaving the clothes to their dreams, she went through the pockets one more time. Slipping her hand into the pocket of the jacket she had worn on the trip from Montana to LA, she felt a slip of paper. It was folded in quarters. She didn't remember putting anything in her pocket, but with all the upset it could have slipped her mind.

Opening it, she saw five numbers. 'Four, one, one, two, zero.' They were followed by the words, 'The sweet kiss on the cheek,' written in Alex's hand. Jules collapsed on the floor and wept inconsolable tears, sobs wracking her body, emptying her until she was depleted, feeling as if she were living in hell.

###

Friday May 1

Jake was in the office early. He called the number for National Bank Services and punched in the extension Alex had given him last night. "Hello, you have reached Thomas at National Bank Services. I will be on vacation beginning May 1st, returning Monday May 11. If you need assistance, please dial zero now." Jake muttered *Damn voice mail*, to himself then dialed zero which routed him to an automated answering response. "You have reached National Bank Services. We are currently closed, but if you know your party's extension, you may dial it now."

Jake decided to call every half hour until he got a live person. He wondered if doing away with live people answering phones frustrated the population in general as much as it did him. ISS was staffed twenty-four seven with a live operator and he expected that of every business. He hated having to wait to do his job. An hour and a half later he still was unable to get a live person. *Where the hell is this Bank? Australia?* He said before he cursed.

About 9:00 a.m. Jules poked her head into his office. As she came in, he told her, "Damn, you look like hell!"

Jules responded tersely. "Didn't get much sleep last night."

"Worried about the trip?" asked Jake, while passing her a cup of coffee from the pot in his office.

"Some. The trip itself is going to be grueling. LA to Dallas for a short stop, then on to Buenos Aires. I have to leave Saturday on a red eye instead of Sunday as I had originally planned. Leaving Saturday gets me into Buenos Aires on Sunday, which gives me all day Monday and Tuesday before I have to fly out Tuesday night to Madrid."

"Where do you go from Madrid?" asked Jake, even though he knew her itinerary was in his mailbox.

I'm flying commercial from here to Buenos Aires, then on to Madrid, but then a private jet has been arranged to take me from Madrid to Peshawar. You know I don't sleep well on flights. Got any sleeping pills?"

"Nope. You know me. I sleep like a baby."

Trying to lighten the mood, Jules quipped, "I should have absconded with a few of Claire's sleeping pills!"

Jake chuckled then asked, "Speaking of Claire, how is she doing? She sounded good on the phone, but that might have been show for her father and stepmother."

"Actually, quite well. She seems to fit into the environment and says she is enjoying working with the horses and, she's getting along with Mickey better than I had hoped. On the other hand, Alex says that she is resistant to the direction Alex wants to take in therapy, so her seeming improvement could simply be due to a change in environment. You know what it was like for her at her father's estate."

Jake's eyebrows arched, signaling his curiosity. "Ah yes. I do. So, you're saying that the relative freedom she now has, and her perception of less parental control may have caused a temporary improvement?"

"Exactly. Her improvement may be short lived."

"How are Sophie and Rick doing with the interloper?" smirked Jake.

"Good. Sophie is bossing Claire around as if she were one of her own. Rick is treating her like a ward, whom he has been assigned to protect." Jules, who was perched on a chair in front of Jake's desk, got up and closed the office door. Before she returned to the chair, she added milk to her coffee, then settled in. "Jake, what progress have you made digging deeper on Elena?"

"Very interesting stuff came up," responded Jake. "Maybe we should have done more than a level one rundown initially but there was no obvious reason to look any deeper at the time." Shaking his head, he went on. "Hindsight is twenty-twenty, no?"

"Um Hmm. What's of interest?" asked Jules.

"Okay. Here's a synopsis of what we previously discovered. Born in Mexico City, mother and father still alive; father a retired banker; mother a retired school teacher. No ties to any particular political factions. Two siblings. Her older brother is married and lives in Mexico City. He's a cardiologist and has a lucrative private practice. Her younger brother is divorced and works for FEADS, the Mexican equivalent of the DEA. When we checked with Immigration none of her family has visited the U.S. for over a year.

"Now we can add that Elena had a baby when she was sixteen and gave it up for adoption. We would have expected a tip off from a sealed record of some sort during the original investigation, but there were no records at all."

"Did your operative just miss them?"

"No. They didn't exist which means either the adoption was a very private affair, or the records were destroyed," replied Jake.

"So how did you discover this?" prompted Jules.

"Well, previously we reviewed medical records and didn't find anything that stuck out but, admittedly, it was a cursory review. We went back through them again. There were no entries for an entire year. I found that odd since Elena suffered from asthma as a child and had medical attention several times a year. So, we thought we'd try and match the year the medical records were in absentia with her school records. Bingo! It matched exactly to a year missed in high school.

"After that it was a matter of gum-shoeing it until we found someone who led us to a rural clinic where her older brother had practiced medicine right out of med school."

Jules thought the information was interesting but doubted it had any relevance. "So how does the fact that she had a child out of wedlock, then gave it up for adoption, play into the possibility that Elena was involved in the kidnapping?"

"What would you say if you learned that Bentworth, through one of his charities, funded the construction of the rural clinic where Elena gave birth?"

Jules snapped to attention. "Shit!"

"Exactly!" retorted Jake.

"You have a working hypothesis?" countered Jules.

"Listen to this. We're still working on it but here's the framework. Suppose Elena was sent to stay with her brother at this rural clinic to have the baby, and what if she didn't want to give the baby up for adoption? Maybe her family pressured her, and she never got over it."

Jules cut in. "You mean that because Elena's baby was taken from her, she has carried some sort of psychosis with her and took Bentworth's child? I don't know Jake. That's kind of farfetched."

"Maybe, but I've seen people do crazy things with a lot less provocation. At any rate, what if we were to add two more pieces of information? One, Elena took a leave of absence from her job when she was twenty-nine citing exhaustion as the reason. Again, there were no records that she was in a facility, but what if she had some sort of psychotic break and needed treatment? Okay, okay, I see your face. It's a stretch but hold on. At the time we did the initial level one, all we did was confirm that her younger brother was indeed a bona fide member of the FEADS. Guess what? He was on vacation for two weeks, the week prior to Claire's abduction and the week after.

"No one knows exactly where he was and there are no Immigration records suggesting he was in the States. However, as part of the FEADS, he might have been able to cross without using a passport or perhaps he just snuck across the border." Jake waited to see if Jules had revised her opinion.

"We need to find out where he was. If he was here and Elena failed to mention it, I'd be inclined to think that your hypothesis has merit." Jules grudgingly conceded that Jake could be right. "God, if this turns out to be true, Bentworth will be devastated. Be prepared to take Elena into protective custody. No telling what Bentworth would do with that kind of betrayal."

"Yeah. I already briefed her bodyguard. I was also thinking that we shouldn't agree to any more calls with Claire until we have more definitive information. Your thoughts?" ended Jake.

"Absolutely. Blame it on me if you need to. Anything else?" inquired Jules.

"Not with this case but, if you have time, I'd like to get your thoughts on a couple other cases." Jake grabbed a pile of folders from the credenza behind his desk.

"I plan to be here all day." Jules needed something to occupy her mind, so she welcomed the work. Jake and she spent the next three hours reviewing active cases before they went out to lunch.

Seated at a local bistro around the corner from their offices, waiting for their orders to arrive, Jules pulled out a manila envelope from her attaché case. Laying it on the table, she faced Jake and asked him if he'd be willing to do her a personal favor.

"Sure. Does it have to do with that envelope?" asked Jake.

"Yes, it does. Look, Jake, let's be realistic about this trip to Afghanistan. There is a chance that I could be forcibly retired, if you catch my drift."

Jake interrupted, trying to ward off any bad spirits. "Now don't go talking like that. Everything is going to go well and besides, you promised that you'd bail if your intuition started acting up."

"I know and I will bail, but just in case, okay? If something happens, I would like you to take this to Alex."

Jake had a quizzical look on his face. Jules really didn't want to explain what was in the envelope but, out of respect for their friendship, which had evolved over the years working together, she told him she had named Alex executor of her estate.

Jake thought about it for a moment, then with respect for Jules said, "You really trust her that much?"

"I do, Jake. Besides her skills will be very advantageous with my parents." Jules had a flash that maybe Jake was disappointed because she hadn't asked him to be the executor. "Jake, I've also named you as an alternate if Alex can't or won't do it. Are you okay with that?"

Ignoring her question, Jake lowered his voice and gently asked Jules, "She's the one, isn't she?"

Jules was thrown completely off guard with his question. Her mind reeled. *He wasn't even around the two of us. How could he know what went on between Alex and me?* Her mind shifted gears and flew into overdrive searching for a way to answer him and, in the end, all she was able to do was say, "Yes, how did you know?"

"I could feel the energy between the two of you. The squabbling between the two of you didn't really feel like adversarial bickering and the way you looked at her when she realized who you were, well, it just seemed more to me."

"More than what?" The feeling of exhaustion seeped into Jules' body again.

"I don't know how to explain it. It was just more than compassion or empathy. At least that's how it seemed to me." Jake was embarrassed. In all the years together, they had never discussed Jules' personal life.

"God, Jake. I didn't know what was happening to me, what hit me, but it's all in the past now."

Surprised again, Jake asked "What do you mean, it's in the past now?"

Jules, trying to control her tears, slowed her breathing before answering. "Jake, it just isn't something that will work out. I can't be distracted by my feelings or any kind of relationship."

"It's none of my business but I'm going to give you my two cents worth anyway. We get to a point doing this kind of work where we expect to sacrifice the personal aspect of our lives but, if I met 'the one' nothing else would matter. If it meant kissing this job goodbye to be with her, I'd do it in a minute."

"My god, Jake. I had no idea!" Jules was stunned. She never would have imagined that Jake would walk away from a job he loved for another person. "Tell me truthfully, Jake, do you think if the 'right one' came along for you, you could have her and this job?"

Jake knew where Jules was headed, and he got there before she did. "I wouldn't hesitate to give it up for 'the one', but I don't think that loving someone and doing this job are mutually exclusive. If she loved me then she'd want me to be happy and would learn to live with the risk. Don't you think?"

"Maybe, but would you want to put her through that agony every time you went on assignment?" countered Jules.

"Would that agony be any more than the agony we'd both feel not being together?"

Jules didn't answer. She was too busy studying the pattern in the tablecloth. Jake went on. "And I bet I can guess what your next question will be." Jules looked up at him waiting. "You're wondering if being in love would jeopardize an operation because you can't get that person out of your mind. For me, I think it would do the opposite. I'd be less reckless; I'd double check everything and take extra precautions. I think being extra vigilant would give me even more confidence."

"And how would you handle having to choose between her and the job?" tested Jules.

"Again, I don't see why I would have to choose, except that maybe I would miss a birthday or anniversary because of a mission and that she'd have to understand that possibility up front." Jake was patient. He could see the torment in her face, so he waited, ignoring the rumbling of hunger in his belly.

"Jake, what if you were on a mission and someone kidnapped her, and you had to choose between her and the mission. What would you do?"

"Realistically speaking, how many of the missions you and I work on fall into that category? One every five years?" Jules nodded agreement. "Okay, then it's not a choice I'd have to make every day, but if it came down to it, I'd have to protect the lives of people we were hired to protect and trust that you or other ISS people would protect the life of my wife." Jake was adamant in his conviction.

"But is it right to put your wife in jeopardy?" opposed Jules.

"That isn't my choice Jules. It's her choice. It goes with the territory. If she wants to be with me, then she has to accept the inherent risk."

"Could you live with the knowledge that your job caused her to be harmed?" The last bastion where Jules had been hiding was about to topple, though Jules had yet to come to this realization.

"My job wouldn't cause her to be harmed. It would be the people who do the maiming and killing. Anything can happen to any of us at any time. What if your parents had refused to teach you to drive because they were afraid you would get into an accident and die? Then what if you were crossing the street and a drunk driver flew through a red light and killed you anyway? We can't insulate people from what might be. The best we can do is teach them to take precautions but, in the end, we are all subject to Providence and no matter how much we try to avoid certain circumstances, it's out of our control.

"If I found someone who shared these feelings, convictions and philosophies, I'd run to her, grab her in my arms and never let her go because I'd know that in loving me, she had accepted the risks and was at peace with them. Call her, Jules. Let her know how you feel."

"I can't Jake. Not now. Maybe after I get back from Afghanistan," replied Jules diffidently.

Jake nodded his head as if he understood her hesitancy. "You don't want to do it over the phone?"

"No. If I decide that I can balance the job and a relationship, I will want to talk to her about it in person, especially after the way I left." Jules chewed on her lip before continuing. "Jake, did you ever meet 'the one'?"

"Once, a long time ago," answered Jake.

"What happened?" Jules was doing it again, changing the topic to take the attention off of her.

"She didn't think I was 'the one' for her." Jake picked up the envelope, folded it in half and stuffed it into his inside suitcoat pocket.

CHAPTER 16 - Tango Bravo Zulu

When you dance the tango, you must give everything. If you can't do that, don't dance.

Ricardo Vidort

Saturday May 2

Jules flew through security at LAX with her special permit, arriving at her gate with thirty minutes to spare. A few minutes later she was sitting next to the window in Business Class. She was hoping that the airline computers hadn't booked a Chatty Cathy in the aisle seat next to her. Just before the door was closed a pleasant looking man in his fifties blew in and, after stowing his luggage in the overhead bin, plopped down in the seat next to Jules. After he buckled his seat belt and ordered a scotch, he extended his hand to Jules and introduced himself. He had a thick Texas accent.

She returned the handshake introducing herself and he asked her what she did. She told him she was a translator for the Associated Press attending a conference in Buenos Aires. He either thought she was beneath him or found her profession boring. After telling her he was going to Buenos Aires on cattle business, with extreme politeness, he explained that he hoped she wouldn't be offended if he didn't talk with her on the flight because he was hoping to catch up on his sleep. Courteously she reassured him that she would be doing the same.

Sunday May 3

Jules' stomach was still protesting the turbulent landing when she walked to the curb in search of a cab. She shivered, feeling the damp stale cold through her raincoat. It was about forty-five degrees and the rain was falling in sheets from a completely overcast sky. May in Argentina is the last month of Autumn before the winter months of June, July and August.

Settled in the back seat of a taxi she told the driver in passable Spanish to take her to the Holiday Inn Puerto Madero Hotel which was located near hundreds of restaurants, shops, and many important corporate and government offices. In addition, it was located a few blocks from the subway and train stations. Using public transportation made it more difficult for anyone to follow, although that wasn't a great concern of hers right now. All she wanted was a hot bath, brunch and a few hours of sleep.

While running a bath she ordered empanadas, little pastries filled with meat, some provolone cheese, fruit and a bottle of red wine. Her plan was to eat, drink herself to sleep then, if the rain let up, walk around later in the afternoon and early evening to scout out the offices she needed to visit tomorrow.

Lying in the steamy, hot, soapy water, she kept going over everything that Jake had said to her Friday at lunch. Essentially it was the same she had heard from Alex, except that it was from the perspective of a person like herself, Jake, who spent his life doing dangerous jobs. Jules knew that Jake was more than he appeared to be at first glance. She asked herself, *how on earth had he internalized those beliefs, and even more so, how had he developed such an intense conviction surrounding them?*

While waiting for room service to bring her brunch, she thought about how difficult it must have been for Alex to remain neutral and rebut her objections one by one without letting her personal stake in the relationship interfere. She hadn't fully comprehended Alex's achievement until now. Alex had managed to guide her through an emotional nuclear meltdown without concern of how it would play out for herself. Jules felt dreadful. She had callously removed Alex from her life without regard for Alex's emotional state.

Deeming her own behavior as despicable, she wondered how she could ever face Alex again after treating her so heartlessly. *Hat in hand and a lot of groveling*, she thought as she heard the knock from room service.

Awaking after four hours of sleep, Jules opened the curtains and noticed that the rain had stopped. It was still gloomy and probably cold, but at least she wouldn't get wet during her exploration of the area. When she passed through the lobby, she stopped for a large cup of coffee to sip as she walked. Right across the street from the hotel, a modern complex occupied three entire city blocks. She located the building which housed many Argentinian government offices, including the Office of Records, which she planned on visiting tomorrow. The lobby was locked so she continued walking like any tourist seeing the sights.

Jules was almost positive that she wasn't under surveillance. She took a deep breath of ozone-filled air, relaxing for the first time in a week, as she watched the shops and restaurants come alive. Checking her watch, she saw it was almost seven. She hustled back to the hotel to change for her dinner reservation at the Rojo Tango in the exclusive Hotel Faena. She was looking forward to the live orchestra, the best tango dancers and singers, along with the international cuisine. Anything to take her mind off Alex.

Monday May 4

Mickey knocked on Claire's door to accompany her to breakfast and she told him to come in. Surprised to find her still in bed, he asked if she was ill. "A headache of the sledgehammer type," she weakly answered him. "I woke up like this and just took some ibuprofen. Go ahead and get your breakfast. Could you please bring me back some coffee and toast when you're finished? Sometimes the caffeine helps with the headache."

"Of course. Be back in a jiff." He flashed his infectious smile and softly closed the door. Flying down the stairs, two at a time, he was in the dining room in three seconds flat.

Rick just finished and was standing up to clear his place. "Where's Claire?"

"She said she's got a bad headache. I'm going to get a plate for myself and bring her some coffee and toast. Do you have a tray?" asked Mickey.

"Sure. I'll get it for you. Do you want me to go up and stay with her until you've eaten your breakfast?"

"I think she's okay alone for five minutes. Don't you?"

Rick shrugged his shoulders. "I agree, but I'm happy to do it if you think we should."

"No, really, I'll be on my way up in a minute. Thanks."

Minutes later, Mickey was on his way back up to Claire's room, thinking how boring the day was going to be if she intended to spend it in bed.

Alex walked into the kitchen from the back door. Rick saw that she had been jogging. "Hey, Doc, your favorite patient has a headache today and didn't get up."

"Really. How interesting," answered Alex.

"How so?" inquired Rick.

"I intended to start a new treatment direction with her today, and she wasn't too happy about it. We had already rescheduled it from Saturday."

Rick asked Alex if she thought Claire was faking the headache to avoid the new treatment.

"Possibly. I'll check in with her after I shower and eat. Catch you later. Oh, by the way, where's Aunt Sophie?" she asked as she turned on her heel to look at Rick again.

"She left right after she finished making breakfast. Went into Missoula for a doctor's appointment. I'm surprised you didn't see the truck missing."

"Rick, is she okay? She'd tell us if she weren't, right?"

"Don't worry Alex. It's just her annual woman checkup," answered Rick, squeamish about the subject.

"Why is she going to Missoula instead of seeing Doc Flanders in Darby?"

"Says his hands shake too much. I guess that could be a problem," said Rick, blushing from the thought of Doc Flanders inserting a speculum into Sophie.

Alex smiled at Rick's embarrassment. It was endearing. "I can see where that would be uncomfortable. Catch you later."

###

Mickey called out "come in" to the knocking on his door. Alex walked in saying, "I understand our guest is not feeling well today?"

"She ate some toast and drank some coffee about forty-five minutes ago. I think she's sleeping now. Do you want to wake her?" Mickey asked protectively.

"Not if she's sleeping, but I'll take a peek. Alex preceded Mickey through the connecting bathroom and cracked open the door into Claire's room. Looking into the room, Alex was confused.

Mickey understanding the look on Alex's face, flung the door open and surveyed the room in less than three seconds.

"She's gone! Damn, I sat with her while she ate, then when she fell asleep, I came back here. I didn't hear a thing! Shit, my ass is grass and Jake is the lawn mower!"

"Wait, Mickey. Check the door. She shouldn't have been able to get out without going through your room. Meanwhile, I'll check the windows," ordered Alex.

"The door to the hall is still locked," Mickey cried out.

"Windows too," responded a puzzled Alex. "Mickey, look in the bathroom, behind the shower curtain," spat out Alex. Mickey rushed past Alex into the bathroom to check.

Back in the room he shook his head, "Nope. Not there."

Alex sat on the bed to think. She motioned to Mickey to sit beside her and talking in sotto voce said, "What about the closet?"

"Why would she hide in the closet, Alex?"

"Mickey, did you hear anything at all?"

"Nothing, Alex. Nothing."

"She could be having a flashback. Since we think one of her captors was a woman, it would be better for you to check the closet. If she's in there and in the middle of a flashback, she'll be confused and maybe combative. Don't bring her over to the bed. Have her sit in the chair by the desk that faces away from the bed."

"Okay, Alex. What do I say?"

Alex thought a moment. "Tell her she's safe, she's been rescued, and you're not going to let anything happen to her. Keep saying it over and over."

"Okay, here goes." Mickey slowly opened one of the closet doors and hunkered down. "Claire, honey, are you here? You're safe baby. I'm here to rescue you. Nothing bad is going to happen." He paused for a moment, then stretched out his hand. "Come on Claire. I see you now. You're safe. I'm here to rescue you. Give me your hand and I'll take you out of here to a safe place."

Alex couldn't see if Claire was reaching for Mickey's hand, but she didn't dare move, fearing that if she startled Claire, Claire might withdraw further into the flashback.

Mickey kept encouraging her, gently and patiently, until she gave him her hand and let him pull her up and out of the closet. Putting his arm around her back, he guided her to the chair and helped her sit down. "Claire, you're okay now. You're at the ranch in Montana and no one can hurt you. Is it okay if I get Dr. Martini?"

Claire was dazed, in some sort of semitrance state. Alex wasn't sure if she heard Mickey. Mickey must have been thinking the same thing, because he asked her again. "Claire, honey, can I go get Dr. Martini now?"

Still staring into space, Claire's answer was weak and barely audible. "Yes, please."

Before getting up, Alex talked to Claire. "Claire, it's Dr. Martini. Mickey told me you wanted to see me. May I come over?"

Though Claire did not turn around, she nodded.

"I'm coming Claire. In a moment you'll feel my hand on your shoulder, then you'll see me. Are you ready?"

"Yes."

Alex approached doing exactly what she had told Claire she would do but thinking that something was off here. While sometimes a flashback can induce a trance-like state, this one seemed different. This seemed more like a hypnotic trance. "I'm here now, Claire. Do you know where you are?"

Claire sprung up from the chair, surprising both Alex and Mickey. Throwing her arms around Alex she sobbed, "I don't know what to do. I like Alex."

Neither Mickey nor Alex understood at first why Claire referred to Alex in the third person. When Claire sprang, Mickey thought she was going to assault Alex.

Then Alex realized that Claire might be disassociating. Alex continued to hold her and told her that she didn't have to decide what to do right now.

"Mickey, I need to get her out of this room and do something to snap her back. I have an idea."

"Okay, Doc. Whatever you say." Mickey picked Claire up and carried her downstairs, following Alex into the great room.

"Set her on the couch and then find that movie Rick, you and she were watching. Pop it in and start it up." Mickey looked at her as if she were off her rocker.

"I know, it's crazy, but do it please." Alex sat down next to Claire and held her hand, repeating that she could rest because she didn't have to try and figure out what to do right now. When the theme song started playing Mickey returned to the couch and sat on the other side of Claire.

"Remember this movie Claire?" The theme song was playing. "You, Mickey and Rick watched it the other night. You said you liked Clint Eastwood. Remember?" Claire's breathing slowed and Alex felt her body relax. "Claire, can you talk to me now?"

Claire moved her eyes from the TV screen to look at Alex. "I remember the movie. Rick and Mickey made fun of me."

"Okay, Claire, that's good. Do you know where you are?"

"I'm at Aunt Sophie's ranch."

"That's right," encouraged Alex, "and do you know what happened to you?"

With childlike innocence she answered, "I think I got scared and hid."

"You're right," replied Alex, "but you know you're safe now. Right?"

"I'm safe now, with you and Mickey." Claire had come out of the flashback and trance state but was still unsteady, both emotionally and physically. Alex couldn't help but remember her own flashback experience with Jules. A pang of angst impaled her heart rendering her speechless for a moment. She collected herself and told Claire that Mickey and she would sit with her for a while. An hour later when Alex was sure that Claire had fully come out of the flashback, she and Mickey put Claire to bed. Alex gave Claire a sleeping pill and Mickey waited until Claire was deep in slumber before he left her and returned to his room. Keeping his door open, he went across the hall and tapped on Alex's door. Alex came to the door and the two of them walked back into Mickey's room.

"My God, Alex. That poor kid. What's going to happen to her? I thought she was making progress, but then this." Mickey was upset, and his feelings were authentic. He had grown fond of Claire and enjoyed being around her.

"Mickey, would you be surprised if I told you I was expecting this?" Alex waited for the shock to wear off.

"What do you mean?" stammered Mickey.

"Do you know what the Hawthorne effect is?"

"I used to, but refresh my memory, please," asked Mickey.

"Most of the research revolving around the Hawthorne effect has been in industrial settings," began Alex.

"Oh yeah, now I remember. Some sort of short-term improvement of productivity by just observing workers?"

"Exactly," answered Alex. "However, it's more. The Hawthorne effect is a form of reactivity. We've been observing temporary change to behavior in response to a change in environmental conditions. Eventually the behavior returns to what it was before the change in environmental conditions."

"Wow. Now what? Will she remember when she wakes up and, if she does, do I tell her everything?" asked a concerned Mickey.

"Most likely she'll remember, and you can tell her where we found her and what we did. However, don't talk to her about her saying that she didn't know what to do. It could trigger additional stress." Alex would have to deal with that in a very controlled therapy session.

"Alex, how did you know the movie would snap her out of it?"

"I didn't. There are many good ways to interrupt a flashback and what works for one person may not work for another. Immersion in cold water almost always works because the brain is shocked and interrupts the flashback to survive what it may perceive as a life-threatening immersion in freezing water. The water has to be very cold to be of any value. Distraction is another method that works sometimes."

"You are one smart doc. Promise me if I ever get an invitation to the 'Cuckoo Show' you'll be the one to treat me," joked Mickey, trying his best to mask the helplessness he felt when he witnessed Claire's episode.

"Okay, Mickey. I promise," smiled Alex. "I'll stick around the house today. Call me if she wakes up." Alex went back to her room, drained from the experience. She would try and sort it out later.

###

After a few false starts, Jules had a productive day. Most of what she needed was public record and, that which was not, she had gotten leads on where to go. She had just finished setting up two appointments for tomorrow and was organizing her notes for tomorrow's interviews, when the phone rang.

"Hey there, had any good steak yet?" Jake sure seemed chipper.

"Yup, buddy boy. Last night, I went to dinner and a tango show. What's up?" Jules was finishing off the bottle of wine she had ordered yesterday at brunch, so she was in no hurry.

"You won't believe what we found, Jules!" Jake took the better part of five minutes sharing information that one of his operatives had obtained.

Jules listened intently, taking down notes now and then. When Jake finished, she answered, "Damn. What about the man from the bank? Did you find him?"

"Yeah. He's just a kid. Said he was paid five-grand to let some dude use his voice mail and go on vacation for a week, but he swears he didn't make the call. Alex's intuition was right!" exclaimed Jake.

"But you weren't able to tie him back to anyone?" countered Jules.

"Not yet, but we're working on it."

"Do you plan on turning him in to his company," asked Jules.

"Nope. First of all, none of my business. Second of all, I want to keep that voice mail box up and running. The kid gave me the code to get in so I can monitor it."

"Good thinking, Jake. Tell me again where the call originated?"

"Los Angeles," answered Jake.

"Today I discovered some very interesting information and by tomorrow, I am hoping to have it confirmed. If it pans out as I suspect, then we have to alert White Bark Ranch, but I don't want to throw them into a panic if we don't have to. You know what Sherlock Holmes says, 'It is dangerous to theorize in advance of the facts.'"

"I hear you, but I'm going to wave a flag if Alex reports anything else suspicious," said Jake with finality.

"Sounds reasonable," trailed off a distracted Jules. "Good night Jake. Good work."

Getting up from the desk in the hotel room, Jules opened the blackout draperies and looked out the window across the Rio La Plata. The Puerto Madero area of Buenos Aires glittered. The area had a reputation as a party city, big clubs with spinning electronic music, sizzling tango shows, and other live music venues dotted the night landscape. Last night, Jules discovered that the locals didn't start prowling until late in the evening. She had gotten back to the hotel well past the bewitching hour and, now as she sat waiting for room service, she reflected on her experience at the tango show.

She had been seated next to a striking man in his late forties. He was a local and he chatted easily in fairly good English describing the history of the tango. When she asked him if he danced the tango, he replied, "The tango is not easy." She assumed he meant the intricacy of the steps. He laughed and told her that the steps were incidental. Passionately, he replied that the Tango required a sharing of power and energy between the dancers and it also required a sensitivity to the musical phrasing.

He told her that the woman must be able to release the energy in her body and surrender her independence to the music as well as to her partner. She could still hear his voice echoing in her head. "The Tango requires maintaining your center, your balance and accepting a partnership without giving up your voice. If you can't feel the ground, if you can't walk, and if you cannot surrender willingly, you cannot tango."

After the show her dinner companion stood up and offered her his hand. "El tango te espera." Even with her rudimentary Spanish she understood him. The tango awaits you. She let him teach her, lead her, hold her, embrace her, until hours later, she viscerally understood what he meant.

As she thought about his words, she wondered if he was really talking about tango, life, or spirituality. Maybe, *all three,* she decided. Taking a pad from her attaché case, she started a letter.

Darling, I have discovered that the tango is much more than a dance. It is a delicate balance between keeping one's own equilibrium and surrendering to the music and one's partner.

She continued writing and when she finished the letter, put it in an envelope and addressed it to Alex, after which she dropped it into a larger envelope with instructions to Jake. She'd give it to the CIA contact in Madrid to put in a diplomatic pouch back to the states. After eating a light supper Jules fell into bed, sleeping soundly for the first time in a week.

###

Keith Woods was packing up his briefcase calling it quits after another boring day at the bank when his secretary came in with a fax. The cover page carried the logo of Bentworth Enterprises. Typed in the middle of the page, the succinct message, resembling a telegram with just the bare necessities said,

Woods, good talking to you the other day. Next page explains what I'd be interested in seeing. Am flying in with the wife Wednesday. Will have my secretary call with flight information. Expect you to meet us and take us to properties on Wednesday and Thursday. Intend to visit my daughter on Friday. Keep confidential. George.

Woods had a plan. He'd show Bentworth properties that did not meet his criteria on Wednesday and Thursday, knowing that once Bentworth saw White Bark Ranch, nothing in the area would satisfy him. Even though White Bark Ranch's mortgage payments were current, Woods had found an obscure loophole in the way the mortgage had been written that would allow the Bank to call the note! He'd then be able to sell it to Bentworth for a profit. *I just have to keep the home office's nose out of the transaction if I want to get that bitch's property,* thought Woods, as he contained himself from dancing around the office. *Finally, I'll get my revenge*!

The house was eerily quiet after Claire's flashback incident. Alex decided to stay in Mickey's room in the event that Claire awoke. She was reviewing about six months of Dr. Metuchi's treatment notes for the second time. In addition to the inconsistency concerning Dr. Metuchi's and Claire's conflicting interpretations of hypnosis, this time she picked up another irregularity. Dr. Metuchi diligently noted that she had been working with Claire to stop the flashbacks but there were no notes on what treatment she was using to teach Claire to intervene in her own episodes.

It was likely that the relaxation and Cognitive Behavioral Therapy or CBT would have a trickledown effect but, if Claire had been suffering flashbacks with any frequency, Dr. Metuchi should have spent time teaching her self-help techniques. One possible explanation for not pursuing self-help techniques was if the flashbacks stopped entirely, there would be no need for them. However, Alex didn't think that was a sound approach. One can't possibly realize all the triggers that were lurking in the subconscious mind or the environment.

Alex pulled out the tapes of the conversations she had with Dr. Metuchi and Claire and listened to them again. She knew she was missing something, but it was playing hide and seek in an alcove of her mind. By the time she finished it was 4:00 p.m. Mickey came up to relieve her, fervently hoping that there wouldn't be a repeat of the morning's episode.

Scrubbing potatoes at the sink Alex heard Sophie's truck drive up behind the kitchen. Moments later Sophie walked in with her arms full of bags. She was as pale as the streaks of white bark on the pine tree down by the pond. Alex rushed to help her. "Aunt Sophie, you look awful. Aren't you feeling well? Come sit down and let me get you a glass of water."

"I'd prefer a scotch, if you don't mind." Sophie sat at the table and said, "Don't ask."

Alex returned with a glass two-fingers full of scotch from the bottle Sophie kept in one of the cupboards. Sophie drank it down in one gulp, setting the glass down in front of her so she could hold her head in her hands.

Concerned, Alex tried again. "What's going on Aunt Sophie? I know something is wrong."

"Honey, I don't really want to talk about it right now."

Alex felt her level of concern leap from *I wonder if she has a touch of the flu to, I hope she didn't get devastating news from the doctor.* "Okay, just tell me if you are physically all right."

"Yes, I'm not sick Alex."

It didn't take Holmes and Watson to deduce that if she wasn't physically ill, the problem was emotional. "Okay, Aunt Sophie. Why don't you go rest and I'll see to dinner tonight?" Sophie, with great effort, got up from the table to go upstairs.

Alex returned to the sink and started playing 'what if'. *What if she had a bad fight with Rick and he's leaving? Nope, that couldn't be it. He was calm and acted normal this morning. Okay, what if she got bad news about the ranch. Not that either. They were current with the mortgage payments. Okay, how about getting bad news from some relative in Italy? Did she stop at the post office on her way into Missoula this morning? Maybe. Or what if she had had an accident and is shaken up?*

Alex ran out to look at the truck. It wasn't damaged. *Damn, what was it?* She grabbed her walkie talkie and called Rick on a private channel. "Rick, Sophie got home a little while go. Something's wrong. I think you should come up and see if you can get her to tell you what's happened."

"Is she sick? Did the doctor give her bad news?" asked Rick.

"No, she says she's fine physically," answered Alex.

"Okay, I'll be up in a few minutes." By the time Rick showed up, Alex had wrapped the potatoes in foil, ready to bake and was peeling carrots. "She's up in her room."

"Sophie, honey, it's Rick. May I come in?"

"Alex called you, didn't she?" snapped Sophie, annoyed mostly at herself for being overtaken by her emotions.

Rick went over to the bed and sat next to Sophie, holding her hand, trying to keep calm. "She was worried about you, that's all Sophie. You know she adores you and you're all she has left, so don't be too upset."

Sophie knew she had nowhere to hide. Between the two of them, there wouldn't be a moment's peace until she spilled the beans. "Okay, maybe you're right. Call her on that damn walkie talkie and tell her to get her butt up here. I'm only going to do this once."

Whatever Sophie had been feeling, she was transitioning back to her usual in-control self. Alex walked in and sat at the foot of the bed waiting for Sophie or Rick to tell her what was going on.

"Before either of the two of you go off halfcocked, let me preface this with I'm physically okay. Understand?"

They both nodded yes. Without hesitating, Sophie launched into it. "It seems that I had a miscarriage yesterday."

If it hadn't been so sad, it would have been almost comical. Rick and Alex looked like they had both been shot out of a cannon. Questions came flying out of their mouths like an attack of Tourette's Syndrome. "What? How? I don't understand. How could that happen? It's not possible! Are you sure?"

Sophie held up her hand to silence them. "One question at a time, please."

Rick's face was turning red, the blush slowly crawling up from this throat. "Ah, Sophie, I thought you couldn't have children and, ah, didn't you go through the change of life?"

"I haven't had a period for ten months, but apparently I didn't stop ovulating," answered Sophie with deep exhaustion.

"So, you can have children?" persisted Rick.

"I didn't think so. I mean all those years trying with Mario and then these last several years with you and 'nada', then this. Doctor said it was just one of those flukes."

"Aunt Sophie, pardon the indelicateness of this question, but do you need to have a D & C?" inquired Alex.

"No. The doctor said it was what they call a spontaneous abortion, probably because there was something wrong with the fetus, but everything was fine. They did a sonogram." Sophie was dreading more questions and now understood how Alex had felt when she asked all sorts of questions about Alex's sexual orientation.

"Aunt Sophie, how do you feel about this?"

"I'm a little sad but, honestly, I didn't even know I was pregnant, so it's not as if I was attached to it. Do you know what I mean?" Sophie saw the pained look on Rick's face.

"Honey," she said, addressing Rick, "Don't misunderstand me. Having your baby would have been a precious gift because I love you so. Please try and understand that even yesterday I didn't have an inkling and it was only today that the doctor told me I had been pregnant. I haven't had a chance to adjust emotionally to the idea I was carrying a baby." Tears were rolling down Sophie's cheeks. Rick took her in his arms and told her he understood and please not to be sad. Alex had many more questions but quietly got up and left the two of them to work it out between themselves.

CHAPTER 17 - Surreptitious Seeds

There is nothing hidden that shall not be manifested.

Unknown

Tuesday May 5

"Mr. Carola, how lovely to meet you." Jules extended her hand to the very old man sitting in a wheelchair attended by a male nurse. "I hope I'm not interrupting your routine."

The old man chuckled and still holding Jules' hand in both of his answered in a frail voice. "What could an old man like me have to do? You are a welcome, eh, how do you say it, divertido."

"Diversion?" offered Jules.

"Yes, yes. I am sorry. I often have difficulty even with the simplest of words. Sometimes I can't even remember what day it is. Young lady try not to get old. It is pathetic," smiled the old man, "and please, call me Roberto."

"Thank you, Roberto. I will," answered Jules warmly. "As I told you over the phone, I'm a reporter. I have identification if you would like to see it." Jules flashed an ID card from the Associated Press which Roberto waved away. He was sufficiently charmed with her manner and looks and didn't care if she was a drug runner, as long as he had someone besides his nurse and housekeeper with whom to engage in conversation.

"Thank you, but that won't be necessary, but would you mind explaining what your story is about again?" Roberto wasn't embarrassed by his lack of short-term memory, though he shrugged his shoulders and tilted his head with an endearing motion. "Please, remove your coat and sit here next to me."

"Thank you. Roberto, I'm working on a story about immigrants from Europe who settled in North and South America around the turn of the century. Specifically, I've chosen to showcase a generational perspective on those families whose children and grandchildren were extremely successful both professionally and economically. I'm attempting to find common factors."

"Ah, yes. How did you pick me?" asked Roberto, curious but not guarded.

"Actually, it was quite by accident." Jules flashed a hundred-watt smile and reached over to touch the back of Roberto's hand which was lying in his lap. "I was working on another story and was introduced to someone that knew your granddaughter. Roberto, would you tell me how you came to live in Argentina?" She patted his hand again to get his attention, then took up her pen.

"You are right about the turn of the century. My wife Gina and I had a very brief courtship. In fact, the marriage was arranged by our parents. I worked in the trades and she was a schoolteacher, one of the few women in that profession at the time. The reason we left was because both our parents meddled in our affairs. After two years of marriage, Gina and I still didn't have children and we couldn't see either set of parents without this becoming a painful topic of conversation."

Jules was curious where Roberto had learned English, but she wasn't going to ask and distract him. She prompted him to go on, "So, how did you choose Argentina?"

"A friend of mine had emigrated around the time Gina and I were married. He wrote and told me to come. He said there was plenty of work, it was easy to learn Spanish. It is so close to Italian, and the pay was good. He offered to help us find a house and get a job. So, we came."

"Go on Roberto. Did you find it as easy as your friend suggested?"

"Si′, Si′." Roberto lapsed back into Spanish for a moment. "Oh yes. I found a job with a building company and worked many hours a day, seven days a week. My wife got bored with me away from work so much, so she went back to school and got her, how do you say, ah, credentials to teach English at the University."

"Did she speak English before coming to Buenos Aires?" inquired Jules.

"A little. She was self-taught. You know, she was a woman far beyond the century, maybe even what you call a Renaissance woman. She was convinced that over time the world would get smaller. She wanted all of us to learn English. So, we did."

"She did so well that she convinced me to go to the University to get my diploma in engineering." A warm smile spread across his face.

"Roberto, so after many years, you had a son?"

"Yes, and it was a glorious day for me when I found out Gina was pregnant. Even if my memory is shredded into a thousand pieces of confetti, I will remember." With a shaking hand he reached inside his suit coat into the inside pocket and took out a worn grimy card. "One of my hobbies as a younger man was gardening. I loved the spring when my tulips pushed their way up through the snow. I had varieties from all over the world but, on this birthday of mine, my wife gave me a large pot of coral colored tulips."

Jules wondered if he had forgotten what he was going to say about his son but decided to wait. It looked like he was enjoying sharing this memory with her. "There was a card, the one you have in your hand, wedged between two of the stems. It said, 'Happy Birthday, Papa.' I immediately knew what it meant!"

Roberto continued. "So, Carlos was born and when he grew up went to medical school and graduated top in his class."

Jules had gotten to the point where she wanted to keep the scope of the conversation tight. "He married later in life, didn't he?"

"Yes. He was very career driven and we had pretty much given up on him ever marrying, but we didn't push him because we did not want to be like our parents. He was often the extra man at dinner parties, but he didn't seem to mind. At one of those dinner parties, he met a woman, a widow. After a few months he brought her around with her daughter. We liked them both and they were married a few months later."

"Did they have a child of their own?" encouraged Jules.

"Yes, a little boy. We loved both of those children and I must confess, spoiled them but then isn't that the job of grandparents?" Roberto smiled ruefully, perhaps wishing that his son and grandchildren lived closer.

"After your son and his family moved to the States didn't you want to move there to be with them?" Jules was curious why the old man had not gone with them.

"At first they were only going for a little while. Then they settled in. Carlos was making much more money than he could here, and he said the education was much better for the children. They asked Gina and me to come but we had our life here. Both of us were still working."

"I'd like to hear about your grandchildren, if you still feel up to it."

Roberto talked for another thirty minutes about the children, the similarities and differences in their personalities, and their likes and dislikes, dreams and aspirations.

Jules could see that he was weary and thanked him for the information. "Roberto, I have sincerely enjoyed spending time with you and learning about your family. It has been a privilege.

Roberto responded to Jules' heartfelt words by taking her hand and bringing it to his lips, kissing it lightly. "Adios Señorita. I hope you will let me know how your story ends."

"I will, Roberto," she promised, knowing with certainty that if it turned out as she suspected, she would never let him know.

###

The taxi she hired this morning was waiting for her. She slipped into the back seat, still feeling affected by Mr. Carola.

"Where now?" asked the cab driver, eager to get on with his day. He had been waiting for an hour and a half and was bored.

"Universidad de Buenos Aires History Department, please," responded Jules.

He nodded and, at breakneck speed, took off. It would be almost impossible for anyone to tail them at the rate of speed they were traveling, weaving in and out of traffic. *No wonder all the cabs and cars seem to have magnetic religious statues attached to their dashes*, thought Jules.

Thirty minutes later the cabbie pulled up to a gray, dingy looking building. He turned in his seat and addressed Jules, "Here we are." She thanked him, located the building she needed and walked through the quad. Entering the building, she hoped this was the right place. Locating a faculty directory, she found the name she had written down. There didn't appear to be an elevator, so she began her climb to the third-floor office. After a false start down the wrong corridor, she located office number three hundred seventeen. Knocking on the door, she waited for a response.

"Siga," said a female voice from behind the door. Jules knew that 'siga' meant continue, so she cracked the door and walked in. The office was small but nicely appointed with a window that overlooked a well-manicured quad. "Ah, you must be Ms. Law, no?" asked the woman behind the desk as she got up and extended her hand to Jules. Jules said "yes," walked in, shook the woman's hand and waited to be invited to sit down.

"Please sit down. Well you already know that I'm Dr. Cabrera, since you found me, no?" She laughed at her own little joke.

"Yes, of course, Dr. Cabrera. Thank you for taking the time to meet with me," answered Jules with a certain measure of attentiveness in her voice.

Dr. Cabrera sat down behind her desk and asked Jules, "What is it that you want to know?"

Once again, Jules spun her story and elucidated that she was gathering background information for an in-depth story and explained that she wanted background concerning Argentina's history of allowing less than desirable political exiles to immigrate into the country.

Dr. Cabrera looked at her watch, sighed and launched into a brief history, starting with post World War II activities of an Argentinian group called the Society for the Reception of Europeans. She explained that this group was responsible for facilitating the relocation of more than two hundred Nazi war criminals, including the notorious Adolf Eichmann, who was seized in 1960 by Israeli agents.

"Is this committee still active?" asked Jules.

Dr. Cabrera continued. "In 1997 the government created a Commission of Inquiry into Nazi activities in Argentina to determine how many of these criminals made their way into Argentina post World War II. This was only done because of global political pressures that came to bear." She paused, looked at the door, then continued. "There is an unsubstantiated rumor that in spite of the government's action to establish an Inquiry Commission, the Society for the Reception of Europeans is still in operation facilitating the disappearance of current day undesirables into the country. Anything else?" asked Dr. Cabrera.

"Just one final question, if you don't mind. Would it be safe to speculate that war criminals from other South American countries would have been able to acquire new identities and live here?"

As Dr. Cabrera stood, signaling that the interview was over, she said, "As long as they had money or other assets to buy their way in."

Jules thanked her and hurried back to the cab, eager to share with Jake what she had learned.

"How is she?" Sophie and Rick hadn't come down for dinner last night and the last Alex had seen of Sophie was when she brought up a tray for the two of them. Rick, looking as dejected as a hound dog who had followed a scent right into a nest of skunks, looked at her, shook his head and said, "Better than I am. She'll be down to rule the world in a little while."

"Oh, Rick," cried Alex. "I'm so sorry. I just wasn't thinking. Please tell me how *you* are feeling?"

He poured coffee and sat down as he said, "Alex, I really don't know. Like Sophie said, it all came up so suddenly."

Alex got up, bent over him and pulled him to her chest, where he cried without shame for several minutes. She said nothing and held him until he was able to compose himself. He looked up at her, wiped the tears from his face and said, "You are so like her."

"You mean Sophie?" responded Alex.

"Yes. Do you remember the night we got here after you were released from the hospital in Germany?"

"Uh huh."

"Remember when I started bawling in the great room?"

"Yes. I think that's when you won Sophie's heart."

"Well, Alex, I feel like that now." He got up and shuffled to the sink where he washed his cup and started laying out an assortment of pastries and muffins on a tray. He was ready to get on with the day's business.

Shortly after Rick had left the house, Sophie came into the kitchen. "How is he?" Sophie asked Alex.

Alex answered, "Why didn't you ask him?" She was a little resentful at having to play the go-between this morning.

Sophie ignored Alex's tone and answered, "Because he wouldn't tell me the truth."

Alex softened. "He's hurting, Aunt Sophie. He's feeling bad for you and bad for himself."

Alex thought, *Wish I were being paid by the hour*, but, in reality, didn't mind the therapy that she dispensed as part of her familial duties. "How are you?"

"I'm feeling fine. There's no bleeding or cramping but the doctor told me to take it easy today. Tomorrow I can get back to normal, though I don't think the doctor has any idea of what normal is around here!" Changing the subject to avoid any more questioning from Alex she asked, "What happened with Claire yesterday?"

Alex gave her a synopsis to which Sophie answered tongue in cheek, "An example of repressed emotions hitting a few days later?"

"All right, smarty pants," chimed Alex. "That's enough disrespect for my profession!" At that, Sophie got up and hugged her niece.

Alex and Claire were in one of the vacant cabins. Claire was not happy about it at all. Alex had pre-empted her activities with the horses and she was sulking with her arms crossed against her chest. Claire was a dichotomy. She was a woman and very sophisticated in many ways. However, she reverted to a child-like creature when she didn't want to do something. Alex thought it might be more than just spoiled brat syndrome.

"Claire, whether you like it or not, I can't let you go back and work with the animals until I'm sure that there's not another flashback in your immediate future. You could be hurt, or the animals could get hurt."

"Fine." Claire either didn't believe her or was so angry she couldn't believe her.

"Here's what we are going to do this morning. First, it's apparent that you're angry and, by the way, it's okay with me that you are. Anger often sits on top of depression, so when we can get angry it allows us to release things or conditions that were making us depressed. What I want you to do is start telling me all the things that make you angry. I'm not going to interrupt you, I'm not going to prompt you, and you can get up and walk around, scream and yell if you wish. All I'm going to do is take notes." That wasn't exactly the whole truth, but it was close enough. "Are you ready to begin?"

Claire looked at Alex defiantly, however it was hard for her to stay angry with Alex. Her calm, patient demeanor always moved Claire to action. "Fine. The sooner we do this, the sooner I can get back to the horses."

While Claire ticked off several things that made her angry, Alex took scarce notes, concentrating on observing Claire. Another thirty minutes passed, and Claire had worked herself into a lather, which was exactly what Alex had hoped would happen. She got up and started pacing the room, raising her voice and using swear words, surreptitiously checking to see if Alex was reacting to her actions and language. Claire went on for another fifteen minutes before she abruptly stopped in her tracks, returned to the couch and flopped down. She didn't resume her defensive posture as she said, "Okay, Dr. Martini, I'm finished."

"Claire, did Dr. Metuchi ever give you an injection?"

It took only a moment for Claire to follow Alex's sudden change in direction.

"Ah, yes. Several times. Said it would help relax me."

"Did it?" inquired Alex matter-of-factly.

"Yes. I usually left her office feeling calmer. It seemed to make the anxiety go away for a while."

Alex gently put her hand over Claire's and asked, "Did Dr. Metuchi ever make you angry?"

"Sometimes," answered Claire truthfully. Alex was bordering on unethical behavior but, if she wanted to help Claire, she had to blur the line.

Alex took on the role of parent and still holding Claire's hand, said "It's okay to tell me, Claire. I'm not going to let anything bad happen to you. It's a good thing to tell the truth and get unsettling feelings out in the open." Holding her breath, she waited for Claire to decide.

"I can't remember. I'm sorry Dr. Martini." Claire had moved her body closer to Alex and her shoulder was pressing against Alex's arm.

"How do you feel right now?" asked Alex.

"Hungry. In fact, ravenous if you want the truth." With that Alex terminated the session.

Alex scheduled a hypnosis session with Claire later in the day. It was productive. She was able to ferret out a better description of the hissing Claire remembered and a smell she recalled, though she was unable to identify either.

CHAPTER 18 - Surprise in the Night

Courage consists not in hazarding without fear, but in being resolutely minded in a just cause.

Persian Proverb

Wednesday May 6

The British Airways jumbo jet slammed onto the runway in Madrid jerking Jules awake. Feeling groggy and tired, she waited patiently for the plane to taxi to the gate. Disembarking, she looked around the gate area expecting someone to meet her as she had been briefed. A man in a black suit, white shirt and patterned tie came toward her.

"Ms. Law, I presume? I am David DeRosa."

She had no reason to doubt that he was anyone other than her contact, but she used the code phrase she had been given. Satisfied by his response, she allowed him to escort her through Immigration and Customs. Once outside, her escort raised his hand and a car pulled up in front of them.

Sitting in a sequestered room at the nearby private air terminal, Jules and David, or whatever his real name was, were enjoying a finely aged scotch while waiting for their dinners to arrive. David put his glass down on the snowy white tablecloth, leaned back in his chair and said, "The mission is really very simple. You'll be met by your contact at the airport in Peshawar. We think that the post office where our package is awaiting transport may be known to insurgent operatives. They would expect a male postal worker to accompany the package. We don't think they'll be too interested in a woman with a team of newscasters."

"Are we in a secure location?" asked Jules.

"Mostly," said David. "Why?"

"Could we dispense with cloak and dagger talk?" implored Jules.

"You want to know who the package is and where he is," blandly said David.

"Exactly. I need to know what I'm dealing with before I'm up to my ass in shit." Jules was purposefully crude. David was taken aback, as she had intended him to be.

"I saw that you read the file I gave you while we were in the car."

"Of course, but it didn't tell me anything other than locations of U.S Troops, suspected locations of the insurgents and friendlies. I know that my mission is to pose as a translator for the Associated Press, grab your man and get back to an undisclosed U.S. Troop rendezvous location."

"You'll learn relevant locations and the identity of your client when you get to Peshawar." David was final in his statement to Jules.

Jules measured David and decided that she didn't want to alienate him. If anything went wrong with the mission, he could just as easily be a foe as a friend.

"All right, David, I'll wait for the briefing in Peshawar but, if I don't get the information I feel I need to get out with my skin intact, then I'm not going to go in. Fair?" She observed his face closely, attempting to determine if his answer was truthful.

"Fair enough, Ms. Law. Oh, by the way, here is your passport. It's been stamped with a Cadiz exit instead of Madrid and it has a Pakistan entry visa stamp and an Afghanistan business visa. You should have no trouble moving around Afghanistan with your credentials. You'll need this letter from the Associated Press."

"One last question, David, can you tell me how I was selected for this assignment?" Jules knew she had been specifically requested, but by whom still remained a mystery, though she had her suspicions.

"That will become evident when you get to Peshawar."

"And how am I to know that the person meeting me is the real contact?"

"You'll know. Use the code phrase." David wasn't going to give up any more information.

After dinner, David turned the small private dining room into a mission room, attaching maps, aerials, and topographical terrain maps to the walls. Jules hunkered down for a long night, passing up a large snifter of brandy.

Promptly at 9:00 a.m., six part-time staffers arrived on the doorstep of the ranch. Most of them knew each other from previous summers and their catching up with each other resembled what happens when a queen bee feels she doesn't have enough room in the hive and enlists like-minded renegade bees to look for a new home. They were swarming all over each other, buzzing with excitement at being in their new home for the summer. Duffle bags and suitcases were strewn every which way, converting the porch into a hazard zone.

Claire had been assigned the duty of checking them in and getting them settled but, even with the help of Mickey, she wasn't having much luck with the rowdies. Rick and Sophie drove up and saw the circus, looked at each other and said in unison, "What on earth were we thinking when we decided to convert to a guest ranch?"

They parked the truck in its usual spot behind the kitchen and walked out to the porch to begin the day's orientation. As soon as Sophie and Rick stepped out to the porch, the kids quieted down. It was obvious to Mickey that these kids knew who the boss was around White Bark Ranch. Sophie introduced Mickey and Claire as part of the family and told them that she expected they would extend the same respect to Mickey and Claire as they did to the other ranch employees. Properly chastened, they lined up their bags in an orderly fashion on the porch and followed Rick and Sophie in for breakfast and orientation.

Alex was in her room trying to call Jake. She had left a message last night, but he had not returned the call. She redialed again, this time hearing his voice. "Jake, I wanted to talk to you about a discovery I made yesterday with Claire. I don't know if it helps with the investigation, but I'll let you be the judge."

"What is it?" answered Jake.

"I had her under hypnosis and she was doing fine until she encountered a, um, let's call it a blockage. She said she heard hissing and a horn, but I don't know what this means yet."

Jake thought a moment, then replied. "Alex, if what we think is right, she was held in a warehouse by the ocean. Her reference to a horn might be a recall of a foghorn. The hissing could have been gas leaking, just before the explosion. We were never able to confirm that the warehouse that exploded the night she was found, was the same as where she was held, but the horn and hissing seem to fit."

"All right, Jake. I'm going to try and find out today what the sounds mean."

"Anything more, Alex?"

"No, not really." Alex was reluctant to end the conversation.

Jake guessed that she wanted to ask about Jules, but didn't know how to broach the subject, so he said, "Alex, she was fine when I talked to her yesterday. She asked about you."

"Thank you, Jake. It was very nice of you to share that with me."

He could hear the sadness in Alex's voice and wanted to tell her to be patient with Jules, but felt it wasn't his place. "Okay, Alex, I've got to go now, but I'll keep you informed if I hear from her. You be careful!" and Jake and hung up

Alex felt like Jake was her only connection to Jules right now and that in some way, talking to him was a substitute for talking with her.

###

Woods, with a sign in his hand, was waiting outside the baggage claim for the Bentworths. He made sure he wore a light-colored suit, so he wouldn't be confused with a chauffeur. As he waited for them, he wondered why a man like Bentworth would fly commercial, when he probably had a fleet of private planes at his beck and call. He watched for someone that looked like the picture he found on the internet and continued to scan people leaving the baggage claim. Five minutes later, a couple walked toward him, the man resembling the photo on Google. He was dressed in expensive clothes, impeccably groomed, and had an air of haughtiness.

"Are you Woods' man?" asked the man.

Woods was annoyed. Bentworth had just treated him as a servant. Carefully controlling his tone, he replied, "Mr. and Mrs. Bentworth, I'm Keith Woods. I wanted to come myself to meet you."

"How nice of you Mr. Woods," replied the woman. Woods thought she was very nice looking but reined in his libido. He wasn't going to screw up a potential multimillion-dollar business deal for a little tail on the side. He graciously responded, "No trouble at all, Mrs. Bentworth. I'll bring the car around while the two of you organize your luggage." After Bentworth's slight, Woods was not going to serve as their porter. He took off before Bentworth could press him into service.

Woods had the hatch of the Escalade open and was standing by the rear of the vehicle when he spotted them dragging two suitcases each. *Hmm, they're only here for three days, what on earth do they need with all those clothes,* thought Woods. While driving south on their way to see two

Page | 302

distressed properties, he got the distinct impression, after trying to engage them in conversation, that they were not very friendly and thought that the reason they were not engaging was that he was not of their social and financial standing.

Lunch at the house was a quick sandwich, salad, and cookie attended only by Claire, Mickey, Sophie and Alex. The six part-timers were chowing down with Rick at the bunkhouse. They'd have an hour after lunch to stow their gear, then back to work. That meant that Sophie had about two hours to rest before kitchen and housekeeping help reported back up at the house.

Sophie looked a little worn out, but Alex couldn't tell if it was the stress of having a bunch of boisterous young people dogging her every step, or if it was due to the emotional trauma of the miscarriage. Sophie caught Alex's appraising look and tried to perk up by asking Claire, "So you got your first experience corralling wild mustangs this morning?"

Confused, Claire responded, "Ah, Aunt Sophie, I wasn't working with the horses this morning. I was trying to get those disruptive kids to pay attention."

"Exactly," laughed Sophie. Alex and Mickey joined in with the joke. Claire pretended that she was annoyed with the teasing. "God, after this morning, I am totally convinced that I never want to have kids! I don't remember being so unruly when I was a teenager! My mother would have whipped my butt!" Claire, despite her tryst with the rowdy kids, seemed to be in good spirits.

Alex decided to use this moment productively. "Claire, what would your father have done, if you had misbehaved as a teenager?"

"He would have complained to my mother," she said lightly.

Alex noted that there was no stress, no hesitation, no antagonistic subtext. *Interesting,* she thought. "Claire, that's funny. Say, I'd like to get together with you for a few hours after lunch." Alex had decided that she was not going to put Claire on a regular schedule for therapy. She did not want Claire having time to 'prepare' for a session. Extemporaneous sessions seemed to be working well, so she was going to stick with her intuition.

"Sure, fine. The cabin?" responded Claire quite agreeably, which was noted by both Mickey and Sophie.

"Yes, 2:00 p.m." said Alex matter-of-factly.

"Okay. We'll be there," said Claire, looking at Mickey.

Woods suggested to his guests that they stop for lunch, then he'd take them to another property. *This should be fun,* he thought. He relished the idea of dragging the Bentworths into the Darby diner. They'd probably freak out, especially since Bentworth was not happy with the first property he had been shown. Woods gladly suffered a berating from Bentworth because the property didn't meet his requirements. *Like taking candy from a baby,* he smirked as he pulled into a parking spot down the road from the diner.

Alex was already waiting in the cabin sitting on the couch when Claire burst through the door. "Hi. I'm ready." She was exuberant, bordering on manic.

"Come sit down, then. I want to get your impressions on how you've been feeling since yesterday."

"Sure, Dr. Martini." Claire thought a moment, then began, "I felt tired last night, and I had no trouble sleeping through the night. I got up this morning with a whole bunch of energy and I'm feeling hopeful."

"Anything else?" prompted Alex. Alex could tell by the look on Claire's face that she was trying to take inventory of a slew of emotions. While Alex might not be very patient with herself or her life, she had infinite patience when a big breakthrough was on the horizon.

"Yeah, there is something else, but I'm not sure I should say it."

"Why is that?" asked Alex.

"Because I don't know if it's allowed, and I don't want to ruin things now that I've finally started feeling better and more in control."

If Alex had been asked to guess, she would have hypothesized that Claire was experiencing feelings of transference and didn't understand what was happening.

"You know, I'm not going to get upset with anything you say."

Getting up from the chair, Claire moved to the couch within arm's reach of Alex. "I felt after yesterday, that we were getting closer."

"And you like that?" asked Alex.

"Yes," answered Claire.

Alex treated the confession as a common occurrence. "Good, then. It's important that you feel good about our relationship and develop a trust with me. I'm really glad you told me this. Do you remember anything about the technique we used yesterday?"

"Yes, I had to imagine a place where I felt safe, secure and good about myself. Then we walked down steps to get there."

"That's right. We are going to do it again today. Ready?"

"Okay," responded Claire as she got comfortable on the couch.

In a few moments, Alex could see Claire was agitated. "Okay, Claire, I'm here with you. Tell me what you see."

"I hear hissing and a horn. Fire, someone coming. I can't move!" She was agitated, scared, and paralyzed.

"Claire, listen to me. You're holding my hand, you're just watching, and you can move. Let's see what's going on."

Alex wanted to be very careful not to plant any type of memory by suggesting that the source was a ruptured gas line. "Tell me, where are we? Are we standing in a room?"

"Yes. Big, cold."

"Is anyone there besides us?" Alex was referring to Claire thinking someone was coming.

"No, gone."

"Do you mean that someone was there, but left?"

"Yes."

"Where's the hissing coming from, Claire?"

"I don't know but I heard something metal banging on a pipe and I smell smoke."

Once again, Claire was exhibiting signs of extreme stress. Alex hadn't expected them to get this far. She was certain that Claire had just been in the room where she had been held hostage. She resisted the temptation to push Claire further, knowing that patience would serve them better in the end and brought Claire out of the hypnotic trance.

Thursday May 7

Sitting around the kitchen table early in the morning, Rick, Sophie, and Alex tried to catch up with each other. Sophie entertained them with tales of her adventures at cross training the kitchen help to fill in for the housekeeping help. Rick commented on Claire's demeanor telling Alex that she must be a miracle worker because in a few short days, Claire's demeanor had been almost magically transformed. Alex then told Rick and Sophie that she was thinking about taking Claire to camp out with the ranch hands and the cattle in the lower meadow.

"Damn, I wish I had you for a therapist," goaded Rick.

"You do? I couldn't stand being with you for that length of time," teased Alex. She was glad to see that Rick's frame of mind had improved. Both of them looked at Sophie and waited for her rebuke, which often followed a serious needling session between the two of them.

"What?" Sophie asked.

"Aren't you going to tell us to behave?" said Alex.

"Hell no. If you two want to punish each other, why shouldn't I sit back and enjoy it?"

Alex was on her way back upstairs to pack a few things for the "sleep over" when Mickey and Claire came out of his room.

"Hey, I have some good news for the two of you. We're going to go on a camping trip today so, after breakfast, pack your gear and meet me at the barn."

Claire was excited. "What do we need to pack?"

"You'll need underwear, a couple of pairs of dry socks, another pair of jeans, a shirt, sweater, and windbreaker." Alex noted the look on Mickey's face. He wasn't as thrilled as Claire. "Mickey, it's only a four hour ride up and when we get there, we'll cook you a big steak!"

"Will I be able to sit and enjoy it?" motioning to his backside with feigned pain.

"We'll bring liniment," cried Claire as she pushed past him on her way down to breakfast.

"Alex," he said, moving in closer to Alex's ear, "what have you been feeding her? She's off the wall with energy and good cheer. I had just gotten used to withering, timid, and glum!"

"Frosted Flakes with extra sugar," teased Alex.

On his way to pick up his new best friends, Woods mulled over how they treated him yesterday. He had invited them to dinner, hoping to use that time to set up the deal he had fantasized about for years. However, they rudely turned him down, saying that they were tired of driving all day and wanted to rest. He didn't have any choice but to acquiesce to their wishes.

They agreed to meet him at 10:00 a.m. in the hotel lobby. He checked his watch again. They were ten minutes late. He helped himself to the complimentary coffee in the Doubletree lobby and sat where he had a view of the elevators. At 10:20 a.m. he spied them getting off one of the elevators. "Good morning," he said pleasantly, expecting an apology for being kept waiting. Instead, he got a gruff response, "Where's the car? Let's get going, I don't have time to waste." Woods clenched his teeth and replied, "follow me." It was going to be another day in hell.

After lunch, Alex loaded up the truck with extra provisions, sleeping bags, and rain gear, even though the local weatherman predicted a dry week, and drove it down to the barn. She asked Dean to get someone to pack up the gear, add grain for the horses and get a pack horse ready. She explained that they were going up to the lower meadow. "What for?" he asked, a toothpick hanging out of his mouth.

"Just for fun, Dean," answered Alex. He shrugged his shoulders as if to say, "to each his own", then asked her if she wanted the riding horses saddled too. "Yes please. I'll take Tommy Boy. How about Sissy for Mickey and Goldie for Claire?"

"Suits me," said Dean.

Alex thought that Rick and Sophie must have the patience of a saint to put up with Dean.

The copilot, a tall, dark skinned man with sharply defined features, roused Jules. He spoke to her in Farsi and told her they would be landing in twenty minutes. She thanked him and looked out the window. It was dark, but she knew that dawn would be coming soon. Stretching, she got up and walked down the aisle to work the kinks out of her muscles.

The Gulfstream taxied for a while and stopped in front of a hanger some distance from commercial and other private jet traffic. Once the door was open, she got up and started down the stairs towards a man in a suit standing at the bottom. She did not recognize him. Speaking in Farsi he said, "Ms. Law, welcome to Peshawar. Please, follow me to the car." He grabbed Jules' suitcase the co-pilot had unloaded and led her to a newer model Mercedes.

Jules' radar was up. She did not know this man, as suggested by David in Madrid. He sensed her hesitancy and said, "Please, your friend is waiting." He opened the back door of the Mercedes. She could see another man in the back seat, hidden in the shadows. She was not getting in without the exchanging of the code phrase. He extended his hand to help her into the car and said, "Ah, my little Jules, give in to love," in perfect English.

"Or live in fear," replied Jules, finishing the quote. Taking his hand to steady herself as she got into the car she said, "Hadi, what are you doing in Pakistan?"

"Well isn't it evident? I'm picking you up and spirting you away for a romantic weekend!" He reached out and hugged her. "You are surprised to see me, no?"

"Yes. I never heard from you after graduation."

"Ah, but I followed your career and pined for you for many years."

"When did you come back to Afghanistan, and why?"

"After I got my MBA. I couldn't stand any more of the Western decadence!" Hadi answered laughing.

"If I recall, Hadi, you liked the Western decadence a whole lot!"

"That is true, but only with you," lied Hadi.

"You're so full of 'mierde', Hadi. I hope I have not offended your new set of values," laughed Jules.

"Of course not. Values are what one adopts when convenient. Let us enjoy our ride now and I will explain everything to you when we arrive at our destination."

Hadi Dostum had taken Jules' virginity. Undergraduate classmates, he was drawn to her partly because she spoke his language and shared a cultural heritage, but mostly because he liked her looks. The more time they spent together, the more he realized that she was much more than flawless skin and a perfect body. He admired her sense of humor, her intelligence, and her passion for doing what was right.

Hadi, however, could never understand her remoteness toward him, even though she slept with him for a semester. This made him pursue and want her more because she never truly gave herself to him. In the end, he knew the relationship would never work, and said goodbye to her as she went off to pursue a career with the military. He was married now, to a woman whom he had learned to love, but he had never felt the passion he had for Jules.

Even if it had turned out that she were straight, she never could have married a man who planned on returning to Afghanistan to work in his family's opium business.

Jules turned her face to speak to him and felt his lips close over hers. She was startled and faltered, "What are you doing Hadi?"

"Don't worry my little Jules. I just wanted to see if your lips still tasted as sweet as they had before," he said mischievously.

Lord thought Jules. *He's going to be a real pain in the ass.* She tried to come up with conversation to stave off his juvenile behavior. "Hadi, do you have children?"

"Yes, three boys."

"You must be happy not to have girls in this time of oppression."

"Not really. We wanted a girl," responded Hadi, seemingly serious.

"Oh, why's that?" Jules was truly curious.

"Because it is the girl who takes care of you when you are old," he said, equally as seriously. "Jules, did you never marry?"

"No, Hadi. I never did."

"Why not?"

"Out of the thousands of people I've met in my lifetime, I've never met anyone who lit the passion in my heart, until recently."

"Ah, that must be why you never fell in love with me!" exclaimed Hadi, returning to a light note. "This person, is he from the intelligence community?"

"No." She toyed with telling him the truth but thought better of it.

"So, my little Jules, you are soon to be off the market?" Hadi continued to tease her.

"Maybe. Too soon to tell, but I do know one thing, Hadi, not soon enough to know I don't miss your kisses!"

Hadi laughed and said, "touché!" They rode in silence the remainder of the trip. When they arrived at their destination, they pulled into a garage and Hadi told her to remain in the car until the door closed. Hadi was now all business. The driver carried her suitcase inside, then left Hadi with Jules in a small bedroom. Hadi said, "Sit down Jules. Do you want food or drink?"

"Tea please, and whatever food you have would be fine."

"I know you are tired and that you leave in a few hours, so let me be as brief as possible so that you can get some sleep," began Hadi. "I am the nephew of one of the former Northern Alliance Generals."

"You're related to Abdul Rashid Dostum?" asked Jules incredulously.

"You might think so, having the same surname, but no. Dostum is a very common name in Afghanistan, but I see you know a little about the former Northern Alliance

"Hadi, is there a bathroom I can use first?"

"Oh, yes, of course, I am so sorry. Right through there," he motioned towards a door.

Jules returned to a steaming cup of tea waiting for her on the table and Hadi started his briefing.

"Are you aware of the delicate balance between Pakistan and the Afghani government?"

"Yes. I believe that Pakistan recognizes and maintains relations with the current official Afghani government because it is essential that the Afghan government be a close ally of Pakistan and willing to fight India if need be. But Pakistan wields a double edged sword. It has allowed insurgent training camps just inside the border, which makes the U.S.A.'s relationship with Pakistan less than ideal."

"Right. So, now to the mission at hand." A knock on the door interrupted Hadi. The driver delivered a plate of food and more tea. Hadi thanked him and waited for the door to close. "Go ahead, eat. I can wait."

"Please Hadi, talk while I am eating. I haven't grown so old that I cannot do two things at once," teased Jules.

"Fine. Recently a man, rumored to be a member of the inner circle of power for the Taliban Insurgents in the South, was captured by the Afghani government troops. This man, whose name I will tell you later, is ill and does not wish to share the same fate that may have taken Osama Bin Laden from this world several years ago."

Jules nodded. "So, this man wants medical treatment and, in exchange for it, has offered to provide information? Unbelievable. What about the Jihad?"

"Apparently his safety and his family are more important than the Jihad."

Jules whistled. "A radical gone soft. If that got out, the Insurgents would suffer tremendous embarrassment."

"Exactly, so they cannot afford to let him live. He doesn't trust the Pakistani government; therefore, he does not want to seek asylum there. He is afraid that since Pakistan maintains loose diplomatic relations with the Insurgents, it would be his death warrant. Secondly, medical care is scarce and, of course, he expects Insurgent members to infiltrate and assassinate him."

"So, that leaves only the U.S." It was not a question.

Hadi smiled and said, "You always were smart."

"Okay, now tell me the plan and don't leave anything out, Hadi."

This is an intense Jules, almost deadly, like a sand viper ready to strike, thought Hadi. He congratulated himself on requesting her. "It is really quite simple, Jules. You are assigned to a Canadian television crew which is going to pretend to conduct interviews throughout the country. At the pickup site, my driver, a highly trained operative will remain behind and be replaced with your ward. He will ride with you to a safe location under the protection of your country and will be flown out on military transport to the States, accompanied by you."

"Does this man have a handler assigned?"

"Yes," answered Hadi. "You have met him."

"David DeRosa?" asked Jules.

"I believe so."

"Hadi, this television crew, are they legitimate?"

"Of course not. Do you think I would send you in alone?" Hadi was mildly amused.

"Hadi, it's easier to fake one identity as opposed to four. That's the only reason I asked."

Hadi's face cleared and he continued, "Two are members of the Canadian CSE Intelligence Organization which is cooperating with your CIA. One works the camera and the other is acting as the reporter. The driver is one of my men, hopefully unknown to anyone. He looks a little like the defector."

"Why are the Canadians helping?"

"I can only assume that they are getting something out of this from your country," offered Hadi.

"Hadi, you must be a very powerful man. Do you have a handler?" Jules wondered if he would tell her the truth.

"I am only a cog in the wheel that fights against the oppression of the day." Hadi had answered her question by not answering it. "Look, Jules, this is very dangerous for you. If your real identity is discovered or if the Insurgents catch wind of what you are doing, you will be killed, or worse. They will beat you, rape you and leave you for the desert animals to finish. You do understand this?" Hadi was waxing apprehensively.

"I think I understood from the beginning, but hearing you say it now is very sobering." Jules felt a coldness come over her. She shook off the chill and continued. "What about weapons, maps, intel?"

"Soldiers at checkpoints will tear your Land Rover apart looking for weapons. All you will be able to carry are sidearms. Maps are different. It would seem logical that you have road and terrain maps. Locations you need to know are disguised on the terrain maps.

"Okay let me take a look. How will I know if they change?"

"They will not change; they were finalized only yesterday. The only wild card is your troop locations. They should be tracking you and intercept you. You have a phone. Do not use it unless there is no other choice. However, if the pickup location changes, you will get a call from a woman identifying herself as Victoria. Talk to her as if she were the production assistant of the Canadian television crew. You will be meeting your television crew in five hours."

Five hours later Jules met the Canadian operatives and the driver. Hadi covered a few last-minute details, then wished them well. The Canadians and the driver were waiting in a Land Rover when Hadi pulled Jules back into the house. "Jules, you know I am not a religious man, but I would like to say a poem for you now."

Jules searched Hadi's face, finding concern and sadness. She wondered if he thought of this mission as a suicide mission and he was already mourning her.

"I would like that, Hadi," she answered realizing that this was more for him than her.

He held her at arms' length, looked into her eyes, and began.

You have seen your own strength.
You have seen your own beauty.
You have seen your own golden wings.
Why do you worry?

"Rumi," responded Jules.

"You know Rumi?" Hadi kissed her on both cheeks. "Trust in your own strength. Now, go my friend and be safe."

"Hadi, why are you involved in this?"

"Because, my friend, my country needs this."

CHAPTER 19 – The Aspirants

Your voice familiar, your words concealing the truth with motive-filled clichés, you are hidden.

Unknown

Friday May 8

They had been traveling for about five hours. Peshawar, Pakistan was less than a hundred kilometers from the Khyber Pass, the main route into Afghanistan. The road was rough and, in some places, blown away. Travel was slow and tedious with multiple checkpoints. They were lucky. No Insurgent or U.S. air strikes took place along the route to Kabul and no one challenged their credentials.

They continued for another ten hours until reaching Kandahar, where they checked into the Amtex Village and Business Park, a small hotel frequented by foreign nationals.

###

"TGIF" thought Woods, as he unlocked his office door to a ringing phone. "Keith Woods, here." He listened, then surprised, sat down. "Really? What time? All right. I'll be waiting in the lobby." After a miserable day with the 'negative nabobs,' Keith had tried his best to convince them to let him take them to White Bark Ranch. They had refused and he felt he had been denied an opportunity to rile Sophie yet another time, but they had changed their minds and called to ask him to take them there later this morning. He had to refrain from clapping his hands in sheer merriment.

###

"Honey, do you realize that last night was the last time we're going to have the house to ourselves for several months?" Rick was nuzzling Sophie's neck while she cut up veggies for a Western omelet.

"You could stop fooling around and help, you know," chided Sophie.

"And miss all this fun?!" Rick went back to kissing her neck.

"All right then, if you insist, do it right!" Sophie turned, leaned against him and tilted her head to the side. Last night, Sophie wanted to make love, but Rick wasn't sure it would be okay. He tried to dissuade her by telling her it wouldn't be a good idea after her 'female parts' had suffered a trauma. When she asked him what was really wrong, he admitted that he didn't think they should 'do it' without a condom and, in case she hadn't noticed, there wasn't a drug store nearby. "Is that what you're afraid of, making another baby?" Sophie asked.

"No, of losing another," he replied. That put a damper on both their libidos for a while but, in the middle of the night, Sophie demonstrating her creativity, had her way with him.

Mickey awoke to the smell of coffee and cooking meat. It was a meat lover's dream come true, up here in the meadows. Steak for dinner last night, and more for breakfast! Claire was curled up against Mickey, still sleeping. It had been very cold last night, and he assumed Claire was looking for a furnace substitute. Mickey remembered his wife constantly pushing him away from her, saying his body was too hot.

Alex's sleeping bag was empty, and Ruby and Rowdy were gone, so he assumed Alex had something to do with the delicious smells coming from outside the tent. He extricated his arm from under Claire's head, shook it to get the blood flowing, carefully slipped out of his sleeping bag, and poked his head outside of the tent. Alex and two wranglers were sitting around the camp fire drinking coffee. Alex raised a cup to him, an invitation he couldn't pass up. He grabbed his jacket and boots, gingerly hopping over pebbles in the dirt.

"Morning, boys and girls," crooned Mickey. Taking a cup of coffee from Alex, he said, "What's the plan for the day, boss?"

"I thought I'd work with Claire for a couple of hours. There's a place within walking distance that's private and has a vantage point where you can keep an eye on the two of us."

Phil was ready to crack eggs into a frying pan. "How many Alex? Mickey? What about for the girl?"

Mickey thought, *Maybe I should change careers. Guarding cows is a whole lot more fun than guarding people.*

This time Woods didn't have to get out of the Escalade. He saw the Bentworths leave the Doubletree lobby, walking at a fast clip. "Good morning are you ready?" he asked politely.

"Well, of course we're ready. Let's go."

Amidst giving instructions to the kitchen help on what to do with the pies when they came out of the oven, Sophie heard a car drive up. The kitchen had heated up with the baking this morning and she had opened the windows. She could hear clearly, "This is it folks." She immediately recognized the voice, rummaged around the kitchen for her walkie talkie, and called Rick. "Get up here now!" Rick didn't ask why. Her tone was clear enough. "Now" meant this instant. He left the barn at a run.

Sophie ignored Woods' knocking, waiting for Rick to get there. Two minutes passed and the knocking became louder and more insistent. Any minute now, Woods would walk in uninvited. She wiped the flour off her hands, picked up her shotgun and walked through the dining room calling out, "Just a minute, I'm coming." By the time she reached the door and saw that disgusting weasel standing there with two strangers, Rick had leapt up the front steps and was saying, "Mr. Woods, I'm surprised to see you here again."

Woods, attempting to hide his contempt in front of his guests, addressed Rick. "Yes, I'm sure you are, but the Bentworths asked me to show them the way down here so that they could visit their daughter." He stopped when he saw his words register confusion, then caution across Rick's and Sophie's faces.

Turning to the man standing next to Woods, Rick said, "Mr. Bentworth, did you clear this through ISS?"

Woods' mouth gathered itself up into a huge smirk when Bentworth, in his usual rude condescending manner, answered, "Of course we did, you idiot! Now, where is she?"

Sophie's finger was itching. She thought she heard the opening theme from "The Good, the Bad, and the Ugly" and wished she had the courage to discharge her shotgun right between Woods' eyes. Rick reached over for the gun, gently taking it from Sophie.

"Mr. and Mrs. Bentworth, I'm afraid your daughter isn't here right now. If Mr. Woods had given us some notice, we would have made sure she was here."

"Then where is she?" spoke the woman with less aggression.

"Ma'am, she's on an overnight camp out and isn't due back until this evening." Rick wasn't inviting them to hang around. No wonder poor Claire was screwed up. Her parents were consummate boors.

"Is she with her bodyguard??" asked the woman.

"Yes Ma'am. She's also with her therapist and two other men. She's perfectly safe, if that's your concern."

Sophie was holding Rick's free hand. He was sure that she had managed to break a few bones.

"Look, I'm sorry about my husband," continued the woman, "We're just disappointed that she's not here. Would it be a great inconvenience if you showed us around the place, then we'll be off. George has to fly out tonight, so we won't be able to stay long."

Sophie was beginning to feel some sympathy for the woman. "It's too bad you missed her. I wonder why ISS didn't call us?"

"I don't know. They should have."

"Would you please excuse us for a moment," asked Rick. He took Sophie's arm and directed her back into the house. Almost in a whisper, he said, "I'm not feeling good about this Sophie. I'll start a tour, but you try to get hold of Jake. I don't buy ISS screwing up and not calling us." Sophie nodded in agreement and Rick went back out to the porch.

"Folks, I'll be happy to take you on a short tour of the facilities. Sophie asked that you forgive her, she's got help in the kitchen and they're getting ready for our opening guest season on Sunday. If you'll follow me, please."

"Woods, we've changed our minds. I think since Claire's not here, we'll just head back to LA." Woods tried to argue, but the couple was adamant. They drove off a few minutes later.

Rick waited for the Escalade to disappear from sight, then went to find Sophie. "Did you get a hold of Jake?"

"No, I left him a voice mail. Where are the Bentworths?"

"They changed their mind about wanting a tour and took off. Woods was none too pleased. I wonder what he has up his sleeve. Would you call me as soon as you hear from Jake? I don't like this."

Mickey's walkie talkie vibrated. He was sitting on a large flat rock, overlooking a grassy knoll where Claire and Alex were sitting on a blanket. "Mickey here. Over."

"Mickey, switch to private channel 2."

"I'm here. Over," answered Mickey.

"Do you know what the Bentworths look like? Over," replied Rick.

"I saw pictures. He's six foot and thin. She's attractive, dark hair, maybe five feet five inches a hundred forty pounds. Why? Over."

"They were just here, looking for Claire. Said ISS cleared the visit. Over."

"Rick, it was my understanding that the Bentworths didn't know where she was. Maybe things changed. Over."

"Did Jake or someone from ISS clear this with you. Over."

"No. Over."

"Would it be like Jake to forget to advise us? Over."

"Nope. He's 'Mr. Precise.' Over."

"I'll call you back once we hear from Jake. We've got a call into him right now. Over."

The couple with Woods fit the description Mickey had given him. Maybe they were going against ISS and had hired someone else to find Claire. God, that would be stupid, but Bentworth seemed like a fellow who did what he wanted. Rick shook it off and went back to work.

Looking down on Alex and Claire, Mickey wondered what they were doing. Claire's head was on Alex's lap. Rick's call had made him a little skittish. His eyes darted around, watching for any movement in the surrounding area.

"I hear clinking, now hissing," said Claire. Alex induced a trance for the third time. "Door closed. Wait, opening again!" Claire's level of panic was escalating.

"You're fine, Claire. Remember, you're just watching a movie." Alex had varied the hypnosis methodology slightly, hoping to get Claire to go deeper. "Girl on bed. Handcuffs."

"What is the girl doing?" asked Alex.

"Listening. Can't see."

"What does she hear?" Once more Alex prompted Claire.

"He's, he's—" Claire trailed off.

"What is he doing, Claire? What's the man in the movie doing?"

"Put something in her hand." Claire's panic instantly subsided.

"Claire, what's happening now?"

"He's, he's talking to her."

"Can you tell what he's saying?"

"The girl. Very groggy."

"Yes, but did she hear what the man said?"

"Don't look. Count to a hundred." At first it seemed like Claire's answer was non-responsive, then it clicked for Alex. *Oh my gosh! I think he gave her a key!*

Brought back to the present, Alex heard Claire say, "I want to go to the barn, please."

"Just one more thing, the movie's not quite over. Did the man talk to anyone else, Claire?"

"No. She called him."

Alex thought for a moment. Did Claire mean that the other person called him by a name or called to him to leave the room? Taking a moment to phrase the question for the maximum effect, Alex asked, "Claire, what did the woman call him?

"Phil."

"Okay, the movie is over for now. Let's go to your safe place."

Alex didn't know if she could sit quietly, while Claire recuperated. She turned from her waist and looked up behind her. Mickey was sitting with a pair of binoculars, scanning the area. She waved her arm, capturing his attention. Pointing to her walkie talkie, she shook her head right and left, letting him know not to use it. Then she motioned for him to come down.

Five minutes later, Claire still in a trance, Mickey broke through the tree cover. Alex laid her finger across her mouth to silence him as he approached. He sat down quietly next to Alex. She signaled him to wait a moment.

"Claire, do you want to come up now?"

"Not yet," answered Claire dreamily.

"Okay. You can stay a while longer, but I need to talk to someone. I'll be back in a minute. All right?"

"Sure," replied Claire.

"Okay, Mickey. We can talk softly now. We've got to get a hold of Jake. We are dealing with a male-female kidnapping team and the man's name is Phil."

Mickey's face scrunched up. "Do you think she confused the man she told you about with your wrangler, Phil?"

Alex's face deflated. "Shit, I was so excited, that I didn't even consider that. Damn!"

"Even so Alex, we need to get the information to Jake. Ah, there's something I've got to tell you." Mickey filled Alex in on the conversation he'd had with Rick.

"Do you think we should stay up here another day?"

"My first impression is that it would be better to go back down. If something is out of whack, Sophie and Rick are sitting targets."

"Shit," was all Alex could say. Mickey got up to return to his vantage point, and Alex went about bringing Claire out of the trance.

"Sophie, this is Jake. Your message sounded urgent. What's going on? You said something about Bentworth visiting?"

"Yes, Jake. He and his wife showed up today looking for Claire. They said ISS had cleared the visit." Sophie could hear Jake sigh over the airwaves.

"It didn't come from this office but let me check in with our Washington office and get back to you. It would be just like Bentworth to call one of the owners in Washington and get them to agree. It may take a while. Meanwhile, can you call Rick and have him operate at heightened security?"

Dinner had come and gone without hearing back from Jake. Rick came into the great room after locking all doors and windows and setting the house alarm. Claire was trying to teach Sophie, Alex, and Mickey to play Euchre, a five-card hand with some similarities to Bridge. It looked pretty hopeless, but Claire kept trying.

A loud knock on the front door startled everyone. Instinctively, Rick, Alex, Mickey, and Sophie reached for their guns. Without a word, Mickey grabbed Claire and threw her over his shoulder, flying up the stairs. Alex, in a commanding voice, told Sophie to go upstairs with Mickey and Claire. One look at Alex and Rick getting into defensive positions was all Sophie needed. She did what she was told.

The knocking continued, shortly followed by an angry, "Where the hell is everybody?"

Rick recognized the voice and motioned for Alex to take up a position to the left of the front door. Rick stood to the right of the door, then moved slightly to peek out the window. He saw the Bentworths who had come to the ranch that morning. Carefully, and without any attempt to hide his handgun, he cracked open the door wedging his foot against it, so it couldn't be pushed open easily.

"I'm sorry, folks. I can't let you in. We haven't been able to confirm that your visit was authorized by ISS."

"God damn it, you fool, if you don't believe us, why don't you get Claire and have her confirm who we are?" The man was very agitated.

"Folks, I'm very sorry, but I can't do that. Not without authorization," Rick replied calmly.

"Do I have to call the authorities to see our daughter?" Even in the pale shadow of the porch light, Rick could see that the guy's face was red with anger.

"Maybe that would be a good idea," responded Rick, not giving an inch.

"Ah, Sir, maybe there is a compromise here," said the woman. "If you're worried about us being who we say we are, have Claire look out a window and identify us. We can step back into the car's headlights. What do you say?"

"Fine. Go back to the car and stand in front of the headlights." Rick waited for them to walk down the porch steps, then he pulled out his walkie talkie.

Before he could make a call, Alex challenged him. "You aren't really considering this are you?" Alex could forget faces, but not voices. She was almost certain she had heard the woman's voice before but couldn't place it.

"I'm considering letting Claire identify them, but not letting them in." Rick cued up Mickey. "Mickey, take Claire to the window and let her look at the two people standing in the headlights of the car parked out front. Ask her who they are. Be very careful, Mickey. Over."

"Got it. Over."

Rick and Alex waited for Mickey's return call. "Rick, she says they are Mr. and Mrs. Bentworth. Now what? Over."

"I don't know. Should we let them in? Over."

"I don't think two people stand a chance against the three of us. Let me ask Claire. Over?"

Claire was sitting on the bed in the corner furthest from the window in Mickey's room. He turned to her and asked, "Do you want to see your father and step-mother?"

She answered, "You mean the Bentworths?" Mickey thought she was confused with the excitement and hoped she didn't have a flashback. "Yes, Claire, the Bentworths."

"Okay," she responded flatly.

"Rick, Claire says she'd like to see them. I think it's okay. Frisk them, though. Over."

"Rick, we could be inviting the fox into the hen house." Alex clearly had reservations. "Tell them to beat it."

"Mickey to Rick. Come in. Sophie just got a call from Jake. They did call Washington to arrange a visit, but Paulson told them they'd have to clear it with Jake, and they didn't. Over."

"Did you hear that, Alex?" asked Rick. "What do you think now?"

"Why didn't the Bentworths wait until they had the go-ahead from Jake?"

"Impatient, rude, spoiled rich cretins?"

Just then they heard yelling. "God damn it, it's freezing out here. How long are you going to keep us waiting?"

Alex sighed. "Maybe you're right. Ask them in, make the two of them sit on the couch next to each other so we can keep an eye on them and then have Mickey bring Claire down. Ten minutes only."

Rick cracked open the door again and yelled out, "Okay folks. You can see her for ten minutes."

Rick held the door open and told them to take off their coats, go over to the couch and sit down. When they were seated and he and Alex were in position, Rick called Mickey.

"Jesus, you people. Put away the guns before someone gets hurt," complained Bentworth.

Mickey came down the steps first, shielding Claire, with Sophie bringing up the rear. When Claire took the last step, Mickey moved aside so she could see her parents. Mrs. Bentworth got up from the couch with her arms open and moved towards Claire. Alex jumped between the two of them and asked Mrs. Bentworth to return to the couch.

"Hello Father, Mother," said Claire without much emotion.

"Hello, Darling," said Mrs. Bentworth. "How have you been?"

Mickey directed Claire to a chair that flanked the couch. "Good. I've done exactly what you told me to do."

"That's wonderful! I'm so proud of you!"

Claire smiled wanly and said, "It's nice you came to see me. Are you taking me home?"

Bentworth replied to Claire, "No, but we thought you might want to spend the weekend in Missoula with us. Would you like that?"

Claire was wringing her hands in her lap and looked conflicted. "If that's what you want."

Rick jumped in. "I thought you said that you were flying out tonight?"

"That was just to get rid of the insipid pest Woods. He's got it in his head that he's going to sell me bank owned real-estate," replied the man.

"How did you meet him?" Sophie asked, curious as to how Bentworth had formed an opinion so quickly.

"Quite by accident. We were having breakfast at a little place by the hotel, and he was sitting in the next booth. He said he saw us looking at a map and talking about White Bark Ranch. We chatted for a while and he offered to bring us down because it would be tricky to find. Bunch of hot air, if you ask me."

"A monumental coincidence," said Alex.

"I suppose so, but he really is insufferable," replied Bentworth. "Do you suppose you can give us some time with Claire? It really is uncomfortable trying to have a conversation with all of you playing Rambo."

"Sorry," answered Mickey. "This is as good as it's going to get."

"Claire," said Bentworth, "maybe these people are right. Let's wait for the ISS folks to contact them tomorrow and then we can visit properly. All right?"

Claire duly nodded her head. Her parents got up and left without any more fanfare. Mickey went over to Claire and touched her arm. She reacted with a startled jerk, as if she were coming back from another planet. "Come on, let's go back upstairs for the night. There's been enough excitement."

Rick showed the Bentworths out and orchestrated a meeting in Sophie's sitting room after Mickey got Claire settled for the night.

"I tell you, something is off with Claire," repeated Alex. "Her reaction to her parents was just a degree above frost."

"Alex, I just thought of it, but when I asked her if she wanted to see her parents, she said, 'You mean the Bentworths?' I thought it was odd but chalked it up to stress. Do you think it means anything?" Mickey mused.

"Alex, did you see how she reacted when they left, and Mickey took her arm to take her back upstairs?" Sophie asked.

"No, I was backing up Rick. How did she look?"

"Startled. She kind of snapped back from somewhere. I thought it odd at the time."

"Guys, and I know this is way out there, maybe as far out as Pluto, but I'd say that those people are not her parents, though she has been made to believe they are." Alex surmised.

"Oh god, Alex, not another one of your wacko way-out-there theories." Rick was tired, frustrated, and was taking it out on Alex.

"Mind control?" asked a speculative Mickey, not wanting to tick Rick off.

Alex appreciated him at least considering her theory. "I don't know enough about mind control except what I've read about the CIA and their experiments, but it is a well-known fact that there are many drugs out there that can cause deep hypnotic trances."

"You think she was hypnotized into thinking someone other than her parents are her parents?" Rick crossed his arms in front of his chest and waited for a rebuttal.

"It does sound draconian, I admit, and maybe I'm all wet behind the ears, but I don't think we should let those people back up here." Alex crossed her arms and stared back at Rick.

"Well, I think we all agree on that," said Sophie.

"I think we should take some extra measures tonight, just on the outside chance that there is something to what Alex says," conceded Mickey.

"All right. What if I stay downstairs for the night?" Rick was already up and moving. "Okay, I'm setting the instant alarm on the exterior and interior of the house as soon as I go downstairs so, if you're looking for a midnight snack it's out of the question tonight." *I wish Alex hadn't left the dogs with the cattle.*

Saturday May 9

Sophie, Rick, and Alex all heard Mickey screaming. It was just after midnight. Rick took the stairs three at a time, not noticing that the alarm didn't go off. Alex was on her feet, gun in hand, crashing through Mickey's door, when Sophie, bathrobe flapping behind her, ran in behind her.

"She's gone. Damn, she's gone! I don't know how she could have gotten past me. Jesus, where the hell is she? I looked all over. At first I thought she might be having a flashback and was hiding in the closet or under the bed, but she's not. Oh my god, how did this happen?"

"Calm down, man. Calm down. When was the last time you saw her?"

"Just before we met in Sophie's room. What was that, about 10:00 p.m.? I set my wrist alarm to check on her again."

"She must have slipped out when we were in Sophie's room. I didn't think she knew the alarm code. Crap." Rick was rubbing his temples. "Obviously something upset her enough that she thought she had to leave. Any ideas where she might go?"

"Down to the barn," yelled Alex, by now on her way out the door.

"Take the pickup," yelled Sophie. "I'll stay here and search the house."

Alex was already in the driver's seat cranking the engine when Rick and Mickey piled into the truck. "Listen you two, please let me go look for her. If she is in the middle of a flashback state, she'll be vulnerable and maybe dangerous."

"All right. We'll follow you."

Slamming on the brakes, Alex barely missed hitting the barn's double doors. She entered through the small door to the side and started walking through the dimly lit barn. "Claire, Claire, are you here? It's Alex. Don't be afraid, honey, you're safe with me." She repeated the same words or some approximate version of them as they searched every stall, the tack room, the bathrooms, and the loft. After close to an hour they concluded she was not in the barn.

"What about the equipment sheds?" asked Rick.

"I don't think she'd go there but, since we're down here, let's check." Alex would have bet money that Claire had gone to the barn. She wasn't in the sheds either.

Piling into the pickup, they drove back up to the house. Rick was the first one in. "Sophie, Sophie, we're back. Where are you?"

Sophie didn't answer. The three of them looked at each other. "Maybe she found Claire and is up in the room with her," offered Alex as an explanation.

"I'm going to look in the basement," said Rick. "You two go upstairs and see if you can find Sophie."

Alex heard Sophie's voice. She sounded strained. "Alex, is that you? I'm in here with Claire." Mickey and Alex opened the door to Claire's room and couldn't believe what they saw. The Bentworths were in the room, watching while Claire held a gun to Sophie's temple.

"Come in Alex, Mickey. Put your guns on the desk and sit over on the bed," said Mrs. Bentworth. "You can see that Claire's a little upset right now, so I wouldn't make any sudden movements."

Mickey was indignant. "What are you doing here? Can't you see that you've upset her and that she isn't in her right mind?"

"Well, you're right about one thing, she isn't in her right mind," responded Claire's father. "Now shut up or Mrs. Martini is history."

"What's this all about?" tried Mickey again.

"Not even you, Dr. Martini, figured it out, did you?" taunted Mrs. Bentworth. Then it clicked. Alex remembered where she had heard the voice. The woman saw Alex's flash of recognition and laughed. "Too late, Alex. By the way, don't worry about Rick coming up. As soon as he opened the basement door, he was history."

Sophie cried out in despair.

"Oh, now isn't that touching," responded the woman. "Don't you think so Phil?"

Mickey caught on but managed not to reveal what Alex's look had told him. He nudged Alex with his arm, hoping she wouldn't move but would understand what he wanted.

"Claire, it's Dr. Martini. Can you hear me?"

"Yes."

"If you think you are going to dissuade her from killing your Aunt, you'll soon see it's useless but, what the hell, we could use a little entertainment," taunted the woman.

"Claire, do you know you're holding a gun?" persisted Alex.

"Yes," answered Claire.

"You don't really want to hurt Aunt Sophie."

"Have to."

"No, you don't. You can leave the gun and go to your barn. You know the way, just take the steps."

"I see you've been successful in hypnotizing her. Nice job Alex. You shouldn't have been able to, but I underestimated you. Too bad, though, she just had a shot of Baradanga. Do you know what that is?" the woman said smiling superiorly.

"It is a long-lasting truth serum that induces narco-hypnosis. Its use is outlawed," replied Alex.

"You are good, isn't she Phil?" Phil nodded his head but didn't take his eyes or gun off of Mickey. "Depending on the dosage, it makes people willing to follow any command and, when combined with Notec, you do know that drug don't you, it turns an unwilling subject into one who is willing to carry out post-hypnotic suggestions for a very long time. I'm afraid your attempt to bring Claire out of the hypnotic trance she's in is useless."

Alex said nothing but noticed that Mickey had crossed his right leg over his knee. He was going for his carry pistol. She had to distract Claire.

"I see your wheels turning," laughed the woman. You're wondering why you didn't find any evidence that mind control techniques were used on Claire. My dear, and I do use that term pejoratively, it is more than conjecture that these techniques can be used, then covered up successfully so that they are impossible to recognize. It is a reality."

Alex felt Mickey nudge her leg. She dove for Phil and simultaneously, Mickey shot Claire. Sophie grabbed

Claire's gun and swung it at the impersonator, shooting her in the back of the head as the she tried to reach the guns on the desk. Alex managed to tackle the man to the floor but was having a hard time restraining Phil on her own. Sophie was up on her feet coming to her niece's rescue. She bashed Phil over the head with the butt of the pistol.

"Mickey are you all right?" Sophie was kneeling over him. He had caught a bullet in the struggle and was down.

"Hurts like hell, but I'm all right. Probably went clean through my shoulder."

Claire didn't seem to be in good shape. Alex thought that Mickey's bullet had caught her in the back. Alex ripped off Claire's pajama top, using it to soak up the blood so she could see where the wound was located. "My god! It went right through her ribs. She saw the slug in the wall, a fraction of an inch from where Sophie's head had been.

"Is she going to make it?" asked Mickey.

"I think so. She may be bleeding internally, but the wound is clean, and I don't think you nicked her lung. Nevertheless we had better get the two of you to a hospital NOW!"

"I'm not going anywhere without checking on Rick." Mickey pushed his way past Alex and Sophie and staggered down the stairs.

"Aunt Sophie, go with him. I can handle it here."

When Mickey and Sophie reached the basement door it was open. Mickey held Sophie back. "Let me check to make sure there isn't another booby trap."

"I'll get a flashlight," answered Sophie already heading for the kitchen 'junk' drawer. She was back and Mickey took the flashlight using it to look for the light switch. All that was left was a hole in the wall.

"Shit," he said out loud. From the smell and hole in the wall, it looked like the light switch had been used to spark a small explosion when the door was opened, and the switch clicked on. He shined the flashlight at the bottom of the stairs where Rick was on the floor contorted, with a gash on his head. Sophie screamed and tried to push past Mickey, but he held her back. "Sophie, let me go first." He gingerly felt his way down the stairs one at a time and when he reached Rick, he called to Sophie, "He's alive. I'm bringing him up."

In spite of Mickey's pain and fueled by adrenaline, he used his good arm to hoist Rick up over his wounded shoulder and carried him upstairs to the couch. He told Sophie to clean and bandage the wounds on Rick's face. "He'll be all right. I recognized what caused the explosion. It wasn't meant to kill him, Sophie, only put him out of commission. He may not be able to see for a while, so don't be afraid if he wakes up and tells you he can't."

Mickey, out of breath from carrying Rick up the stairs, took hold of the banister and pulled himself up to help Alex. Claire had come to and was moaning. Mickey noticed that Alex had bandaged up both the entry and exit wound to staunch the bleeding.

"Rick?" asked Alex.

"Okay. Superficial head wound from a home-made explosion. We're lucky there wasn't a fire."

"Mickey, do we call the police or get to the nearest hospital and explain later?"

"Can you bandage me up while I talk to the Feds? Jules had talked to the local FBI field agent before Claire came out here."

"I'll find some more gauze pads while you dial."

Phil, the man on the floor was coming to. The lump on his head was visible under his thinning hair. Mickey smiled and noticed that Alex had trussed him well with strips of ripped sheets. *Guess her experience roping calves at the ranch had paid off. Phil wasn't going anywhere.*

Alex worked on Mickey while he talked to the FBI field agent. She was listening to half of the conversation and understood that they were to go directly to a designated medical facility and the agent would take care of the rest.

"Mickey, I need to call Dean to help carry Claire to the truck." Mickey nodded in agreement.

"Dean, this is Alex. I'm sorry to call you so late, but we have a situation here at the house. Can you and one of the boys come up as fast as you can? I'll explain when you get here."

Four hours later, Mickey and Claire were in surgery at Marcus Daly Memorial Hospital in Hamilton, twenty-five miles north of the ranch. Rick's head, face, and upper chest had been stitched up and the ER doctor told Sophie and Alex the burns on his face and neck weren't serious and would heal without complications. The gashes and cuts were caused by the tumble down the stairs. When they asked about his eyes, the doctor said they would have to wait until tomorrow to tell for sure, but that he thought the damage was temporary. He wanted to keep him for observation.

Sophie and Alex found the surgical waiting room and checked in with the attendant, who told them that Mickey was in recovery and doing well. There was no news on Claire yet. While Sophie was on the phone with Dean, Alex's phone rang. It was Jake.

"Alex, I'm sorry to call so late, or early as the case may be, but I had to reach you. You were right about the people who came to the ranch. Don't let them get anywhere near Claire. They're imposters."

"Too late Jake. Sophie and I are here at the hospital waiting for Mickey and Claire to come out of surgery."

"My god, what happened?"

Alex gave Jake a run down and promised to call him as soon as she saw Mickey and got word on Claire. He told her he was going to call the Bentworths, the FBI agent in charge, then catch the first flight out that he could.

###

"Aunt Sophie, Jake said he was flying out as soon as he could. What did Dean say?"

"That the place was crawling with cops. They took the man away almost immediately, and then the body of the woman. He also said that the Feds were processing the room and then were going to seal it off as a crime scene."

"Aunt Sophie, I'll be okay here if you want to go up and sit with Rick." Alex was numb. Her mind was barely functioning, but she didn't need Sophie to sit with her while she agonized over Rick.

"Okay, baby. Come up when you find out about Claire." Sophie stiffly got up off the couch and for the first time looking like an old woman, slowly made her way to the door. Minutes after Sophie's departure, the Surgical Waiting Room attendant told Alex that Claire was out of surgery and doing well in recovery. "She'll be brought up to the surgical floor wing, along with your friend Mickey, in about two hours. You can check with the floor nurse for their rooms." Alex thanked the attendant and left to find Sophie.

###

Alex felt a hand on her shoulder. Slowly, the room came into focus. Jake was standing over her in Claire's room. When he was sure she was awake, he bent over and hugged her, lifting her to her feet.

"Dr. Martini, I'd like you to meet the Bentworths."

George Bentworth came forward and took her hand in both of his. "I understand you saved my daughter's life."

"Along with my Aunt Sophie, Mickey, and Rick," she said humbly.

Bentworth reached for his wife. "Dr. Martini, this is my wife Elena."

Elena put her arms around Alex and hugged her briefly. "Thank you so much. Finally, we can breathe again."

Alex turned to look at Claire, who was still knocked out from the residual effects of the anesthesia and pain killers. "She's going to be fine."

Bentworth moved to the side of the bed, reaching out to touch Claire's hand. He looked at her with a trace of regret, but it was clear he loved his daughter. "Dr. Martini, since she won't be awake for a while, do you think we can go get a cup of coffee?"

"Sure," answered Alex, not understanding why.

"We have a private nurse who will look after her. Please, come with us. There's so much to talk about." With that, Bentworth took Alex's arm. She nodded and followed him out of the room.

Seated around a Formica topped table in a little mini cafeteria on the surgical floor, they drank terrible coffee without complaining.

Bentworth took the lead. "Dr. Martini, Jake told us that it was your idea to go back and look at Dr. Metuchi as a possible suspect."

"Please call me Alex, Mr. Bentworth."

"Only if you call us George and Elena," responded the man with warmth.

"Thank you. Ah, yes. There were some minor inconsistencies that I found in Dr. Metuchi's records that got me thinking." She wasn't about to tell the Bentworths that she had also asked Jules and Jake to take another look at Elena. It appeared that Jake shared her thoughts. "The biggest tip off was a conversation I had with Dr. Metuchi concerning her treatment plan. I wondered why she didn't try hypnosis with Claire.

"Hypnotherapy is recognized as a viable treatment for PTSD. Dr. Metuchi told me that Claire absolutely refused, and she felt she couldn't bend her ethics and do it without the patient's agreement. Then I asked Claire why she refused hypnosis and found their answers didn't quite jive. I wasn't convinced that the discrepancy was due to Claire's mental state, and when I was able to hypnotize her, she was very responsive and we had good results, which threw even more doubt on what Dr. Metuchi had told me." Alex wasn't sure how much further she should go.

Bentworth said, "Jake told us on the trip up here this morning what Jules had discovered in Argentina lead him to uncover Dr. Metuchi's motives." That was Jake's cue to explain to Alex.

"Jules had a hunch after you made her promise to take another look at Metuchi. She discovered, through public records, then an interview with Dr. Metuchi's grandfather that Dr. Metuchi's mother was married to a Chilean general, who after the 1973 coup in Chile, sought exile in Buenos Aires. He was assassinated in 1974. Dr. Metuchi's mother married Carlos Carola, who ironically had the same first name as her late husband. Dr. Carola adopted Laura."

"Go on, Jake," encouraged Alex.

"Okay, so Dr. Carola got a fellowship at Princeton, took his family with him, and ended up staying. We knew that part but, what never came out was that Dr. Laura Metuchi, before she was married and after she did a residency at Stanford in psychiatry, was recruited by an unknown agency to resurrect mind control research that the public thought had been definitively shut down in the seventies."

"That explains her ability to control Claire, but what was her motive?" asked Alex, revived by the caffeine.

Bentworth took over. "I don't know how much you know about the Chilean coup in 1973 and its aftermath but, my father, who ran the munitions business at that time, supplied much of the weaponry used during the coup. Laura, Dr. Metuchi, blamed my father for making her father a target of the new government."

"Unbelievable," said Alex, looking at Mr. Bentworth. "So, you're thinking that she held this grudge all these years and kidnapped Claire to get back at you?"

"We think that she held the grudge, but that the crime may have been one of opportunity," offered Jake. "She met Elena at the Club, found out to whom Elena was married, and thought she had struck gold!"

Alex was shaking her head in disbelief. "She's one sick puppy."

Jake corrected her. "She *was* one sick puppy."

Alex nodded her head somberly. Alex was pretty sure that Sophie had never killed anyone before and when the numbness wore off, she'd need some counseling. "Who is Phil?"

"We're not quite sure yet about his story, but he's told the Feds that he used to be a patient of Metuchi's." Jake waited for Alex's head to spin around like in the 'Exorcist'.

Alex was sick to her stomach. She got up and began to pace.

Jake asked, "Alex, how is it that a person so warped can have a successful practice for so many years?" George and Elena looked at her expectantly.

Alex wanted to say, *Damned, if I know*, but by the looks on George's and Elena's face, she knew she'd have to phrase it better. "I suppose there could be any number of theories, but I honestly don't know enough about her to theorize. We'll probably never know."

George and Elena nodded their heads gravely. Elena reached across the table and took Alex's hands. "You must be exhausted. We should let you rest, but first I know George has something to ask you."

Alex turned her attention to George. He cleared his throat, "Dr. Martini, I mean Alex, I don't want this to come across the wrong way, so I'm going to rely on your sensitivity." He paused before he went on, "You and your family have given us our daughter back and we'd like to give you something in return. Please, anything you want, just name it."

The sincerity in George's eyes spoke far more than his words. Alex did not take offense at what might have been perceived as a rich man trying to pay off a debt.

"George, Elena, there are only three things I want," spoke Alex with equal sincerity. "First, I'd like you to honor our agreement and settle the ranch's mortgage."

Bentworth interrupted her. "That goes without saying. I mean something above and beyond that. I'll build you a clinic, or whatever you want."

"That's very generous, but that won't be necessary," said Alex, "but what I would like is for you to allow me to continue treating Claire when she gets out of the hospital for the rest of the summer. Her brain has been re-wired by malevolent hands and she deserves to be treated by someone who really cares for her. At the end of the summer I will find her someone good in your neck of the woods so she can continue with therapy as needed."

She appraised the Bentworths. There was no surprise on their faces. "The last thing I would ask is to have Mickey stay at the ranch during her treatment. She feels safe with him and it's going to be a long road to undo the damage that Dr. Metuchi did. I think his presence would be helpful." Alex waited for the Bentworth's response.

"That's all?" asked George, a little choked up.

Alex wearily nodded.

"Just remember, Dr. Martini, any time, any place, anything you need; you call me. All right?"

"George," said Elena, "If Claire wants to stay, I think it's the right thing to do." Elena turned to Alex, "Now let our driver take you and your Aunt back to the ranch."

CHAPTER 20 - Heads or Tails

Are wars anything but the means whereby a nation's problems are set, where creation is stimulated, there you have adventure? But there is no adventure in heads-or-tails, in betting that the toss will come out of life or death. War is not an adventure. It is a disease.

Antoine de Saint-Exupery

Saturday May 9 (cont.)

Jules and the faux television crew headed northwest out of Kandahar in the middle of the night to Chora, a small town at the foot of the Hindu Kush mountains. Only the driver knew their exact destination. After three hours of driving, they reached Chora, driving through the sleepy town without incident. Shortly, they veered off the paved road and spent over an hour bumping along a winding washboard dirt road, everyone vigilant for other vehicles or movement at the sides of the road. An hour later, kidneys aching from the constant bouncing, the driver turned off again, this time on to no more than a path. Had it not been for seatbelts, the vehicle's passengers would surely have sustained concussions.

After what seemed like an eon of narrow misses with a date for death as they careened down the mountain, Hadi's man slowed and pulled off the path. "We wait now," he spoke in Farsi. Jules translated for the Canadians, then asked the driver if they could get out and stretch their legs. He agreed as long as they promised to stay close to the Land Rover.

They spent about thirty minutes munching on granola bars and walking around the vehicle so many times that they wore a path around the Land Rover. The driver called to Jules in Farsi, "We are ready to leave."

She wondered how many more hours of agony they were about to endure.

###

Even in the dark, Jules was able to discern that the Land Rover had stopped in a naturally formed bowl surrounded on all sides by arid hills. Within seconds, the vehicle was surrounded by men with weapons, opening the doors and giving them directions in Farsi. Jules, flanked by the soldiers, and followed by the Canadians, also surrounded by soldiers, was directed by the driver to a tent about twenty-five yards from the Land Rover. He motioned her to follow him inside. The soldiers stopped the two Canadians by stepping in front of the tent flap after Jules and the driver went in.

"This is General Adeeb Zahir Daud." The driver made the introduction in Farsi.

"It is my humblest and deepest honor to make your acquaintance," repeated Jules in Farsi.

General Daud invited Jules to sit at a table, lit only with a candle. "So," he continued in Farsi, "You know my nephew, Hadi?"

"Yes, I knew him when we attended the university together. We were classmates."

General Daud poured tea and offered a cup to Jules, which she accepted with effusive courtesy. "Jules," the General continued, "Hadi has great faith in you. What did you do to impress him?"

Jules knew that the answer to this question would determine if General Daud would turn over his prisoner to her and the Canadians.

"I do not submit," she answered simply, waiting for the next chess move.

The General, driver, and three other men in the tent were quiet for a moment, then simultaneously broke out in raucous laughter. She remained watchful, not knowing if their laughter was derisive, believing that they could make any woman submit at any time, or if they were laughing because she had pleased them with her answer.

"My nephew is right about you, Jules." General Daud motioned to one of his men, who told one of the door sentries to bring in the Canadians. "You must be tired. You will eat and rest for a few hours, then we will talk about your upcoming journey." He got up, walked by the Canadians without more than a glance, and left. Two of his men stayed behind to guard Jules and her companions. She knew that the General and his cohorts left to discuss their feelings about turning over the "package" as DeRosa had described her soon to be ward. She explained this to the Canadians as they calmly waited for the food offered by the General.

Jules gazed at her watch; three hours had passed since the General had left them in the tent. When the tent flap opened, cold air blew in almost extinguishing the stub of a candle left on the table. General Daud spoke to her.

"Tell these men to go wait outside. I will talk to you alone." She did as she was asked, and when the General and she were alone, he pulled a stool close to her. "In my country, we would never trust a woman with business such as this, but then, you are not from this country and your people think differently." Jules wondered if he was baiting her. "Hadi has told me that you are a decorated soldier. Is this true?"

"Yes, General Daud. It is true."

"You have killed before?" continued the General.

"Yes, when I have had to do so." She understood the General's line of questioning. It was inconceivable that a woman Hadi met in the states was on par with the General's concept of warrior. "And I would do it again, if my mission required it."

"What will you do if the Insurgents have discovered our plans and capture you?" The General's black eyes peered at her.

"What you would do, General."

"And how do you know what I would do, Jules?"

"Would you not attempt to escape, even though it means certain death?" Jules waited patiently for this cat and mouse game to conclude.

"And what would you do with the prisoner?" asked the General.

"If you wish, and give me instructions to do so, I would kill him." She casually sipped cold tea from the cup she left on the table. She had no intention of carrying out any order from this man, but he had to believe she would.

"I do so give you the order to kill him. I will have you meet him now." General Daud left the tent with purpose in his stride.

General Daud came back into the tent, followed by a man, who resembled their driver slightly, though clearly more fragile. *Passible, possibly,* thought Jules.

Wasting no time, the General, introduced the man to Jules. He barely looked at her and disregarding her presence, angrily asked General Daud, "Are you incompetent, trusting my safety to this Western whore?"

The man stumbled backwards from the force of Jules' backhand blow across his face. "You have two choices, Esmat," growled Jules. "We release you to your cohorts and tell them that you defected, or you trust me to fulfil our contract. You choose."

General Daud nodded his approval of Jules' aggressiveness. Esmat shifted his gaze to Jules, then back to General Daud. He nodded his head slightly. General Daud addressed him once again. "You will follow her orders, or she will kill you. Do you understand?" Again, Esmat nodded his head.

It was late afternoon before their driver took them back to the dirt road, got out of the Land Rover and disappeared into the surrounding rocks. Henry, one of the Canadians, had been tasked to memorize the way in. He was pressed into service to drive them back to the main road. If they were stopped, their 'driver' was ill and could no longer handle the Land Rover.

It was daylight now and they were returning to Kandahar. They expected to rendezvous with U.S. troops between Kandahar and Kabul. Without warning, they were blinded by an explosion in front of their vehicle. Henry swerved the Land Rover to avoid the newly created crater in the road. Then they heard it, a helicopter. Henry rolled down his window. "Sounds like a Russian model," he shouted over the noise. "What should we do, try to outrun it?"

From inside, Jules grabbed the roof of the SUV and pulled the upper part of her body out of the window. She looked up, trying to identify the chopper. What she saw made her scurry back inside, as if the vehicle's roof could protect them against what they faced. "There are two choppers, one keeping pace with us, right above us, and another flying higher behind. The one above us is a Chinese Z-10s. The other looks Russian." Esmat's eyes told the story. The Chinese supplied the Insurgents with weapons and aircraft, and it looked like both had waited for them to travel far enough from the mountains that turning around to find a small canyon in which to hide was impossible.

Jules tried to remain calm, clicking off their options. *If they're trying to rescue Esmat, they won't target us, yet. If they know that Esmat defected, we're all dead whether we try to outrun them or if we stop. Toss up. Heads or tails!*

Through Henry's expert handling of the vehicle, they dodged huge pot holes in the road and continued heading toward Kandahar. Jules, based on nothing but instinct, decided, "We're going to keep moving. Henry, can you drive a zig pattern?"

"Yeah." They all knew it was a matter of time before a rocket launcher would take them out.

###

Sunday May 10

Awaking to a noise across the hall, Alex looked at the clock. It was already 10:00 a.m. She leapt out of bed, stubbed her toe while trying to hop into a pair of jeans, and flew down the stairs yelping in pain.

"Nice to see you're so exuberant this morning," said Sophie tongue in cheek. "I called the hospital. Mickey is up and around, spending his time between driving Rick crazy and camping out in Claire's room. Rick is as antsy as a fire ant swarming around its dirt hole. He said the doctor was there this morning and removed the bandages from his eyes. He can see light and some shadows, so he thinks he's ready to come home."

"That's great news! And Claire?"

"Rick said Mickey told him she was doing very well physically but asking for you. You made quite an impression on that poor girl."

"Aunt Sophie how are you?" Alex treaded carefully.

"I don't have a choice. I've got fifteen people coming in this afternoon and no time to moon over what's happened. Water under the bridge." Maybe it was best that she didn't have time to consider the fact that she took another person's life. "If you are worrying about how I am feeling having killed that psycho doctor, I can sum it up in a few short words. Good riddance. She tried to kill Rick and had that poor girl ready to kill the rest of us. So, if you're thinking for one moment that I have any regrets, put another nickel in cause I don't. She deserved what she got." *Sophie's personality didn't lend itself to PTSD*, Alex mused.

"How long have you been up? I can't believe I slept almost twelve hours." Alex took the cup Sophie offered.

"I've been up for three hours or so, getting ready for this afternoon."

"Do you have everything under control here?" asked Alex.

"We do. Dean's got the schedule Rick worked out for picking up the guests and he's pressed two of his guys into running the shuttle service. Jeanne, Lord help me, and Matt are going to get the guests to their cabins and then deal with supper. Oh, which reminds me, Jake called this morning. He canceled Bill and Marcy, so we'll have a cabin open. Let's eat. I'm starving!"

Typical Italian, thought Alex. *Whatever the crisis is, feed it.*

Charles, one of the wranglers, dropped Alex off at the hospital on his way to the airport to pick up the first batch of guests scheduled to arrive at two o'clock. Walking to the main entrance of the hospital, she heard her name. Turning she saw Jake running across the parking lot. For a big man, he sure could hustle.

"Afternoon. How are you and Sophie holding up?" Jake put his arm around Alex's shoulder and walked with her.

"Sophie is hiding behind her rough and tumble mountain woman façade and isn't letting anyone in. I, on the other hand, admit that I am exhausted both mentally and physically." Alex gave him a squeeze.

"I've got some news back from the agent in charge. Let's share it with Rick and Mickey." They rode up the elevator to the third floor in silence. Jake's arm was still around her shoulders.

Knocking lightly on Rick and Mickey's door, Alex stuck her head in and said, "You two want any company?"

"Please," exclaimed Rick. "This man is driving me nuts. He keeps saying that he's beating me at cards, and I owe him a year's salary."

"I thought you were only seeing shadows right now," Alex responded.

"Exactly! I have to rely on him to tell me what cards I have." Rick was in good spirits. "Any more news?"

"Yup. That's why I stopped by. You didn't think it was just to visit with you two pathetic pals!" needled Jake. "Get comfortable boys. We know that Alex was right; the real motive was personal, not monetary. However, Phil, who happens to be Philip Warshaw, a convicted felon for burglary with a dangerous weapon, was in it for the money. Besides the kidnapping, he now is cooperating with the Feds on a string of fine art robberies from private collections and galleries in LA. He served time at the California State Prison in LA County, where guess what?" Jake didn't wait for anyone to answer. His question was rhetorical. "Warshaw participated in a program for substance abusers who committed violent crimes."

"Is that where he met Metuchi?" asked Alex.

"Bingo. Give the woman a prize," sang Jake doing a pretty good imitation of a carnival worker. "Okay, boys and girls, Metuchi couldn't believe her good fortune when she met Elena at the country club. She then dreamt up a scheme to grab Claire and enlisted Phil to help out. He's telling the Feds that he didn't realize that Dr. Metuchi intended to kill Claire during the kidnapping and, when he did, he wanted no part of it so he slipped Claire the key to the handcuffs right after he disconnected the gas line and lit a candle to cause the explosion at the warehouse." Jake saw that Alex wanted to say something.

"This matches up to what Claire told me under hypnosis, though it was cryptic at the time."

"Oh, yes, I almost forgot, Phil told the Feds that Metuchi drugged Claire every few hours. So, Phil says that he had been watching the Bentworth house and the day Elena and Claire went shopping he followed and called Metuchi.

"Metuchi went in for Claire knowing that Claire knew her from casual interactions at the Country Club and that she would willingly follow her. Any questions before I get to the good stuff?" Jake waited.

"Yeah, how did they find us?" Mickey asked.

"This really bugs me after we spent tons of Bentworth's money to come up with ironclad covers and security. Alex talked to Metuchi on the phone a couple of times. Metuchi looked her up, found her easily in Seattle, had Phil call her office and was told she was on leave. It wasn't hard to find Alex after that. Martini isn't exactly a common name." All four of them shook their heads in disgust at their own incompetency, or at the very least, their oversight.

"Okay, I can admit that we screwed up by not hiding the trail better, but how the hell did they get into the house with all that sophisticated alarm equipment? We never gave the code to Claire." Rick's emotional state was somewhere between dejected and furious.

"Good question. We don't know. She could have easily observed someone punching in the numbers, unless the code was written down somewhere and she found it. Remember, Claire was still under the mind control of Metuchi and Metuchi's and Phil's visit reinforced it or triggered it and she either got it that night or had it for days. Would that be an accurate statement, Alex?" Jake turned to her.

"Most likely," answered Alex.

"So," said Jake, "once she had the code, we can only assume she snuck out while you all were meeting, hid somewhere upstairs, then when you went to bed turned off the alarm on the panel at the top of the stairs. We won't know for sure unless her memory of that night comes back."

"We didn't look everywhere upstairs, guys," said Alex. "We missed the pull down stairs to the attic." She felt sick to her stomach all over again. "Shit."

Rick's 'damn' followed Alex's 'shit'. "And I had just oiled the hinges so they wouldn't squeak! I'm afraid to ask how they actually got in past the deadbolts."

"Remember Phil was a burglar? Easy pickings once the alarm was off. They parked their car about a half mile down the road and walked to the bridge. Before crossing, they spray painted the camera lens and walked right up to the back door and went directly to the basement, where they booby trapped the light switch in case someone came down before they were ready to grab Claire. They counted on most of you going outside to search for Claire and if you did search the basement, well, you experienced the results."

"So, what exactly caused the explosion?" asked Rick, interrupting Jake.

"Sugar. Powdered Sugar with a little C4." Jake saw Mickey nodding his head. "You smelled it Mickey?"

"Yup. I thought so, but didn't take the time to check it out," replied Mickey, satisfied that his guess was right on the money.

"Powdered sugar?" questioned Alex and Rick in unison.

"Yeah, really quite ingenious. Sugar dust is highly explosive. The tiny particles burn up almost immediately because of their high ratio of surface area to volume."

"Speak English," said Alex.

Jake apologized. "Sorry, that surface area ratio stuff isn't important, but a little particle, sometimes called a nano or micron sized particle of sugar is very susceptible to a spark and a spark generated by a light switch can supply enough energy to set off a small explosion. However, it only really becomes dangerous in environments that have a lot of sugar dust and lots of oxygen, like a sugar silo, so they had to combine the initial primary explosion with some C4 to create a secondary explosion, the one that actually caused the damage to you, Rick. You are lucky that neither of the explosions triggered a fire. They should have."

"How did they get C4?" inquired Alex.

Jake shrugged his shoulders. "One day when you have some time, type in your web browser, 'how to make C4' and hit search. There are lots of recipes for C4-like compounds. Disturbing, but true."

No one moved or talked for several minutes, each of them assimilating in their own way how lucky they all were to be sitting together in the room. Metuchi's diabolical sickness almost devoured five people's lives. Alex spoke first.

"I'm sitting here pondering all the security measures we took and, in the end, we were vulnerable to a mad woman's twisted mind. It just goes to show you that no matter how much one tries to protect themselves from danger or pain, it may never be enough." It was a sobering thought that left all of them feeling depressed.

"What's next for Claire? Is her father taking her back to LA?" Mickey asked.

"Nope, Mickey," answered Jake, taking advantage of the question to brush off the funk that had settled in the room. "Alex asked Bentworth to allow her to stay at the ranch and continue treatment and he agreed."

Mickey nodded. "And," continued Jake, "Bentworth wants you to stay until Alex decides she's okay to go home."

Mickey's mouth slowly formed a smile; he poked Rick in the ribs and chirped, "Guess I'll have two years of your salary before I'm finished Ricky-boy!"

"I'd love to sit here and listen to you two boys drive each other nuts, but I'm going to see Claire. I'll come by tomorrow to see how you're doing." Kissing them both on the cheek Alex said, "bye" and left.

"Jake, I didn't want to ask this while Alex was still here. She looked like she'd just finished ten hard ones in the slammer but, I was wondering, is there any evidence that there may have been other people involved?"

"Good question, Mickey," replied Jake. "At first blush it doesn't appear so, but we don't know for sure. The Feds are going through Metuchi and Warshaw's houses as a precaution. We're going to run down any other released prisoners with whom Metuchi may have come into contact as soon as the Feds turn over the information we need."

"Then we still need to keep up the precautions?" asked Rick.

"Yes. We're not taking any chances that there might be someone else out there for now," answered Jake.

Both Rick and Mickey nodded their heads in agreement. "Best we get better fast, Mickey-boy. I'm not liking Sophie and Alex alone at the ranch."

"All right you two, behave. I'm going to visit Claire, then chat with the Bentworths and catch them up. Talk to you tomorrow."

The door to Claire's room was open, but Jake knocked just the same. Alex was sitting on the bed with Claire and the Bentworths were on the couch situated parallel to the bed and under the window that overlooked the parking lot. The private duty nurse had left the room.

"Mr. and Mrs. Bentworth, would it be possible to see you for a few minutes?" Jake stood in the door way so that they would understand that he wanted to talk to them away from Claire.

"Certainly," responded George. He and Elena got up, told Claire they'd be back in a bit, and followed Jake down the hall. Alex went to the door and closed it, returning to the bed.

"Dr. Martini, please help me. My dad and Elena are driving me nuts. They are here all the time and keep asking me how I feel, what do I remember, but they won't tell me anything."

"They're concerned, Claire. You know that."

"I know, Dr. Martini, but I'm feeling pressure to remember what I can't."

"Do you want to remember?" Alex wondered if the amnesia was induced by the drugs or the trauma. Probably both.

"I do want to remember, and Dr. Martini, if I did something bad, I need to know about it," Claire said bravely.

"Okay, Claire. Here's what we're going to do. I'll get your parents off your back for now, then when you're back at the ranch, we'll deal with it." Alex was too worn to suggest any kind of intervention today. She knew Claire would probably be discharged in a couple of days.

"What I don't understand, is why no one will tell me what happened?" Claire was insistent.

"Honey, do you still trust me?" asked Alex with infinite patience.

"Yes, yes I do. I, uh, feel good when I'm with you," answered Claire.

"There are two reasons no one wants to tell you the details of what happened. One because they are thinking of your physical recovery right now and two, they don't want to upset you." Alex was honest with her.

"But, Dr. Martini, can you tell me just a little so I can understand what's going on?"

Alex weighted her options carefully. Right now, while Claire was in the hospital, Alex wasn't authorized to treat her. She didn't have privileges at the hospital. If her actions caused any kind of further trauma to Claire, she would be liable, and something like that could ruin her reputation and career. On the other hand, what was right for the patient? In the end, she fashioned a compromise that she hoped would work until Claire was discharged.

"Claire, what have your parents or Jake told you?"

"That the kidnappers tried to take me again at the ranch and you, Mickey and Sophie stopped them before any harm was done, but Dr. Martini, I can feel it. They're not telling me the whole story."

Again, Alex opted for complete honesty. "You're right. They are not telling you the whole story. They think you're fragile and don't want to cause you emotional harm."

"They think that if I know the truth, I'll go off the deep end?" Claire was subdued, but not frightened.

"Yes. That's what they think."

"And what do you think, Dr. Martini?"

"I think there is always that possibility," responded Alex with total candor.

"Am I that damaged?" Claire asked with a perception that surprised Alex.

"Honey, I'm pretty sure your kidnappers used mind control drugs and techniques. We don't know right now what post hypnotic suggestions may still be active and we can't take a chance right now." Alex sighed heavily. She was truly sad.

"You're saying that my mind is not even my own anymore. Right? First they take my body and emotions, and now they have my mind too?"

"Try not to get too agitated, Claire. What you said is not exactly correct. They don't have your mind. However, there may be lingering effects that we have to try to uncover."

"How long will it take to hunt out the damage?" questioned Claire.

"Hard to tell, maybe a couple of months." Alex did not want to tell her that they may never uncover all the damage Metuchi had done. She'd have to be significantly stronger to hear and accept that piece of information.

"So, you won't tell me who the kidnappers were either?"

"Not today, but I promise I will when you are discharged and back at the ranch. Now let me go and see if I can get your parents to give you some space, okay?" Alex patted her shoulder and went in search of the Bentworths.

She found them with Jake in the little cafeteria where they talked yesterday. Before she had a chance to sit down, George asked her, "How is she?"

"I think she is doing very well for the trauma she's been through this year. However, she told me that she feels pressured to remember, so I'd like us all to be sensitive to this fact and not say anything that she could interpret in that way. The good news is that she does want to remember, and she will, as soon as I can start treatment again mid-week."

Alex explained to the Bentworths her suspicions on post narco-hypnotic suggestions lingering in Claire's mind and what she planned to do to address the situation.

George studied Alex carefully. "I appreciate your candor. My daughter trusts you, refuses to see anyone else, so you have carte blanche to do what you think is right."

"George, I appreciate your offer to sign off on a treatment plan, but unless you have court ordered custodial care of Claire, she's the one who is going to have to sign off."

He puffed up and Alex thought he was going to say something to the fact that if that's what was needed, he'd get a court order. Instead, after Elena laid a hand on his arm, without rancor, replied to Alex. "Doctor, I appreciate your ethics, and maybe you're right. It is high time Claire started taking control of her life. Whatever you and Claire decide is fine with me, and I want you to know that whatever monetary resources you need, they will be available. Will you please excuse us now? We promised Claire a milk shake."

###

After they left, Jake and she stared at each other, until he broke the silence. "What power do you have over people? I've never seen him so meek."

"That was meek?"

"You know what I mean, Alex. Don't be so humble," offered Jake.

"Truthfully, I just don't know, Jake. Sometimes I feel like I'm outside of my body, watching someone else do the talking," answered Alex.

"Well don't tell anyone else that, or they'll take you over to the psych ward!" teased Jake. "Oh, the Bentworths gave me these for you."

She took the envelope Jake offered and opened it, pulling out two checks, made out to White Bark Ranch. Jake told her that the first check was to pay off the mortgage and the second to cover Claire's extended stay at the ranch.

Monday May 11

Monday was unseasonably warm for Montana, and Sophie had all the kitchen windows open, breakfast scents floating out the window. The guest crowd had come and gone with little incident and Sophie had rounded up Matt to handle the lunch traffic while she and Alex went to meet with Keith Woods. Sophie was singing "Before He Cheats," a tasty revenge song, pretty much off key, subsequently driving Matt and the kitchen help crazy. Matt mouthed, "Thank you'" when Alex came to collect Sophie for their trip to First Territorial.

"Give me the keys, Aunt Sophie. You are enjoying yourself entirely too much and I'm afraid you'll sing us into a ditch." Alex appreciated her Aunt's disposition. Though she was happy that Woods and First Territorial would be out of their lives, she had a dark cloud hanging over her, but she wasn't going to dampen Sophie's good time today. "Are we still planning on picking up Rick and Mickey on the way back?"

"Rick called earlier and said the doctor had discharged the two of them and would we please pick them up sometime after eleven and before four. I told him you and I were going up to First Territorial. He asked if we'd put it off a day or two, because he wanted to go along." Sophie started humming again, more off key than her singing.

"Aunt Sophie, what did you tell him?"

"I told him that I was sorry, but that this couldn't wait and no matter how much he begged me, I was getting it done today." Sophie under no circumstances, including her love for Rick, was going to pass up the revenge she had been plotting for years.

Entering the bank, Sophie bypassed the tellers, various assistant managers, and loan officers sitting in a bull pen area. She was dressed to kill. Alex hoped it wasn't literal, but no one stopped Sophie when she opened a door at the back of the bank. Alex followed not knowing what to expect.

"I want to see Keith right now, Esmeralda," spat Sophie. Esmeralda assessed whether or not she would be successful in turning Sophie down and decided that she would interrupt her boss.

"Mrs. Martini, please wait while I tell him you're here."

"The hell I will," answered Sophie. "I know that weasel has a back door out of his office to the parking lot. You'll stay right there and keep your hand off the phone." Sophie pushed her way around Esmeralda and swung open the solid oak door leading to Woods' inner sanctum. He looked up in surprise and told the person with whom he was talking on the phone that he'd have to call him back.

"Well, well. What do we have here? Annie Oakley and her trusty horse, Target?" Woods laughed enjoying the smoke coming out of Sophie's ears.

Sophie's green eyes had narrowed and deepened in color. Alex was glad she was not on the receiving end this morning. "Get Esmeralda to prepare a release of mortgage, you twit. We're settling up right now!"

Woods, in no particular hurry, tried drawing out the conversation. "I heard you had a little trouble down there at the ranch. Sorry to hear Rick was injured; be a shame if he never sees again."

Sophie measured her next words. "Keith, there's been bad blood between the two of us since Mario's death. Then with that stunt you pulled a year later, well, let's just say that the sight of you turns my stomach. Now get Esmeralda to get the release form ready or you are going to see what happens when that bad blood begins to boil."

"What are you going to do, shoot me?"

Sophie was trying to keep control, but the asshole was really pushing her buttons. "I should have let Dean shoot you when you tried to rape me, you no good bastard! You want to get into that now?"

Alex's jaw dropped. She wondered if Sophie knew what she had divulged.

"That's all in your head, Sophie. It never happened and even if it had, it probably would have been what you needed to cure your insatiable bitchiness. Maybe that's what your lesbo niece needs too, a good fucking!" He was on his feet shouting, but he hadn't moved from behind his desk. Alex couldn't believe the restraint Sophie was showing. Maybe the thought of finishing out her old age in prison was enough to keep her in line. Never the less, Alex held her arm.

"Mr. Woods," began Alex, "I think you should calm down and do what my aunt is asking. There is no reason not to provide her with a mortgage release. Do you want to ask Esmeralda to get it ready, or do I call the Sheriff?"

Woods picked up the phone and tersely gave the orders to Esmeralda. He told Alex to take her aunt and wait outside.

Sophie answered, "Hell no, you no good pole cat. We're staying right here. As soon as you get the papers, we'll hand over the cash."

Woods sunk into his executive chair that dwarfed his small stature and busied himself with shuffling papers from one side of the desk to another. Sophie took a seat right across from him and Alex stood by Sophie's side. She had a hundred questions but knew better than to fan the fire. Ten minutes later, Esmeralda brought in a document. Woods read it, then unceremoniously, tossed it to Sophie. She took time to read every single word, which infuriated Woods even more.

"Looks like it's in order. Sign it." Sophie was giving orders now.

"Not until I see the money," retaliated Woods.

Pulling out Bentworth's check, she handed it to Woods, careful not to touch his hand. He looked at it, then smiled. "I'm afraid you're going to have to wait until it clears. It's made out to you, not the bank." Woods was gleeful, but it was short lived.

"Call this number and ask for Robert McNally. He's the president of the bank the check was drawn on. He's prepared to make a wire transfer as soon as you call him."

Woods picked up the phone and dialed. He confirmed with McNally what Sophie had told him, gave McNally the routing and account number and hung up. "All right Sophie. You've won this round, but believe me, I know the Bentworths and I intend to make trouble for you."

"Is that a threat, Mr. Woods," asked Alex, her hackles up.

"Yeah and what are you going to do about it. I'll deny everything," Woods said as he signed the four copies of the mortgage release document. He passed the four copies to Sophie, who pulled out her own pen when he offered her his. She was done in less than a minute, taking one copy and putting it in her purse.

"Thank you, Mr. Woods," said Sophie as she got up to leave. "By the way, I've recorded our conversation today, perfectly legal in Montana if at least one of the parties to the conversation agree, and I believe, Mr. Woods, we have two of the three parties in agreement. There is one more thing I thought you should know."

A knock on the door interrupted Sophie. Esmeralda was frantic. She could barely talk. "Ah Mr. Woods, there are some gentlemen in the office for you, something about a kidnapping."

Sophie and Alex recognized the FBI agent in charge as he and another man walked in and read Woods his rights. He was being charged for aiding and abetting the Bentworth imposters, and though the charges probably wouldn't stick, they'd be enough along with Sophie's recording, to get his superiors to can his ass. Rick had filed two complaints the day he harassed them at the ranch.

Alex still in a semi-daze, followed Sophie through the bank to a teller, where she promptly withdrew the small amounts left in her personal and White Bark Ranch accounts. The majority had already been transferred to new accounts opened at another bank days ago.

"Alex, give me the keys. I don't want us ending up in some ditch," needled Sophie as they walked to the truck. "You can close your mouth now."

"Man, Aunt Sophie, I hope I don't ever get on your bad side!" said Alex with a renewed appreciation of her aunt.

"I know you want to know about the attempted rape, so buckle up and I'll tell you on the way to the hospital and then I don't ever want to think about it again. Got it?" Sophie stepped on the gas and peeled out of the bank's parking lot.

"Yes, ma'am," replied Alex, holding on to the grab handle for dear life.

"A year after your Uncle Mario died, I started getting proposals. You know, men wanted to court me. I turned them all down, and for the most part, all of them were gentlemen." Sophie was watching the road intently.

"You mean to tell me that Keith wanted to court you? It's unbelievable that he would think a person like you would hold the slightest interest in him. Go on, Aunt Sophie."

"Well, his ego is so big that he thought he was the cat's meow and any woman would fall for him. When I repeatedly turned him down, he started showing up at the Ranch uninvited. One night, it was after dark, he showed up with enough alcohol in him to give him courage. He bullied his way in and wouldn't take no for an answer. In spite of his small stature, he was strong and had me pinned on the couch of the great room.

"I didn't know how Dean heard me screaming, the bunkhouse is a quarter mile down the road, but he did and came in to find Keith with his pants down on top of me. Dean yanked him off me and slugged him in the jaw so hard, he broke it." Sophie paused to get her breathing back under control. "Later I found out that Dean was taking a walk to get some distance from his wife. You know what I mean."

"Then what happened? Why didn't you press charges?" prompted Alex.

"Alex, times were different then, we owed the bank a lot of money, and he threatened to press charges against Dean. Who were the police going to believe, an esteemed member of the financial committee or an immigrant woman and a red neck cowboy? We cut a deal. I wouldn't press charges, and neither would he. Now you know why I have my shotgun near the door." Sophie finished the sentence with a finality.

"My god, Aunt Sophie, no wonder he loved taunting you. It was his revenge for not getting his way with you, so to speak. And Dean, he never said a word to anyone?"

"Nope, Dean has kept the secret for years. I suppose you're right about Keith relishing taunting me. However in my heart of hearts, not to mention my dark moments, I always thought that he'd get what was coming to him. What is it that you call that?" Sophie was smiling.

"Karma, Aunt Sophie. You know, what you sow, you shall reap, or whatever cause you put out, there will be an effect."

Alex thought it interesting that Sophie had been willing all these years to allow the universe to mete out the exact punishment that Woods deserved. That started Alex on an introspective trip thinking about how Jules and her paths had crossed. *Was it karma that brought Jules and me together and if so, for what reason? Why is the attraction so strong? Did we know each other in a former lifetime? Will we get the chance to play out what fate has in store for us? Do I pursue her even though she says she's not interested? How will I know unless I act?*

"Alex, we're here," announced Sophie.

Coming out of her meditative state, Alex asked Sophie. "Do you believe that people come and go in our lives for a reason?"

Looking at her quizzically, Sophie responded, "You talking about anyone in particular?"

"Not really, just in general," Alex told her.

"Yes, I think so, Alex. Look at this whole situation. Go back over it and see how it is impossible for everything to have lined up without some sort of greater purpose. Jules saving your life, you dragging Rick out here, Claire being abducted, Bentworth hiring Jules, Jules choosing White Bark Ranch? Don't you think that this tapestry is too tightly woven to just be serendipity?"

"I didn't even consider looking at it from that perspective. How'd you get so smart, Aunt Sophie?" Alex smiled warmly.

"I learned it from my niece the psychologist," retorted Sophie with a hug. "Let's go get the boys."

Mickey and Rick were waiting for the clothes that Alex and Sophie were bringing. It was the last hurdle to getting out of the hospital. They pounced on the duffle bag Alex tossed on Mickey's bed. It was comical to watch two grown men try and sort out whose underwear and socks belonged to whom. Mickey helped Rick into the bathroom and stayed with him. Shortly, they both came out dressed in blue jeans, patterned shirts, and boots.

"Let's go," ordered Rick. "I can't stand another minute in here."

"Hold on there you two. We want to go by and see how Claire is doing. Coming?" Sophie didn't wait for an answer, as she already knew they had no choice. The keys were in her pocket. Coming down the corridor, they met Jake.

"I see you two are up and around. How's the vision, Rick?" asked Jake amiably.

"Getting better by the hour," replied Rick. "Where are you heading?"

Jake told them that he was flying back to LA later in the afternoon and was on his way to an appointment with the FBI agent in charge.

"Any more news?" asked Mickey.

"Nothing new, but I'll keep you posted," tossed Jake as he continued down the corridor towards the exit. "Bye, all!"

CHAPTER 21: The Letter

I can't control my destiny, I trust my soul, my only goal is just to be. There's only now, there's only here. Give in to love or live in fear. No other path, no other way.

Jonathan Larson

Monday May 11 (cont.)

It was late when Alex's phone rang. She picked it up and saw the caller ID. It was Jake. She wondered why he was calling this late. Rick, Sophie and Mickey had all gone to bed around 9:00 p.m., but Alex decided to read for an hour or so. "Hi Jake, what's up?"

"Alex, honey, I have some bad news and I'm not quite sure how to tell you." The distress in Jake's voice was apparent.

"Oh no, Jake, no, please don't tell me what I think you're going to tell me." Alex thought that if she continued to talk, Jake wouldn't be able to deliver bad news.

"Alex, I'm so sorry. We just got word. Jules' mission went bad and she is MIA, most likely dead." He heard Alex sob, so he waited.

"Jake, how?"

"Honey, we don't know much right now, but it appears that her Land Rover was shot by a rocket launcher on Saturday."

"When did you hear?" asked Alex between sniffles.

"A few minutes ago. I got a call from our boss. He got the call about an hour ago. Alex, I'll be there tomorrow as soon as I can."

"Jake, it took them two days to notify you?"

"I'm so sorry, Alex. The government moves slowly sometimes."

"Is there any chance—"

Jake cut her off. "I don't think so. They found a half-burned passport with which she was traveling along with partial passports of two of her companions strewn several yards away from the blast site. If the rocket hit them squarely, they would have been vaporized, so to speak. I'm so sorry, sweetie."

I've got to go now Jake. You understand, I hope."

"Of course, but Alex, please don't tell Mickey or Claire. I'd like to do that, but you can tell Rick and Sophie if it will help. Bye, and call me at any time if you need anything." Jake put down the phone, covered his eyes with his hands and let the lost feeling take him over for a while.

"Come in," answered Sophie. The table lamp was still on and Sophie had a book cracked open across her lap. "What is it Alex?"

"Jules is MIA; probably dead. Jake called me." Alex began to sway, then collapsed on the floor. Sophie yelled for Rick, who came thundering up the stairs. Rick burst in, saw Alex being held by Sophie, who was kneeling on the floor. He picked up Alex and laid her on the bed.

"What happened?"

Sophie told him that Jake had called to tell Alex that Jules was MIA or worse, dead. Sophie continued to cradle Alex in her arms on the bed. Rick did not know what to do. He wiped his eyes and said, "Ah, Sophie, maybe I should go downstairs."

"Don't you dare. We're family and she needs us both right now. Sit down on the bed until she comes to."

Rick did as he was told, though he felt uncomfortable. Alex came around in a few moments, moved her head as if trying to figure out where she was, then sighed and laid her head back in the crook of Sophie's arm. Sophie talked to her gently. "Honey, we're here with you, both of us. Just rest now. You don't have to tell us anything until you're ready."

Alex took a few moments then started, "Jake called. He doesn't have much information, but they think the Land Rover she was in was hit with some sort of rocket and she and her companions were killed. He's coming tomorrow. He hopes to have more information."

Sophie held her tightly. "You loved her, didn't you?"

"Yes." Alex was sobbing, feeling a loss greater than she had ever felt as an adult. Sophie and Rick did not try to tell her that everything would be all right, because they knew it wouldn't. When Alex stopped crying, Rick got up from the side of the bed, made his way to the recliner settling in for the night, keeping watch over the two people he loved most.

Tuesday May 12

Contrary to the absolute certainty that the sun wouldn't come up in the morning, it rose in the East, saffron color against a perfectly clear cerulean sky. There was a certain oddity this morning, as the pale moon was still visible for a while, then disappeared behind the western mountains without a complaint.

Sophie and Rick were sitting in the kitchen alcove after the breakfast rush when they heard a knock on the back door, then Jake's voice calling out, "Sophie, Rick, are you here?" He strode into the kitchen and at first glance, he looked like he had been up all night.

"How did you get here so fast?" asked Rick.

"I chartered a flight and left before dawn. I wanted to be here early, though I'm not sure what I can do." Jake slumped into a chair. He was unshaven, his shirt tail was hanging out, and his eyes were bloodshot. Sophie thought that he had to have taken the news hard too. "You got some coffee I can pour down my gullet to kick start me?"

"Coming right up, Jake," answered Sophie. Rick's vision was improving, but she didn't trust him to pour hot liquid into a cup opening four inches in diameter. "Do you know any more than what you told Alex?"

"No, Sophie. I don't know how much more we'll know. I was told that what we know was pieced together from the forensics. Would it be any different if we did know more?" Gloomy cynicism had crept into Jake's demeanor. No one held it against him. "Is Mickey up yet?"

"Yeah. He decided to go down to the barn and watch the circus. It's the second day for the guests and saddling up the horses can be amusing. Do you want me to call him up here?"

"No, thanks. I'll walk down and talk to him, then hang around up here until Alex gets up. I have a package for her." Jake took a long draw from his coffee cup.

"What kind of package?" asked Sophie.

Jake played it cool. He felt that Alex should have the choice on whether or not to share what was in the package with anyone else. "Jules gave it to me before she left. I really haven't read the contents." It was true, but Jake knew he was bending the truth a little.

"How did Mickey take the news, Jake?" Rick was sitting on one of the couches in the great room when Jake returned from the barn.

"Like the rest of us. He's in shock. Said he was going for a walk. Any sign of Alex?"

"Sophie checked right after you went down to the barn. She was still sleeping, and Sophie didn't want to wake her. Do you have to be somewhere else?" Rick looked at his watch and saw that they'd have to clear out shortly for the lunch crowd.

"No, not really, I wanted to talk to the Bentworths today, but I can do that later. God, what a summer, huh?" Jake allowed his body to sink deeper into the couch giving himself up to the fleeting pleasure of a soft, enveloping cocoon.

Jake heard his name and felt a hand on his shoulder. He cleared his head and found himself looking up into Alex's empty eyes. He jumped up and cradled her in his arms with a delicateness that few men could produce. He allowed her to cry softly against his chest, then gently asked if they could go somewhere and talk privately.

She managed, "My room."

Walking by her side, he lightly supported her with one arm as they climbed the stairs.

"Alex, I don't know any more today than I did when I called you last night. I'm sorry that I had to tell you over the phone, but I thought you would want to know right away," he apologized.

"I'm glad you called, Jake. How are you doing? I know you were friends for a long time." Alex in her grief was still able to consider the feelings of others who cared for Jules.

"Ah, Alex, I don't know," he said with a sigh. "I know life goes on, but life without her just isn't going to be the same. I can't help thinking that I should have done more to dissuade her from going."

Alex realized that Jake was blaming himself for Jules' death. *Poor fellow* she thought. "Jake, you know as well as I do, that when Jules made up her mind, there was no talking her out of it. You can't put that kind of blame on your shoulders. It was her decision. Of that, I'm sure."

"Alex, I know that at some rational level, but my gut isn't buying it. I felt bad about this operation from the get-go."

"Do you mean you had a premonition?" asked Alex.

"Not exactly. I've known Jules for a long time. She was always the warrior. You know, gung-ho, adventure-seeking, with a touch of wanderlust, all that stuff usually associated with testosterone. Don't get me wrong. I loved that about her. I had met my match and it was exciting to work with her. But something changed in her recently and I think whatever it was, frightened her so much, that she took the assignment to find ground where she felt secure."

"How do you know this, Jake?"

"If you mean did she tell me this, the answer is no; but before she left, we spent time together and I got a sense of what I'm telling you now."

"I see," said Alex not wanting to consider that what happened between the two of them played a part in Jules' choice to accept a risky operation.

"I see it in your eyes, Alex. Don't go there. She loved you."

"What?" Alex didn't know if she had heard Jake correctly.

"She loved you," Jake repeated.

"How do you know, Jake?" asked Alex, whose grief was momentarily replaced by astonishment.

"She told me," responded Jake, thinking it was a good segue to the package he carried.

"I'll be damned," said Alex, anger rising. *She couldn't admit it to herself, she couldn't tell me, yet she tells Jake, then runs away. God, what a waste.*

Jake's voice snapped her attention back. "Alex, before she left, she gave me an envelope to give you in case she didn't make it back." He took the manila envelope from his briefcase and laid it on Alex's lap. She stared at it, but didn't reach to open it, so Jake told her, "When you're ready in a week or so, I'll help you settle her affairs, all right?" In a state of bewilderment, Alex nodded her assent.

"There's one more thing," said Jake as he reached into his briefcase once again and pulled out a regular white envelope. Alex didn't take it from Jake, as if her refusal could change that Jules was really gone. She put her arms around her stomach and doubled over, pain cutting through her chest once again. "I can't, Jake. I can't," she cried.

"Yes, you can. You have to Alex," replied Jake. "You don't have to read it now, but this was important to her." Jake was scarcely bearing his own pain right now, but seeing Alex so overcome with grief, for a moment, he experienced his loss with a pain he didn't think he could endure. He took one of Alex's hands, held it in his and said, "It's okay, Alex. Go ahead and take it Alex." She reached out with her other hand and shaking, took the envelope from Jake.

"Promise me, Alex, that you'll read it soon. Promise me." Jake's heartbreak touched Alex and in a moment of clarity, she thought that perhaps Jake, at one time, had been in love with Jules too. Their shared grief was the impetus for her promise to him. "I'll read it, Jake. How can I not?"

###

Friday May 15

Currents of sorrow ran through the house since Monday like electricity through the circuits, only there were no switches to turn off. Sophie's anguish was tied directly to her niece's grief. She knew that grief would hit Alex over and over again like a tidal wave pounding the shore and demolishing everything in its path, uncovering an emptiness so deep that it would drain away the hues of the day, leaving her with only shadows lurking in the recesses of her mind.

If only I could suffer this for you, I would gladly endure the despair swirling around ready to pounce on what's left of you, but I can't. You will have to find your own way and seek out a flicker of light to comfort you among the ruins of your heart. Sophie wasn't a religious woman, in spite of her Catholic upbringing, but she repeated her home-made prayer time and time again, hoping that a higher power would take pity on her niece.

Mickey and Rick had brought Claire back to the ranch yesterday. Alex considered calling Bentworth to advise him that she wouldn't be able to continue Claire's therapy. She didn't think she had the strength but in the end, convinced herself that the distraction would be welcome. After the session this morning, she began to formulate a new treatment plan. Sitting at her desk, out of the corner of her eye, she saw the envelope, still unopened, on the edge of the blotter. Her chest heaving, she got up and looked down, trying to see beyond the tears. In a moment of swift decision, her hand swooped down, lifted the envelope to her heart, and walked out the door. "Aunt Sophie," she called out, "I'm going to the Falls." Sophie hustled out of the kitchen to catch a glimpse of Alex's back as she ran down to the barn.

###

She had been sitting for a while on the mossy ground fingering the letter, trying to diagnose why she was so afraid to open it. For three days she had left it sitting on her desk. *Did opening it mark the end of the road or was it more that it would mark the beginning of the years that stretched ahead, bleak and cold without her? Maybe both.* It was no use. Her mental faculties were short circuited, synapses burned from the fire of emotions. She pulled out a pocketknife, and carefully cut open the envelope, removed the letter, and put the envelope in her back pocket. Unfolding the letter, she took a deep breath and began reading Jules' last words to her.

Darling,

I have discovered that the tango is much more than a dance. It is a delicate balance between keeping one's own equilibrium and surrendering to the music and one's partner.

If you are now reading this, I imagine your heart is aching and I regret not understanding everything we talked about sooner. I know you love me. You were not the coward;

I was, and now I ask you to summon the strength to read what I have to say to you.

Your essence has been moving in and out of my consciousness leaving me with alternating moments of profound joy and excruciating pains of separation. I am flooded with intoxicating memories of you; the way you move, how your hair takes on multiple hues of lemony gold in the sunlight, the compassion in your eyes, and how love seems to move through you, sublimely touching everyone in its path.

Sometimes I think the world will stop on its axis if I never feel the warmth of your hand on my cheek again or experience how you held me the last night we were together. How can I refute that you reached me in places I never knew existed? You kidnapped my heart from the very beginning.

How can I deny that the love emanating from you washed over me and opened my heart to the greatest joy I ever felt? I look in the mirror and all I see are dead eyes, my eyes. I try to search them for that moment of recognition when I knew, but they are clouded with discomfiture and shame. Your teary eyes and the agony in your voice haunt me, punishing me for the cowardly way I left you.

Now, I have left you once again, but not as a coward. If it was written somewhere that my destiny was to leave this human life form now, then I depart, my darling, wrapped in a cloak of my love for you. Please forgive me.

Love and Devotion,
Jules

The wind had shifted, and Alex could not tell where the tears ended and the mist from the pool on her face began. Doubled over with her fists clenched and pressing into her thighs, a desolate sob escaped her lips. Somewhere in her periphery, she knew that it had startled Tommy Boy. With great effort, she stood, folded Jules' letter and tucked it into her back-jean pocket along with the envelope to protect it from the moisture whirling in the air. She soothed Tommy

Boy, holding his bridal with one hand, stroking his neck with the other, and kept repeating that everything was all right. Tommy Boy nuzzled her face and even though Alex knew he was tasting the salt from her tears, his soft nose and mouth against her cheek comforted her.

After moving him to another spot where he could graze on low hanging branches laden with leaves, she went back near the edge of the pool and laid down on her stomach with her head resting on crossed arms. She turned her head toward the falls, watching the shadows of light running in and out of the mist. The thundering roar lulled her into a deep sleep.

Alex opened her eyes but didn't move when a hushed voice, coming from behind her, partially muffled by the thunder of the falls asked, "Are you ready to forgive me?"

The voice was familiar, though distorted by the cascading water. *What is this?'* Alex questioned herself without turning around. *Is this a dream within a dream? I don't know which is true anymore, the dream or reality.*

She heard the voice again, this time clearer. "I'm here." Slowly turning, Alex gasped with fright. She scrambled to her feet backing away, crying out, "Don't do this to me. It's too painful. Please, let me wake up!"

The apparition gradually moved toward Alex, who was now frozen at the edge of the pool with nowhere to go. "Alex, I'm here. Touch me," said the figure calmly and gently. "Come, touch me."

Barely able to see through her tears, Alex desperately tried to wake up. "This can't be. This is impossible! Please, please, just let me wake up," she pleaded.

"You're awake, love. Just reach out. I'm really here." Jules was aching to feel Alex pressed against her, but knew Alex was still trying to integrate whatever she had been dreaming with the new reality of her awake state. Slowly,

Jules moved closer to Alex, searching Alex's eyes for comprehension.

Hesitantly Alex reached for Jules and felt her hand captured in warm fingers, then kissed by soft lips. She placed her hands-on Jules' chest, sighed and said, "Jules, I don't understand this, but if I wake up and you're not here, I intend to haunt you into eternity." Alex's words were humorless. Wrapped in the haze of this strange pseudo mystical experience, she was dead serious.

Jules suspected that the shock was wearing off and a wave of anger was finding its way into Alex's consciousness. She raised one of Alex's hands and gently touched her lips to Alex's palm. "Darling, I'm here in this moment, and I will be here in all the moments to come, if you let me."

Alex put her arms around Jules' neck and moved her body closer until there was no space between the two of them. "You have some big explaining to do."

Jules tilted her head and grazed her lips against Alex's mouth. "I know, but first, come away from the edge." Jules grabbed the blanket Alex had been on and spread it out in one of the few rays of sun penetrating the forest cap. She sat down and reached for Alex, who was still in a partial stupor. Willingly, Alex sat down and let herself be pulled between Jules' legs, her back against Jules' chest with Jules' arms and legs wrapped around her.

"How long had you been watching me?" asked Alex.

"Not too long. I didn't want to startle you," responded Jules.

Alex thought a moment, then plaintively asked, "Why didn't you call to tell me you were alive? I thought my grief would consume me and leave nothing behind."

"So terribly sorry, darling, but I couldn't. The operation was secretive until last night, when I landed in Los Angeles. All I wanted to do was come to you, thinking I'd have a better chance of you taking me back, if I came in person."

Alex, turning her head, could see the pain through the tears in Jules' eyes. Jules gripped her tighter and desperately kissed Alex's lips, trying to repent for causing Alex's sorrow. Her passion was a genuine physical need to be forgiven for causing Alex's agony.

As if Alex had read her thoughts, she turned to face Jules and kneeling in front of her, took Jules' face in both her hands, kissing her eyes, her forehead, the corners of her mouth, and then, with tenderness, she covered Jules' lips with her own. Alex pushed Jules down on the blanket, her lips never losing contact.

"Let me hold you, Alex," whispered Jules.

Laying her head in the crook of Jules' arm, Alex hurried to unbutton Jules' shirt. She began caressing every inch of exposed skin. As Alex slipped her hand under Jules' bra, she kissed her neck, cheek, and corners of her mouth before she crushed her lips with a hungry kiss, her chest aching with desire, her heart thundering with love.

Jules was rubbing Alex's back and felt the sensuousness of Alex's brushed Chambray shirt under her fingers until she was satisfied no longer with just the softness of the fabric. Yanking the shirt out from Alex's jeans, she felt her own jeans being unbuttoned and unzipped. Alex's mouth was everywhere, moving from one sensitive spot to another like a tornado, changing course at will. Feeling Alex's fingers enter her, Jules moved against Alex, moments later arching her back and crying out. Alex absorbed her into her arms, protecting her from the chill that had snuck in when the rays of sunlight were busy dancing in their hearts.

"Alex, it's going to be dark soon. We should go back, or your aunt is going to send out a search party."

"Not on a Friday night. It's campout night for the guests, but you're right, we should get back and, you still owe me an explanation." Alex reluctantly got up, helping Jules to her feet.

"Can it wait until we get back to the house, so I only have to tell it once? Sophie was gracious enough not to detain me before she took me up here, but I know she must be wild with curiosity."

"Wild isn't strong enough. Besotted is more like it!" They both took their time enjoying the return of Alex's sense of humor. "Where's your horse parked, city girl?" asked Alex laughing.

"Why, you want a ride?" retorted Jules.

"Actually, I was thinking, we'd take Tommy Boy's saddle off and together, ride him bareback to the barn." Before Alex finished the sentence, Jules was off to fetch Goldie, assuming correctly that Goldie would carry Tommy Boy's saddle back.

"Jules, you haven't said a word in close to an hour. Are you okay?" Alex felt Jules' arms tighten around her waist as their bodies moved rhythmically to the roll of Tommy Boy's walk.

"Yes, I was just being contemplative."

"And, if I'm not too nosy, what were you contemplating?" Alex's voice had a teasing lilt to it.

Jules ran her hands up Alex's abdomen, coming to rest on her breasts. "I was wondering if I could make love to you while riding," Jules answered flippantly.

"Liar," retorted Alex. "Really, honey, what were you thinking?"

"All right. I know you won't leave me alone until I tell you," said Jules with mock resignation. "I was thinking how different I feel when I'm with you."

Alex could have said many things but chose to stay with something simple. "Don't underestimate the power and beauty of love."

Sighing in carefree surrender, Jules laid her head on Alex's shoulder and for once, didn't worry about anything.

Dusk had settled over the main compound when Alex and Jules rode in. By the time they settled the horses, the sun had fully set. The air was still and quiet, punctuated only with an occasional whinny of a horse, campfire singing that floated in on a breeze, the chirping of a cricket, and an unexpected laugh coming from the house. Standing on the porch, Alex and Jules faced each other, kissed, and squared their shoulders before they entered. They removed their boots and walked through the great room and dining room in their socks, delaying the announcement of their arrival until they went into the kitchen. Sophie, Claire, Mickey, and Rick were sitting around the kitchen table waiting for Alex and Jules' return by the looks of the two extra chairs at the table.

Sophie leapt to her feet, hugging both Alex and Jules at the same time. Rick, Claire, and Mickey waited their turn, not daring to intrude into Sophie's territory.

"Hungry?" Sophie asked. Though Sophie had told them all of Jules' miraculous return, they all were dying to hear the details of her resurrection.

"Yes," Alex and Jules chirped simultaneously.

"Is warmed up chicken enchilada casserole okay?" asked Sophie.

"Yes," both answered.

"Okay. I want to know what the hell went on, Jules," said Sophie. "We were freaked out!" Everyone looked at Sophie, laughed at her uncharacteristic use of slang, then looked back at Jules.

"You heard the lady," said Rick.

"Okay, but when the food comes, I'm stopping to eat." Her audience nodded their heads in unison. "I went to Afghanistan to bring-in an Insurgent operative. In essence, he defected and wanted U.S. protection. There were three of us, plus the defector and on our way out of the mountains north of Kandahar, two helicopters overtook us. One fired a rocket, which landed in the road ahead of us. We thought the Insurgents had gotten wind of the man's defection, and intended to either kills us or capture us, then kill us."

"Were you scared?" asked Claire.

"Petrified, but we kept moving," responded Jules. "I had a satellite phone and used it to call for backup from Camp Dwyer but knew that it would be too late. Then the two choppers flew ahead of us. Our passenger was terrified. He recognized the maneuver. They were going to turn around, fly towards us in a closed "V" formation, hitting us with rockets or other weapons from both sides."

"Then what happened?" Mickey knew his boss, and figured that even in dire circumstances, she had a plan.

"I ordered everyone out of the Land Rover, and we ran far enough away to escape being struck with flying metal if they decided to destroy the jeep. All we had were sidearms, but I thought we had a better chance out of the car than staying in it like sitting ducks."

Rick set the food in front of Alex and Jules, both of them not delaying in shoving a couple of bites into their mouths, before Rick asked, "Was there anywhere to take cover?"

Jules put her fork down and answered. "No, the area was flat and desolate and from our vantage point, we saw that both choppers changed their direction and were headed towards us. We waited."

She picked up her fork again and took another bite. Everyone was peering at her, as if they were waiting to pounce on her if she didn't continue. She ignored them and took another bite, chewed, swallowed, and continued.

"The helicopters were still in their 'V' formation but did not fire. They landed. They stirred up a bunch of sand, but we were able to hear through a bull horn. From the Chinese chopper, someone yelled in Farsi, "Lower your weapons." We did as we were told and in a second, were surrounded by troops dressed in non-descript fatigues and traditional Afghani headdresses. I immediately pulled the defector towards me, raised my Glock, and aimed it at his head to kill him.

"I watched another soldier jump out the other chopper, which I looked like a salvaged Russian chopper. It was clear he was in charge. He came up to me, then the impossible happened. He pulled the scarf from around his face and said, 'Coronel, Captain Eric Weston, 809th Expeditionary Red Horse Squadron, at your service. Give me your passports now. I don't have time to explain'."

"What was going through your head? You must have been blown away. Oh, sorry, no pun intended," apologized Claire.

"Truthfully, I don't remember. Captain Weston was shouting orders to his troops and to us. We were hustling. He took our passports and carefully burned them, leaving just enough to identify us. Then they spilled some red liquid over the sand, shot the Sat phone to pieces, and did the same with the camera equipment and suitcases two of the troops had lugged from the Land Rover. They scattered the half-burned passports, camera equipment, and clothes across the sand. Once we were in the Russian chopper and flying north towards Bagram, a U.S. base, the other chopper fired a missile at the Land Rover and blew it up.

"Captain Weston told me that the original rendezvous point had been compromised and they had to intercept us before we reached it. He explained that the story concocted by U.S. officials and released to the press was that my team, the prisoner, and I had been killed by an Insurgent attack. Some hours later we reached Bagram.

Sophie reached out to Jules and said, "Eat, honey," then with amusement, "Don't let these war mongers rush you."

Jules did as she was told, noting, along with Alex, that Sophie had called her "honey." After another bite and a swig of water, she continued.

"When we arrived at Bagram, we no sooner touched down on the runway, than we lifted off again in a C27J transport plane. We were told that we had to remain dark, in other words, our survival had to be kept secret for a few days so that the rouse would work. Twenty four hours later, we arrived at Fort Brag, North Carolina. After they let us shower, change into clean fatigues, and eat, they flew us to Andrews Air Force Base near Washington, D.C. They kept us until yesterday."

"I don't understand why the vehicle was destroyed and they made it look like you were all killed," commented Claire.

"The Afghani government feared that the mission had been compromised. I wasn't told how, but I had to assume that word leaked out. Our troops posed as the Insurgents and faked the attack. I have no idea how they got a Chinese and Russian chopper, but it had me convinced. I imagine that the Insurgents have been confused for days."

Everyone had questions, including how Alex reacted when she saw Jules, but Alex, held up her hand and said, "That's all for tonight. Jules hasn't slept in days, and it's time I take her to bed."

There were a few snickers from around the table and it dawned on Alex exactly what she had said. She was mortified, blushing only as blonds can do.

Jules stood up and taking Alex's hand said, "Pay them no mind. I can't wait to tell you all the parts I left out." Everyone started complaining as Jules and Alex made their exit post haste.

The almost full moon provided enough light to see each other's faces as they let the night bathe them in peace. Drowsily, Jules whispered, "Alex, darling, this all seems so impossible, doesn't it?"

Alex, ready to sleep, roused her mind for a moment. "No, honey. It doesn't." Remembering a famous quote from Sherlock Holmes, Alex replied, "Once you eliminate the impossible, whatever remains, no matter how improbable, must be the truth."

THE END

We hope you have enjoyed our collaboration on "Kidnapped Hearts." If you would like to read more books by Morgan Elliot and Erin Wade, please let us know. We have enjoyed working together and hope you agree that our writing styles complement each other.

Thank you for reading "Kidnapped Hearts." We hope you had as much fun reading it as we did writing it.

Our sincerest appreciation,

Morgan Elliot
Erin Wade

If you like our book, please let us know by writing a review at https://www.amazon.com/dp/B08D73JRTL

You can follow us at:
www.morganelliot.com or www.erinwade.com.

Below are the first five chapters of our next book *Never Speak of Tomorrow,* scheduled for release in December, 2020.

Never Speak of Tomorrow
By Morgan Elliot & Erin Wade
Coming December 2020

Chapter 1

Keaton Springfield wedged herself between the dumpster and the brick wall of Callaway's, a known hangout for Peru's sleazy underworld. She pulled her Glock from its shoulder holster, positioned the mask over her face, and waited.

The back door of Callaway's swung open and four burly men filled the alley. Each carried a bound woman who had obviously been drugged. "Prop them up in front of the dumpster so they can see what they are getting for their money." A gruff voice commanded. "The blonde one will bring a pretty penny."

A black Cadillac Escalade slowly crawled down the alley stopping in front of the dumpster. Four well-dressed men got out of the vehicle leaving the doors open.

"What do you have for us tonight, Pepe?" the tallest of the four asked.

"Two Americans and two beautiful native girls, Señor Cole," Pepe replied. "All prime. They should bring top dollar anywhere."

"A hundred bucks for the blonde," Cole bid.

"Señor, you are not renting her for the night," Pepe wheedled. "You are purchasing her for resale when you finish with her. Starting bid on the blonde is one thousand dollars."

The four newcomers discussed the price among themselves. "Five hundred," Cole declared.

"Take her back in," Pepe instructed his henchman. "I can make more than that off her in one night and still sell her many more times."

"Okay, okay," Pepe acquiesced. We'll pay a thousand for her, but no more than two hundred a piece for the other three."

"Oh, sixteen hundred." Pepe feigned disappointment. "These are classy women, not putas. Take the blonde, we'll traffic the others."

"Two thousand for the lot," Cole bid.

"Prime merchandise," Pepe reminded him. "I make you a deal, twenty-five hundred cash for the entire group."

The four businessmen nodded in agreement. "Load them in the back of my SUV." Cole directed Pepe's men.

Cole counted the bills as he paid Pepe. "We need eight more to fill the cargo container going out in two days. Can you handle that?"

"Si Señor."

"I need you to deliver them. Picking them up here is getting too dangerous for us."

"There will be a delivery charge," Pepe bargained. "Five thousand for eight of them plus delivery charge."

"Fine, fine," Cole grunted. "Deliver them to Pier 12 after midnight on Wednesday. My boys will meet you there and lead you to the container."

Keaton waited for the alleyway to empty than stepped from behind the dumpster and began speaking into her open body mike. "Black Cadillac Escalade, LP number 25Charlie, Echo, X-ray192, headed to Pier 12."

"Following them now, boss." Came the reply.

Calloway's door swung open and two of the thugs stepped into the alley lighting their cigarettes. "What the hell?" they chorused reaching for their guns.

"Don't do it," Keaton warned. "Don't pull out a gun unless you want to die."

As if on an unspoken signal both men rushed her. Keaton fired twice dropping them just feet from her. *So much for the twenty-one feet rule*, she thought as she pitched two chess pawns between the men and sprinted from the alley.

###

"Nice job, Springfield." Captain Carlos Risso entered the observation room. "We picked up everyone involved in tonight's little sex-trade operation.

"There were ninety-two women in the shipping container. All are in bad shape, starved, dehydrated, and abused. With the recording from your open mike and catching them red handed with the drugged women in their vehicle, we'll have no problem getting a conviction on these bastards."

"I love it when an operation goes smoothly," Keaton replied. "But it seems like every time we take down one operation another springs up in its place."

"You must be psychic," Risso exclaimed. "We've got a problem at Pontifica Universidad Catolica del Peru in Lima."

"The private college?"

"Yes, three girls have disappeared in the last four months. We think traffickers are targeting the women attending our local colleges. The University is hosting a fund-raising gala the Saturday after next. All of Lima's movers and shakers will be there. I want you to attend. Black tie."

"Sir, you know how I hate black tie affairs. Can't one of the other units handle this one?"

"I need your team on this. One of the missing women is the daughter of the Mayor of Lima. We need his support. It will be a real feather in our cap."

Risso held out a scrap of paper. "Here's the name and number of the woman who filed a report. It seems two of the girls were in her class. I think she's a Peace Corp volunteer teaching at the college."

Keaton read the name on the note. "Remi Navarro. Probably some boring academic. I'll try to catch up with her tomorrow afternoon, Sir. Right now, I'm going to get some sleep."

###

"Good morning Professor Navarro. She's waiting for you." Sister Clara was as old as the hills, but somehow still managed to make her way from the convent to the Administration building every day.

Remi nodded, took a deep breath before lightly tapping on the oversized orange agate door and turning the ornate doorknob. Mother Superior beckoned her and told her to take a seat in front of her desk.

"You sent for me, Mother Superior?"

"Yes, Remi. How is this term going?"

Remi relaxed a bit and said, "It started out about the same as last term, but the girls settled down much quicker. Maybe they will actually learn some chemistry that will help them in their nursing profession."

"You are no longer so exotic," grinned Mother Superior.

"I think they are beginning to see me as just another boring professor instead of some mysterious woman from the country where the streets are paved with gold and movie stars. In fact, as I learn about the history of your country, I think that Peru should have the moniker of the country with roads paved with gold."

Mother Superior was in essence the dean of the newly formed Nursing Program, which right now had about 90 women enrolled. She was a formidable woman and usually very serious, succinct, and lacking in humor. However, she must have gotten up on the right side of her bed today because she was congenial, and a very slight sense of humor was attempting to emerge. That made Remi even more suspicious of Mother Superior's reason for calling her in this morning.

"Remi, I know you have received many invitations from the families of our students to dinner and other social events in their homes. I have heard that you make a good impression on the parents. Is this something you enjoy?"

Remi knew that Mother Superior was setting her up, but she couldn't quite figure out her motive. She answered cautiously, "I enjoy getting to know the families; however, I am not one to look for glamor and glitter, and these families are the glitterati."

Mother Superior's lip curled upward. "Well, Remi, we'll have to fix that. You are aware that we have a huge gala scheduled the Saturday after next. Right?"

Remi nodded her head, waiting for the shoe to drop. Mother Superior smiled, took a sip from her coffee cup and continued. "This gala is an important fund-raising event and we hope to obtain enough donations to construct a building dedicated to our nursing program. All the glitterati, as you put it, will be there, hopefully with their checkbooks open."

"Yes, Mother Superior. I can imagine. I'd love to have a real classroom with a well-equipped lab instead of that prison cell I swear doubles as a classroom."

"Remi you can help make that dream a reality. I'd like you to be the keynote speaker."

Remi bounced up from her chair and began pacing, all the while saying, "No, no, no, not going to happen."

Mother Superior signed deeply and with an air of authority said, "Sit down Remi and listen."

Remi unhappily complied and said, "Mother Superior, I don't do public speaking."

"But Remi, think how impactful you could be. A young woman such as yourself who agrees to give up a promising career and come to some third-world country to help prepare girls for an admirable career, especially during this global shortage of nurses. They will be shamed into writing big fat checks—just what we need."

"So, the end justifies the means?" Remi was sick to her stomach, but held her tongue, lest she say something very offensive.

"I am afraid that this is what the Rector wants, and you can't say no to him, Remi."

"But I don't have anything appropriate to wear." Remi knew it was a useless last-ditch effort.

"Not to worry, Remi. Sister Clara's niece is a top-notch seamstress. Tomorrow you will go with her to pick out an evening gown design, material and get measured. Her niece will custom make a gown that will be the envy of everyone."

Mother Superior sat back waiting for Remi to try another excuse. When Remi remained silent, she continued. "I also have secured an escort for you. My brother's son will be at your disposal."

Just kill me now. Remi repeated those words over and over as she left the office. On her way out, Sister Clara gleefully shouted, "Did Mother Superior dress you down, or perhaps, was it dress you up?"

Chapter 2

Keaton searched through the wastepaper basket in her office. *Please let it be here*, she prayed.

"What are you looking for?" her Uncle Lucho Dapelo asked.

"That invitation. You know the one inviting us to some gala at Pontifica Universidad Catolica del Peru."

"You threw it away?" Lucho exclaimed. "I told you it was important for us to be represented. The crème of Peruvian society will be there. The people who purchase your extremely expensive Peruvian saddles. Keaton, you must take our social and civic obligations more seriously."

"Fine, Uncle. I'm going but if it's so important why don't you go?"

"I hate those things." Lucho grinned. "No one wants to be there, but they go for fear someone else will show them up. It's a zoo."

"I'll go." Keaton sighed loudly. "But I no longer have an invitation."

"Oh!" Lucho waved an engraved invitation in the air. "I salvaged it from your trash."

"Keaton," Office Manager, Ava Calle, called flourishing a memo, "This call just came in. A Professor, Remi Navarro, has invited us to visit the facilities at Pontifica Universidad Catolica del Peru to see the condition of the wing they are raising funds to replace. I hear it's very dilapidated."

"Us? Does that mean you'll accompany me?" Keaton asked hopefully.

"No dear, I'm just delivering her message. I gave her your email address so she can send you a map of the University grounds."

Keaton groaned. "When is this show and tell?"

"Tomorrow," Ava laughed as she left the room.

Keaton carried the invitation and memo into her office, closed the door, and called Stryker Nelson on her cellphone.

"Hey Keats, what's up?" Stryker answered.

"I want to ask you on a date," Keaton teased.

"I love you dearly, babe." Stryker chuckled, "But you're really not my type. You know I like the dark-haired ladies."

"That's why we work so well together," Keaton replied. "Seriously, the Captain wants . . . no, ordered me to attend a shindig at Pontifica Universidad Catolica del Peru next week. I need a date, so get your tux out of mothballs and air it."

"Why are we being assigned to the University?" Stryker queried. "One of the sisters running drugs?"

"No, but three female students have disappeared recently, and the local authorities have asked Captain Risso for help. I'm taking a tour of their facilities tomorrow as the representative of Springfield Exports. The company will contribute to the fund-raising gala. I'm trying to get my foot in the door and find an excuse to hang around the University."

"You could enroll at the U," Stryker suggested.

"I'm a little old for a student," Keaton pointed out. "And I do need to carry my weight at Springfield Exports."

"Do you need me to go with you tomorrow."

"No, I can handle a tour alone." Keaton laughed. "I just wanted to update you on what I'm doing."

Keaton arrived an hour early for her appointment with Professor Remi Navarro. Dressed in her navy business suit and crisp white blouse, she was the epitome of an American entrepreneur. She pushed back the blonde strands that had escaped her ponytail and now curled around her face, added fresh lipstick, and slipped her dangling earrings into place. She repositioned her rearview mirror looking around to see if anyone was watching her. She hoped to observe Professor

Navarro in a classroom situation. To get a feel for her. Using the map provided, Keaton quickly located the women's nursing facilities. She slipped into the class and took a seat at the back of the room. Professor Navarro had her back to the class writing an assignment on the blackboard.

Nice derriere, Keaton thought as she watched the five-foot-five woman stretch to add something to the top of the blackboard. She surprised herself by wondering what the professor's hair would look like if she pulled the pins from the French braid and let that glorious dark hair stream down the teacher's back. *It's been too long.*

Navarro talked as she wrote on the board and Keaton found her voice to be calm yet enthusiastic as she discussed her subject.

"Good morning ladies. I am happy to tell you that now we have finished our review of basic chemistry, we are going to start learning about Biochemistry."

Groans and boisterous protesting rose from the class.

Navarro turned to face her students. *Nothing special there,* Keaton thought. Tortoise shell-framed glasses perched atop a perfect nose above generous lips just waiting to smile at her class. *But oh, those lips.*

"Settle down, you'll like this. I promise. You need to remember that the roles of nurses have changed. The expression "high tech, high touch" reflects the need for you to have the ability to combine humanistic skills with scientific knowledge. What we cover the rest of the term will be very useful in your clinical work, specifically in the knowledge of how the body metabolizes different drugs, dosage and concentration, the disposal of byproducts of toxic drugs, and other bodily reactions to disease or illness."

Geeze, a snore fest, Keaton thought. *I hope I can keep my eyes open.*

"I can see you all are about ready to take a siesta, so let's talk about some biochemical reactions you might already know. How many of you have a significant other?"

Most students raised their hand snickering and giggling.

"Now, promise me that you are not going to talk to Mother Superior about this lecture, because we are going to talk about kissing. Yes, that's right, kissing. Promise?"

"We promise." The girls tittered

"Ready?" Remi took a deep breath and plunged ahead. "Imagine it's Saturday night and your parents have taken your siblings out to dinner and a movie. You feigned an upset stomach and begged off. Now, as soon as they are out the door, you text your significant other that the coast is clear and you run around the house turning off lights, lighting candles, and putting on some soft romantic music."

A soft murmur ran through the classroom as the girls became totally engrossed, as did Keaton.

"I see you've done this." Remi laughed. "As soon as your significant other gets to your house, you both scramble to the couch and start kissing. At first you are gentle, tender, enjoying the closeness. Then what happens?"

Keaton discovered she was squirming in her chair.

"Things get heated and more passionate," one of the girls answered.

"Yes, that's right. Does your body actually feel warm?"

"Oh yeah!" Someone breathes and the rest of the class laughs knowingly.

Remi continued. "What you are experiencing is a biochemical reaction. Dopamine, an organic brain chemical is released during a kiss and can stimulate the same area of the brain activated by heroin and cocaine. As a result, we experience feelings of euphoria and addictive behavior. Oxytocin, another organic chemical, otherwise known as the 'love hormone', fosters feelings of warmth, affection and attachment."

A girl shouted, "Yeah, addicted to love." Sending the class into a riotous laugh session.

"Hold on girls, we're not finished yet. What might happen next during your necking session?"

A girl from the class interrupted and shouted out, "Something gets hard!" The rest of the class went nuts.

"Settle down. You guys are going to get me fired."

Remi's statement set off the class on another laughing jag. Keaton couldn't stop the smile spreading across her face as Remi's glance sent a wordless apology to her visitor.

"That isn't quite what I had in mind, but since you brought it up, that is an example of a combined biochemical and physical reaction. Now go ask your Biology teacher for specifics." Remi laughed, shaking her head at the girls' antics.

"Let's try that again. The question was, what else happens during kissing? I am going to give you the answer and for your homework, you are going to write two paragraphs why this happens and why it is beneficial."

The girls groaned at the thought of homework.

"Kissing lowers cortisol levels. Cortisol is another organic compound that you should get to know intimately. Too much or too little can cause serious problems in a human body. Does anyone have a question?"

One of the girls raised her hand.

Remi nodded at her. "Yes?"

"Professor Navarro, do you have a boyfriend?"

"I didn't mean that kind of question." Remi blushed. I meant about your homework."

"Oh, come on Professor," the other girls joined in asking for more information about their teacher's private life. "Tell us?"

"I don't have time for romance right now," Remi mumbled. "I'm married to my job and believe me, getting all of you through three terms of chemistry is a full time job! Class dismissed. See you tomorrow."

###

Remi picked up her lecture notes and put them into her briefcase while the students were leaving the classroom. Once the room had cleared out, she turned her attention to her visitor. *Wow! Did heaven just send me an angel? Who is that?*

She stepped off the dais, almost tripping over her own feet, but caught herself before landing face down and making a fool of herself. Gathering herself, she approached her visitor, and extending her hand. "Hi. I'm Remi Navarro. Who might you be?"

Keaton took Remi's hand and told her that she was Keaton Springfield and before she could explain any further, Remi interrupted her.

"I'm so glad you came. We invited many people to come and look at the deplorable conditions in which we are working, but not many accepted our invitation. Let me take you on a short tour and we can get to know each other. This way please."

Keaton walked out the door followed closely by Remi, who seemed to be having trouble keeping her attention on the task at hand, which was to emphasize how bad the conditions were and how much better the educational experience for the students would be if they had better facilities.

Keaton stopped and turned towards Remi. "Which way?"

"Let's start down this hallway," answered Remi. As they were walking Remi ticked off the statistics, hoping to show this potential donor just how much of an impact her contribution would have. "This is the first year for the nursing program. The Board of Regents from the University decided to establish a nursing program to meet the needs, particularly of the rural areas, where medical care is sparse."

Keaton asked her how many students were enrolled and was surprised to hear that it was close to a hundred. "Why so many students right out of the gate?"

"I suspect the need is so great and the Board of Regents offered tuition free if applicants pledged two years of rural work post-graduation. That is a huge motivator for girls that normally wouldn't have the resources to attend a private university."

Keaton wondered if now would be a good time to ask about the girls that disappeared. She made sure she remained relaxed and casually asked, "I heard that there were three girls that disappeared from the school. Did you know any of them?"

"Yes. All three were in the nursing program and came from wealthy families. At first I thought they had been kidnapped for ransom, but there never were ransom demands. Now I can't help but think something worse befell them." Remi started to tear up. "I had been to each of their houses, met their families, and even tutored one of the girls who had a problem learning basic chemistry."

Keaton took a clean handkerchief she had in her breast pocket and passed it over to Remi. "I'm so sorry. Did you get involved?"

"Yes, to some extent, and thank you for the hanky. The police interviewed me several times, but the only information I had that was relevant was that the girl I was tutoring one evening, never made it home. They asked me if I thought she could have run away from home, but Keaton, I don't think she was the type. She was really dedicated to getting through the program."

"What did the other girls say? I suppose there's talk after a life changing event." Keaton reached out and brushed away a tear that had strayed down Remi's cheek, surprising them both. "I'm sorry Remi, I didn't mean to startle you."

"Thank you, Keaton it's fine. I've been with these girls for six months and have grown close to them, but to answer your question, there was a lot of chatter, but nothing useful as far as I could tell." Remi sniffled a bit then composed herself. "So, now we're going to enter the so-called lab. She held open the door for Keaton, noticing how her pencil skirt hugged her curves.

"This looks pretty dilapidated to me," observed Keaton. The benches look like they are made from scrap wood and the chairs look pretty rickety. It's been a long time since I studied chemistry, but it doesn't seem like there is enough equipment to go around."

"You are exactly right. Ideally we should be able to have teams of two working with one Bunsen burner, but right now, six girls have to share. They learn by doing, not observing."

"Remi, you mentioned that you had grown close to the girls and I could see that from the rapport you had with them. I meant to tell you that I was very impressed how you got them to pay attention. Your analogy was spectacular and I for one, won't ever forget the Dopamine and Oxytocin, or what did you call it, the 'love hormone'? I bet they won't either." Keaton reached out and gently touched Remi's shoulder. "You have a gift. I wish I had teachers like you when I was in school."

Remi blushed, and managed a shy, "Thank you."

Keaton smiled at her. *I wonder what she would look like without those glasses.* So, Remi, what else is there to see?

"You have seen one of the better classrooms. Would you like to see the rest, though they are currently in use? Also, the professors in the program don't have offices and we have to rotate classrooms so there isn't a permanent place for us to store our materials and meet with students."

"I'll take your word for it. How about if you show me the plans for the new building?"

"Sure, we can do that. I signed out a copy of the plans and we can go down to the cantina and look at them over a cup of coffee. What do you say?"

"I say let's go."

Remi lead the way to the stairway. They went down two floors and ended up in a small lobby. The cantina was situated in a room right next to the lobby. As they walked in, several students called out to Remi.

"Hi Professor Navarro! How's it going Professor Navarro? When are we getting our tests back, Professor Navarro?"

"You seem to be on everyone's mind, Professor." joked Keaton.

"Yeah, just what I need. A bunch of 18-year-old girls dogging my every step."

Keaton, mildly flirting said, "And what's wrong with that?"

"Seriously? You must be joking! Spend a day in my shoes and you will know exactly what I mean!" Remi chuckled, pulled out a folded packet from her briefcase and said, "Keaton, would you like to open these and spread them out on a table and I'll get the coffee? How do you like it?"

"Americano, but please let me get the coffee."

"Really, Keaton, it's the least I can do, because next Saturday you are going to write a big check, right?" teased Remi.

"Will you be there?"

"Yes, I will. I'll be keeping my eye out for you." Remi flashed a smile and headed to the coffee bar where she placed their order. *I wonder if she is going alone or if she has a date.*

After they reviewed the ambitious plans, Remi looked at her watch and apologized to Keaton. "I'm so sorry to have to cut our time together short, but I have a class in about 15 minutes."

"Of course, I've taken up enough of your time already. You have been very generous." Keaton helped her pack up the blueprints and as they were about ready to part she asked Remi, "Do you suppose that if I have any more questions we could set up another meeting?"

Remi looked at her quizzically, but in the end said yes, though she had no idea why. *Keaton Springfield is way out of my league.*

Chapter 3

Keaton knocked on the doorframe of Captain Risso's office before entering. "Come in and close the door," Risso instructed. "How did your meeting with the professor go?" Risso asked as Keaton settled into the chair in front of his desk.

"Fine. She has a good rapport with the women in her classroom. If anyone can instill trust, she can. She's lowkey and very nondescript."

"Not a looker, eh?" Risso laughed. "Comes with the territory, Keats. Old maid schoolteachers are rarely beauties."

"I'm not looking for someone to date, sir. I'm looking for someone who can get the women to open up to them. There is no way three women can go missing and that group knows nothing. They seem to be a close-knit bunch."

"You're usually right," Risso agreed. "Just keep your ear to the ground."

"I will, sir. I need to spend some time at the export business this week. I must carry my weight there."

"Then get out of here. I don't need to see you again until you have something to report."

"Have we identified all the women taken from the cargo container?" Keaton asked.

"Stryker is working on that now. Over half of them are still hospitalized. They were in bad shape but none of them are the girls from the Universidad Pontifica. As soon as they are strong enough, we'll question all of them."

Keaton walked into her office at Springfield Exports to find her uncle ranting in Spanish. "Calm down, Uncle," she admonished. "Tell me what is wrong."

"Your girlfriend," Dapelo sputtered. "She is a demanding, self-centered—"

"Say no more," Keaton interrupted. "I'll handle Carmen."

"Apparently you don't handle her often enough," Dapelo grumped. "She is on her way here right now."

"Just send her into my office," Keaton said unlocking the door to her suite and flipping on the light. She left her door open so nothing would stand in Carmen's way when she stormed into the company.

A sultry dark-haired beauty Carmen Tacona gave a whole new meaning to the term hot blooded. Keaton knew she was about to be lambasted for her failure to return Carmen's calls.

The doors flew open and employees moved out of her path as Carmen stormed through Springfield Exports. "Keats," she purred intimidatingly reminding Keaton of a big cat just before it devours its prey. "Why the hell haven't you returned my calls?"

"I've been working night and day," Keaton explained, closing the door. "I've been out of the office for the past four days. Unlike you, I must work for a living."

For the first time Keaton was thankful for the stacks of mail and work orders piled on her desk.

"No matter," Carmen walked around the desk and kissed Keaton breathless. "You will take me to lunch, no?"

"I'm terribly busy. I—"

"You will take me to lunch." Carmen growled.

"Yes, of course." Keaton gulped. "I'll make reservations. Where would you like to go?"

"Astrid & Gastón of course," Carmen replied. "But, umm, first we stop by my apartment."

"I only have a narrow window of time," Keaton pushed Carmen's hands away from the buttons on her blouse. "I have appointments all afternoon."

"I also need to discuss business with you," Carmen smiled salaciously. "Perhaps you can cancel your appointments for the rest of the day, and we can combine business with pleasure."

"I can't do that," Keaton sighed opening her office door. "Ava, please make reservations for two at Astrid & Gastón. Tell them we'll arrive there in thirty minutes."

Keaton took Carmen's arm and escorted her from the building to her Jeep. "Must we ride in that thing?" Carmen demanded.

"Yes!" Keaton smirked. "You know any vehicle will be destroyed in Lima's traffic. Peruvians consider traffic lights and signs mere suggestions to be ignored. They would rather die than yield to another vehicle. If it were legal, I'd drive a tank."

"Keats, you are so funny." Carmen slipped her arm through Keaton's and hugged the blonde's arm into her breasts.

Keaton stiffened. "Um, you have missed me," Carmen hummed.

I'm exhausted, not dead, Keaton thought. Her body jerked involuntarily as the thought of mousy Remi Navarro crossed her mind.

"We will discuss business on our way to the restaurant," Carmen declared. "Then you may spend your time over lunch convincing me that I should forgive you and sleep with you tonight.

"As you know, Papá oversees the National Peruvian Paso Horse Competition at the Mamacona show grounds every year."

Keaton nodded.

"He wants everyone that has anything to do with the Peruvian Horses to be represented at the show grounds the entire week of the show," Carmen continued, "breeders, trainers and of course vendors".

"And you want Springfield Exports to be front and center with a huge display of our goods," Keaton added.

"Of course, darling. You are the largest exporters of Peruvian leather goods in the country and Papá approves of you."

"Consider it done." Keaton smiled. "I'll have Santos arrange it. Springfield Exports will make you proud."

"But Papá wants you to be there, love, especially for opening weekend. It is the biggest event of the year."

"Carmen, I will be there opening weekend. Now I have a favor to ask of you. I must represent Springfield Exports at some black-tie event Uncle Lucho has roped me into. I have no choice. I'd like you to meet me there and bring your checkbook. And I'm truly sorry I haven't returned your calls."

"Um, well, you have all night to beg my forgiveness." Carmen blew softly into her ear.

Remi was finished dressing except for putting on her grandmother's emerald earrings. She had decided earlier to let her hair hang loose. Tossing it to one side, while she put on one of the beautiful earrings, she wished she didn't have to go, even if she might run into Keaton again. *Stop dreaming, girl.* Finishing with one ear, she draped her hair over her bare shoulder and put on the other earring.

Standing in front of the full-length mirror, she liked what she saw. The glasses she wore at school had been replaced by contact lenses. Her makeup was understated but brought out the best of her naturally attractive features. She was amazed at how perfect the dress was. It was an asymmetrical off-the-shoulder, form fitting dark emerald green cocktail length dress with a moderate slit up the left leg. The left side of the dress covered her shoulder and was capped with a tasteful mini ruffle. Her right shoulder was bare. The back of the dress dipped about a third of the way down her back, so that if she were forced to dance, her partner would not have his hand on her bare skin.

The doorbell to her flat sounded. She looked out the peep hole before opening the door. Mother Superior had given a description of her nephew. The man on the other side of the door was definitely Rolf. "Come in Rolf. It's so nice of you to come for me and it is a pleasure to meet you."

He offered his hand. "I have been looking forward to this evening for a week. My aunt Beatriz, or Mother Superior to you, told me what a wonderful teacher you are, but failed to mention how lovely you are."

"Thank you for the compliment, Rolf. Let me get my wrap and evening bag and I will be ready." A moment later she walked out the door, locked it and was escorted to his chauffeured car.

Once settled, Rolf spoke. "I understand that you are giving the keynote speech tonight. Are you excited?"

"More like petrified," answered Remi honestly.

"Don't worry too much. By then everyone will be feeling no pain and all you have to do is show a little leg and cleavage and they will be tripping over themselves to hand you a big fat check."

"Maybe I should get your check now, before you are feeling no pain," answered Remi icily.

"Don't be such a prude, Remi. I was only telling you how these things go. Let's talk about something else. All right?" *Damn, I am going to have to work hard to get her in bed tonight!* Rolf tried to repair his faux pau and began asking her the usual 'first date' questions: Where did you grow up, where did you go to college, what did you do before you came here? Remi answered politely, only out of respect for Mother Superior and what they were trying to accomplish this evening. *How do I get rid of this jerk? He makes my skin crawl.*

The Gala was being held at the Country Club Lima Hotel located in a residential district of Lima. It had been declared a Peruvian Cultural Monument and was the perfect marriage of architectural charm, history, and modern comfort. One of the gala organizers had told her that many of the attendees had reserved rooms for the night so they could imbibe freely without concern of getting home safely. Remi wondered if Rolf had reserved a room. She shuddered at the thought.

They stopped at the Gala registration table to sign in and receive directions to their assigned table. As soon as they found it, situated next to the stage at the front of the ballroom, Rolf turned down the champagne a circulating waiter offered and left in search of something harder. Remi was content to sip her champagne without him. Her people-watching was interrupted when Mother Superior, Bishop Calabria, the Rector of the University, and two other couples joined her. After the introductions, Rolf, seemingly in better spirits, reappeared. Remi could smell the alcohol on him as he sat next to her, slinging his arm around the back of her chair.

A man came out from the stage wing, walked over to the podium, introduced himself as Monsignor Duarte, and welcomed the attendees. He briefly went over the night's program, then announced that dinner would be served. Remi, good naturedly, withstood a mild interrogation by her table mates until their first course arrived.

While the food was excellent, Remi couldn't eat. Her stomach was in knots. *Is my stomach full of butterflies because in thirty minutes I am going to have to talk to all these people or is it because I don't see her?* Mother Superior must have noticed her looking out over the room and quietly asked her if something was wrong, to which Remi replied, "No, I'm just a little nervous." Mother Superior patted her hand and told her she would be fine as soon as she got up on the stage. *That didn't help much.*

###

"Keaton, I'm so sorry. I think that ceviche I had for lunch was bad," Stryker explained as the two of them were walking toward the Hotel's main exit.

"Stryker, are you sure it wasn't the pisco sours you had with it?" Keaton had to agree he looked a little green around the gills.

"Maybe the combination." offered Stryker shrugging his shoulders. "Look, I don't want to ruin your fun. I'll take a cab and leave you my car so you can get home after this shindig winds down."

"It's okay Stryker. Let me drive you home."

"Keats, how long have we been partners? I can get home. Besides, I know you saw something you like? Why don't you go back in and see if you can get her phone number?"

"I thought she was coming, but I haven't seen her. Was I that obvious?" Keaton sighed.

"The teacher you met last week?"

"What makes you say that Stryker?" Keaton was surprised.

"Keats, you never go out, you never date, except for that wild woman Carmen now and again, so it was just a matter of simple deduction. The teacher is the only woman you've recently met." Stryker gave her a key fob and the valet ticket, both of which she slipped into her evening bag, and he hugged her goodnight. The valet flagged a cab and Stryker was gone.

Keaton went back to her table, which had been cleared of the meal, and turned her chair to the stage where Monsignor Duarte was introducing Bishop Calabria. The old wind bag droned on and on for what seemed like eons. He spoke about the plans for the new building and how much money they already raised through public support and how much more they needed. He was followed by Mother Superior who talked about the students' progress for a few minutes, then segued into introducing Remi.

Keaton's breath caught. She couldn't believe what she was seeing. Her mouth was still open as she blinked her eyes, making sure they were working properly. *That can't be the same Remi I met last week. My god, what an unbelievable transformation! She's absolutely stunning. Her hair. Her eyes-what happened to the glasses? Her bare shoulder.* She was mesmerized, but as Remi began to talk, her attention was drawn to Remi's words and she became engrossed just as she had in Remi's classroom.

Good evening everyone. Thank you all for coming and thank you Mother Superior for that warm introduction. Remi walked away from the podium to stand in the middle of the stage. She began,

I was born and raised in Santa Fe, New Mexico. My grandparents came from Colombia during the early years of La Violencia to seek a better life for themselves and the family they hoped to have. I reaped the rewards from their courageous actions. After I went to Nursing School, followed by completing my advanced degree, I was somewhat undecided as to the next steps I wanted to take.

My father said to me, the best way to discover who you are is to immerse yourself in the service of others.

I said, Dad, I've worked four years in two different hospitals. Isn't that service to others?

He said, yes of course, but you still seem to be floundering. Maybe the way you get meaning in life is to create something that gives you purpose and a sense of accomplishment.

So, I started looking for opportunities where I could devote myself to a community that needed me. Did I have illusions of changing the world? Of course not, but I believed that I might be able to help a small group of people who did have the capacity to change the immediate world that surrounded them.

When the Peace Corps offered me the opportunity to come to Peru and be part of a bold new venture that had the

potential to make a significant impact on improving health care for many, I jumped at it. I am proud to say that I am honored to be part of a four-year journey along with your daughters, who are truly thoughtful, committed citizens dedicated to enriching the lives of others.

You should be proud to have raised daughters who have embraced the difference between what we do and what we can do. They know what they are capable of doing and they have embraced the idea of active charity and willing service to others. These are the young women who are capable of changing the landscape around them.

Remi paused for a moment, looked out at the crowd and continued.

We care a lot about our mission, which is extremely important, but I love focusing on understanding the people behind it. You are the people behind this mission. You will make it possible for these students, your young women, to accomplish the goals that are set in front of them.

Tonight, you have the opportunity to make a difference, not only in the lives of your daughters, but in the lives of many people who will be touched by your daughters in the future. I humbly ask you to be as generous as you can so that your daughters can reach their full potential.

Remi looked at the audience, took a breath and continued.

I leave you tonight with a quote from Winston Churchill: 'We make a living by what we get, but we make a life by what we give.' Thank you for your gracious attention and your generous gifts.

Remi stood in the center of the stage for a moment as the applause continued. The audience was on its feet, the clapping encouraging Remi to take a small bow. She kept eye contact with the audience and waved goodbye as she walked across the stage. Just as she reached the podium, she caught sight of Keaton. *Oh my god, could she be any more stunning? That dress...Of course it's black. Her cleavage—*

I want my lips there. The slit up her leg, oh god, it's just short of X-rated. Remi stumbled slightly and grabbed onto the podium for a moment before hurrying off the stage.

Father Duarte helped Remi down the stairs and guided her to an alcove where University employees were receiving donations. She shook hands and answered questions from the donors for about an hour, occasionally looking over the crowd, hoping to catch a glimpse of Keaton, but she didn't. Finally, she was able to extricate herself from the hubbub and find her way out into the hotel lobby. She decided to go to the coat room, grab her wrap and take a cab home. Rolf was stinking drunk, and she wanted nothing further to do with him. There was no one attending the coat room, so she entered. As she was removing her wrap from a hanger, she felt someone come up behind her and grab her around the waist.

"Finally, I found you," slurred a very intoxicated Rolf. He dragged her over to a dark corner, turned her around in his arms and forcibly kissed her. Remi was able to free one of her arms and slapped him hard.

"Is that how you want it, you tease?" Rolf reached for her dress and in a flick of his wrist, tore the shoulder of Remi's dress and began to slobber across her chest. She struggled and managed to poke one of his eyes. He yelped, but did not let go, moving one hand to her throat and the other under her dress. Remi managed to bite his hand and he slapped her. She was scared, more frightened than she had ever been.

"Rolf, let her go right now!" Remi recognized Keaton's voice but thought she was imagining it. Rolf looked over his shoulder, still clutching Remi's throat and pushing her against the wall with a hand on her chest.

"Keaton get out of here; this is none of your business," hissed Rolf.

"I won't ask you again, Rolf. You know I'm more than capable of taking you down."

Rolf relinquished his hold on Remi and whirled to face Keaton. He aggressively reached for her and found himself on his knees with his arm twisted behind his back.

"Rolf, I'm going to let you go if you promise to get out of here and leave Ms. Navarro alone." Keaton applied more torque to Rolf's arm, bringing it close to the point of snapping.

"Do we have a deal? You'll be in a cast for months if you don't agree." Keaton tightened her hold just to make her point and be sure Rolf knew she was serious.

"All right, all right! I promise, now let me go." Keaton released Rolf and stepped between him and Remi. Rolf staggered toward the door, turned, and spat out a threat to Keaton.

"You American women are all alike, whores! You tease and then cry wolf. You just want her for yourself. Yeah, I hear the rumors. Just know that you will pay for this, Keaton." Rolf whirled and stomped out.

Keaton quickly walked over to Remi, who clearly was in shock. She picked up Remi's wrap and evening bag which had fallen to the floor during the attack. She draped Remi's wrap around her shoulders and pulled it across her chest, put her arm around Remi's waist, and said, "Let me take you home. Okay?"

Remi nodded her head and walked with Keaton without a word. They waited briefly while the valet brought around Stryker's car. Even after getting into the car, Remi was semi-catatonic. Keaton reached across her and fastened her seat belt all the time wondering if she should take Remi to the hospital. Then she remembered that Stryker carried a flask in the glove compartment. Once more reaching across Remi, she removed the flask, opened it and told Remi to take a sip.

Remi did as she was told followed swiftly with a sputtering and coughing fit. Keaton told her to take another sip, which she did without any argument. The color was coming back into her face and her eyes weren't quite as glazed over as they had been in the hotel.

"Remi, may I have your address?" Keaton asked. At first Remi just stared at her, but then she seemed to understand and recited her address as Keaton punched it into the GPS. Remi didn't speak again until they were nearing her flat.

"It's on the right, three houses down. You can park in the driveway. It's a pretty safe neighborhood."

Keaton parked and as she walked around to the passenger side of the car, the door opened, and Remi swung her legs out. Remi was still unsteady, so Keaton held onto her until they reached the door. Remi was able to retrieve her keys from her evening bag, but her hands were still shaking, and she couldn't insert the key into the lock. Keaton gently took the keys from Remi, opened the door, guided Remi inside, and locked the door behind her. She helped Remi up the stairs and into her bedroom over to the bed, where she asked Remi to sit.

"Do you want to take a shower or just change clothes and go to bed?" Keaton asked gently.

"Shower please," answered Remi but not making a move toward the bathroom.

Keaton entered the bathroom, found a robe on a hook behind the door and returned to help Remi disrobe—her hands now trembling. Remi let her take her wrap, remove her shoes, and unzip the ruined dress. With watery eyes, she turned to Keaton, thanked her, and said that she could finish. Keaton nodded, went to the door and said, "I'll wait for you in the living room."

###

While waiting for Remi to finish showering, Stryker called. "Keats, I wanted you to know that I'm at urgent care. I got worse after I got home, and they are keeping me overnight as a precaution. Will you please come get me tomorrow when they release me?"

"Of course, Stryker. Did they say what is making you sick?"

"Yes. Food poisoning. I should be better by tomorrow morning. They have me hooked up to an IV right now. Where are you...still at the Gala?"

"No. You won't believe what happened. I was calling it quits, went to fetch my coat and walked in on Rolf assaulting Remi Navarro, the professor who gave the keynote speech."

"Did you tell her about his reputation?"

"I didn't get a chance, Stryker. She was in shock. I took her home and plan to stay the night in case that drunken bastard shows up."

"I'm glad she's okay. I'm going to try and get some sleep now that I am not running to the bathroom every five minutes. See you tomorrow."

Remi walked into the living room, swathed in a bathrobe, her hair hanging loose still wet from the shower.

"Thank you for staying Keaton, but I'm all right now. I don't want to keep you from the rest of your night."

"Does Rolf know where you live?"

Remi nodded her head, "He picked me up this evening. Do you really think he'll come back?"

"Remi come sit next to me," she motioned to the couch. Once Remi was seated next to her, Keaton told her of Rolf's reputation, not only of being a player, but also of being a date rapist who so far had gotten away with his degenerate actions by bribing police and justices.

"Keaton, how do you know this?"

Keaton was worried that Remi might be homing in on her "secret career", so she chose her words carefully.

"Remi, the Import/Export business is a small ecosphere here in Lima. Everybody knows everybody's dirty laundry. I can't stand Rolf, yet his family's shipping business is the best and most reasonably priced in Lima. My uncle has been doing business with them for years. When I first came from the States to join the business, he tried to put the moves on me. I kicked him in the groin, and he went down. My uncle witnessed the whole encounter, picked up Rolf by the scruff of his neck and in no uncertain terms, told him what would happen if he tried it again. He also called Rolf's father. Since then, Rolf has given me a wide berth."

Remi tried to speak, but she was overcome with emotion again. Keaton took her in her arms and let Remi cry on her shoulder until regained control.

"I'm sorry Keaton. You must think I'm a baby."

Keaton wiped the tears from Remi's cheeks with her thumbs and said, "I don't think you are a baby. I think you were almost raped, and you are upset with good reason. I'm going to stay here tonight, just in case he decides to come back and harass you. Do you have something that I can wear? I'm thinking that this dress won't be too comfortable."

"Keaton, that is so nice of you, but I think I'll be okay. You don't have to ruin the rest of your night." Remi sighed, wishing she hadn't told Keaton she could go.

"Remi, I don't have other plans, so if it's the same with you, I'd feel more comfortable staying. The couch will do fine." Keaton's eyes were earnest and sincere. Remi took her hand and led her to the bedroom, where she pulled out clean T-shirt and sweatpants.

"Please feel free to shower if you like. There are clean towels in the linen cabinet and new toothbrushes in the middle left drawer of the vanity. Use whatever you like. I'm going to make tea. Would you like some?"

Keaton gave her a thousand-watt smile and joked, "Only if you make your tea with whiskey and honey!"

"I can do that," quipped Remi. "See you in a few."

Keaton's long curly blonde hair was slicked back from her face. Remi handed her a mug of hot tea, laced with whiskey and honey. *She is so adorable, and she doesn't seem to know it.*

Keaton sipped cautiously, smiled widely, and said, "This is perfect. Thank you."

Remi grinned, "I'm glad you approve. I made up the couch, but why don't you let me sleep there and you take the bed?"

"That's very sweet of you, but if Rolf does show up, I want to be the first one that intercepts him. You don't happen to have a firearm, do you?"

Remi looked back at Keaton with big eyes, reminding her of a Margaret Keane painting. "You're kidding, right?"

Keaton shook her head "no" but then grinned and said,

"Yes, I'm kidding, Remi," But she was gravely serious. Rolf was dangerous. "We're safe. Do you need me to tuck you into bed? joked Keaton." *I'd like to do more than just tuck her in.*

Remi smiled lightly, shook her head "no", said good night, and went into her bedroom.

Keaton couldn't get comfortable. She had been tossing and turning for over an hour. *Remi was right. The couch is horrible. I wonder why she hasn't changed out this torture rack...unless the place came furnished.* The room was too light. The flimsy curtains did nothing to prevent the moonlight from spilling into the room, disrupting her sleep.

A movement in the hallway pulled her from her grumpy reverie. She quickly sat up and was just about to launch off the couch when she caught a glimpse of bronze legs bathed in the interloping moonlight. *Remi.*

"What's wrong Remi?"

"I can't sleep."

"You are perfectly safe."

"No. Keaton, I can't sleep with you out here on that god-awful sofa." Remi took Keaton's hand, looked into her eyes and said, "There's room for the both of us in the bed. Besides, it has a new mattress."

She tugged Keaton's hand and pulled her toward the hallway and bedroom. Remi pulled back the covers, got into the bed and held the covers open for Keaton, who was trying her best not to hyperventilate as she looked at Remi's bare legs.

"Keaton, it's okay. Please get in, it's cold."

"Are you sure Remi?"

"Of course, I'm sure. I feel safe with you nearby."

Keaton climbed into the bed, lay on her back, and tried to get her impulses and breathing under control. *I don't know what it is about her. I've never felt such an instant connection. Being with her is strangely comfortable and at the same time makes every ounce of my body vibrate in need.* Keaton's thoughts were interrupted by a whisper.

"May I sleep next to you? I'm still a little freaked out." Remi started to move closer to her without waiting for an answer.

Keaton summoned all her self-control and simply answered, "Yes."

Without hesitation, Remi curled up next to Keaton, resting her head on Keaton's shoulder, her arm across Keaton's abdomen and her leg thrown over Keaton's. Keaton knew this was not an attempt at seduction. Remi was vulnerable and scared. *Maybe that's what has me in a lather, her vulnerability and innocence.*

Within minutes, Remi's breathing slowed, became deeper, and her body relaxed. Keaton knew Remi was asleep. *There is no way she is into women,* Keaton thought. *She couldn't possibly be sprawled all over me like this and go to sleep if she liked women.*

Keaton was stunned by what she did next. She slowly lowered her head and placed a soft kiss on Remi's forehead. She was amazed at her own emotional reactions. Keaton took a breath, put her arm around Remi and let herself drift into a deep sleep.

Remi woke and glanced at the clock. She couldn't believe that she had slept until noon. *Where is Keaton?* Remi got up, cleaned up a bit and donned a pair of jeans and an off-white Henley. Walking through the flat and not finding Keaton, she felt a little deflated. Entering the kitchen, she saw a piece of paper and what looked like a creased check on the kitchen table.

Dear Remi, I'm sorry I have to leave. My friend Stryker called and needs me to pick him up from urgent care. I wish I could have stayed until you woke up; I really do. I hope that you are feeling better this morning. I'm going to have a talk with Rolf later today to make sure he doesn't bother you again.

Also, I never got to leave my check for the building fund at the Gala, so I hope it is okay to leave it with you. Please reach out if you need anything. Keaton

Remi looked at the check and almost fainted. She never expected so much. A million sol was the equivalent of about a quarter of a million U.S. dollars. The Import/Export business must be very lucrative.

###

"Professor Navarro, may I speak with you?" Angela, one of her chemistry students stayed after class.

"Yes of course, Angela. What's up?"

"I have been too afraid to tell anyone until now, but I think I might know something about Elena's disappearance."

"Sit down Angela and tell me what you know." Remi took her arm and directed her to the teacher's chair while she sat on the edge of the desk.

"Professor Navarro, I think I know where she went after class and tutoring. She met this guy...he was older than she. She had been sneaking around to see him for a couple of weeks. I saw them getting into a black Cadillac Escalade. Maybe she ran off with him."

"Angela, is there a reason why you didn't tell the police about this?"

"Yes, I'm sorry to say, and now ashamed I didn't say anything. I had told my parents I was going to be studying with Mariana and then spending the night with her. But I didn't. I stayed with my boyfriend because his parents had left for a week."

"All right Angela. I'm glad you told me. I think I have a friend that can help me with this. Try not to worry now and I will get back to you in a few days." Remi gave the girl a hug and sent her on her way. Quickly she looked up the phone number for Springfield Exports.

"Springfield Exports. How may I help you?"

"May I speak to Keaton Springfield please?"

"Yes, would you mind giving me your name?"

Remi told the receptionist who she was and before she knew it, Keaton was on the line.

"Remi, I'm so glad you called. I felt terrible leaving you Sunday morning.

"Keaton, you did more than I ever expected. Thank you and thank you for the very generous donation to the building fund. I also have another reason for calling. Could you possibly meet me this evening? I want to get your input on how to handle something I learned today, which may be related to the girls who disappeared."

"Yes, of course. Where would you like to meet?"

"How about dinner at Café Museo Larco? Do you know it?"

"You have good taste, Remi. How does 6:00 p.m. sound?"

"Sounds perfect. I'll see you there. Bye Keaton."

Chapter 4

Where did the day go? Remi had to hustle if she were going home to change, then meet Keaton at the Café Museo Larco in a couple of hours. As she was dashing out the door to grab her scooter, her cell phone rang. Annoyed she answered, "Hello. This is Remi."

"Remi," this is Mother Superior. I was wondering if you could stop by my office before you leave."

"Oh, I am so sorry Mother Superior, I already left. How about tomorrow morning before my first class?" Remi didn't think the little white lie would land her in hell, at least not yet.

"All right Remi. I'll see you at 8:00 a.m. tomorrow. Hope you have a good evening."

The scooter cranked at the very first try and then Remi was off, flying through the afternoon traffic like a Peruvian veteran. She made it home in fifteen minutes, unlocked her door, flew up the stairs, and started disrobing before she got to the shower. Ten minutes later she climbed out of the shower, ran a comb through her hair, wrapped a towel around her and went to her closet to choose an outfit. She took out three to mull over as she put in her contacts and makeup.

What difference does it make what I wear? She won't care, but I wish she would. Remi picked up the first outfit, turned it around on the hanger, and threw it down. *Lord no. That looks like a burlap sack.* The next one she picked up was a navy business-like suit. It looked great on her, but she didn't really want this to be a business meeting, even though that was exactly what it was. *Nope.* Finally, she looked at the third ensemble. *Yes! The suede!* The straight skirt was heather green suede and fell to her mid-calf. *Perfect with my brown suede high boots.* The matching jacket was as soft as butter and perfect for the cooler weather. She layered it with a simple white, deeply cut V-neck top. *Perfect!*

Remi pulled out a wide belt that matched her boots and picked out a pair of conservative earrings and necklace that hung perfectly on her chest just above the V-neck of her top. After putting on her Tag Heuer watch, a gift from her father, she gave herself a final once over in front of the mirror. She sighed loudly and summoned up a little self-assurance as she left the flat to wait for the ride share she had arranged earlier in the day.

It wasn't a long ride to the Café Museo Larco. She arrived with plenty of time to spare and decided to go into the attached museum and browse before going into the restaurant. However, the period paintings that had been curated in the museum were not to her liking, so she walked over to the restaurant, gave her name to the hostess, and took a chair to wait for Keaton.

Keaton burst through the doors like a whirling little dirt devil that was so common in New Mexico. She seemed a bit frazzled. She caught Remi's eye and briskly walked over to her apologizing for being late.

She looks so good. Okay Keaton, focus.

"Keaton, you are only five minutes late. I think I can forgive that," Remi joked.

The hostess noticed that Remi's companion had arrived and invited them to follow her to their reserved table.

"Is this table okay for you, Keaton?"

"Yes, it's great. I like that it is tucked away from the main traffic. I think it will be okay to talk. Don't you?" Keaton waited for Remi to respond.

"Yes, I'm comfortable here."

A server, with a printed name tag announcing he was Antonio, came by, filled their water glasses, gave them menus, and asked if they would like a bottle of wine or perhaps they would prefer a pisco sour. They both said "wine" at the same time then began to peruse the wine and dinner menus.

Antonio told them he would give them a minute to decide on their dinner choices and then he could recommend a wine.

When he came back, both Keaton and Remi were ready to order. Remi chose a grilled sea bass in brown butter with risotto. Keaton chose a shredded duck leg accompanied by a pumpkin risotto. Before Antonio could suggest a wine, Keaton told him to bring a bottle of the Peruvian Tacama Gran Blanco. She turned her head to Remi and asked, "Okay?" Remi nodded and Antonio disappeared.

The noise of the busy restaurant fell away, and they were both silent, neither knowing how to start the conversation, yet neither one finding a need to fill the silence with idle chatter. They seemed to be lost in watching each other or maybe in their own daydreams.

Keaton smiled at Remi deciding that the only course of action was to help Remi feel comfortable enough to tell her what she had learned.

"Remi, you look absolutely lovely tonight. That color compliments your eyes beautifully."

Blushing, Remi answered a simple "Thank you."

"Remi, you said that one of the girls in your class told you she knew something about the disappearance of one of her classmates. Tell me about it."

Remi, looked around the immediate area, leaned across the table and lowered her voice. *God, I can't concentrate around her. Concentrate, Remi.*

"Keaton, I don't know how this will help the police, but since you asked me if I had been involved in the police investigation, I thought I would share with you what one of the students told me and see if you could tell me the best course of action. You have been here much longer than I."

"Yes, of course. I'm glad to help. Tell me what she told you." Keaton's attention kept wandering to Remi's neck.

She couldn't quite figure out what kept drawing her to look at the left side of her neck. *Hey, you wanted her to talk. Pay attention.*

"This morning, before I called you, one of the students, Angela, asked to talk to me. She told me that the night one of the girls disappeared, she saw Elena, with a man she had been seeing for a couple of weeks. They got into a black Escalade and drove off. I asked her why she didn't tell the police this and she told me that she was afraid her parents would find out that she stayed late at school and then went to spend the night with her boyfriend instead of her study partner."

"Remi, was there anything else?"

"No, but I got the impression she might be able to identify him if she saw him again. Keaton, what should I do with this information?"

"I have a friend in the police department. I'll talk with him and we'll go from there. Is that okay Remi? Will that work for you?"

"Yes. Yes, it will, Keaton. I don't know how to thank you. That takes a load off my mind."

Antonio returned with the bottle of wine, uncorked it and Keaton tasted it. She nodded her head and Antonio poured them a glass.

They chatted easily now that the ice was broken, and they tossed questions about each other back and forth until Antonio served their dinners. Over dinner, Keaton noticed that Remi kept touching her neck and finally decided to ask.

"Remi, I see a mark or something on your neck and you keep touching it. What is it? You can tell me."

Remi took a deep breath and said, "Finger marks. The ones Rolf left behind. I've covered them with makeup, but all that does is cover them up. My neck is still tender."

Keaton felt the anger rise and take control of her. *How could that brute do that to this sweet woman? I just hope he gives me a reason to kill him.* Remi watched her closely, seeing her eyes burn, but said nothing. Keaton got her murderous rage under control, leaned toward Remi, and took her hand across the table. It was intimate and they both knew it.

"Oh god Remi. I am so sorry. You must go to Mother Superior and tell her, show her what happened. If you want, I will go with you. Please don't let him get away with this. Remember, you had a witness. Promise me, Remi."

"How can I possibly tell Mother Superior? She's his aunt?"

"Remi, you have to tell her. I bet you she will be in your corner. Trust me on this. I know I'm right."

"All right Keaton. I'll think about it tonight." *How can I resist Keaton's impassioned plea?*

"Will you call me and let me know how it goes?"

"Of course. Now how about some dessert?"

During dessert, Remi entertained Keaton with her students' antics and the politics of the University.

"You know, Keaton, I never thought there could be so much politicking at a University. Boy was I wrong. You either get dragged into it, or if you can resist, the minute your back is turned, you get stabbed.

"Do you get dragged into it, Remi?"

"Pretty much they leave me alone. I'm kind of the wild card and they can't figure out where my loyalties lie."

Remi looked up and saw a sexy, dark haired woman closing in on Keaton. If flashing eyes and a fake smile meant trouble, the woman was a walking time bomb.

"Is this your work?" The woman demanded.

Keaton stood. "Carmen Tacona this is my friend Professor Remi Navarro. Remi was the keynote speaker at Saturday night's fund raiser for the nursing college at the Pontifica Universidad."

Carmen calmed and was civil. "I'm pleased to meet you Professor Navarro."

"You remember the fundraiser?" Keaton continued. "You were supposed to meet me there but never showed up."

Carmen look properly chastised and Remi's heart fell into her stomach. *She is far too familiar with Keaton,* she thought.

"However, I'm certain Professor Navarro will be happy to accept your check right here, tonight."

Carmen's eyes flashed again, and a seductive smile played on her full lips. "And what will I get for my check?"

"Professor Navarro's undying gratitude." Keaton smiled sweetly.

Why don't you two get a room, Remi thought controlling her own temper.

"What if I want more than the professor's gratitude?" Carmen flashed perfect white teeth and sensually raked her teeth over her lower lip.

"Why don't you match my donation and see?" Keaton lowered her head and looked up at Carmen through long lashes.

Damn, that's the most adorable little girl look I've ever seen, Remi thought squirming in her chair.

Without breaking her gaze with Keaton, Carmen pulled a checkbook from her purse. "How much for what I want?"

"Springfield Exports donated this amount," Keaton pulled a pen from her jacket pocket and wrote a figure on the napkin.

Carmen glanced at the seven-figure donation. Without a blink she wrote a check for the same amount and handed it to Remi. Remi glanced at the check. It was from Buenaventura Mining, Peru's largest silver mine.

"This is very generous of you Miss Tacona. Thank you," Remi said as she thought, *I'd tear it up if I knew it would guarantee you won't have Keaton in your bed tonight.*

"Carmen and her family are very supportive of the Universities in Lima," Keaton pointed out. "I believe one of your buildings is named after her father."

Turning her attention back to Carmen, Keaton said, "If you'll forgive us, Professor Navarro and I were discussing important business matters and it looks like most of your friends have found their way to the bar without you. I believe that one is most antsy about your absence." Keaton nodded toward a tall, skinny redhead who was glaring at Carmen and Keaton.

Carmen waved her hand to indicate how insignificant her date was. "You were busy," she huffed at Keaton.

"So, any port in the storm, eh?" Keaton snickered signaling for the server to bring their check. "I must see Professor Navarro home."

###

"I need to call a ride share or taxi," Remi said as they stood by the table.

"Nonsense," Keaton exclaimed. "If you don't mind riding in a Jeep, I'd be delighted to take you home."

Remi's heart sang. "I love Jeeps," she murmured.

Keaton slid her hand down Remi's back coming to rest at the small of her back and gently guided her through the now crowded restaurant.

Keaton's hand on Remi's back sent fire shooting in all directions through her body. Remi prayed her knees wouldn't buckle. *God I want to be with her, but it is obvious she is involved.* She tried to drive from her mind the thoughts of Keaton's firm hands and long fingers strumming her body but failed miserably.

###

Keaton turned to Remi, "You don't live very far from here if I recall correctly".

Page | 423

"You have a good memory, Keaton. Do you need the address again?"

"No thank you. Once I have been to a location, I can easily find my way back."

"Seems like a handy skill to have. I'm just beginning to feel comfortable finding my way around the city," answered Remi.

"Perhaps you will let me show you around sometime. I like making new friends."

Remi's stomach fell to her feet and clawed its way back up. *Well that settles it. She definitely is off the market.* Remi answered politely, "Thank you Keaton, but I rarely have time for sightseeing." Remi turned toward the passenger window and didn't say another word until Keaton turned into her driveway.

Keaton felt the icy silence and knew exactly what was wrong but didn't have a clue how to handle it. She was sure that Remi had realized Carmen and she were involved, and as much as she would like to extricate herself from Carmen's talons, she knew she couldn't; not yet at least. She was also reasonably sure that Remi was interested in her more than in a friendly way. And then, a miracle happened.

Remi turned to her, thanked her for the ride, and asked if she would like to come up for a night cap.

Keaton didn't have to think twice. "Yes, I would, and I want to explain what you witnessed tonight."

"Remi said, "You don't owe me an explanation. Your life is your life and you don't have to justify it to me or anyone else."

"But I want to; I need to explain. Please?"

Remi began walking to the door and stopping to look over her shoulder at Keaton. "Are you coming?"

Keaton made a beeline to the door and stepped inside as soon as Remi opened it.

Remi took Keaton's coat and her own jacket, hung them in a small coat closet near the top of the stairs. "What would you like to drink? I have whiskey, as you know, pisco, cerveza, and a Malbec from Chile."

"The Malbec please. Is there anything I can do to help?"

"No Keaton, make yourself comfortable."

A moment later Remi came into the living room and joined Keaton on the lumpy couch. Keaton could not resist.

"Why do you keep this lumpy couch? Did the flat come furnished?"

"Yes, It did, but honestly, I just haven't gotten around to exchanging it. I've only been here six months and I have been working nonstop at the University."

Keaton nodded her head, sipped from her glass, and decided to push forward. "Remi, why did you invite me up here tonight? It was obvious you were upset with me."

"I was annoyed with the situation, and I want to apologize to you. May I be honest?"

"Please do."

"Do you remember the night of the gala, the night you saved me from that despicable Rolf?"

"Yes of course. How could I forget? Have you decided to tell Mother Superior?"

"Yes, I have a meeting at 8:00 a.m. tomorrow, but let's not get off track. Keaton, do you remember what he said when he left?"

"I think he threatened me, right?"

"Yes Keaton, but he also said that you wanted me for yourself, that he had heard rumors." Remi waited, curious to see if Keaton would admit that she remembered.

"I do remember, Remi. I'm surprised you did."

"From the very first moment I met you Keaton, I felt an inexplicable connection to you and the night you stayed here to take care of me, I thought you might have felt it too. Even tonight, until your, ah, friend came, I thought we were connecting. Was I wrong?"

"No. You weren't wrong. I've been powerfully drawn to you, but I didn't know you felt the same, until just now."

"I would like to see you, explore this, um, "thing" between us, but I can't, no I won't as long as you are with someone else, Keaton."

Keaton seemed to deflate right in front of Remi, who sat immobile while Keaton determined what she was going to say, if anything at all.

Keaton moved closer to Remi and took both her hands in hers. "I want the same thing, but the situation with Carmen is complicated."

"Aren't they all? She's a boor and you know it. Why are you with her?"

"I'm not really with her. She thinks she is with me."

"Keaton, what does that even mean?"

"Remi, I'm not going to lie to you. Having an association with Carmen has been advantageous to my line of business." *But not the one you know about.* "I have been trying to let her down easy, but she just won't take no for an answer."

"Are you in love with her?" Remi pulled her hands back.

"No. No. It's never been like that for me and clearly it isn't like that for her." Keaton took a big gulp from her glass.

"Then why? I just don't understand." Remi shook her head from side to side.

"I can't explain right now, but I want you to believe me when I say that she means nothing to me."

Remi got up and paced, whirling around in front of Keaton. "That's what a lot of people say. How many times have I heard, "It's just sex, she means nothing to me?""

Keaton captured Remi's hand and pulled her towards her. "I know you don't have any reason to believe me. I get that, but I beg you to give me time to fix this."

Remi let Keaton hold on to her hand, thought a moment, and said, "You can't have it both ways. You know where I am when you make up your mind, but don't take too long. I don't have much patience for cowards!"

Keaton dropped Remi's hand, the words feeling as sharp as any slap ever was. She had two choices. She could storm out and leave Remi in the dust, or she could be understanding hoping that somehow Remi would reconsider.

Getting up, Keaton thanked Remi for the nightcap, retrieved her jacket and said goodnight. She had descended one step, when she felt a hand on her shoulder. She looked up at Remi, whose hand was still on Keaton's shoulder.

"Keaton, this isn't casual for me. I just wanted you to know." Remi bent her head, placed a tender kiss on Keaton's cheek, and said goodnight. She followed Keaton to the door and locked it behind her. *Well that couldn't have gone any worse.* She sighed and headed to bed.

###

Keaton walked to her jeep and sat down. One thing was certain, Remi liked women. She even liked her. Keaton fought the urge to bang on Remi's door, make her promises and make love to her. But she knew she couldn't. Things weren't that simple where Carmen was concerned.

Keaton had been undercover associating with drug and human traffickers for so long she sometimes forgot that a world made up of Remi Navarros even existed.

She liked Remi's no-nonsense truthfulness. The brunette's straight forward approach to their relationship had surprised her. "I like Remi Navarro very much," she said out loud. "But I don't dare tell her the truth."

The truth would put too many people in harm's way. If the traps the department had been setting the past year were ever made public a lot of undercover drug enforcement officers would lose their lives. Keaton had to play the role assigned to her or endanger others. No matter how badly she wanted Remi Navarro, she could never speak of tomorrow.

Chapter 5

Remi marched into Mother Superior's office at 7:55 a.m. ready to say "no" to whatever she wanted now. Sister Clara said good morning and waved Remi in.

Remi was astounded to find Mother Superior in civvies and even more surprised when she saw Keaton fixing coffee.

"Remi, come in. I take it you know Ms. Springfield?"

Remi was speechless and wasn't sure she could recover from both shocks. Mother Superior was dressed in a black pant suit and white button-down blouse, looking pretty sharp. Her hair was pulled into a loose ponytail at the back of her neck. *Do nuns even have long hair? I thought they chopped it all off.*

Keaton was standing to the side like a cat who had just swallowed a canary. *What is going on here?* Remi mused.

"Good morning Remi," Keaton said as she handed her a cup of coffee. "I'm sorry to surprise you like this, but I thought you might want someone to back up what happened to you at the Gala."

Remi's eyes threw daggers at Keaton but pulled herself together enough to politely thank her for the coffee.

"What's this situation that happened at the Gala? Please enlighten me?" Mother Superior asked.

"Mother Superior, there is no gentle way to say this. I wish there were. Rolf got very drunk and assaulted me in the coat room. If Ms. Springfield had not come along when she did, he would have raped me."

Mother Superior was shocked. "Are you sure you didn't misinterpret his actions, Remi?"

"No. Absolutely not. The marks of his fingers on my neck are still visible." Remi rolled down the turtleneck sweater she had worn and approached Mother Superior, who tentatively touched the bruises and turned pale.

"Ms. Springfield, you were there? You witnessed this?" Mother Superior was ashen.

"Yes, I did. It was exactly how Professor Navarro described it. I pulled him away, brought him to his knees and told him to leave her alone. He left and I took Professor Navarro home."

"Damn it! That boy is going to be the death of me. I'm so sorry Remi that this happened to you. I will see to it that it never happens again. I thought he had grown up and would treat you like a gentleman, but obviously I was wrong."

Keaton asked Remi, "Do you want to press charges?"

Mother Superior visibly paled even more. She stuttered while saying, "Let's keep this in house and I promise I will take care of this and make it up to you."

Remi didn't want the hassle and nodded her head in agreement. She remembered Carmen's check and passed it to Mother Superior. "Ms. Springfield convinced Ms. Tacona to donate to the building fund. Here is her check. Now may I leave?"

Mother Superior accepted the check and looked at it. "Ms. Springfield, you must be an excellent persuader to have Ms. Tacoma match your company's donation."

"Glad I could help Mother Superior. If you don't mind, I need to take my leave. It was a pleasure to see you again."

Mother Superior shook her hand and walked her to the door while Remi uncomfortably waited in the hot seat.

"Remi, please let me say that I am appalled at my nephew's behavior and rest assured that I will take care of it. I'd like to try and make this up to you. Would you like to accompany me to the Peruvian Paso Horse Show and Competition this weekend? It really is a marvelous event, and everyone should attend once in their life. What do you say?"

Remi knew if she turned Mother Superior down, it would be a huge insult, so she agreed, excused herself, and made her way to her classroom before another disaster befell her. She was surprised to find Keaton waiting in the hallway outside her classroom.

"Remi," Keaton spoke softly, "may I have a moment of your time?"

Remi made a show of studying her watch then said, "My class starts in five minutes."

"Remi, I would very much like to date you," Keaton ducked her head and looked at Remi through long lashes. *Dear God, did you have to let her look at me that way*, Remi thought as her stomach performed a double pike.

"I know you have reservations about me, but please get to know me before you mark my name off your dance card."

Remi ducked her head trying to hide the smile that threatened to spread across her face. *Damn she is so cute.*

"I thought that perhaps—" Keaton faltered. "That maybe you could accompany me to the President's Ball in celebration of the opening of the annual Peruvian horse show. I have an invitation for a plus one and I thought you might enjoy the festivities. Err not as a date, of course, that sort of thing is frowned on in high places. Just as a friend."

Remi watched Keaton's lips as she spoke. She had never wanted to kiss anyone so badly in her life. "I assumed you would be escorting Carmen," Remi lashed out.

"I have no desire to escort Carmen."

"Did she collect her pound of flesh for her donation?" Remi couldn't stop her bitter tirade.

"I'm sorry," Keaton mumbled. "It appears I've made a mistake." She turned on her heel and walked away.

Remi watched her. *There goes the woman of my dreams*, she thought.

"Keaton," she called, "I'd love to be your date for the ball."

Keaton turned to face her as the school bell clanged and nodded as a huge smile spread over her face.

###

Beatriz stormed through the doors of Berger Shipping. She was livid and it showed. Everyone quickly moved out of her way as she headed toward Rolf's office. She barged past Rolf's secretary, flung open the door, and yelled, "What the hell is the matter with you? Are you a complete imbecilic moron?"

Rolf stood, nonplused and said, "Auntie what are you doing here and in civvies too?"

"Rolf, you good for nothing imitation of a man, don't pretend you don't know why I'm here. Your behavior was appalling."

Smiling like a Cheshire cat, Rolf said, "To what are you referring, Auntie?"

"I don't have time for games and if you do, I'm going to go directly to my brother about this." Mother Superior's chest was heaving.

"All right Auntie Beatriz don't get your panties in a ruffle. I just had a little too much to drink and misread your precious Professor Navarro's signals. It won't happen again. I'll stay away from her."

"Rolf, you did not misread Professor Navarro's signals. There was a witness, one of our largest donors that came to my office to corroborate the assault. Now, I'm going to have to bend over backwards to repair this, especially if she decides to press charges or even worse report it to her Peace Corp bosses."

"Auntie, you are making too big a deal of this. Water under the bridge."

"Listen to me you sniveling brat, you are going to do exactly as I say, or I am going to make sure that you no longer have a place in this company."

"Okay. What do you want?"

Mother Superior outlined her plan which included a letter of apology and a huge bouquet of flowers delivered to the University. She shoved him out of the way and left as forcefully as she had entered.

###

Keaton called Remi that evening to tell her the date and time of the ball. "It's formal." Wanting to impress on Remi how formal the ball would be she added, "I'll be wearing a Trumpet/Mermaid off the shoulder evening dress with beading sequins and heels, of course."

"What color?" Remi asked.

"White."

"I'll be sure to wear a different color, so we don't look like the Bobbsey Twins," Remi giggled.

Keaton laughed out loud happy to hear Remi's giggle. "I'll pick you up at 6:30 p.m."

Remi hung up the phone in a tizzy. She had nothing to wear. She hoped she could hire Sister Clara's niece and pay it out over time. *I must wear a dark purple dress or maybe navy blue*, she thought. She hugged herself then thought how good it would feel to have Keaton's arms around her. She fell asleep planning things that would steal Keaton's heart and make her forget Carmen Tacona.

###

The next morning Remi approached Sister Clara and spoke with her about the ball dress. Sister Clara shook her head and said, "Child, my niece can sew for most events, but the President's Ball is a different story all together. I don't think she sews that spectacularly. I'm afraid you would be embarrassed but let me show you something breathtaking. It was donated last year by the American ambassador's wife who has returned to the states. She only wore it once. It is from The Dress Boutique in Miraflores. It is custom made and exquisite!"

"What color is it?" Remi asked following the old woman to the back of her office.

"Deep Purple with exquisite beading on the bodice. It will look stunning on you."

Remi caught her breath when Sister Clara unzipped the bag protecting the dress. It was indeed unique. "Oh, Sister Clara it is beautiful."

"And it looks like just your size," Clara noted. "I've been saving this dress for someone special going to a significant event. You fit the bill. Take it home and try it on. If it needs adjustments, my niece can help with that."

"I should pay for it," Remi insisted. "The school could sell this for a great deal of money."

"Ridiculous," Sister Clara hissed. "You wear it to the President's Ball, have it dry cleaned, and return it to me. The school will still get its money. Please take it."

Remi nodded her head and took the dress.

Stryker turned over the body and shook his head as he pushed the button on his cellphone designated as boss. Keaton answered on the first ring.

"Gallegos is dead," Stryker said. "You'd better come."

"Damn. Where are you."

Stryker gave Keaton the address. I'll wait until you get here to call Mattie," he added. "You might want to bring a barf bag. It isn't pretty."

"On my way." Keaton hung up searching for an excuse to give her uncle for leaving. She walked into Ava's office as the secretary was transferring a call to Lucho. *My lucky day she thought.*

"Ava, when Uncle Lucho gets off the phone, please tell him I had to make a sales call."

Ava nodded and Keaton sprinted from the office to her jeep before Lucho could get off the phone and catch her.

Stryker was waiting for her in one of the seedier parts of Lima. The body was on the roof of an apartment building surrounded by other crumbling structures.

Keaton made her way through garbage thrown on the roof from surrounding buildings and found Stryker standing over the remains of a man she guessed to be over three hundred pounds.

"Tiny Gallegos," Stryker said.

"He's the muscle for Buenaventura Mining." Keaton noted. "What happened?"

"The tenant heard something heavy hit the roof and came up to see what it was."

Keaton looked around noting the roof was surrounded by taller buildings. "Let's call Mattie. You know how bent she gets if we rifle a corpse before she has a chance to look at it."

Stryker laughed as he pulled out his phone to call. "I sure do."

They walked around the roof looking at debris that had been tossed onto it. "I can't believe they throw their trash onto the roof," Stryker commented as he nudged a sack of garbage with the toe of his boot.

"Lima is so crowded," Keaton noted. "Over eleven million people. That's seven thousand people per square mile. That's staggering, Stryker."

"Yeah, they can't control the traffic nor the garbage," Stryker noted.

"Any guess from which one of the rooftops Tiny was chucked?" Keaton asked. "How in the world did he land right in the center of this roof?"

"Maybe he wasn't tossed off a roof. Maybe he was placed here," Stryker surmised.

"Do you see how flat he is?" Keaton pointed out. "I'll bet a month's pay every bone in his body is broken indicating he was thrown onto this roof."

The door to the roof opened and Lima's Chief Medical Examiner Mattie Ramos and her entourage joined them. "Bag everything on this roof," Mattie instructed her team.

She turned her attention to the two DEA officers. "Thanks for making me the garbage collector today."

"We didn't kill him Mattie," Stryker defended.

"Do you know who he is?" she asked as she lifted his jacket to get to the inside pocket.

"Tiny Gallegos," Keaton answered. "He works for Buenaventura Mining."

She checked the wallet she pulled from his pocket and nodded in agreement. "What's this?" She held up one of the chess pawns Keaton had tossed between the dead bodies of the human traffickers.

"A turf war," Keaton huffed.

"They're beginning to kill off each other." Mattie grinned. "Life is good."

"Mattie do you have any idea how the body could land right in the center of this roof?" Keaton asked.

Mattie looked around. "He wasn't thrown from the buildings surrounding this one. Give my team a chance to go over everything with a fine-toothed comb and I'll let you know what I conclude." She slid her hands under Tiny. "Judging from the jelly consistency of the body, I can tell you he is pulverized."

Keaton looked at herself in the mirror one more time and thought, *Dress to die for, check. Blonde hair anyone would want to spread out on a pillow, check. Heels guaranteed to make legs look even longer, check.*

She suppressed her thoughts of Remi slowly unzipping her dress, slipping off her shoes and admiring her silky blonde hair as the she leaned above her.

She had invited Remi to a function guaranteed to keep Keaton on her best behavior.

###

Printed in Poland
by Amazon Fulfillment
Poland Sp. z o.o., Wrocław

63225986R00246